SURVIVING
VENICE

SURVIVING VENICE

ANNA E. BENDEWALD

HUDSON-IVY PRESS

I was raised in a deeply religious family. My grandfather was a minister, I went to a church school, and I was in church several times a week. And while I feel that church provides a cohesion of community and values and spiritual direction, the church I attended was so rife with hypocrisy and dogma that even as a young girl I knew I was being manipulated and I saw the lies.

—Anna Erikssön Bendewald

SURVIVING VENICE

"The snake that cannot shed its skin must die, and the mind that cannot change its opinion ceases to be intelligent."

—*Friedrich Nietzche*

1

Raphielli fought her way out of a dark sleep that clung to her. Reaching for her phone on the bedside table her fingers found something else. She picked up the chunky thing and held it up in the dim light. Salvio's ring. Detective Lampani had taken the Scortini heirloom off Salvio's dead hand last night. She glared at the horse and boat emblem before dropping it back on the table with a clunk.

Her head started pounding and her eyes felt like dried fruit. Then she remembered how she'd acted last night and cringed. Detective Lampani told her Guiseppe had died, and she'd wailed like a baby. When he told her Salvio had hired hit men to kill her, and in an attempt to do just that they'd broken into her Porto delle Donne women's shelter and killed three of her staff members, she'd gone into hysterics and tried to run over there. But most unforgivable was her reaction when he told her Salvio had been shot to death behind their palazzo—she'd thrown her arms up and shouted in triumph like a crazed sports fan.

She was a horrible person, piling up a despicable cache of sins these past weeks.

She rolled over and saw Alphonso looking at her. His smooth skin glowed caramel against the white sheets, and his long muscular limbs were lean and hard. She peeked under the covers at her own short pudgy body, the cellulite on her big hips, her oversized floppy breasts.

How had one lunch with Giselle Verona and her uninhibited French friends gotten her to toss aside twenty years of righteous living? She'd taken Alphonso, the private detective on her husband's payroll, as her lover, started wearing expensive clothes, and acting as if the head of the Sicilian Mafia, don Giancarlo Petrosino, was her errand boy. "Take Salvio away! Release him! Now, come kill him!"

"Looking for your phone?" Alphonso was smoothing long snarls of her dark curls away from her face. "What are the odds I can get you to sleep for another hour?"

"None." Her voice sounded flat. "And stop talking about odds, you gave up gambling." She was surprised at the petty dig that came out of her mouth.

"*Mi dispiace*, a figure of speech," he said softly.

She squinted around the bedroom area of her suite. Alphonso must have undressed her because her clothes were folded neatly over the back of the nearby settee, whereas her maid, Rosa, would have taken them to be laundered. She blinked slowly. "My eyes feel like raisins."

Alphonso got up and walked across the heated carpet

runner, got some water from the mini-fridge, and brought it to her.

"Here, you're dehydrated. Can I get you something for your head?"

"No." She downed the water and placed the glass on the nightstand. "I deserve this pain. I'm a terrible person. My mother and *nonna* were right. I'm kidding myself to think that I belong in this big palazzo. I'm infertile, a complete failure as a wife. I couldn't even make Salvio like me. What other wife is so terrible that her husband kills half of Venice trying to murder her?"

"You're starting to grieve the people you've lost—go easy on yourself, okay? As for your mother and *nonna*—ha! The Dour Doublet snatched you out of your quiet life in the abbey and married you off to a monster. If they're right about anything, it certainly isn't you. They don't even know you."

"They know my kind. I'm as common as dirt and shouldn't pretend to be grand."

He put on a robe, then held one up for her.

"Come on, let's get you into a shower and then I'll take you out for breakfast on your way to the shelter." He stood there, all towering broad-shouldered, long-haired manliness, and gave her a worried look as he picked up the remote control, ignited the fireplaces, and opened the shades revealing a sleet-frosted wall of windows. The wintry glaze didn't obscure the arresting view of the lagoon, nor the ominous storm bank bearing down on the Lido from out at sea.

"Raphielli, stop thinking this was about you. Salvio was a maniac. He killed people who were admired. Count

Gabrieli Verona yesterday, that marble artist Reynaldo Falconetti back in the fall. He kept trying to kill Giselle who has adoring fans around the world. Everyone who came up against Salvio became a victim. Except, of course, don Petrosino, who I'm sure put those bullets in his head." Then, as he helped her into her robe he muttered, "Which I'll never repeat as long as I live." To her he said, "I can't get Lampani's words out of my head from last night. You're still in danger. Have you considered his suggestion?"

"What suggestion?"

"Getting a bodyguard."

"Gabrieli had one. It didn't keep him alive, and weeks back Salvio killed Vincenzo's bodyguard. And he killed two of my shelter guards." She bit the words off as her throat closed up in a sob and Alexi's face came to her so fresh and earnest.

"Petro bought Vincenzo enough reaction time to save his life," Alphonso reasoned.

"I'm not getting a bodyguard. You already walk me to and from work, and I have people around me all the time. Frankly, it's getting claustrophobic." Again, her meanness startled her.

"We only want to keep you safe."

"I know. I'm not myself this morning. Forgive me."

She let him lead her to the shower, and after she made herself presentable, they walked through the cavernous black marble halls. Living alone with her tiny staff...now one less...in Venice's largest and second-oldest palazzo, it felt like an ancient tomb that went on forever. What she wouldn't give for a warm wooden banister for her hand, or floors that creaked every now and then under her feet.

Alphonso cleared his throat. "Last night I told Rosa and Dante I'd take you out for breakfast."

"They must be devastated." Her elderly maid and butler had worked with Guiseppe, Salvio's valet, for years.

"They're very sad," he said as they reached the cloak-room. "I checked on them while you were in the shower. They're in the kitchen, the cook just arrived and she's making them eggs."

They let themselves out the big front door into a blowing icy mist. Now, out of habit, she glanced around looking for one of Salvio's assassins ready to finish the job, but no men in black were lurking about. It was the *acqua alta* season and large sections of the city were under water after another surge in the early hours. Wooden risers had been placed along the sub-merged *calles*, and planks spanned the risers making temporary bridges. She pressed close to Alphonso, and he put a protective arm around her as they passed a *tabaccheria* with newspapers in the window. Headlines proclaimed VENETIAN BUILDING SCION MURDERS COUNT AND VALET, and SCORTINI MURDERED DURING CRIME SPREE!

They moved past without comment. Then a woman's voice called, "Alphonso!" and they heard the sound of heels clacking on the raised boards over the flooded *calle*. Before Raphielli knew what was happening, a woman with an orange face and a teased platinum hairdo wearing a leopard print rain slicker strutted up to Alphonso like it was her own private catwalk and practically knocked Raphielli off the plank into the water. Raphielli shrank behind the wall that was Alphonso, trying to avoid the woman.

The floozy opened the collar of her coat—an odd thing to do with the biting cold—and out heaved impressive orange cleavage from a low-cut blouse.

"Where've you been? I've missed you! I should be mad, but that's no fun!" She flung her arms around him, kissed him full on the mouth...and lingered!

Alphonso detached himself gently and held her at arm's length. "Donatella, nice to see you. This is Raphielli."

He reached back for Raphielli's hand, but she kept it firmly inside her pocket as she stepped back. She looked down at her sensible winter coat and boots, and felt plain. They were nice, but no one would notice her in this glamazon's presence.

The middle-aged hussy didn't glance her way. She was batting fake eyelashes at Alphonso and cooing, "Ooh! I'm picking Rigo up at the groomers right now. Come with me, he misses his daddy. And I've missed you. We'll catch up."

Raphielli started to burn as the woman tried to link arms with him.

"We don't have time right now, but it's good to see you." He succeeded in grasping Raphielli's arm, and as they moved off, Donatella called, "I still live in the place you got me. You have my number."

As they proceeded through the slushy *calles*, Raphielli felt herself coming unhinged. Finally, she whirled on Alphonso and glared up at him.

"I don't need you to shepherd me. I'm not a sheep or a child. Go catch up with her."

He looked caught off guard. "Don't be silly."

"One of your girlfriends?"

"No," he said softly. He tried to take her arm to walk on, but she shook him off.

"Who is she?"

"A while back, I was hired by a politician's wife to prove her husband had a mistress." Raphielli arched a brow. "That was the mistress?"

His eyes narrowed, and he studied her with his keen private-eye skills. "What makes you ask that?"

"Only desperate women paste on lashes like that...wear clothes like that."

"What?" He sounded uncertain. "She dresses like Carolette."

"My friends don't dress like hookers," she said while silently conceding that Carolette would have drooled over Donatella's ensemble.

"You're not yourself this morning. It isn't like you to be mean. Anyway, *sì*, she was the mistress, and the politician was a psychopath who killed people who crossed him. Donatella risked her life to help me."

"Sounds cozy if you gave her your dog."

"I got her a dog from the kennel for protection. She needed it. She allowed me to get photos of her in bed with the politician, giving the wife leverage in the divorce. She spied on him for me and got me the key evidence I needed to hand him over to the police. She was brave."

"You got her an apartment?" She was so angry she wanted to hit him.

"He had men trying to kill her, so I found her a safe place."

Instead of this making her feel better, she felt a wave of inferiority as she recalled Donatella's sexy mannerism. Intense jealousy crashed down making her almost burst into tears. Donatella was probably pushing thirty and knew tricks in bed that Raphielli hadn't learned.

"She helped you because she was in love with you."

"*Sì*, but I didn't love her, and I never led her on."

Apparently saving ladies from killers was a regular thing with him, and he didn't have to love them to do it. Visions of Alphonso and Donatella having sex ran through her mind, and she backed away from him. "I need a break from you. Go away! Leave me alone!"

"Elli...*per favore*..."

She ran off as fast as she could, skidding over the planks where the water was deepest. She ran all the way to the next *sestiere* before the sky got darker and a wind whipped up with such force that she had to lean into it. She slipped and fell down on a slush-covered bridge, but there was no one nearby to help her up. Fighting tears, she recovered her purse, picked herself up, and ran on until she was standing breathless in front of the Aman Hotel just as the rainstorm arrived with a vengeance. She had a bad stitch in her side and pressed one hand to it while she pulled out her phone and called *him*.

"Eh, Raphielli."

She could always hear the smile when he said her name.

"Gio...I..."

"Are you all right?" She could tell he'd gone on high alert when he heard her tone. "Where are you?"

"I'm standing outside the Aman. I heard you mention it to Primo. Are you inside?"

"*Sì.*" Then he said to someone nearby, "Raphielli's outside, bring her in." Then into the phone he said, "Primo's coming. You can't be outside right now. Salvio has a hit out on you."

A minute later she saw his son pop out a side door of the hotel, and he ran straight for her. Once he'd hustled her into his father's room, he stepped out closing the door behind him.

Gio was wearing a heavy silk robe over pajamas made of some soft material, and his feet were bare. He had nice feet.

"Ah! You're soaked! Come 'ere."

Raphielli ran to him and buried her face in his neck. His arms were strong and he smelled incredible.

He held her and murmured into her hair, "*Povera ragazza innocente.*"

"Gio, forgive me. I've behaved like a spoiled, depraved..." She couldn't think of all the terrible things she needed him to absolve her of.

He laughed lightly, pulled her away from his chest, then unzipped her jacket and peeled it off her shoulders. "You? Never."

"I pitted you against my own husband."

"No, you didn't."

She looked up and saw that he was smiling down at her. "And I'm dripping all over your robe and your floor." Now she started to smile, too.

He maneuvered her over to a sofa and sat her down.

"If you wanted to come see me, I'd have sent Drea in the boat to get you. How'd you get so wet? Did you swim here?"

"Everything's flooded and...I thought the storm would hold off on the way to the shelter. I have to check on my residents. I lost people over there, too."

"Here, let's get you dry. We don't want you catching your death of cold, I'm trying to keep you alive." He said the last words quietly and very near her ear as he lifted her wet hair off her neck. "They have very nice robes here..."

Her wet sweater felt too tight. She reached for the side zipper drawing it upward, then raised her arms above her head, offering him a silent invitation with her eyes. As he undressed her, she felt a languorous glow. He offered her his robe, and when she saw the stark desire in his eyes, she pushed the robe away and reached for him.

Thunder rattled the windows as she gave herself to the hard man who always looked at her as if she melted him. He was a revelation, so sure of himself, with none of the boyishness of Alphonso. He took her again and again as he marveled at her body, pleasuring her while offering little twinges of pain to bring her nerve endings to attention in a way that was light years from the torture she'd experienced beneath Salvio.

Lying in his arms afterward, she felt restored to sanity. She'd gotten a grip on her emotions, and now she needed to return to work. The women in her shelter needed her to be strong. Gio had aroused deep feelings in her since she'd first laid eyes on him, and now she knew the feelings were mutual. Remembering the morning's flights of anger and guilt, she realized the sedative she'd been given last night must have messed with her head. But now her head felt clear. She watched Gio as he twirled ringlets of her black hair.

"I know a private place we could go for lunch," he said.

"I haven't had breakfast, and I could use a cappuccino."

He picked up the room phone. "*Continental service, un cappuccino e una caraffa di caffè espresso. Subito.*" Then he tossed the phone aside, scooped her up, and began nuzzling her neck. "Let's go to Palermo this afternoon. I'll take you home. You'll be safe there."

"Mmm?" Her mind reeled at the proposition as her body responded to him.

"I'll take care of you."

"What? Aren't you married? I mean, doesn't Primo have a mother?"

"*Sì*, but I have the perfect house for you, with a nice flower garden and a view of the harbor. I'd move in with you—mostly."

She thought of Vincenzo and Leonardo's apartment that publicly belonged to Leonardo alone.

"Gio, I can't leave Venice. This is my home. My work is here, I've just got my women's shelter up and running and we're finally at full capacity. Today I should be searching for replacements for the staff that were murdered last night."

"A job for your manager," he countered. "What's her name?"

"Kate."

"Let Kate manage while you get away...at least until someone cancels the orders Salvio's killers are marching to."

"Someone?"

He gave her an innocent look. "Well, that detective...Luigi...Lampani...he has a lot of clout with Police

Chief Inspector Laszlo. And because Salvio made a fool of him, he won't stop till he's dragged everyone involved with Salvio to jail. Luigi's smart, maybe he'll get these guys. Then again, after our trip to your underwater temple it sounded like the Vatican might stop Salvio's killers. That cardinal of yours, Negrali, and the pope knew a whole lot about Salvio's religious mania, his Alithinían Church, and there's nothing more deadly than a holy war."

She shivered in his arms at the memory of the pope thrusting that sword down the pipe Salvio had disappeared through and found herself agreeing. "The three of them did use the word 'inquisition' liberally."

He grazed his lips over her shoulder before pulling her in for a delicious kiss. "Okay. Stay here and save your women. I'll stay, too, see what I can find out about the Alithinían Church, get a better understanding of who'd be loyal to Salvio. Or, maybe he just put a hefty bounty on your head."

"That can't be it. A while back I took charge of the entire Scortini estate."

"Good for you. You're the last Scortini. It's yours."

"So, I don't see where he could get the money to pay people to kill me."

"None of this makes sense yet. He certainly wanted the Veronas dead. It stands to reason they're still in danger, too." Gio pulled one of her bare legs across his and stroked it thoughtfully.

"Well, if you find out who he paid, let them know I'll pay more to stay alive."

"Buy your way out of a contract? That usually isn't done. But maybe he hired mercenaries, and then you could just make your fee more attractive to them. He's not alive to hire any others."

"Either way, I'm not letting a plan hatched by my late husband stop me from living my life. I've got plans of my own. I've asked Genero Tosca to help me turn part of my palazzo into another women's shelter."

He looked impressed. "Tosca? The new head of the Venetian Builders? He's the man."

"*Sì*, he and Mayor Buonocore helped me get the last one built."

"You've got powerful friends—and plenty of spunk, little girl."

A brief flash of lightning brightened the room, illuminating him on the bed. Without his conservative business suit, Giancarlo Petrosino looked like a darkly handsome angel. She registered that a big part of her attraction to him was the way he looked at her—like she was the most beautiful thing he'd ever seen, like she was precious to him. The haunting sound of the *acqua alta* siren began blipping four tones outside the windows, and it echoed crazily between the buildings.

"Hear that? You're not walking anywhere. The water is deepening. Soon, people will be mid-thigh out there." He gripped her thigh with a powerful hand and kissed her neck.

There was a knock on the door and Primo announced, "Your breakfast. Want me to bring it in?"

Gina felt a wave of relief when she turned in her exam booklet. She'd been struggling to ignore distractions all morning in school.

One: The storms that had been drenching Venice the entire month of November suddenly intensified, shaking the ancient windows of Ca' Foscari University and making the lights flicker ominously.

Two: Most of her fellow students reeked of wet wool and body odor, so she'd had to keep flicking droplets of homemade fragrance onto her arm to make the overheated classroom miasma bearable.

Three: Beatrix Knutsdatter—who hated her for some reason—had selected a seat next to Gina's. Every time she completed a question, she let out a *Heh!*, tossed her overly-styled blonde hair, and grinned a veneer-toothed grin at Gina, as if this exam were a competition and each exclamation meant "Top that one!" But this test was critical, so Gina had let her chin-length brown bob fall in a curtain to block Beatrix from view and tried not to think about the fourth thing.

Four: This afternoon she was going to have sex with the most glamorous man in Venice, the only son of Venice's founding family, Count Vincenzo Verona...and his secret gay lover, Leonardo Trentori. Well, she wasn't sure what Leonardo's role would be precisely and had to keep forcing her mind to return to her exam.

After handing in her booklet, she moved to the door to claim her long hooded coat from a peg and heard her friends hurrying behind her.

"Gina, are you coming with us? Or do you have to work at the flower shop?"

"You smell delicious! Another new concoction?"

"Think you got another perfect score, Gina?"

Then Beatrix's haughty-yet-bored German accent. "She did not have Contessa Verona to take ze test for her, so maybe she failt."

Diego got defensive. "Gina *doesn't* cheat. She probably knows more about the phytochemicals in flower pollen than *il proffesore*. In case you didn't know, her whole family works in natural chemistry."

Dot's voice joined. "*Sì*, Gina's great grandfather attended Ca' Foscari the year it opened."

"Ugh, zen I guess Great Grandpa No-Von-Cares vas too far in his grave to git her into Ca' Foscari. Zuh queen of Venice hat to do zat."

"You're just jealous because Gina and la Contessa Juliette are friends," Diego shot back.

"Dunt be stoopit, Juliette Verona gave Gzzh-een-ah charity for zih same reason she opent zat homeless shelter. She takes pity on pitiful people. Zay are not friends. Gzzh-een-ah is just a Verona groupie."

Gina zipped up her coat as she answered the questions posed to her. "I have a commitment, I'm sorry, I can't join you. I'm wearing a scent Marie Antoinette used to wave under her nose when unwashed dignitaries sat near her. And I think I did fine on the test."

Gina maneuvered around students who were struggling into wet galoshes. She was wearing shiny thigh-high black rubber boots that looked like patent leather. Almost as fabulous as the ones Juliette wore, these had a modest heel and looked beautiful even when dodging puddles but, most importantly, kept her socks dry. She'd saved up for four months to buy them.

She followed the flow of bodies into the hallway, but before the cacophony of squeaking boots and thudding feet drowned her out, she heard Beatrix say, "I dunt know vat commitment she could have. Can't be a guy. No von vants to fuck a titt-less boy-girl."

Gina ignored the jab at her lack of curves and pulled her hood up. Outside, the pedestrian flood platforms were higher in this area, but the water rose above them in some places. Like her fellow students, she rejected umbrellas as torture devices used by tourists to gouge at the eyes of Venetians and avoided tourist areas whenever possible. Instead, she traveled less-known *calles* with her hood up looking like a one of many druids moving anonymously through the stormy Veneto. Excited now, she sloshed a secret zigzagging route toward the Grand Canal, avoiding the lower *calles* that were completely submerged. Hurrying past homes whose first floors were flooded, she took pity on an old man who was climbing out his window and stopped to help him safely down into his boat, which was floating at the height of the windowsill. Waving off his offers to pilot her home, she knew the *vaporetto* would be the fastest way to the other side of the city. She'd have just enough time to shower and change before her first surrogacy appointment. *Is that what I'm calling it?*

The Veronas had been an obsession of hers since her first evening in Venice. She wasn't a groupie...was she? She certainly wasn't unique. Everyone in Venice was crazy about their founding family. They were the ultimate in subdued style and gracious manners.

She'd just moved into the little apartment in the Arsinale *sestiere* over by Campo San Martino and had been walking to Ca' Foscari University when she saw the Verona Palazzo all lit up. People were greeting a handsome man in his fifties, Count Gabrieli Verona, the unofficial king of Venice. He called back to each of them by name and got into a friendly conversation with a group of people when his wife, Contessa Juliette, approached just as Gina was passing. La Contessa had slowed down to ask how people were doing, inquired after people by their names, and opened her arms for a child who promptly climbed into them. Impromptu *al fresco* gatherings happened regularly in the shadow of the fairy tale Verona palazzo.

When it had come time to look for a job, Gina applied at the flower shop diagonally across the canal from their palazzo. Being in close proximity made her feel somehow connected to them, more than just an admirer who followed their comings and goings in the local news. But she'd never dreamed Contessa Juliette would be her first customer and become her most trusted friend. The day after they met, she received her first call from Ippy, Juliette's secretary, inviting Gina to accompany Juliette to a social event. Similar invitations continued with surprising frequency and regularity, but nothing prepared Gina for last night's intimate and urgent invitation.

Juliette had called and asked Gina to bear her a grand-child by Vincenzo.

"Why are you asking this? Vincenzo has a wife who's pregnant with his child."

"No. Vincenzo is a homosexual, and Giselle is his..."

"Beard?"

"*Sì*, a disguise. The child is not Vincenzo's, and for reasons I will share someday, it is crucial that the house of Verona lives on…in particular Vincenzo's bloodline. With that murdering Salvio hunting us, we cannot wait any longer. Is this a good time of the month for you to try to conceive?"

A quick glance at her calendar showed she was just entering her window of fertility and, without giving it much thought, she'd agreed to be the mother of Juliette's grandchild—which Juliette had explained needed to be done the old-fashioned way. As devout Catholics, medical intervention for procreation was strictly prohibited.

Now, the thought of sex with Vincenzo kicked Gina's heartbeat into a herky-jerky rhythm almost in time with the heavy raindrops drumming on her hood. In less than two hours, she was going to the apartment Vincenzo secretly shared with Leonardo—who was his accountant and so much more.

Vincenzo was twenty-four, tall, dark and more beautiful than handsome, with big brown eyes rimmed with sweeping black lashes, and he topped every "sexiest man" list published. Until last night, Gina had believed that Vincenzo was happily married to his high school sweetheart, French bad-girl *artiste du monde* Giselle Forêt, whose beauty took Gina's breath away. Although it wasn't public knowledge, Gina knew Giselle was pregnant. While Vincenzo and Leo worked tirelessly donating millions to humanitarian and environmental causes, Giselle donated every cent from her sculptures to similar causes.

And now Gina would be family! Sort of.

She got into line at the *vaporetto* stop and held her transportation card, a gift from Juliette, up to the scanner just as the boat approached and its slickered crew performed the treacherous dance of lashing it to the pier with ropes. As she stepped aboard, the boat heaved, and a sheet of water cascaded off the roof. The sound startled her, but she stayed dry, unlike nearby passengers lacking hooded long coats, who let out shrieks as icy rainwater poured down their collars and into the tops of their boots.

She found a seat for the twenty-minute ride to her side of the city and thought about Vincenzo's call late last night. Gina had only seen him a handful of times at society functions she'd attended with Juliette.

He'd sounded tired. "Gina, it's Vincenzo. May I put Leonardo on speaker with us?"

She'd tried not to sound too eager. "Of course."

"*Ciao*, Gina." Leonardo's voice was softer than Vincenzo's.

"I understand my mother has discussed our situation with you." Vincenzo sounded uncertain, which made him seem vulnerable.

"*Sì*, and may I say how sorry I am for your loss? Your father was a great man."

"*Sì*, we're still in shock."

"Juliette told me Salvio Scortini is hunting your family."

"I've just learned Salvio's been killed."

"Well, that's a relief."

"But the police just told us I'm still in danger."

"Oh, no. That's not good."

"No. So, it's time to have a child in case something happens to me."

"I'm absolutely up for it. The women of my family are very fertile." She'd clapped her hand over her mouth and stifled a groan. What made her say that?

Leonardo said, "Gina, Juliette tells us you're able to start trying tomorrow."

"*Sì*, tomorrow's the first day of my...er...fertility phase." This was such a new subject, the words sounded strange. "She asked me to promise to try for six days straight to ensure the best chances of pregnancy."

"*Sì*, we promised the same." Vincenzo let out a long exhale and then said in a small voice, "I've never been with a woman...but I made a promise to mama that I'd make it good for you." His voice trailed off.

"Ah, *sì*, that was considerate of Juliette."

"If you don't mind," Leonardo began, "I could help put you at ease and hopefully make it enjoyable for both of you."

"Ah, okay." She'd fallen back against her pillows thinking she must have fallen asleep while studying. She'd pinched herself as Vincenzo asked her to come over the next day. "Would four o'clock work for you?"

"*Sì*."

She was startled back to the present by an old man's cry. "Who the fuck was that rat Scortini? Nobody knew him!"

An angry voice shot back, "Thought he was too good for people! Why he gotta kill the count?"

The Verona palazzo came into view and the buzz of regular ambient conversation died away. The *vaporatto's* pilot tolled his bell as they passed the palace, whose rooftop balustrades and gates were now draped in black.

Murmurs of "*Riposa in pace, Gabrieli*" rose around her, and hands fluttered as people crossed themselves.

She thought of Salvio Scortini, the madman who'd been targeting the Veronas. Headlines announced that he'd been shot in the head last night, but not before he'd stabbed his own valet to death. Everyone believed he'd killed Count Gabrieli, but police had little evidence in that murder. The papers said there was an investigation into all of Salvio's probable crimes and whether he'd acted alone.

Gina thought of Juliette, so tireless and generous. Her graduation gift to Gina had been a fully paid tuition to university with a seat in the prestigious advanced chemistry and biology courses which had been Gina's reason for coming to live in Venice. While she was confident she'd earned the place on her own, she had no qualms about allowing Juliette to cement the position through her influence. Gina's mother always said, "When Providence opens a door, never hesitate to walk through it."

The *vaporetto* conductor called, "*Arsinale!*" as they docked at her stop. She grasped the handrail as she stepped onto the rocking platform that was attached to the pier. Not only were the waves heaving it with rhythmic jolts, but the temperature had dropped, and a thin sheet of ice glazed the surfaces. Her side of the island was relatively deserted with few tourist shops and no locals sitting out in the *campos*.

Arriving at her little apartment, she stripped, showered, and changed into a slate-blue skirt with a smoky purple sweater set. She pulled on fresh warm socks, then her boots, and crossed the minutely slanting floorboards to her vanity table. A quick brush of her precise chestnut-brown bob and she was done with her hair. She decided to take a cue from Vincenzo's wife, who never wore any makeup, and forgo attempting to apply cosmetics. She looked down at her hands. Her nails were shaped and buffed—she was proud of her hands—and right now she was grateful they weren't shaking.

What if I can't get pregnant? What if I over-promised and I let Juliette down? What if my womb is stubborn and refuses to produce? She mentally shook herself. *That's not helpful. I'm going to do everything in my power to live up to my promise.*

The chirping alarm on her watch told her it was time to go. She turned to the selection of handmade fragrances on the low glass shelf before her and selected a flacon filled with a mixture she'd whipped up as soon as she'd gotten off the phone with Juliette last night. It was one of her great-grandmother's recipes that she'd retrieved from her box of supplies and ingredients sent from an apothecary in Avebury in Wiltshire where her family had lived for generations.

This fragrance was an exquisitely subtle, and incredibly long-lasting mixture of lavender, verdant herbs, citrus oils, human male pheromones, and a touch of wolf essence that had been procured by massaging the underbellies of wolves—immediately after coming off females—with cheesecloth and then distilling those oils.

She unscrewed the silver cap, withdrew the applicator and stroked the wand along her wrists, the back of her knees, and along the back of her neck. Then, in the spirit of today's adventure, she lifted her skirt and stroked it across her lower abdomen, then parted her legs and stroked the insides of her thighs for good measure. Time to get pregnant.

As she stepped outside, the last of the early winter sun vanished, extinguished by a bank of clouds sliding across the darkening sky. Far off thunder rumbled, and fat drops of rain made *plotter-plottering* sounds on her hood as she pulled it over her head.

It had been three months since she'd had sex with her friend Diego's older brother on the night before he moved to Spain. It had been very nice, and she hoped what was about to happen would be enjoyable. Gina headed to the toniest apartment building in Venice's most exclusive *sestiere.*

———◦◦◦———

Mateo leaned over the kitchen sink and splashed cold water on his face, his fingers scrubbing over the beginnings of stubble on his cheeks. He slid his hands up to his scalp and felt the beginnings of stubble there, too. He took a deep shuddering breath and tried to swallow around the hot lump in his throat, almost choking as the tears came back. *Dio mio! They've murdered Salvio! After the eons in hiding from Peter's assassins, they're closer than ever to wiping us out!*

He stared out the safe house's rear window and could barely make out the trees of Parco Savorgnan through the sheeting rain. The park was flooded and deserted so, conveniently, nobody had seen one of their church members use a trellis to cover the broken window in the back bedroom. Yesterday they'd plummeted from the heights of elation when Salvio had finally succeeded in killing Gabrieli Verona, to the pit of utter desolation when they'd lost two men inside Raphielli Scortini's women's shelter, then another two men in France where Benjamin's brother Bernardo was arrested, and then someone had assassinated Salvio. The night had ended with the horrible discovery that Benedetta—possibly carrying Salvio's child—had broken out of the safe house and run away.

The moan of the water garage's hinge and the familiar chuffing of a boat motor signaled Benjamin's return. Mateo dried his face with a clean kitchen towel, then spooned espresso grounds into the stovetop pot and took two cups down from the cupboard. Benjamin came in from the water garage, hung up his raincoat, and sat on the bench to remove his boots.

"Can this really be it?" he asked. "Rome commands people to mindlessly procreate until the planet can't sustain us while they prey on their faithful, pilfering every cent from their pockets, and now after two thousand years they've murdered our last tie to Saint Paul?"

"If we doubt, we're dead. We have to have faith. I believe Benedetta's pregnant. Salvio made a baby with her. San Paolo's lineage is safe," Mateo said.

Benjamin took a deep breath and let it out. "I have faith. But what now?"

"We need to get her back. How'd it go at the police station?"

"A real fiasco." Benjamin pushed his feet into slippers and stood. He smoothed a palm over his thin pomaded hair and turned frightened eyes on Mateo. "Benedetta's parents are dangerously unbalanced. We should never have chosen that family to continue Salvio's holy bloodline."

"They've always been solid, devout, quiet."

"I wish they'd go back to quiet. You wouldn't believe the things that came out of their mouths this morning. You'd think they hadn't been Alithiníans their whole lives, the way they blabbed about being hunted by the Vatican."

"What?" Mateo was stunned. "They said that to the police?"

"Not to the police. No." He eyed the coffee pot. "We've been up all night. Let's have some espresso and I'll tell you."

Together they went to the stove, filled their cups, and returned to the table.

Mateo said, "It was a simple plan: Report her missing and get the police's help locating her. How'd things get messed up?" He tossed back his espresso in one scalding gulp.

"Well, by the time I got the Amendolas to the police station, they couldn't keep their story straight."

"Oh, no." Prickles of fear scrabbled up Mateo's back.

"Right, well, as planned, I stayed outside so the police wouldn't connect me to them. When they came back out, they'd filed a missing person's report and spoken to a reporter who arranged a press conference."

"A *what?* She's only been missing a few hours!"

"Well, that's the thing. They decided since no one has seen her since they'd brought her here to stay with us, there was no harm in saying she'd been missing since then…" Benjamin downed his espresso.

Mateo gave that some thought. "Yeah, it's true, no one's seen her for about two weeks, so that would work."

"But hang on. They told two versions to the police. One, that she'd been missing for two weeks, and another that they'd last seen her twenty-four hours ago when she went out for a jog…"

"A jog? During the *acqua alta*? Venice is submerged!"

"…near Parco Savorgnan," Benjamin finished with a groan.

"What? Here? Near the safe house?" Mateo felt himself losing his temper, and he was not a man to lose his temper. "I told them to say she'd last been seen walking away from them in Parco Biennale on the other side of the city! Now the police are going to be crawling around over here! What were they thinking?"

"They weren't thinking. When they came outside and met me in the Piazza San Marco, they couldn't keep their voices down and started complaining to me that Benedetta was stolen by the Catholics to get the holy seed from her womb."

"*Dio mio!*"

Benjamin returned to the stove to make more espresso. "We made a terrible choice with those two. They're unstable. You should've heard them. 'You made our daughter a sitting duck! What kind of safe house doesn't have bars on the windows? The pope's men broke in and took her and the Messiah's seed! He'll kill us all! The Inquisition is happening! Mateo needs to wake up!'"

"They said all this loud enough for people to hear?"

"*Sì.* You wouldn't believe how loud those two can talk, but I didn't see anyone take notice. We were standing a few meters from the door of the police station."

"What did you do?"

"I got my arms around their shoulders, pulled them into a huddle, and said, 'We've survived the Inquisition for over two thousand years through secrecy!'"

"And?" Mateo asked.

"I told them you and I would handle this. We aren't alone, we have the Alithinían faithful who'll help us get Benedetta back."

"Did they calm down?"

"*Sì,* but they told me they'd deviated from our plan in other ways."

"*Oh, Dio.* How?"

"Instead of just reporting Benedetta missing and letting us handle the rest, they called all her friends, both hospitals..."

"You and I already searched the hospitals. Did you tell them we peeked into every room dressed as orderlies? She's not hospitalized."

"...before deciding she must have run to Porto delle Donne."

"No!" Mateo jumped to his feet. "They've got to stay away from Raphielli's shelter! We lost two men there yesterday! And since we killed her staff, the place is hot!"

"I told them exactly that. Their response was, 'The police expect us to look everywhere for her!' I reminded them that Raphielli's shelter is private, and they'd have no chance of bullying their way inside without a court order."

"Did that shut them up?"

"*Sì*, they headed home to get some rest before their press conference."

"Sweet Jesus, a press conference. Let's pray it doesn't amount to anything. Listen, Benjamin, we can't stop now. We can still do this. I'll bail your brother out of that French jail."

"*Grazie.*" He looked relieved. "Maybe the French police don't have anything on him. It's not as if he was at Giselle's estate, he was just coordinating logistics."

"So, a slight change of plans. Now, y*ou'll* go to France and dispose of Giselle and her child while I stay here and get rid of Vincenzo. I mean if you can't take out a skinny little artist in stilettos, and I can't dispatch a pretty-boy whose idea of exerting himself is dabbing his oars in the canals, then we aren't trying."

"Salvio already took out Gabrieli, and that alone may be enough to topple the pope. Once Vincenzo dies, Leopold XIV won't have a crutch to prop himself up with, and that whole rotten cult of personality in Rome will implode. We'll get Benedetta back and Paul's bloodline will live on. Do we know what happened to Salvio's ring?"

"According to Lydia, Detective Lampani gave it to Raphielli."

"We've got to get Paul's ring back."

"First we've got to get our little Madonna—Benedetta."

"Call Lydia and find out what the police know."

Taking his cup back to the stove, Mateo felt tears spring to his eyes. "This must be what the disciples felt when Jesus was killed. What I wouldn't give to have one more day with Salvio. We never got to know him."

They were silent for a while, and then Benjamin said, "All right, I'll arrange to get on the next plane to France and make a new plan to get Giselle."

"I'll try to get a grip on Benedetta's parents and form a plan to get at Vincenzo—he's been so erratic lately." It wasn't lost on Mateo that it was probably due to them killing his father.

"Faith without works is dead," Benjamin said as he got to his feet.

"And God helps those who help themselves."

———— ❦ ————

Detective Luigi Lampani was in a foul mood that matched Venice's weather. He'd been working on the case against Salvio Scortini for weeks now, and the more puzzle pieces he clicked into place, the more unbelievable the picture became—like he had it all wrong. This case of one founding family apparently trying to wipe out the other was making him doubt his instincts.

His headaches were increasing in ferocity and regularity, threatening to incapacitate him. Hungry and exhausted, he went down the hall to the vending machine and stared at slot F6 where the Pocket Coffees were supposed to be. In their place were something called Marshmallow Fling! Like a true addict, he craved the rich, caffeinated hit of espresso and dark chocolate of his Pocket Coffees. But, incredibly, he was staring at a neon blue wad of sucrose that looked like it could choke a goat.

Robbed of his preferred energy source, he stalked back

through the relatively quiet headquarter halls to the hive of activity that had become the homicide department. And not an orderly hive—it was a hive someone had jammed a stick into.

The last son of the beloved Scortini building family had gone berserk. For weeks he'd evaded Luigi while relentlessly hunting his own wife and the Verona family—even sending hit men to France hunting Giselle Verona—and murdering innocent bystanders like young Reynaldo Falconetti. Raphielli Scortini had only survived his attempt to hang her because she was young and strong enough to cling to the rope until her maid found her.

But now Luigi was certain that Salvio had been able to elude him since early fall because there was an informant inside the department. From now on, he'd keep everything close to his chest, and to that effect he'd asked the head of the French investigation to communicate exclusively with him. At the same time, he was withholding key information from the French, that the amber-colored rope they recovered from the hit men's murder kits was the same special rope used to drown Count Gabrieli Verona here in Venice at the Verdu Mer construction site yesterday morning.

For privacy, Luigi went out onto the balcony to call the mother of one of the French hit men who'd just died while attempting to kill Contessa Giselle Verona. He'd been systematically going through the list of associates his French contact had given him. He spoke excellent French and had spoken it more since eleven o'clock last night than he had since his year as a foreign-exchange student in Nice.

Halfway through the conversation, the storm strength-ened and rain started coming at him sideways as he stood with his phone pressed to his ear, and his notebook pressed flat against the wall, scribbling notes as fast as the woman on the line could talk. And she was a fast talker. Never mind that he couldn't recall the last time he'd slept, he silently cursed the bad reception, the foul weather, and the fact that his pen was only emitting ink sporadically. He knew from years of experience that when a material witness talks, you capture every word and you don't ask if you could call them back on account of weather or faulty writing implements.

He'd been lucky to get the woman on the phone, and now that she'd answered some of his questions she was starting to repeat herself. He cast his net wider. "By any chance, was your son Catholic?"

"I didn't raise Miguel to be religious," the woman's voice crackled via satellite. "He went through a phase of trying to find God as a teenager and decided he couldn't stand Catholics. 'A bunch a crooks,' he said. I agree. Not that he wasn't a crook, too. Such a disappointment to me."

The disapproving mother apparently didn't live in a glass house, the way she threw stones at the Catholic Church and her ne'er-do-well son.

Luigi glanced through the window at the police running around inside headquarters. Lydia, a detective on loan from the bullpen, was looking at him. When their eyes met, she waved and made some gestures asking if he wanted coffee. He nodded and turned away to concentrate. Privacy aside, he stood a better chance of hearing over the thunder outside than he did over the raised voices and ringing phones of the investigation that was currently sending shockwaves across Italy and France like a bomb—his office was ground zero. And he knew in his bones Salvio Scortini had thrown it...before he'd gotten shot in the head. Luigi was as far under the roof overhang as he could manage, but his shoes were getting soaked.

"What'd you say killed him?" Miguel's mother asked.

"He ran into a sculpture studded with a lethal chemical."

"Leave it to Miguel to die in a stupid way, always reckless. When he was eleven, he..."

By the time Luigi hung up and went back inside, he was drenched from the knees down and his shoes were ruined. On the short trip to his desk, his socks squelched inside his shoes. He sat down and completed his notes by tracing over the partial letters with a fresh pen as his pants dripped a puddle under the desk. Investigators came and went, dropping reports in his inbox and giving him staccato updates on their progress.

"Prelim forensics from yesterday's four murder scenes," Lydia said as she turned away, then yawned and called over her shoulder, "Coffee's on the way. Going to order some breakfast *panini*. Want one?"

"Absolutely," he said.

She paused mid-stride. "Hey, did the Porto delle Donne team miss something?"

"I haven't read the report yet."

"Just asking cuz I saw you coming out of there this morning...you went back over."

He quirked his head and gave her a dead stare. He didn't know her from Adam, and he didn't like being probed. "You worked the Scortini palazzo crime scene with me. What were *you* doing over by Raphielli's shelter?"

"My boyfriend lives in that *sestiere*. I'm pulling a triple shift, so when I got my one-hour break I went there to take a quick nap and a shower. I was surprised to see you going inside as I happened past the shelter."

"I checked on the manager," he lied. There was no way he was going to divulge that he'd been interviewing a victim of serial rape that'd been orchestrated by her own parents.

Another detective dropped his report on top of the in-box stack and said, "Prelim from the medical examiner on Salvio. All three bullets from one gun. He bled somewhere else on the *calle*, the rain erased it. He was down about a liter from the bullet to his gut when he took two more bullets to the head." That detective started to leave Luigi's desk and had to dodge another cop approaching with more folders.

"Photos from the women's shelter, statements from the resident women and Kate the manager. But you know the place is owned and funded by Salvio's young widow, Raphielli Scortini, right?"

"*Sì.*" Luigi was watching every cop with suspicious eyes now.

He didn't need to look at the photos from Porto delle Donne. He'd never forget the bloody scene he'd walked in on there. He'd questioned the residents who'd survived the attack, coming away with a great respect for those women.

When Kate had called him later in the wee hours of the morning asking him to come back to the shelter, he'd arrived after the crime scene team had left and as the private cleaning contractors were starting to mop up. He found Kate in a back room with a frail girl with long flowing hair and big pouty lips, who was wrapped in a blood-spotted sheet.

He introduced himself to the girl. "I'm Detective Lampani, but you can call me Luigi. What happened to you?"

Kate was bent over the girl, using a powerful lamp as she tweezed splinters of glass from the tender skin of the girl's hands, arms, neck, legs and feet. She didn't look up. "Thanks for coming, Luigi. This is Benedetta Amendola. She's sixteen and was a virgin until her parents locked her up with Salvio Scortini to get her pregnant. I haven't called SVU yet, but they'll need to do a rape kit on her."

The cop in him was elated. *This girl is the key!* The next breath, his heart dropped into his stomach and he felt a sad sympathy for her. Her innocence ripped away by a madman. "Benedetta, how long were you trapped with Salvio?"

"I lost track of time. They kept me locked in a back bedroom without any clothes," she complained. "My parents said I'd be treated special."

"Can you estimate the time?"

"About two weeks. They made me tell all my friends I was going to visit my aunt in Pisa so nobody'd miss me. But Salvio's crazy. He hated me, threatened me, it was awful. The first time I was sure no one was in the house, I broke out."

"It wasn't just your parents helping Salvio?" He held his breath in suspense.

"He has helpers, but I was blindfolded so I don't know who they were."

He clamped down on his disappointment. "How many?"

"A bunch. But from what I overheard, only like, a handful who are willing to kill for him."

"Any helpers with French accents?"

"No."

"If I call your parents and we tell them..."

"NO!" The girl flew out of her chair, causing Kate to fall to the floor. The sheet fell away, and his heart broke looking at the girl's skinny frame covered with blood and bruises. She held one hand awkwardly as if she'd broken it. Kate picked up the sheet and covered her again.

Luigi held a hand up. "Okay, you're safe here if you can keep all of this a secret for a while. The police can't be involved at this point or they'll return you to your parents, so swabs and photos will have to be taken by Kate."

Kate nodded, and the girl looked relieved.

"How does that sound?"

"All right."

"Why would your parents hand you over to Salvio? Money?" He watched a veil of disinterest descend over her eyes that told him he wasn't looking in the right direction. "Are you guys Catholic?"

Boom, just like that he'd lost her. She pretended not to hear and instead appeared to be consumed in Kate's ministrations, and then made a hissing sound. "*Ssss-Ow!*"

He'd left so Kate could do an examination, but Benedetta had profoundly touched him.

Now Luigi spread the reports across his desk then unlocked the drawer where he kept his Salvio file. Reaching all the way to the back, he retrieved the last square of Pocket Coffee. He savored it as his eyes devoured the information in the new reports. It was half an hour later when he heard Chief Inspector Laszlo bellow, "Lampani! I need what you've got!"

Luigi pulled everything together in a neat stack, added his notebook and phone on top, and carried it all to the hotbox that was Laszlo's office. The big man, who was a perfect combination of Bela Lugosi's Dracula and Elvis Presley, sat at his desk fuming. Luigi dragged the guest chair over to the open window for some fresh—albeit wet—air.

"I'm making a statement at the top of the hour. What am I saying?" Laszlo swigged some chalky liquid from a plastic bottle and then screwed the cap back on with such force Luigi heard the big man's neck crack.

"That didn't sound good. Laszlo, you're falling apart."

"Looks who's talking? You look like you're taking chemotherapy."

"The Pocket Coffee's been replaced in the vending machine. You didn't have anything to do with that, did you?"

"No. If I had any pull with vending machines, they'd be filled with Pan di Stelle. Now, what am I saying to the public?"

"I recommend keeping it brief. 'Last night Salvio Scortini was shot dead near his palazzo. He was armed.

We're seeking the public's help in identifying the shooter, who may have acted in self-defense.'"

"I can't believe this. This isn't Venice, California. We don't have people shooting each other here."

"We did last night. Somebody with a gun put an end to Salvio's murder spree, and they may have done it when he came at them with a knife. Apparently, he didn't know they were armed with a superior weapon."

"And what am I saying about the attack at Porto delle Donne? Those murderers used guns with silencers."

"Give that place a break. You don't need to mention that—it isn't what people are asking about. *I know* Salvio sent those hit men there to kill Raphielli, and any negative publicity her shelter receives would be unfair. There's no benefit to addressing Porto delle Donne at this time. It'd be tabloid fodder."

"You don't think the public has the right to know?" He twirled the bottle on his desk.

"Actually, no. The families of the victims have been notified. The public will have enough to chew on with Salvio Scortini's return from the dead, escape from police custody, and murders of Count Gabrieli Verona and his own valet before someone killed him."

"What do you know about Salvio's accomplices?"

"I don't know how he selected them, but he hired hit men here in Venice and in France, five in total. I've questioned families and landlords of the two men killed at the shelter, Rajim Aksal and Carlos Promulotti. My gut tells me Salvio assembled a group of anti-Catholic assassins."

"*Anti-Catholic?* Are you kidding me?"

"No. It came up when I asked Carlos' landlord if he was friendly with his tenant, and his response was, 'No, I'm Catholic.' When I asked him what he meant, he said Carlos hated Catholics. So, I did some checking, and Rajim hated Catholics, too. I made sure to follow that up with everyone else. I just learned from one of the French hit men's mothers that he fit the same pattern."

"That's the most bizarre thing I've heard in an already bizarre case."

"I'm getting used to being on the other side of the looking glass with this one."

"Tell me you've changed your mind and Salvio's murder plot is finished. Tell me it's over now."

"I wish I could, but no."

"No?"

"I think Salvio set a plan in motion to kill his wife and the Veronas that's still being played out. I believe Raphielli and the Veronas remain targets. I think it's bigger than just Salvio somehow."

Laszlo looked angry. "That's not what I want to hear from you."

"No one's sorrier than me. Also, the hit men were all wearing black, head to toe, including the one who tried to get into Raphielli's shelter back when the young guard, Alexi, was killed. Head-to-toe black with shiny shoes."

Laszlo grunted, unimpressed. "Anyone trying to commit a crime wears black, it's non-descript."

"Not true. Crooks wear regular shoes, jeans, greys. But all black, and shiny shoes? It's like they wore a special uniform."

"That doesn't interest me, let's get back to Giselle Verona." The big man's brows knit. "Where is she now? Has she come back from France?"

"She's disappeared, but I have word from Contessa Juliette Verona that she's safe."

"What is *with* this case?" Laszlo lost his patience and threw his hands up. "Contessa Verona stashed her daughter-in-law somewhere for safekeeping?"

"*Sì*, and since this was Salvio's second attempt to kill Giselle, I can't say I blame her." Luigi glanced down at his tall stack of intel and knew it didn't tell him what he needed to know. "I haven't gotten to the bottom of what's going on here, and until I do, I'm afraid it's a race to prevent more murders."

"You mean Raphielli Scortini, and the young Veronas—Count Vincenzo and Contessa Giselle?"

"*Sì*."

"He just killed Vincenzo's father, and last month he almost killed Vincenzo. What is it about that family Salvio hated so much?"

"I thought it was because the Vatican awarded the Verdu Mer construction project to Gabrieli. But now with the anti-Catholic hit men, I don't know. The Veronas are very tight with the pope."

"What about Raphielli? Salvio's dead. Even if he was angry enough at his wife to kill her, why wouldn't the contract be nullified by his death?"

"Dunno, but she wasn't telling me the truth last night when I questioned her and her associates at her home when the valet was murdered."

"Associates?"

"She was with Zelph Vitali, her security contractor, and Alphonso Vitali..."

"The private detective who gets the dirt on all the white-collar crooks?"

"*Sì.* They told me some crazy sequence of events, and I could tell they were making it up on the spot."

"All right, I'll keep my statement about Salvio's murder basic and leave Raphielli's women's shelter out of it. Keep me informed. I want you to go home at the end of this shift. Get some sleep, will you?"

"Sure, you too. Maybe see a chiropractor, your neck sounds bad."

"Don't worry about my neck. Get me something better than an anti-Catholic conspiracy. Practically the whole country is Catholic, and when it comes to sheer power, Rome is nothing but a suburb of Vatican City. Rome's got two and a half million people, but the pope has over a billion followers. I want to avoid running afoul of the Church."

"If I promise to be discrete, can you get me into the Vatican for Gabrieli's funeral?"

Laszlo stared off into the middle distance as he considered it, and then said, "I have a contact, I'll arrange it. But the more important funeral for you to attend is Scortini's here in Venice."

"Right, I'll check with Cardinal Negrali about that service. Since I've been surveilling Raphielli, he visits her every single day and sometimes accompanies her socially. He's attached himself so thoroughly to her he might as well be welded to her. I'll bet he's handling Salvio's service."

———◦◉◦———

Giselle woke up to the sound of jaunty knocking on the door and Markus answering sleepily in Ukrainian. Yvania's voice prattled back in happy-sounding Ukrainian from the other side of the door. He stretched and, teasing his substitute mother, said, "We are not currently having sex. Come in."

The door opened and Yvania locomoted her way into the abbey's secret guest quarters with clogs clacking, the rhinestones on her cat's-eye glasses glistening dully in the gloom, and the aroma of dark-roasted coffee preceding her. This would serve as Giselle and Markus' new home until the French or Italian police could stop the recent onslaught of hit men trying to kill them.

Juliette had come up with this inspired plan for her and Markus to hide out with the monks of Abbaye d'Orval just across the Belgian border on the edge of the great Ardennes Forest. And Yvania had come for several reasons: to keep their spirits up, to help as Giselle's pregnancy progressed, and because Yvania was incredibly helpful at times like these—hit men didn't scare her.

Giselle asked, "How'd you sleep?"

"Goot! I am sleeping just down the hall in a monk's cell so very, er, *clean.*"

Giselle and Markus's quarters were cozy and comfortable. Although designed originally in the Middle Ages to provide safekeeping for people who were being persecuted, the quarters had also been pressed into use during both world wars. Yvania had the stature of a fireplug, even with the extra inches provided by her clogs, so she looked perfectly proportional under the low ceilings. However, Giselle, at almost five-foot-nine, and Markus, at six-foot-two, needed to duck in places. Not that she was complaining—she was grateful for these ingenious monks' protection and accommodations.

Yvania set the coffee pitcher on a sideboard, stepped back out into the stone tunnel, and returned bearing a tray laden with stacked dishes. The picture of grandmotherly care, one would never guess that she used to be an underground resistance fighter for the Chechens in their struggle against Russia. And she'd saved Giselle on more than one occasion without hesitating or even losing a hairpin from the ubiquitous bun perched atop her head.

"Come lovebirds, you must take the food," she said in her heavy Ukrainian accent.

"I'll eat whatever's on that tray." Giselle sat up and Markus handed her the shirt she'd worn yesterday, which she pulled on.

Giselle rubbed her bare feet against Markus' warm leg under the covers and said, "*Mon amour*, if there's a place to hide that has better food...I don't know where it could be." She eyed the array of homey breakfast breads, jams, hard-boiled eggs, and what looked like herbed cottage cheese. Lifting a little cone-shaped lid off a pitcher, she spied her favorite treat, a deep red-orange persimmon compote that tasted like a warm fall sun dipped in dark sugar. It made everything it was drizzled over delectable. "Here, it is! *Goût du ciel!*"

She took a slice of baguette, swiped on a dab of fresh churned butter, then tipped the fat pitcher so a dollop of the gooey persimmon pulp anointed the bread. Settling into the crevasses, the flesh of the fruit slumped into the compote liquid like a jewel covered in orange varnish. She offered it to Markus' lips while holding a hand underneath to catch any drops of nectar. "It's incredible on everything."

"Taste of paradise? I cannot say 'no' to that." He took a bite, and after the crunch of the bread's crust, he closed his eyes and chewed. Then he opened his eyes, took the remaining bread, and popped it in his mouth.

Giselle licked dribbles off her hand. "I once ate a bag of horse treats with *goût du ciel* on them."

"Really?"

"I was way out in the countryside for a picnic and I'd forgotten to pack the crackers. I let my horse graze, so we were both happy."

"No wonder Juliette loves these monks!" Yvania said. "They are most talented at preserving that I know anywhere! This morning I was helping with the goats for the cheese making! I am not happy you are in danger, but I am *so happy* with being here for some time! So happy you two have a baby coming and soon will be married!"

There was a timid knock on the open door and a man's voice called, "I have a message. May I come in?" It was Daniel, the monk who'd been tasked with taking care of them.

"*Da*. I mean, *oui*," Markus called.

Daniel entered, looking nothing like a stereotypical monk. He'd said he was forty-something, but looked a decade younger, and his dark blonde hair was slightly longer than the ultra-tight shaved head that Markus maintained—who wasn't a monk in any way, shape or form. He said, "I have news from Juliette. Salvio's been shot. Dead."

"Fantastic!" Markus cried. Giselle felt him relax next to her, releasing tension he'd probably been holding since Salvio first started spying on her back in September, even before Salvio had threatened to bash her head in with an iron bar.

Yvania applauded the news by clapping her hands with a hearty *smack-smack-smack*. "Finally! The worlt is good rid of that nasty man! I thought I am killing him once before, but he came back still with the murdering!"

Giselle stopped short of clapping, too. "What about Vincenzo?"

"Your husband is unharmed, safe in Venice."

"*Dieu merci*." She felt a wave of relief, but then thought of her friend. "I hope Raphielli's okay."

"Juliette said aside from killing Gabrieli, Salvio went after his own valet, who didn't survive."

"How horrible. Raphielli must be a wreck."

"Now that the monster is dead? Raphielli is goot I am sure," Yvania said. "Not for worrying about that leetle goddess of love. Men will line up for trying to take care of that girl."

"Need coffee cups?" Daniel eyed the coffee pitcher and walked over to the kitchen, a time capsule containing a crude bee-hive oven built into the stone wall, wooden shelves stocked with dishes, pans, glasses, cups, urns of silverware, an ice chest, and small wooden table.

Daniel came back with cups and arranged them on a table next to the bed. "Your friend Fauve called. She says your local police friends were fine with your story, and she wants to bring you some clothing today. To keep your location secret, I'll make the exchange in an out-of-the-way town in case anyone follows her."

"*Merci,* Daniel," Giselle said. She reached a hand out to accept the coffee Markus had poured for her. "Now we'll just wait till the French and Italian police catch the rest of Salvio's band of killers. I can't imagine how Juliette's holding up with Gabrieli gone."

Yvania said, "Yesterday before I left Venice, she was busy arranging for a Verona grandchild. Today Vincenzo will be taking Gina to bed for the trying."

"*What?*" Giselle almost spit out her coffee. She stared at Yvania and then flicked her eyes toward Daniel in a signal for her to clam up in front of an outsider.

"It is okay I am saying anything in front of Daniel. Juliette said to trust him like we would trust her—absolute."

Giselle found that surprising, but then back to the initial shock blurted, "Gina, the schoolgirl from the flower shop?"

"Oh, *da.* I did not say anything last night because we were making the getaway. But having a Verona heir—it got Juliette out of her mourning like a miracle cure. It is a purpose. Somehow a new Verona baby will save the pope, but I do not know how."

"None of us do, Yvania." Markus waved a hand in exasperation, and a devilish smile appeared. "Ride 'em, Gina."

Giselle couldn't picture it. "Little Gina with the arm-loads of books, and the fussy pearls, and pencil skirts, and scrubbed nails, and the precise knife-edge hair? She seems so anal."

Markus raised an eyebrow. "Then she is perfect," he said drolly. "But that will not make a baby."

Daniel looked uncomfortable and straightened some books on a shelf at his elbow.

Yvania flipped a pudgy hand. "Juliette asked Gina for this favor of carrying on the bloodlines. Vincenzo should be okay with this. Gina does not have such a woman's body—more like a boy."

As Markus was busily buttering a piece of bread for Giselle, he said under his breath, "Except she is not Leonardo."

"True..." Yvania said slowly and took a drink of her coffee. "Perhaps she will be the first time Vincenzo will be with someone who is not Leonardo."

"Oh, I'm positive of that," Giselle said. "I can't wait to talk to him."

She eyed her cell phone plugged into a charger that was plugged into a converter that was plugged into the oldest electric outlet she'd ever seen—and having been raised in a château built in 1730 that had gotten electricity in 1836, that was saying something. This place was primordial.

"Daniel, we'll get dressed now. Can you come back in a few minutes and give us a tour of the areas it's safe for us to explore in the daylight? Before you go meet Fauve?"

"Of course."

"How cold is it outside?"

"Cold enough that the snow is not melting, but not too windy right now." He eyed her clothes draped over a chair doubtfully.

"I was doing yoga when the killers came for us," she explained.

"Near the end of the tunnel is a closet with heavier coats, scarves, hats, and gloves. You're welcome to what's there. I'll come back for you in ten minutes."

2

Raphielli arrived at Porto delle Donne feeling more herself after her...*um*...breakfast with Gio. She approached the security cage adjacent to the shelter's front door and saw that Azure was on duty. His face was solemn as he pressed the button requesting her admittance from Kate in the office. "Good to see you unharmed, Signora Scortini."

"*Grazie.* Call me Raphielli."

They both knew her last name would be forever associated with murder. "*Sì*, okay. Raphielli."

Once inside, the reek of cheap disinfectant hit her. She sat on the lobby bench to remove her winter boots. Looking over at her work shoes in their cubby, she felt an eerie vertigo—they'd been mute witnesses to last night's violence. While putting them on, she heard Paloma's raised voice in the nearby multi-purpose room.

"But we *didn't* die, we fought *back*. I didn't survive all the shit I've endured to be bumped off by some weirdoes dressed like funeral directors."

"One had on the nurse's lab coat," Ottavia said.

"*Sì*, but over his black...uh...uniform." Shanti sounded creeped out.

Paloma reasserted herself. "Why sit around discussing something I'd do again in a heartbeat? I thought I was about to see Leona's throat slit."

"You were!" Nanda cried.

"Just a tiny prick," Leona said. "I'm fine with my Band-Aid."

"Poor Kate was being choked till her eyes bulged—we had to do something," Paloma said.

"Some of you are very quiet," Dr. Risinger said. "Margarita, Meryl, Jasmine, Grace, Abrienne how do you ladies feel?"

Raphielli started to tiptoe past the open door, when Nanda cried, "Raphielli!" They all ran to her, but a wave of guilt reached her before her residents did. She'd been the cause of last night's mayhem. Surprisingly, they weren't blaming her for the attack and murdered staff. They huddled around, patting her on the back and petting her hair, all of them talking at once. "You're okay! They didn't get you! We saved Kate! You should've seen it—there were two of them! They had knives and guns!"

Raphielli's eyes met Paloma's, and she saw no judgment there. Paloma mouthed, "You're safe now."

As Mia and Dr. Risinger got the women settled back into their chairs, Raphielli excused herself and moved toward the office, but hesitated just outside the door when she heard Kate saying, "Ah, *sì*, Alphonso, she just arrived. You didn't give me a chance to...I just buzzed her in." There was silence and then, "How should I know where she's been? Well, you shouldn't have let her run off. She's in shock. We're all in shock to some degree. The drug you say the paramedics gave her last night can have serious side effects—psychotic episodes, thoughts of suicide, impaired judgment." She listened some more and then sounded angry when she said, "Well if you say she was acting erratically you should have..."

Raphielli could hear someone coming down the hall, so she cleared her throat and entered the room.

Kate muted her phone and said, "It's Alphonso, he's worried about you. He and Cardinal Negrali have called every half hour this morning. Do you want to talk to him?"

Another wave of guilt hit her. She took the phone and with eyes lowered to the scrubbed floors said, "I didn't know you'd worry, I..."

"You weren't answering your phone," his voice was hoarse with emotion. "I thought you'd fallen off a bridge when you didn't arrive at work."

"I just needed a walk."

"It started pouring!" He sounded incredulous, and then his voice was tender. "I'm so glad you're safe."

"I needed a break."

"*Ti amo*, Raphielli. I'm sorry."

"I'm sorry, too. Look, I've got to get some work done. I'll see you tonight."

"Call me when you're ready to walk home."

"Okay. *Ciao*."

Handing the phone back to Kate, she looked over at her desk. There was nothing on it. Her computer and files were all sealed inside transparent blue bags. She felt that eerie vertigo she'd felt seeing her shoes. Did evil leave a residue?

"It's unbelievable how far blood can travel," Kate said tiredly. She wrapped her arms around Raphielli in a warm maternal hug from behind. "I'm so glad you're here. I'm glad Salvio's dead. I never met the man, but I'm sorry you got stuck with him." Kate sniffed deeply. "You smell great. New soap?"

Raphielli realized Kate smelled Gio on her and changed the subject. "I wanted to come over here last night as soon as I heard, but they gave me something to calm me down and I'm afraid it knocked me out." Pulling back and turning to face her, she saw the bruises and claw marks on Kate's neck. Her hand flew to her mouth in horror.

"Oh, *sì*, my neck. Not as bad as yours was. When I finally go home, I'll borrow your trick and cover it with a scarf."

"Are you in pain?"

"I'd like to book a few sessions with your physical therapist. I'm too old to be beaten up."

"Is that your only injury?"

"Also a few stitches in my scalp. I have a hard head."

"*Per favore*, go home now. I'll send you my therapist's contact information. If you have any resumes that I can start reviewing for our...temporary replacement staff." She choked past a fresh lump in her throat. "I can't believe they're gone. So senseless."

"It's all taken care of for now. Luigi told me in confidence that he believes you're still in danger, so I brought in some of my family to cover the positions until the coast is clear. People I know I can trust. My aunt's in the kitchen cooking up a storm, my cousin Constanza is a registered nurse and has taken over our medical dispensary, Azure will work double shifts at the guard post, and my nephew Gilly will cover the rest."

"You've got a lot of relatives."

"We are legion. Oh, and Cardinal Negrali's been calling, probably about the funeral. But first things first. We have a new resident." Kate withdrew a roll of Mentos from her pocket and popped one in her mouth.

"New resident?" Raphielli blinked. "You did an intake last night of all nights? We're at the limit."

"Trust me, we need to keep this one. She's a sixteen-year-old kid but she looks about fourteen. She was naked and bloody when she turned up in the rain."

"Poor girl!"

"Held captive and serially raped for more than a week, but the pregnancy test was negative. I put her in the nurse's quarters because all the beds in the dorm rooms are in use. Also, Detective Lampani wants her to stay there so he can sneak through the kitchen to visit and question her as needed."

Rapheilli followed Kate down the back hall behind the kitchen. "What's her story?"

"Her parents took her to a house and left her there to be raped...by Salvio."

Again, that vertigo feeling of doom. *He was still trying to make an heir.*

Kate knocked lightly on the door. "Benedetta? It's me, Kate. May I come in?"

"*Sì,*" came a soft voice.

Kate opened the door to reveal a girl wearing one of the shelter's sweat suits. She had dark red cuts and scratches on her pale forehead and hands. One hand was splinted and bandaged. She was lovely, long and slim in a coltish way like a twelve-year-old in the midst of a growth spurt. She looked achingly vulnerable. Dark brown hair cascaded over one shoulder pooling in her lap, she had big pouty lips and looked at Raphielli with inquiring eyes that were somewhere between brown and green.

Kate gestured to Raphielli. "Benedetta, I'd like to introduce..."

"I know who you are," she said without glancing at Kate. "You're the barren wife."

Raphielli had been unguarded because of the girl's frail appearance, and she felt the label like a slap.

"You have no idea what you are talking about." Kate's voice was firm. "Apologize *per favore.*"

Raphielli said, "Kate, can you give us a moment?"

"I'll be right outside." She looked upset and left reluctantly.

Raphielli regarded the girl who now looked both sullen and smug.

"You're pleased you got a reaction from me."

The only reply was a little cock of her head that conveyed, *And what if I am?*

Refusing to be baited into an adversarial exchange, she sought to align herself with her newest resident as best she could. "You're correct. In the two years we were married, I was unable to give Salvio a child."

The girl continued to look her over in a rude manner.

"So, my husband raped you?"

"*Sì.*"

"You think you're superior to me. Why is that?"

"My parents considered it an honor to offer me up to have the Scortini heir."

"So did my mother and *nonna* when they married me off to Salvio."

Her whole demeanor brightened. "So, you *are* one of the faithful."

Raphielli looked at the girl with new eyes. "I take it you don't mean a Catholic."

The girl shut down. "Never mind, forget it."

"Okay, I'm going to draw something, and you can tell me if it's familiar." Raphielli went to the desk in the corner, took out a pencil and paper, and quickly sketched the symbols that had recently become so familiar to her: a sun, a moon, and the earth in a lunar eclipse, and a figure of a man standing in a boat. Handing the paper to the girl she asked, "Mean anything?"

"Oh, *sì.*" She looked relieved and less like an angry child. "You *are* one of us. You were just trying to throw me off with the Catholic comment."

"Did Salvio ever sneak you into our palazzo? Possibly through a secret passage?"

"To the water temple?" Her eyes lit up, and then she looked disappointed. "No. I've never been inside the Scortini Palazzo. My grandparents went there, but I only worshipped in the little temple under the safe house that I told Luigi and Kate about last night. Hey, will you take me to your palazzo so I can see the big temple?"

Raphielli felt protective over this girl who was apparently even more innocent than she'd been. "*Certamente*, Benny, I'll show you the temple. Can I call you Benny? But, it's important that we keep this as our secret."

"Sure." Benedetta flipped a hand in dismissal. "I know never to speak of the Alithiní with outsiders. Not even Luigi, and he's really cool for a detective."

"You can call me Elli. My friends do, and I'd like us to be friends."

The girl smiled and then picked at the tape on her splinted hand.

Raphielli had heard Salvio refer to the Alithiníans last night. She was sure this was the first person she'd come across who was actively devout to the religion the Catholics considered so dangerous. "Listen Benedetta, I know what Salvio did to you was savage...if it's what he used to do to me."

"*Sì.*" Her lips pressed together, and her nostrils flared in anger.

"And since you still have both eyes, I know you followed his rules."

"He threatened to cut one out if I looked anywhere but the ceiling...during..."

"Benny, what happened to you wasn't an honor. You were trafficked by your family, and it's because of what I endured with Salvio that I founded this shelter. You can stay here as long as you like. We'll keep you safe. I promise."

"*Grazie*, I'm planning on staying for a while. I'm not going back there, but I know the Alithiníans and my parents are looking for me. They'll want to return me to Salvio."

"Salvio's dead."

"Oh." The girl balled her good hand into a fist and scrubbed her knuckles along her knee. "Good. I mean, the faithful are going to freak, but *I'm* glad."

Kate opened the door, poked her head in, and pointed to their office mouthing, "Cardinal Negrali."

Raphielli wasn't in the mood to confess all the sins she was racking up and felt a strange woozy feeling. Maybe she was tired or it was an aftereffect of last night's sedative. But there was no putting him off now.

She found Cardinal Negrali sitting on the office sofa waiting to hear her confession.

"*Padre*, I wasn't expecting you today, not after everything that's happened."

"I had to see you after last night. Your trials just keep coming. I'm at your side through all this."

"*Grazie, padre.*"

"The police questioned you?"

"*Sì.*"

"The police didn't find the temple, did they? We can't have word of that dangerous cult getting out."

"No. But then, I've lived in the palazzo for years and never suspected it was there. The police have no idea."

"*Bene, bene.* Your mother and *nonna* have not come to pay a condolence call to you?"

"No, they would only come to take over my household. There'd be no condolences."

"Were you able to sleep?"

"*Sì.*" She neglected to tell him she'd taken a drug.

"Any nightmares?"

"No. I slept...deeply."

"Really? That's good news, and very unusual." He was staring at her intently.

She caved. "I became hysterical when I heard who died, and the medics gave me a sedative."

"Understandable. Has the Mafia don contacted you? Giancarlo Petrosino?"

"No. Now that he's killed Salvio, I expect he'll return to Palermo," she lied.

"All the better. Now, before we pray for the souls that were lost last night, is there any other burden you have to share with me, my child?"

Today her sins were heavy, but she was absolutely not ready to share them. "I want an annulment," she blurted and was surprised to hear herself say it.

He gave her a disappointed look and ran his hands over his cross and gold chains. "A grave request."

"But *padre,* Salvio has to have been one of the worst husbands in history." She couldn't believe she had to plead her case. If he knew her at all, he'd know she'd want to put that awful time behind her.

He fixed her with a look of paternal kindness. "*His* failure to be a good husband has nothing to do with *your* fidelity to the lifelong contract *you* made before the Almighty. Now, let us pray together..." He knelt down on the floor and brought his hands together. She joined him on her knees as he began to pray, "Absolve, we beseech thee oh Lord, the souls of thy servants who are dead to this world..."

As soon as he left, she went and found Paloma. The poor thing had only just started to come out of her shell in the last few days, and since the cathartic cry the two had shared, they had a special bond. "I'm glad I found you. You know we have a new girl?"

"*Sì*. I got a glimpse of her as Kate took her into the nurse's room. Just a kid."

"Well, I only have permits for ten residents and..."

"She makes us eleven."

"Right."

"Does one of us have to leave?" Paloma's bruised face sagged. "Oh, shit. Is it me? Oh shit."

"I was hoping you'd come live with me."

"Wuh-wuh...live with you?"

"Your bedroom would be at my home, but you'd still come here every day."

"Pinch me!" She held out an arm. "I mean...I really like it here, and the women are growing on me...even their kids...but I'm psyched to live with you and come here every day. I promise I'll be a good roommate."

"Kate'll handle the paperwork. Pack your things and you'll come home with me tonight."

"You're the coolest, Raphielli." As Paloma moved off toward the elevator, her limp was less noticeable. She really was improving since her arrival.

When Alphonso came to walk her home, she introduced him to Paloma who looked up at him and said, "You're even more handsome up close."

He gave her an embarrassed smile as she explained, "All the gals inside gather around the security monitors in reception when you come to pick Raphielli up."

"I had no idea you were all so bored in there," was his shy response.

They walked slowly to accommodate her pace. Since it wasn't raining, it was a nice stroll through the *sestiere*, with the lamplights illuminating wispy winter fog. Approaching the palace, Paloma said, "I can't believe I'm going inside Palazzo Scortini. It's friggin' huge, like an airport...and spooky."

Inside, Dante took their coats and offered a courtly bow to their guest. "*Signora*, welcome."

Paloma pressed a hand to her healing ribs and bowed stiffly. Then she realized it wasn't called for and blushed. "Call me Paloma. Signora's my mother's name."

He chuckled and turned to Raphielli. "Zelph is waiting for you in *la Sala Baùtta*."

"*Grazie*, Dante. I've called Domina, and her team's delivering a fresh bed for that orange and gold room by the nautical observation gallery."

"*Sì, la Sole Vista* room. Her team already delivered the bed, and also boxes of items Domina wants Paloma to have."

"I'm in *la Sole Vista* room?" Paloma breathed. "Sounds nice."

"It is, and it's on this floor not far from my suite. Most of the rooms are upstairs on the second and third floors, and are not only a long way away, but haven't been used in years."

Paloma stood uncertainly as Dante disappeared with her tiny suitcase.

"Why don't you relax with me, Alphonso, and Zelph before dinner," Raphielli suggested.

As they walked off toward *la Sala Baùtta*, they passed

through enormous halls and rooms, all of them dark. Paloma said, "Wow! Your fireplaces are the biggest I've ever seen."

"We don't use most of them."

"My father was a chimney sweep. As a kid I used to work with him, clean brushes, go into tight spaces because he was pretty fat. I could tell you all about yours if we ever get so bored you'd want to hear about them," Paloma said with an edge of pride to her voice.

Alphonso perked up. "That'd be helpful. We're learning about the layout of this place."

"We're doing some updates," Raphielli explained. "Installing security, things like that."

"I don't see servants running around."

"No."

"Kinda crazy I know, but I imagined that musical where servants would do everything for me."

"Sorry to disappoint."

"I'm not really disappointed."

"I have a maid, Rosa, and you've met Dante, and I have a part-time cook," Raphielli said.

"A real knockout of a cook," Alphonso sighed.

"Well, that's something," Paloma said while squinting at another fireplace as they passed.

<hr />

Giselle was grateful for the heavier clothes Daniel had loaned them. She, Markus, and Yvania followed him through low stone tunnels strung with naked light bulbs overhead as Daniel unlocked and relocked several doors. They'd come this way last night, but she hadn't taken much notice. Finally, they came out from behind an ivy-covered trellis in a cloistered stone courtyard that housed plants in boxes of all sizes. It was an ancient stone garden that was sheltered, and the stones radiated the sun's warmth back to the plants.

Markus asked, "Daniel, you say we are safe here. Even from your public visitors?"

"Quite safe."

"Who has access to us?"

"The property is vast, extending out to the motorway and deep into the forest. The visitors roam many areas, but nowhere near here. The gates to the public areas are open between ten and six o'clock every day. Down the hill, visitors have access to the shops on the east side of the property, the small chapel just over another hill, a restaurant. Also our petting zoo, and cheese house near the main parking lot, which you cannot see from here in the main abbey compound. Buses park there, and the tourists stick to those areas. The people who venture out around the east grounds are going on nature walks, bird watchers, or the painting society. No one has permission to move inside the compound's wrought iron fencing, come west approaching the abbey's hill, or toward the west sector where our actual farm is."

Giselle was itching to call Vincenzo. "How's the phone reception?"

"In and around the abbey, it's excellent. We have new technology in the bell tower, and when I return from town,

I'll have disposable phones for you. I must ask you not to use your personal phones for safety reasons."

"Certainly." Markus stomped his feet against the frozen ground and exhaled a plume of vapor.

"You won't be bored here. We can keep you busy. There's plenty to do in the barns."

"Happy to help," Giselle said. "I remember coming here every year for school trips. Do you still have big draft horses?"

"*Oui*, but nothing glamorous like yours. These are workhorses."

"You know my horses?" She was surprised.

"What kind of a mother-in-law would Juliette be if she didn't show us pictures during her visits? Juliette is my oldest friend. We grew up together."

"I didn't know that."

Making their way down the stone pathways out of the courtyard, through more locked doors and gates, they left the grand abbey via wide granite steps down to the private west grounds and headed toward a cluster of white and red barns.

"Juliette never said she knew you personally, though now I know it's another reason she never missed a chance to come here whenever she visited me and Vincenzo in Gernelle. I thought she'd forged a friendship with the monks here over cheese and preserves."

"Ah, she does have a special love of our old way of making food, but we've always kept in touch. Actually, when it was time for Vincenzo to travel for school, I was the one who suggested Aiglemont for him. Such fine schools there."

Giselle shot Markus a 'See?' look and then turned back to Daniel. "So, you grew up in the South of France?"

"*Oui*, in Rennes-le-Château where Juliette's family lived. We were closer to Barcelona than Paris. Our families have been friends for generations. When Juliette and I were sixteen, she went to Venice for school and I came here to study theology."

"I thought Juliette was from Italy," Markus said.

"No, she's from a very old French family called Clairvaux," Giselle said. "She doesn't talk about her family much though. After going to school in Venice, she fell in love with Gabrieli and never left."

They arrived at the horse barns and saw a monk waving his arms. "Help me gather the sheep!" he shouted. "Something pushed the fence over, and they're moving toward the road!" He gestured toward the far-off four-lane motorway.

"*Oui, venaient!*" Giselle yelled. "Coming!"

"I'll get them onto horses!" Daniel called.

They rushed into the barn, and when Giselle grabbed a bridle from a hook and started nudging a horse out of its stall, Markus said, "Let me and Daniel go. You are pregnant, and a fall could—"

"Ridiculous!" she cut him off. "Every woman in my family rode during pregnancy until their last trimester when they couldn't get up on their mounts. There's no danger to my pregnancy. First, I'm not going to fall off a horse while shepherding sheep. But even if I did, I'd still be pregnant. The worst that could happen could be a broken arm. Our little embryo is snuggled deep within my body."

He caught the bridle Daniel tossed at him, and before he could argue further, she'd finished bridling her horse. "I'll take the gentler of the two and promise not to jump over any fences." She made a clicking sound, backed the bridled horse out, and tossed the reigns over a fence post. Then she moved to Markus' side, took the bridle from him, and had it on the big horse in a few quick movements. She jogged it out to Daniel and asked, "Which is mine?"

"This one is very docile," Daniel said. He made a stirrup of his hands and gave her a boost up. "Can you ride bareback?" he asked Markus.

"I have strong legs."

"Kick them straight into a lope, and they're very smooth." He gave Markus a leg up and handed them short brooms of thin dried sticks strung with reeds. "These make a howling hiss that the horses are used to, but the sheep run from. Get between the sheep and the road, then swish your broom so they'll run away from you and come back here." Daniel opened a gate to the pasture.

Giselle gripped her broom and kicked her horse into a lope with Markus right behind her. When they got between the sheep and the busy road, the herd stopped, confused, and one wave of her broom sent the herd running back the way they'd come. It didn't take long before they'd gathered the sheep back in their grassy field where Daniel and the other monk had propped the fence up to secure them.

Giselle loved being out in the country, so far removed from the vogue persona she had to assume as Contessa Verona in the cities at art events or on Vincenzo's arm.

Here she didn't have to worry about French tabloids reporting her every move, or the art world gossiping about her mental stability based on her dangerous sculptures.

Here, the scents wafting from the Ardennes Forest grounded her. It was the same forest that butted up against her property in Gernelle. Deep and magical, mossy and alive, especially in the dark recesses beneath the canopy of boughs where the sunlight failed to penetrate.

Comfortable within the borrowed coat, she took a deep breath and loped alongside Markus. The sight of him riding across the untouched winter landscape, his legs gripping the big Belgian draft horse, made her ache for him. He hadn't grown up with horses but had learned to ride while staying with her in France. She was impressed at how firmly he sat astride the enormous grey horse. She was riding a smaller Ardennes draft horse, and while she had strong legs, the broad girth of this beautiful mare's back was about her limit. God help her, despite losing Gabrieli, she felt happy—and that made her feel guilty.

When they got back to the horse barn, they met up with Daniel and he walked them to the pasture where they released their horses to graze. "I have requests from the farmhands. Can you give some attention to the kids, lambs, and piglets?"

"Of course," Markus said.

"And can you help gather eggs in the hen house?"

Giselle said, "I'd be happy to."

"Where is Yvania?" Markus asked, looking around.

"She's in the barn helping the vet tend to the goat who broke the fence."

"Are you off to town now?" she asked.

"*Oui.*"

They went to check on Yvania. She was in one of the larger barns with a veterinarian who was cleaning a gash on the front shoulder of an adult goat. Yvania was handing clean gauze to the vet and tossing soiled medicated strips into a bucket. Then she picked up an aerosol can and shook it. After the vet dried the wound, Yvania stepped close and said, "You will take hold so he does not bite?"

The vet held the goat's head. "Got him."

She said, "Hokay, I am going to spray now." And with a burst of aerosol mist, she shellacked the wound with a thick white glue. The goat jumped once, then took the offered apple out of the vet's hand, fright forgotten, and chomped contentedly. As Yvania placed the can back on a shelf, she commented, "So much better than putting tree sap on the wound, this liquid skin."

"They use it on humans, too," the vet said. "It fuses to the skin and stays in place until new skin grows and the old sloughs off. For this adult, it'll last about a month. Plenty of time for the wound to heal."

"If I had a cut, I would love to try on me," Yvania said enthusiastically.

Giselle admired the old-world-meets-new-world tableau, and Markus said, "I love that at her age she is excited by new things. She will be good with our children."

Giselle took a deep breath, inhaling the cool scents of fresh hay bedding for the little goats and the tang of goat milk in the air. "Let's get animals for our property. I'd like to raise our children around animals."

Yvania heard and responded, "*Da!* Is goot for children."

After helping clean out the pens and groom the kids and lambs, Giselle wondered if her hormones were making her baby-crazy. She was feeling positively maternal toward the little beauties. Next, they headed over to the pigs, who adored being brushed and scratched. Finally, Giselle headed off alone to gather eggs.

The henhouse was a yellow wooden structure with three levels of shelving, and each nest was packed with fresh straw. Ducking inside she spotted a monk scooping feed into a bucket. "I've come to help you gather eggs."

He nodded as if he already knew who she was, then pulled a folded card from inside his wool cassock and handed it to her. It read: I HAVE TAKEN A VOW OF SILENCE.

He was about sixty years old, tall and lean. Giselle nodded and returned his card. After showing her how to feel around each perch for eggs and place them in slim old-fashioned crates, he left the hen house to spread food around the hen fields.

About ten minutes later, she'd just fallen into the relaxation of her task when she heard heavy footsteps on the wooden walkway just outside the thin wood-slat wall. They sounded ungainly, and something tentative about them made her hyperalert. *Someone sneaking up on me?* Being hunted had made her paranoid.

Looking through gaps low down in the siding, she saw big black boots and thick legs in dark pants. Someone had stopped, and they were facing the wall as if sensing her. Soundlessly, Giselle set her crate aside, sank to her knees, and got low so she was eye level with the gaps. Peeking out between the weathered slats, she could see the boots more clearly, but not who was wearing them. Perhaps if she got lower, she could look upward and see their face or whether they had a weapon.

Her pulse pounded as she lowered herself flat against the straw, praying she wasn't crushing unfound eggs. This view was no better. She glanced around for a weapon and snatched up a handheld metal claw used for raking the nests. "Who's there?" she called.

"Oh! Someone's talking in there?" a surprised voice called back. It was a gruff local Châlons-en-Champagne accent, but the end of her sentence had a neighboring Ardennes-Metz slur. No way Salvio could convince a local woman to take money to kill her. Not a chance in this tight-knit region.

Giselle swung the door open to reveal an old woman writing something on a chalkboard hung on the wall. She had a stack of empty egg crates under one arm.

Giselle said, "I'm gathering eggs. Daniel said I could help out."

"Ah, our special guest. I won't ask your name," she said. "I've already met Yvania. I'm Ida, the cook's assistant. I came for eggs. Usually, it's the boy, but he's busy churning butter. My joints don't like churning when it gets this cold."

Giselle gave Ida what she'd gathered and returned to her chore. It seemed such a strange thing to be hunted by Salvio Scortini, a man she didn't know, and to have him hire hit men. It wasn't something she'd have believed if they hadn't come racing onto her property trying to murder her and Markus yesterday. Those disturbing thoughts were interrupted when she heard Daniel talking to Markus just outside and went to join them.

Daniel turned to Giselle. "I have news. First, Juliette said Gabrieli's funeral is the day after tomorrow in the Vatican, and that while it breaks her heart, she and the pope agree that it's too dangerous for you to attend."

"*Merde!* I was afraid of that! Now I hate Salvio even more, if that's possible! He cracked Vincenzo's head and killed Gabrieli, and now he's kept me from..." She took a shuddering breath. "I understand...I'm fine. Just really...*really* angry."

Daniel handed her a disposable phone. "Okay, second is your friend Fauve spotted a man who looks just like Bernardo, the hit man she drugged. But she checked with the authorities, and he's still in custody."

Markus tensed. "Where did she see this new man?"

"He just arrived in Aiglemont. She encountered him in the general store near her hotel. He was asking questions like what they knew about the recent story in the news of the men who targeted you...and if anyone knew where you were."

"Oh, my..."

"Fauve says his questions sounded casual, like small talk. He has an Italian accent."

"What'd she do?"

"Your friends are quite brilliant, actually. She texted her husband, Henri, to look out the window of their hotel and watch for someone who looked like Bernardo. Then they called everyone in the area, and now all the locals are keeping an eye out for this man. He's wearing all black, driving a silver Peugeot with a rental sticker. The text group keeps expanding and they're getting constant texts from neighbors reporting where he is and who he talks to. They've included your new burner numbers in the group, so both of your phones will give you the latest updates."

Giselle looked down at the new disposable phone, and there were indeed group texts on it. The latest reports were of the snack he'd just bought at a fuel station; a tin of sprats, plain crackers, and a bottle of Volvic mineral water. "They're calling him 'Spratman'?"

"Your country folk are very perceptive."

"You're too nice to say 'nosey,' but you're right. We don't miss a thing when it comes to life in our neck of the woods. So, here's another hit man who looks like the one Fauve drugged yesterday. I'm glad we're here until the coast is clear."

"Strategically, we shouldn't leave this hired killer lurking about the countryside. I'll think of a trap for Spratman," Daniel said as he hefted a suitcase. "Now, let's take your clothes to your quarters, and then eat."

Markus put his phone in his pocket and said, "Yvania is making her bread. You monks here are in for a treat."

"It's good?" Daniel asked over his shoulder.

Giselle was suddenly hungry. "It's life-changing!"

The three of them climbed the path up to the abbey.

———◦◦◦———

Luigi had been working for more than thirty-six hours and he was exhausted. He'd gone home for a twenty-minute nap and a shower before hurrying back out through the storm to the Hotel Londra Palace for the Amendola's press conference. He squeezed into the lobby and found reporters from various news programs in front of a phalanx of locals who were volunteering to look for the missing teen.

The event appeared to be orchestrated by the news program Notizie Now!, a popular new cable show that promised news but delivered outrage and sensationalism. One of the show's correspondents was speaking into a microphone behind the podium on a small temporary stage. She was asking for everyone's help in finding Benedetta while Signore and Signora Amendola stood frozen nearby. Luigi saw their behavior for what it was; they were terrified someone would discover their crime.

When it was the couple's turn at the podium, they mumbled that they were praying for Benedetta's safe return, and the event concluded with the correspondent urging attendees to search for Benedetta and take flyers bearing her photo. Luigi moved to the stage and helped the coiffed correspondent down. Up close, he could see her thickly applied makeup. It looked outlandish in person, but the HD cameras must read it as flattering.

"I'm Detective Lampani. I have a few questions." He was looking past her and right at Benedetta's parents. "Signore et Signora, you reported your daughter missing after twenty-four hours? Or two weeks? Which is it?"

Their eyes bulged, and he ignored the correspondent's protests as he maneuvered around her to prevent the Amendolas from leaving the stage.

He pressed, "The missing person statement you filed

with us early this morning said you saw your daughter go jogging last night. Was she in the habit of jogging during rain storms? You don't live near Parco Savorgnan, so why were you there last night?"

"We meant to say, Parco Biennale..." the wife began to say, when the husband spun her around and she almost fell.

The correspondent was objecting over Luigi's shoulder. "Don't upset them. They've been through enough, and I'm about to film an interview with them." She then addressed the Amendolas. "We're set to film upstairs. Come this way. You can talk to the police afterward."

Luigi stepped aside, but his questions had spooked the couple into coughing up a third story. As they hurried past, he couldn't resist tossing some bait to see if they went for it. "You said you're praying for her return. You're Catholic?"

The two flinched in unison but recovered in a flash. "Of course! Good Catholics," they stammered.

"Which church do you attend? You know, where you'll hold the prayer vigil?"

"*Ehi fermi questo!* This is harassment!" the correspondent objected and hustled the couple toward the elevator.

Luigi could have marched the couple down to headquarters, but at this juncture he didn't want his interest in this missing person's case to become known to his department or even Chief Inspector Laszlo.

There were three Catholic churches in the Amendola's *sestiere.* He'd check to see if they attended services. Benedetta had refused to answer his question about her religion. His hunch was they were part of the anti-Catholic group Salvio had surrounded himself with.

He headed over to Sestiere Canaregio to find Cardinal Negrali. Luigi had seen him hovering around Raphielli's daily routine for weeks now, and it was time to become better acquainted with the Vatican power player who, as the most influential cardinal in the world, was touted to be a shoo-in as the next pope.

Cardinal Americo Negrali was the head of Chiesa di Santa Maria dei Miracoli, which the local Venetians called "the Little Church"—sort of tongue in cheek. And while the cardinal could have attached himself to any cathedral in the world other than Saint Peter's in the Vatican, Negrali had an apparent soft spot for this church.

He'd set tongues wagging and headlines flying over a ten-year period when he spent almost four million euros to have the church's marble exterior removed, rinsed inside stainless-steel tanks of distilled water to remove some of the natural salt content from the stone, and then reassembled.

Stepping into the Little Church's narthex, Luigi veered around the tall figure of Christ on the cross and over to the font of holy water, into which he dipped his fingers and then crossed himself as he studied the impressive stairway leading up to the altar. Maybe Negrali liked being so high above everyone else.

"You cannot come in here," a firm voice declared.

Luigi turned to see two elderly monsignors pointing a scantily clad woman to the door.

"I can put my coat on," she whined.

"You certainly can, just outside," was their response.

She dragged a fur coat over her bare shoulders, and because her dress was so short, she appeared to be naked beneath it. A relieved young man put a cigarette between his lips and followed her out.

Luigi approached the monsignors. "*Scusi*, I'm looking for Cardinal Negrali."

Their bright eyes sized him up. "Is this official police business?"

"At this time, no."

"We will tell His Eminence at once. Your name?"

"Detective Luigi Lampani." To show respect, he added, "I should have made an appointment."

"He is always happy to help the police."

"*Grazie.*"

One of the men moved so swiftly and smoothly, his black robes fanned out behind him like wings. He disappeared through a door in the back while the other stood staring at Luigi. After a beat, he said, "*Sì*, it does well to aid the police. The Mafia is feasting on the rest of Italy, we must help the police keep strong here in il Veneto."

"True."

"That Mafia trial in September had us on the edge of our seats," the old man continued.

"It surely did."

"Too bad don Giancarlo Petrosino was found 'not guilty.'" It was said with such neutrality, Luigi wondered if it was a condemnation, but decided he was too tired to care.

The monsignor continued, "Well, he cleared off back to Sicily, so I think he got the message. *No Mafia! Venezia è sacra.*"

Cardinal Negrali came hurrying toward him at the same pace as his subordinate, his red robes streaming out making him look like a Christmas bell. He sported the biggest cross Luigi had ever seen on a person's chest. He must have missed it when he was surveilling Raphielli because the cardinal had always worn a coat.

"Detective."

Up close, Luigi was reminded of a bird of prey, maybe a hawk. "*Eminenza...*"

"I'm on my way to Chiesa di San Canciano. If you accompany me, we can speak as we walk."

"*Grazie, bene.*"

"Is the rain holding off?"

"For the moment, *sì.*"

Luigi waited while one of the old monsignors helped Negrali on with his coat, then followed the cardinal out the front door and around the edge of the canal before falling into step with Negrali along the *fondamenta.*

"How can I help the police?"

"I'm sure you're aware of the recent local murders, in particular, Salvio, the heir to the Scortini building dynasty."

"*Sì.*"

Luigi felt the tingle of perception. The cardinal should have asked about details, started pumping him for information, but he was monosyllabic. He was hiding something.

"You're acquainted with that family?"

"I'm a scholar of Saint Vincent Ferrer, patron saint of builders, and have been the Scortini family's spiritual patriarch for years. I'm Raphielli Scortini's father confessor."

"Oh?" Luigi feigned surprise. "As the head of the College of Cardinals, I wouldn't think you had time, what with the recent scandal on birth control and that bad business with Cardinals Arguelles and Klerk in the news."

The look of pious pain that settled on the old man's face was worthy of a painting.

"The church will return to the conservative teachings and things will right themselves."

"So, you find time to hear the confessions of a twenty-year-old heiress?"

"I find time for those to whom I've made a commitment. Raphielli is young and naïve, and I'm serving as executor of her estate."

Ah, now it made sense. Luigi knew from a banker friend that Raphielli was now probably the wealthiest woman in the world, and that Vincenzo Verona was helping her create a gargantuan trust. Negrali, being the kind of man who used the offerings of the Catholic faithful to desalinate the marble of his favorite church instead of feeding the poor, wouldn't hesitate to pounce on Raphielli's money.

"So, you'll be able to tell me who I should speak to about Salvio's funeral arrangements."

"I'm personally handling that service."

"There won't be a lot of friends coming, I'd assume."

"Salvio didn't have any, no. But his father and his grandfather had many, many friends. They'll come out of respect."

"When is it?"

"The day after tomorrow. I'll be in Rome for Count Verona's sunrise funeral, then back on the train to preside over Salvio's that evening."

Luigi would do likewise. "Where will it be?"

"Chiesa di Santa Maria dei Miracoli at seven forty-five."

They'd arrived at San Canciano as rain began to spatter, so Luigi tossed out a final hook. "I'll be attending both funerals, part of our surveillance to identify the hit men who conspired to kill Gabrieli and are still hunting Raphielli."

"Hit men? It was Salvio." He started to say more but started coughing. A priest, who'd been watching from the church door, came running out with an umbrella and after positioning it over the cardinal's head, he clapped him on the back a few times.

"*Grazie, Eminenza*, I'll see you in Rome." Luigi took notice of Negrali's alarmed expression before turning and splashing hurriedly across the *campo. Ha! I made the greedy old cleric choke. Scholar of the patron saint of builders, my ass.*

There was a good chance this mighty cardinal would get himself bumped off by a hit man if he got too close to Raphielli. Luigi had never met anyone more shy than Raphielli Scortini. The unfortunate girl probably had nothing to confess to this power player—she was ripe for exploitation.

Ripe was a good word for Raphielli. She was a delicious mixture of fresh innocence in a body that wouldn't quit. And now that she'd updated her wardrobe—no longer wearing some old woman's cast-off clothes—she was positively arresting. Nothing showy, but last night in Salvio's office, her wet clothes hugged her curves in a way that was downright primal. Sure, she had a big sweater pulled over the ensemble, but Luigi's powers of perception were superior to a cardigan's power of concealment.

Next, he visited the area churches to see if the Amendolas attended or if they planned a prayer vigil. Zilch. Then he went back to headquarters and called every Catholic church in Venice and the surrounding areas. Nothing. While chewing aspirin tablets to stave off a headache, he read every page in every file on the Scortini case, then logged into the computer system and found everything he could on the Amendolas...which was nothing.

Now, with a headache blooming behind the bridge of his nose, he plodded home to get a proper nap.

⸺⸺◈⸺⸺

Gina would never forget her first time with Vincenzo. Arriving at the luxury apartment building, she'd done as Vincenzo had asked and told the doorman she was visiting Leonardo Trentori. After being admitted, she took the elevator to the third floor and walked along the plush runners to the boys' unit. She gave the doorbell a poke and had just enough time to take a deep breath before the apartment door opened wide. Vincenzo stood before her in a button-down shirt, dress pants, and driving moccasins. He was taller than she remembered. He looked happy to see her, and he was even more beautiful than she'd remembered.

Her mouth went dry. "*Ciao, Vincenzo.*"

"*Ciao,*" he said. "*Per favore,* call me V." He hesitated, appearing nervous.

Not good, nervous isn't going to help him perform. Break the ice. "Okay, V." She peeked over his shoulder. "Your place is beautiful. You know, whenever you and Giselle were in town from Paris, I thought you two lived in the palazzo with your parents." *Ooh! Why did I bring up his parents! I don't want to make him cry!*

"Yeah, well, for obvious reasons, Leo and I never told anyone that this was *our* apartment. We've led everyone to believe that when I'm here, I'm visiting my best friend and accountant, working on financial transactions."

"That's right, he's your accountant. Well, you both did an excellent job of keeping up appearances. Where's your bodyguard?"

"He's around," he said waving vaguely to the building's public hallways behind her.

"Invite her in and let's have some refreshments," Leonardo called from somewhere behind Vincenzo.

V ushered her into the living room. All the furnishings had clean modern lines. Everything was oversized and custom made to fit the grand proportions of the rooms without looking ostentatious. The sofas and ottomans were generous, but the place didn't look like a hotel lobby. It looked homey, filled with mementos from their travels and life together. Vincenzo made her coat disappear into a closet as she moved toward Leonardo, who was coming out of the kitchen with a tray.

"We can't thank you enough for doing this," Leonardo said. He was smiling serenely as he set a tray of cut fruit, chilled wine, and bottled water on a table. "When you've been at Juliette's side, I never really looked at you. You're lovely, Gina."

"*Grazie.* I guess I like my hands."

Vincenzo took one of them and led her to the couch. "*Sì*, your hands are beautiful, and so are you."

"*Grazie*... Should we get started, and then get to know each other afterward?" Her voice faltered. "Sorry, that sounded so lame and pushy at the same time."

"No, you're right. Trying to make this into a seduction would be an awkward failure, I'm afraid."

"No seduction needed, I'm ready to...oh gosh...what do I say? Receive you?" She cast about for something to do with her mouth other than talk. She plucked a grape from the tray and nibbled it.

Vincenzo said, "We think we can make the whole experience pleasant and enjoy the situation we find ourselves in. Let's begin so we don't become even more inhibited." He poured a glass of wine for himself and one for Leonardo. "What would you like to drink, Gina?"

"Water, *per favore.*"

As Vincenzo poured she said, "That's a nice sweater, Leonardo."

"*Grazie,* and call me Leo."

"Would you take it off?" she said as she unzipped her boots.

She felt Vincenzo's eyes on them as Leonardo started to undress. She stood to help him, and they ended up slowly undressing each other. He knelt to remove her boots and she lay back on the big couch admiring him. His chest and shoulders were sculpted perfection. Both he and V had a reputation for championship sculling on the Venetian canals and the rivers of France. His upper body showed how effective rowing was as resistance training.

Vincenzo placed her glass of water on the table and came to stand behind her. He stripped his clothes off, nosed the nape of her neck, and inhaled deeply. Gina felt him shiver minutely as a wave of arousal hit him. He inhaled again and kissed the back of her neck while Leonardo stood in front of her. She put her arms around Leo, and he pressed fully against her, enfolding her completely. Vincenzo felt Leo's hands reach out and stroke him as he bent forward and started nibbling on Vincenzo's neck. They stood with her sandwiched between them, both reaching between her parted legs, explored her body, stroking, and kissing her while teasing each other.

Her knees went weak and she moved from between them to sit on the couch and watch them kiss. After a bit, Leonardo came and knelt in front of her, kissing her inner thighs, and stroked one of her socks off with smooth caresses down her calf. Vincenzo knelt and kissed her thigh as he began drawing her other sock off. Leo slipped her panties down, and Vincenzo removed them and began to knead and nibble her thigh as she let it drop to the side to make room for what Leonardo was doing. He appeared to be fascinated by her privates, touching, stroking, and then reached for a small item on the table, which she realized was a vibrator.

"I bought this for you. Is it okay if I touch you with it?"

"*Sì.*"

"It's on the lowest setting, and I'll start with your thigh, okay?"

"*Sì.*" She closed her eyes and reached for Vincenzo's hair as he nibbled his way toward her hip and watched.

Leonardo was like a child with a new toy as he applied the vibrator lightly and asked her to guide him with it. Vincenzo stood up and finished undressing. Gina watched him with hooded eyes, and he enjoyed her eyes on him—he was aroused by how attractive she appeared to find him. He drank in her desire for him, and then she looked back down with hungry eyes at Leonardo, who was still kneeling before her. He had moved the device upward and appeared to have learned quickly how to control her breathing with what he was doing between her legs.

Vincenzo was incredibly aroused as she turned her attention away from Leo and beckoned the naked Vincenzo to come closer. She reached out and took hold of his cock and stroked it in a way Leonardo never had, soft, and yet strong. She took him in her mouth and it felt so good he had to steady himself. Leo looked up from biting her thighs, and while the device hummed quietly, he slipped a finger inside her and said, "I shouldn't have worried. You two look like you're having fun."

"Oh, Leo, she's really good at this. Gina, you're amazing at giving head."

"Will you do it for me?" Leo asked and removed his finger from her wetness.

She gave Vincenzo a final lick before saying, "*Sì*, stand up, *per favore*."

Turning off the device, he stood next to Vincenzo and said in a voice tight with desire, "I believe I have you ready. Can you take Vincenzo now?"

She nodded, and Vincenzo sank to his knees between her legs. She guided him inside her as she took Leonardo in her mouth. Vincenzo found himself stroking inside something he'd never felt before, and it was glorious. Her body was fit, spare, nothing jiggling or curvy. Her skin was creamy pale like a pearl next to his and Leonardo's olive skin. She undulated her hips in a rhythm that he joined in, and she watched as Leo leaned over to kiss Vincenzo passionately.

Leo was on the verge of coming and pulled back to watch. Both men were overcome watching the other taking pleasure from Gina. She'd opened her thighs wide and was scratching Vincenzo's back while pulling him in. Then she began to shudder, and he lost all control as she wrapped her legs around his hips. Leonardo withdrew from her mouth and turned to let Vincenzo finish him off as Gina cried out something unintelligible. The three collapsed in a heap on the couch.

"Wow!" she panted. "You two never did that with Giselle?"

"What? *No!* She's like our sister," Vincenzo said.

She fanned her face. "Some sister."

Leonardo seemed surprized. "Oh-ho! What's this? *You* like Giselle?"

"Are you kidding? Every man in the world—except you two apparently—wants her and every woman wants to be her. But yeah, I have a girl crush on her."

"A girl crush? Really?"

"Anyone else?" Vincenzo asked.

"Mmm...I recently met Raphielli Scortini."

"You find Raphielli desirable?" Leonardo lifted his head from Gina's stomach and stared at her. "You certainly don't have a type. She's nothing like Giselle."

"She isn't tall, but there's something larger than life about her. That delicate pale skin, dramatic brows, big dark eyes, and voluminous black ringlets falling below her shoulders..." Gina made a little sound like a cat purring. "She's shaped like a fantasy woman with those big breasts and round hips."

"Have you ever been with another woman?"

"No, so you could just call it an attraction, I guess." Pooching her lips out in thought, she closed her eyes before saying, "A big part of the attraction is their accomplishments. Giselle and her dangerous sculptures taking the art world by storm, and Raphielli is just out of her teens and establishing her own women's shelter...both so ballsy."

"You're a very interesting person, Gina," Leo said as he stroked his palm across one of her nipples, making it harden. "And very candid."

Vincenzo lazily lifted his head from Gina's thigh. "I think this baby making will provide an enjoyable six days."

"I agree." Gina looked down at him as she ran her fingers through Leonardo's hair feeling the silky thickness. His short black curls were lush. "This was the best sex I've ever had."

Leo smiled. "Glad to hear it."

"Mmm, this was good for me... more fun than I expected," Vincenzo said. "It's like you're somehow familiar." Vincenzo rolled over to lie on his back, watching her admire him.

"I was just going to say that. She's somehow familiar."

"Have you had much sex?" Vincenzo asked her.

"No. And this is my first unprotected sex."

"Leo and I have only ever been with each other. We were young, virgins."

Leo glanced up at the clock. "We need to get cleaned up and over to the palazzo for dinner with your mother."

The boys took a quick shower and then she hopped in to rinse off. When they left the apartment building a bodyguard appeared from the shadows and stayed close as they walked to Vincenzo's boat.

In the lamplight she saw that the steps to the palazzo were mounded with flowers from mourners. Photos of Count Gabrieli drooped inside plastic sleeves hung from light posts and placed on benches. She'd been to the Verona palazzo a handful of times—always enjoying the lively atmosphere—attending charity events held in various formal rooms. Now, the halls were quiet and the servants were somber, moving silently along thickly carpeted stairs that wound like a wedding cake up four grand floors stacking opulence on top of grandeur. Servants took their coats and then disappeared.

Vincenzo moved at Gina's side, keeping his hand either at the small of her back or her elbow in a familiar manner that was intimate in a courtly way, something she'd seen him do with Giselle. She was conscious of Leonardo trailing behind, a long-practiced trick of keeping a woman between them to discourage the mental picture of the boys together. Leonardo already seemed a bit protective of her, and she wasn't even carrying the baby yet.

They walked through the private family areas of the palace and she found her eyes wandering high up on the walls to portraits of people in formal costumes. They passed through an enormous marble gallery, past suits of armor standing in groups and against walls, up on pedestals, and the occasional breastplate or sword on display. She eyed crests that looked like the Knights Templar shields she'd seen in history books.

"I didn't know the Veronas were...um...warriors."

"These are from my mother's ancestors."

When they reached the parlor, they found Juliette waiting for them. She jumped up from a couch. "Was everything good?" she inquired, like she was asking if Gina had enjoyed a concert.

Gina found herself grinning and dimmed it down to be more appropriate. "*Sì, molto buono.*"

"Ah! *Bene, bene!*" Juliette looked relieved.

Vincenzo bent to kiss his mother's cheek. "*Sì,* Mama, it was good."

"I would like several grandchildren, so I hope this will be a long-standing arrangement."

Gina thought that was some serious chick counting before hatching but was saved from responding as an elderly man using a walker came in. His gleaming silver hair was slightly damp, and he was dressed in heavy grey wool clothes complete with charcoal cardigan. "*Ciao,* my dear," he said in a heavy eastern European accent as he reached for her hand. "I am Ivar Czerney. A friend of the family."

"Gina," she said as one of his strong, calloused hands enveloped hers and the other patted the back of her hand in an endearing way. "Pleased to meet you. I'm a family friend, too."

He nodded and released her hand. His walker clinked softly as he went to take a seat at the bar that took up the wall to the right. Gina let Juliette lead her past the tables with chairs for card games and chess, and they took a seat on the sofa in the center of the room. A blazing fireplace was warming the room from the back wall. Vincenzo went to the bar and began making refreshments as Leonardo made himself comfortable on a stool next to Ivar.

"And you, young people...I would ask what you have been doing, but I have been made aware." Ivar had a twinkle in his eye as he looked at each of them and then zeroed in on Gina. "May you be blessed with a healthy child."

Vincenzo handed drinks over the bar to Leo and Ivar before bringing her and Juliette glasses. "I believe you'll like this Gina. It's non-alcoholic."

"I love mint and lemon verbena," she said as she reached for it.

Leo looked impressed. "Good guess!"

"No guess. I have a good nose."

"I'll say!" He sniffed at his glass of wine, swirled it and then sniffed again. "I can never identify notes of anything that's in my glass."

Juliette looked on proudly as she sipped her drink. "Gina is a student of natural chemistry and biology. In England, her family have been chemists for generations. They have a line of *biologique* creams and herbal cures."

"Very impressive." Vincenzo looked at her with admiration. "A bit like Giselle's family."

"No dangerous chemicals, right?" Leonardo asked, his face becoming serious.

"Not dangerous in my hands. But nature has exquisite toxins, everything from numbing agents to a wide cadre of lethal poisons like belladonna or the mushrooms that grow wild near my family home called destroying angel."

"Such beautiful names for killers," Ivar mused.

"Speaking of herbal cures," Juliette said, "I will make us appointments at a vitamin spa. It helped Giselle get pregnant. I believe it will benefit you, too."

"*Grazie,* vitamins sound great," Gina said. Then looking at Ivar's wet hair she asked, "Did you just come from outside?"

"*Da,* I was at the Verdu Mer construction site. You know it?"

Gina nodded. "Of course, the big site where the slum used to be. I'm surprised you're still doing construction during the cold and rainy months."

"This weather has no effect. We are sinking pilings for the new foundations. It is always cold and wet under the lagoon."

"That makes sense."

"Today we had a meeting on how to proceed now that Count Verona is no longer leading the project," Ivar continued.

"Who manages the consortium now?" Leonardo asked.

Ivar's eyes went to Juliette who said, "I will."

Vincenzo's drink paused midway to his lips. "Mama? You?"

"*Certamente,* I know your father's vision, and I was privy to the political maneuvers he made to pull the experts together. I may not have Gabrieli's special gift, but I can be very persuasive. Today I was elected by the Verdu Mer Consortium, and after two days of mourning, we will continue construction on schedule with me at the helm."

"A decree from the pope has just solidified the consortium's commitment to follow Juliette's lead," Ivar said. "The team respects her accomplishments with her homeless shelter. It will be a smooth transition."

"Then, I propose a toast to Juliette's new job." Leonardo raised his glass and they all drank.

Juliette raised her glass again and said, "More importantly—to future Verona children."

After they drank, she continued, "I have been doing more research and have learned the best way to avoid missing the window of fertility is to make attempts for *eight* consecutive days. Then we will go see Doctor G. Please do this for me."

Gina's loins clenched involuntarily and she nodded.

"*Sì*, mama, seven more days of trying," Vincenzo said and looked at Leo, who appeared to be thrilled.

Ivar was looking at Leonardo. "You are like my wife and Juliette are about babies...crazy."

Leonardo blushed. "*Sì*, I know it's silly. I have no right to, but I want a child more than anything." He looked at Gina. "This is my fondest dream. I'll be forever grateful to this incredible woman for making a child for us."

Gina said, "I'm happy to be part of this effort. It's all happened so fast, I feel like I'm going to wake up from that same dream you're having Leo." Then she stifled a yawn and asked, "Juliette, may I switch to a coffee? I promise to only have one cup a day after I get pregnant."

"*Certamente,* you are tired?"

"*Sì.* After dinner I have a ton of homework, and I get up at four-thirty for my shift at the shop."

Vincenzo was aghast. "Why so early? You go to work when it's so dark and stormy? Alone?"

"The flower deliveries arrive early. I work a half shift, then hurry to my first class."

"A good work ethic. I admire that," Ivar said.

———◆———

Hierotymis "Hiero" Karno sat back in his chair. He eyed Cardinal Americo Negrali, who had just caused a scene in Ecclesia Dei, Vatican Intelligence's outer office. After gaining access to this inner sanctum where no visitors were allowed, Negrali parked his embellished skull cap on the corner of Hiero's desk and started flapping his thin lips, emitting pious nonsense.

Hiero cut him off. "What do you want?"

Negrali's eyes darted around the room. "You know what I want."

"Speak plainly. This is the only room in the Vatican State I haven't bugged."

"I already told you."

"Then you already have my answer. Now get out of my office."

"What about Vincenzo Verona being a faggot?"

"He's not."

"I'm pretty sure Salvio called him one...or a pansy."

"Salvio was a useless mental defective."

"And an Alithinían."

"So you say." Hiero laced his fingers together and stared at Negrali.

"What are you going to do about them?" Negrali looked wary and licked his lips, pointy tongue darting.

"It sounds like you're checking up on a job that my department's been doing since the year 1250."

"But the pope's order to end the Inquisition..."

"Pope Leopold may believe he ended our efforts to eradicate enemies of the church, but he's mistaken. I don't report to him, so that decree has no effect on Ecclesia Dei's solemn order to protect the church."

Hiero had had time to reconsider the brief conversation he'd had with Negrali last night. He'd agreed too quickly to the wily cardinal's demands. Negrali had spent decades climbing to the top of the College of Cardinals. Now he was poised, one beating heart away from becoming the next pope. But Hiero wasn't an errand boy. He wasn't going to do Negrali's bidding. If he did this one thing, there would be no end to it.

"You said you'd take care of Vincenzo."

"Did I?"

"You said we didn't need any more mind-bending Veronas undermining our Vatican affairs."

"That's true."

"You said you could solve our common problem with a gun."

"I never said I'd shoot a Verona."

"Well..." Negrali spread his hands out, jeweled rings flashing. For someone who wore such ostentatious rings, the man should get a manicure; he had the cuticles and nails of a gardener.

"You're still sore because Verona made you give back those stolen villas, aren't you? Oh, such a look! Of course, I know you stole those German properties and sold them to buy two villas. You're getting more audacious in your old age. Now you'd like me to rip the Verona support out from under the pope and let him fall."

"*Sì!*" Negrali shouted, looking half exasperated and half elated, as if Hiero were offering him a gift.

"That would be sedition—spiritual anarchy. Why would I take away the pope's armor, so you could stab him in the back like Juan Fernández Krohn?"

"I share Krohn's ultra-conservative devotion, but I don't have to put a knife in Leopold. I just need to cut him off from the Verona power. Then it's easy to use his words against him. While the pope is busy focusing on the world's youth, I'm going to get Arguelles and Klerk off the hook and put him on it."

"Oh? You're going to put the baby-selling scheme in the pope's lap?"

"*Sì*. While he's singing 'Kum ba yah' and asking spotty children to recycle, I'm going to bring his Chicago speech back to haunt him."

Hiero didn't follow the logic. "That was about daycare."

"If you take some passages literally, he is commanding us to take responsibility for a child, put them into the arms of others when their own family is without means."

"And the babies that were taken?"

"From impoverished, blighted regions. Completely

without means."

"Sounds like you've got the throne in the bag."

"You don't know the half of it. I won't repeat the mistakes of my predecessors. I have my eye on Peter's throne. *I'm* going to bring it to the Vatican and sit on it."

"Eh? That's just a figurative term."

"No, Peter's throne has been in the clutches of an archbishop on an island in Venice, and I'm going to commandeer it to rule from. No pope has ever had my all-encompassing foresight."

"How does this concern me?"

"Are you asking...what's in it for you?"

"What could you possibly offer me to help you?"

"What do you want? I'll give it to you."

"Generous for someone whose sum total of wealth is sitting on my desk right now."

They both stared down at Negrali's jeweled rings.

"Oh, and how can I forget that Herculean cross on your chest. Can't be solid gold, it would be an anchor." He prodded, "Negrali, you live well because you suck on the Vatican's teat. You live in your cushy residence attached to your Santa Maria dei Miracoli Church and eat well because no one will refuse you, but you don't have anything I want."

"Now that Salvio's dead, I'll have the Scortini money. That estate is easily two thousand years old..."

"And is now in the possession of that young widow, that girl who was raised in the abbey..."

"Raphielli, sì. I'm her spiritual advisor. I'll oversee everything for her now."

"Ah, getting a finger in every pie? I hear you're going to make a play for the Verdu Mer project, too."

"It makes sense. Gabrieli's dead, and it's an epic Vatican project in my own backyard. Of course I'll take that over."

"Squandering a mint on your little church makes you a real estate titan?"

Negrali's eyes narrowed, and Hiero could see he'd touched a nerve. The old man's eyes turned malevolent, but he said nothing.

"Find me an enticing piece of property in Scortini's estate, and if I like it, I'll see about taking care of your problem."

"'Problems'—plural. To be clear, the problems are Vincenzo, Giselle, his pregnant wife, and la Contessa Juliette."

"Why Juliette? She's not a Verona by blood, she's French."

"Have you just had a stroke or something? She's a shoo-in to take over Verdu Mer! She needs to be disposed of!"

"My price just went up. I want an island from Raphielli's estate, and I hear the Scortinis have paintings by Caravaggio. I want *two* of the best they have. That's for that stroke comment. Now, get your cap off my desk and get out of my office."

When Negrali was gone, Hierotymis took out his communicator, entered the personal code that would be changed in four hours, and switched to voice mode. "Checco, I want to see the team within the hour."

Disconnecting, he sat back and considered the bright prospect of a world where he could run his agency without interference by the do-gooder Veronas. He then set his mind on precisely how he would make the deaths of Giselle, Vincenzo, and Juliette Verona appear to be accidental.

He went over to the vault door and pressed his hand against the scanner, causing a *blip-blip* of approval before he swung the door open and headed for the Verona files. He'd review their family history. Someone must have already been killing them off, or that bloodline wouldn't have trickled to one drop away from extinction. Could the Scortinis have been waging a covert extermination effort? The prospect was intriguing.

He needed to refresh his memory about the Boatman, Marcion of Sinope. He'd been a sort of posthumous secretary of the apostle Paul, gathering up all of Paul's writings. The early Greek followers called their church *Alithiní*, meaning "true," and they were incredibly tenacious in clinging to their belief that the Catholic Church was a bastardization of Jesus' true teachings. They believed water had intelligence and considered it a sacrament, even if it wasn't blessed. Whenever possible, they worshipped standing in water and loved to settle in watery areas.

Venice was about to lose a few citizens. This would have to be done carefully. Ecclesia Dei was unknown outside the Vatican because they didn't make mistakes.

On the morning of Gabrieli's funeral, Gina woke up with Leonardo molded to her side. She looked around, momentarily disoriented, the eyes the Madonna and child staring at her from a painting, and then it came back to her. She and the boys were at the Vatican in Count Gabrieli's bedroom in the papal apartment.

Before boarding Vincenzo's jet for the late-night trip to Rome, she'd put on a touch too much of the scent, and the boys had been fixated on her during the flight as Juliette and Ivar sat oblivious nearby going over Verdu Mer business and making phone calls.

The drive from Leonardo DaVinci airport through the dark streets of Rome was a blur, and the Vatican halls were likewise a blur as the boys whisked her toward the bedroom. She'd been floored to see Pope Leopold XIV striding toward them in crisp white vestments, and he gave her such a knowing look she cringed inwardly. He took her face in his hands tenderly, solemnly, then lifted his eyes upward and said, "*Dio ti dia un bel bambino*." He made the sign of the cross above her forehead and pressed his palms together in front of his lips. "Now, to bed with you, beautiful one."

Vincenzo's bodyguard stayed stationed outside as the boys drew her into the room, and as they tore her clothes off, she clung to their muscled shoulders.

"Did the Pope just order God to give us a child?"

"*Sì*, and he was *ex cathedra!*" Vincenzo enthused as he nuzzled her neck, inhaling deeply.

"Doesn't he have to be on a throne to be *ex cathedra?*" she asked.

Leonardo was busily ripping Vincenzo's clothes off as he said, "No, *ex cathedra* means with the full authority of Saint Peter's chair. The Pope can be *ex cathedra* at any time if he uses his ecclesiastical authority."

Vincenzo stopped stroking her belly, picked her up, and carried her to the big bed. "No one can actually sit in Peter's throne anyway. The chair is a relic that's mounted high up on the wall in the apse of Saint Peter's Basilica. It's a worm-eaten wooden decoration that couldn't support anyone's weight."

Gina enjoyed their attempts at an heir until they all fell asleep, leaving whatever beds she and Leo were supposed to be sleeping in vacant. Now she heard a faint knocking on the door and felt the boys stir beside her.

Vincenzo called, "*Chi è?*"

"Just me." Juliette came in bearing a thermal coffee pot and three cups. "I am so pleased you had another attempt last night." She was smiling broadly. "A bright spot to focus on as we prepare to lay Gabrieli to rest. The funeral will be in less than two hours. Time to get showered and dressed. Meet me in the papal receiving room where there is food. Our friends are starting to arrive from around the world."

Gina and the boys got ready and then hurried to the receiving room. Through tall windows, lamp light illuminated the statues atop the colonnades on Saint Peter's Square and glinted off the snow-covered ground.

Standing at the big breakfast buffet, Gina recognized some of the "friends" in the room as kings and queens, and she dropped the oatmeal ladle when the president of the United States brushed shoulders with her on his way to greet Juliette on a sofa. The president was overwhelmed.

"Poor Juliette! He was my best friend! He reached out to me when I was just a campaign volunteer. I can't believe he's gone! *Murdered!*"

Uncomfortable in the midst of such private sorrow, Gina shuffled along the table, spooned her oatmeal into her mouth, parked her empty bowl on a bus tray, and inched toward the door. Passing the pope and Vincenzo, she heard the Holy See speaking in a low voice.

"You may be wrong. We've been in their temple. We know the Alithinían exist. I will go to the archives and revisit everything we have on Marcion of Sinope."

"Then I'm afraid for them. Could Salvio have been right? Is our Alithinían Inquisition still underway?"

Her ears pricked up at the killer's name, but she didn't want to spy and left the room. Hovering around the marble hall as people came and went, she was looking up at the blue domed ceiling, soaking up the feeling of being in the Vatican, when she felt the hairs on the back of her neck prickle. She turned her head and saw someone had come up behind her.

"You're with the House of Verona." The look he gave her made her feel like a moth on the head of a pin.

She backed away from the man. He was wearing a no-nonsense suit in deepest charcoal, on his lapel was a small pin of a bird crushing arrows in its talons, his greying hair was cut *en brosse*, and he had cold eyes that raked her over with something more than intelligence. Cunning was the word that came to mind as another man in a dark suit came striding toward them. When her inquisitor folded his hands in front of his chest, the man took note and veered off in another direction. She felt certain he'd given a signal.

Unable to hold his penetrating gaze, she dropped her eyes to his hands where thick hairs sprouted from his clasped fingers. "*Sì*, I'm here with Juliette." She realized she should have used her title, but too late now.

"And what is your name?"

"Gina."

"In what capacity are you attached to the Verona household, Gina?"

"Gina, can you come with me?" Ippy's voice cut in, and she appeared at Gina's elbow. Juliette's personal assistant was always there when needed.

He turned on her. "Why, Ipanema, I didn't see you there. So, Gina's a ward of la contessa?"

Ippy pooched out her lip in casual rejection of his assumption. "Not a ward. Nothing formal, just part of la contessa's charity outreach." And without another word she put her hand on the small of Gina's back and steered her toward the reception room.

Once again at the breakfast buffet, Gina whispered, "Who was that?"

Ippy made a face and said *soto voce*, "Hierotymis Karno, head of secret Vatican security. He scares the shit out of me. I hope you don't mind my fib about charity. I didn't want him to know how close you are to the Veronas. Better he thinks you're not worth his attention. I keep away from him, which usually isn't difficult because I stick to Juliette, and he avoids the Veronas like the plague."

"Then I'll stay close to the family, too."

"Be sure you do. When I spotted you in the hall, he was right behind you, and I swear he was sniffing you." Ippy gave her an expression of mock terror. "Like he might eat you. With the Vatican being above international law, I don't know if anyone could prosecute him if he did. You know people have disappeared from within these walls."

"Recently?"

"Oh, well, popes have been getting bumped off for ages. You know about John Paul the Second getting shot and stabbed, right? Pope Urban and Pope Celestine were murdered before they were even consecrated onto the throne. No one's safe here."

The King of Sweden approached the buffet with his family, and Ippy changed the subject. "How did you like your vitamin treatments yesterday?"

"Fine. They don't seem to be doing for me what they do for Juliette."

"I can't get over how she's turning back the clock with those vitamins. But then, she also does her exercise regimen every day."

"Is it safe for me to use the restroom?"

"Oh, certainly."

Gina went in the direction Ippy indicated and discovered there was a line for the restroom. She didn't have to go that badly, so she paced around the area, being sure to keep Ippy in sight across the long hall. Behind a pillar, she found a statue of an angel wielding a sword like a superhero. She overheard two men speaking in hushed tones on the other side of the wide pillar.

"There's nothing to be anxious about, Marconi. I'm days away from controlling the Scortini estate."

"When you have it, you'll have my vote."

"*Grazie.*"

"And when you're Pope, I want Germany."

"You'll have it. I'm making big plans."

"Oh?"

"First thing I'll do is move Peter's throne here and rule from it."

"His throne? But you can't..."

"There's nothing I can't do."

As they moved off, Gina peeked from behind the pillar and got a good look at the men. Both cardinals. When the coast was clear, she used the restroom and then went back to where she'd last seen Vincenzo. He and the pope were speaking to someone, so Gina went and stood near them. Not wanting to intrude, she maneuvered herself next to an enormous antique chest of drawers and waited. When the man moved on, the pope turned to Vincenzo.

"I am shocked he would bring up such a subject on a morning...of mourning."

"He couldn't help himself. The emergency is mounting in his country."

"So many emergencies. The Arguelles-Klerk travesty, the natal plague in his country and all its neighbors have millions of faithful threatening birth control, conservative bishops going rogue..."

"My father should be here to calm the waters."

"That was your father's gift. Through their hearts he changed their minds. If he were here, he would meet with these men, and they would not only see reason, they would repent and mend their ways. The Veronas are the Holy Spirit of God."

"He never explained it to me like that. I don't have the same gift. Well, maybe to a slight degree."

"You have it. You have never fully opened your heart. You must love everyone as God loves them."

"Maybe being in the closet my whole life dampened my fully loving..."

"I regret the Church got that part wrong. We should not decree who someone can love. Wherever there is true love, we should celebrate. We need more love, not less. It would be the ultimate irony if Papal law rendered my Verona *persona non grata*."

Vincenzo said, "I've studied Genesis where everyone points to saying homosexuality is a sin, but that story was about the rape—brutal dominance—of outsiders, and most of the rules set forth in Leviticus don't make any sense to me..."

The Pope interjected, "Which brings to mind what we

saw inside the Scortini temple. The only thing Paul's followers were, er, *are* following, are the words of Jesus."

"But Jesus says nothing against homosexuality. In fact, there are six references to John being the one that Jesus loved. And, then to the point of our South American Catholics, Jesus said nothing against birth control."

"You must have spent more time with Markus than I thought," the Pope said. "His analytical style has rubbed off on you."

"You may be right. Both Markus and Ivar urged me to press you about reform. I thought they were..."

"Heretics," Leonardo finished. He'd walked over to claim them. "We should be getting to the chapel. Where's Gina? Your mother needs her."

She was about to step out of hiding, but hesitated, not wanting to be caught eves-dropping.

"And speaking of Gina," the pope said. "I believe that she is the dream Gabrieli saw right before he died. It is your child with her that will change the world."

"I'm pretty sure that's your job," Vincenzo said in a self-effacing tone.

Gina slid out from behind the bureau as if she'd been passing by, and as Leonardo led her away, she heard the pope say, "I have discovered who put the bank numbers into my papal pouch."

"The ones that exposed Marconi's theft of the property and villas?"

"It was myrrh."

Gina wondered what incense had to do with the cardinal who she'd just overheard demanding control over Germany.

Alone on the flight from Venice to Rome, Raphielli had time to think. She was grateful for her invitation to sit with Juliette and her family at Gabrieli's funeral. Publicly embracing the wife of your husband's murderer, Juliette was literally going to save her from becoming a social pariah. She was Salvio's victim, too, but the whole world would take their cues for how to act toward her from Juliette. This was the second time the contessa's goodness and generosity had changed the course of Raphielli's life. And, it was the effort to emulate the contessa that had inspired her to open her women's shelter.

Just yesterday, the head of the Venetian Brotherhood of Iron Workers, Genero Tosca, had come to Raphielli's home for a meeting. She thought it went well. He'd recognized Alphonso when she introduced them.

"You're the private investigator who brings down the dirty politicians," he said, offering his hand.

"*Sì*, that's me."

Then both men had settled into chairs and given her their full attention.

"I'm ready to turn part of my palazzo into a shelter for women," she said. "It'll be the second location of Porto delle Donne."

Tosca looked pleased. "I'd hoped that was why you called me. On behalf of the Venetian Builders Society, I accept the job."

"When are you going to start?" Alphonso looked from her to Tosca.

She answered, "I want to begin right away. I'm happiest when I'm working on a big project, and I can't wait to help more women. I mean, ten is something, but I'm capable of helping so many more."

"I'll look into upgrade options," Tosca said. "Any chance you have blueprints of this property? From what I've seen, there's nothing like it in the world."

"No, but we've been able to map out much of the building. We can give you our hand-drawn diagrams and measurements." She thought about the temple and said, "There are only a few areas that'll be off limits to your crew and the eventual residents. My new suite of rooms, and the wing behind the dining room."

Tosca gave her a big smile. "My dear, you have far more space than you'll need for a new shelter. I'll get back to you soon.

"*Perfetto.*"

The flight steward came to offer Raphielli another blanket, which she accepted and then pushed herself deeper into the chartered jet's seat. Now the sunrise was a sliver of yellow far out in the night sky. It felt good to start another big project, but she was kidding herself. She was nothing like Juliette. Juliette would never have taken Gio's call yesterday, or agreed to go to his room, or let him...

The Devil makes work for idle hands, but her hands couldn't be busier. Yesterday she'd had three consultations with Tosca, completed Salvio's death paperwork at city hall, and met with Vincenzo and Leonardo so they could process payments to the relatives of her murdered staff. She was incredibly busy—even before sneaking off to see

Gio—unfortunately, too busy to spend time with Paloma yesterday. She'd need to make more of an effort.

Late last night when Carolette and Fauve called, she'd only mentioned the first three innocent efforts. Although it was no effort being with Gio, it was sheer luxurious pleasure, sort of like being worshipped...thoroughly...in ways that didn't occur to Alphonso.

She snapped back to the present when the attendant asked if she'd like anything to drink before landing.

"Cappuccino, *grazie*."

She thought about the cappuccino she'd shared with Alphonso just a couple of hours ago in the private air hanger's café. Famous people were coming and going with their families and assistants—some with more fuss than others—and Alphonso had asked again to accompany her. She wanted time alone and had reassured him, "You're putting me on a jet, and Vatican security is taking me off the jet. I'm perfectly safe."

She could read the hurt in his eyes, but he'd made a face that was somewhere between disappointment and worry. "Okay, then I'll be back here to meet your plane this afternoon, and we'll go to Salvio's funeral together."

She didn't know why sometimes she felt the immediacy of that free-floating danger, and other times she felt she could take care of herself. She wasn't a fearful or flighty person, and mostly she was only scared when she saw one of those strange men watching her. The rest of the time she felt secure, and Alphonso's giant presence was becoming a bit oppressive.

Raphielli looked out the window. Rome was a shimmering

masterpiece, twinkling white in a blanket of snow, the first streaks of dawn turning the plane's wing peach as they dropped low on the airport approach. She knew the Veronas hopped back and forth between Rome and Venice like they were just taking a boat over to Murano. Perhaps she should start getting out more.

When the plane came to a stop, she stood up, smoothed the black and cinnamon dress that Ava had overnighted to her, and let the attendant help her on with her coat. It was another Ava design, and as she stepped off the plane and hurried beside security, she was thankful for the dramatic plush collar that rose up to her cheekbones.

By the time she was sitting in the back of the car Juliette had sent for her, all the beauty of Rome left her mind. She sat in the ugly reality that her husband had killed the finest man imaginable, Count Gabrieli Verona. She'd tried so hard to prevent Salvio from accomplishing it in the fall, and somehow everything had gone wrong. He'd done it anyway—or maybe it was one of his hired hit men.

What was it that Luigi Lampani had told her? Mad men have a knack for getting through defenses and killing their prey.

———※———

It had still been dark outside when Luigi walked down the Venice Termini platform passing posters bearing Benedetta's face. She was all over the local news, and it was a relief knowing she was safe with Kate at the shelter. Today was going to be another long one. To Rome for Gabrieli's funeral in the Sistine Chapel, then back to Venice for Salvio's funeral at the Little Church this evening.

He'd climbed aboard the train to Rome feeling a twitchy restlessness, like an athlete seconds before a competition. He'd still been unable to find Pocket Coffee anywhere in Venice, so he had a light breakfast and packed a small satchel with three good pens, his notebook, and a phone charger. Funerals provided invaluable opportunities for detectives who kept their wits sharp and their eyes open.

He looked around the train car and saw a number of familiar faces, people that he'd interviewed during this investigation. The heads of Venice's building associations were sitting in groups, and Genero Tosca beckoned him to the empty seat across from him.

"Detective Lampani, join us."

"*Grazie.* Such a sad occasion," Luigi said to the group in general.

"I don't like having to travel all the way to Rome to say goodbye to the patriarch of Venice," Genero Tosca said.

"Then we come back for Salvio's funeral."

"What's the world come to?" Marco Falconetti said. "We all know Salvio killed Gabrieli. Like he killed my son."

"We're not going out of respect for Salvio, we're going out of respect for his great family—the House of Scortini that gave each of us and our fathers, and our grandfathers, our start," Genero said. "And to show our support for Raphielli. We owe her a great debt."

"Salvio's father and grandfather were like parents to each of us," a man Luigi didn't know added.

"But Salvio was no brother to us," someone behind him said.

"Piece of shit," Marco said, his face red. "I'm not attending his funeral."

"We owe Salvio's wife. That girl got us our patents back..." the man fell silent when two of his associates gave him overt looks to shut up. Then he finished firmly, "Raphielli has us behind her one thousand percent. We'll show up to let her know she's not ostracized because of what her husband did."

Luigi looked over at Marco and he knew he was thinking of his son, a talented marble sculptor whose skull Salvio crushed for no reason at all.

At Roma Termini station they all filed off the train, and Tosca and the Venetian builders moved off to find their drivers at the curbside limousine queue. Luigi was supposed to wait for the Vatican-attached monsignor Inspector Laszlo had arranged to be his guide. He saw a stocky Asian man hurrying toward him across the frigid platform. He was dressed all in black, his crisp long coat encased him like a shell, and he had the face of a shogun warrior.

"Detective Lampani?" he asked.

"Monsignor Nuur," Luigi said in greeting. Offering a hand, he discovered the cleric's hands were encased in heavy black gloves. "Shoveling snow?"

"Ah, no, I will leave it on the ground," he said in perfect Italian, but with a heavy accent.

"I wouldn't have recognized you as my Vatican liaison. I was looking for a priest's collar."

Nuur unzipped the top of his coat to reveal the rigid

white collar. "And I thought I was looking for a police uniform."

"Yeh, well, I'm a detective, so no uniform." Then Luigi laughed and nodded. "But you pegged me anyway. Looks like you'd make a good detective."

"You flatter me. Are you ready? I have a helmet for you, but did you not bring gloves?"

"Helmet? Are you kidding?"

"No. Heads of state have reserved every car available to the Vatican, so my only option for traveling outside the Holy City is my motorcycle. You will thank me. For a few minutes of cold, we can bypass the traffic nightmare and be inside to watch people arrive."

Luigi followed Nuur to where his motorcycle was parked, turned his collar up, fastened the helmet, and climbed on behind the big man. Luigi clung to the monsignor's solid frame as they shot through the stopped traffic on the exit rotunda and through the predawn Roman roads like a pinball hurtling the landscape of a machine. Icy wind bit at his face, and his hands ached for a few moments before numbness took hold. They came to a grinding stop where several car bumpers had come within a centimeter of one another, and the drivers were honking in a cacophony of horns. Luigi figured Nuur would hop the sidewalk, but he took a quick peek over the monsignor's broad shoulder and saw cars parked across the sidewalk all along this stretch of Via Isacco Newton.

Luigi asked, "Did you grow up on scooters in China?"

"No, I am Siberian. Dirt bikes are the main transportation where I grew up. Very rugged terrain. Here with roads, a Siberian three-year-old would be a better Vespa driver than anyone in Rome."

With that, Nuur shot through a slim opening, and Luigi feared for his elbows as they flew between the mirrors of the trucks and limousines stopped on the bridge over the Tiber. They hurtled toward a side Vatican gate where Roman police stood guard on the outer perimeter and Vatican police were visible inside. Luigi had to grip the monsignor with his thighs and bear-hug him when the brakes brought them to such an abrupt halt that he felt the back wheel leave the road.

Nuur greeted the police who were already lifting the gate for them. A nun wearing a serious expression and an old-fashioned wimple approached them with a clipboard. "Monsignor Nuur, I see you have found the Venetian detective...Lampani?" She made a little tick on her sheet and nodded. "Detective, you are welcome to join us in mourning Count Verona." She choked up on the last word.

"All of Venice mourns with you," he said. "Count Gabrieli Verona was a great man."

She nodded and waved Nuur on, and Luigi almost ripped the monsignor's coat from his shoulders as the front tire came off the cobblestones. They accelerated straight for a dark slit in the block stonework of a building, which looked too narrow for them. Lampani clenched his teeth and fought the urge to jump off the back of the little rocket as they slid into the frosty darkness, stone brushing close to them on both sides. Nuur let off the throttle, but the downward slope of the stone pavers carried them silently at a high rate of speed. They entered a drainage tunnel between Saint Peter's Basilica and the Sistine Chapel. Nuur didn't turn on his headlamp, and within moments he braked to a stop.

"From that little flight of steps, we can watch the guests of honor and His Holiness move to the chapel if you like."

"No, it's too cold. Can we get into the chapel now?"

"I know a back way. Have you there in no time."

True to his word, within minutes they were in the Sistine Chapel and had an excellent vantage point of everyone's comings and goings.

"Give me the lay of the land," Luigi whispered to Nuur.

"The choir will be there, the count's casket will be brought to that draped platform, the Verona family will be in that front row, the College of Cardinals will fill that section, those two sections are for world leaders, this area just beyond us is for important Venetian guests like the gentlemen you arrived with, and the public will be on the other side of those railings."

"I assumed there would be a bullpen for the press."

"Never."

"You can't keep the press out of something like this."

Nuur gave him a pitying look. "There is no free press in Vatican City. We are sovereign."

"But the news eats up everything that happens here."

"We have our News.va staff. They're responsible for capturing news and disseminating it to the media in conjunction with the Holy See's press office."

"Where are their cameras?"

"There, there, there, and there." He pointed at pillars and the chandeliers.

Luigi watched as the choir filed in with white robes fluttering and the big space began to fill up. The Verona contingent was at the head of the crowd that stretched out the doors.

"Look away so you can say truthfully that you didn't see. I've got to take my first photo."

"I can tell you who those women with the Veronas are. Ippy is la contessa's secretary, very capable, been with her for years. Next to her with the severe brunette bob, impeccable coat, and fierce boots is Gina, la contessa's new protégé, and then Raphielli Scortini."

"Sitting with the Veronas?"

"*Sì,* la contessa insisted she be allowed in the family section."

"A clear message that she doesn't blame the wife for her husband's acts."

"You know la contessa?"

"As much as any Venetian knows a Verona. I tried to convince her and her late husband that Salvio was alive and dangerous. She stopped speaking to me as I continued investigating Scortini's crimes. She's been in mourning, but I don't know that she's warmed up to my efforts, which she interprets as meddling. She's unbelievably private for someone so approachable by the masses."

"She is formidable yet loving. Like steel wrapped in kindness and a disarming scent of hibiscus."

Luigi chuckled at Nuur's apt rundown. "Exactly."

"Do not get me wrong, I love Juliette."

"What are people saying about Giselle Verona's absence?" Luigi asked.

"Everyone knows about the attempts on her life and that la contessa is keeping her safe."

"Do you know where?"

"No."

Luigi watched as world leaders entered, and he could see the grief on the faces of the presidents of America and France, and the Prime Ministers of England and Australia. Finally, the public pressed close as the first strains of "*Il Mio Signore e Mio Pastore*" began to swell from the organ. The choir stood and began to sing.

The coffin approached on the shoulders of the pallbearers, and Luigi noticed that among them were Vincenzo and Leonardo Trentori. Ivar Czerney, the Verona's Ukrainian houseguest, followed using a cane instead of his usual walker. His stubby little wife, who'd cracked Salvio in the head with her shoe last fall, was conspicuously absent. Perhaps she was with Giselle? The College of Cardinals flocked behind with black crepe scarfs fluttering around the necks of their red robes. They looked devastated.

Next came the widow, Contessa Juliette Verona, her face and hair draped with a black mantilla, holding hands with Pope Leopold XIV.

After parking the coffin, which Luigi noticed had been borne on a hydraulic lift—no chance of stumbling and dropping a Verona—the pallbearers sat in the family pew with Vincenzo next to Juliette, and the cardinals moved past the family in a line and all appeared to be saying the same thing.

"Some are taking Juliette's hand, but others are specifically reaching for Vincenzo."

"Ah, *sì*. I personally would seek out Vincenzo's hand. His father's touch was indescribable, and I would want to see if the son has the same power."

"Power?"

"We do not talk about it, but I will tell you. It is love. It comes off the Veronas like...well...it heals is the best way I can describe."

They watched an intense-looking man in a charcoal suit with grey hair cut in a military style. Luigi read the look on the man's face. He was repelled by Juliette and Vincenzo.

"Who's that guy? He's moving to the outside of those three cardinals."

"Hierotymis Karno, head of Ecclesia Dei."

"Secret service? He's avoiding the Veronas."

"Mmm."

"Tell me about him."

"Personally, he makes me feel like a rabbit..."

Luigi turned and gave him a questioning look.

"...and he is a badger about to flush me out of my warren... into the blinding sun...to be shot."

The pope delivered a eulogy and broke with tradition by finishing with, "And while I do not weep for Count Gabrieli, for his soul is in heaven with our father, I weep with his brothers and sisters on earth. I rend my garments for the terrible loss of one of our greatest gifts...a treasure..." He ripped one of the sashes draped at his neck and sobbed in front of the people packed into the chapel and outside in the cold morning sun watching on Vatican news monitors. Then came a high-pitched keening as everyone let loose their grief and sobbed. It was as if it was contagious, and white tissues appeared before everyone's faces. Luigi had never experienced anything like it, a physical feeling of heart-breaking sadness being cathartically released. He scanned the room and spotted one man with dry eyes. Hierotymis Karno.

That evening a very different scene played out in Venice's Little Church. Luigi had been trying to dry off after being soaked in the icy downpour outside. He was just inside the entryway, dripping on the floor mats, when Raphielli arrived with Alphonso Vitali and the look-alike cousin Zelph, who was probably the smoothest liar Luigi had ever questioned.

"Detective, it was good of you to come," Raphielli said.

Zelph gave him a collegial nod. "Getting a look at the funeral attendees, Luigi?"

"Perhaps you three have reconsidered your version of the events at the palazzo on the night of Guiseppe's murder."

"Reconsidered?" Zelph seemed nonplussed and then looked around as if just noticing where he was. "The place is empty except for those little *nonnas* who look like they prefer funerals to a night at the movies. Nobody's gonna come pay respects to Salvio."

The first group of builders arrived and walked straight to the font of holy water, touched their foreheads, made the sign of the cross, and failing to see the widow behind the two massive Vitali men as they passed, they walked up to Salvio's coffin. From their hand gestures, it looked like they were cursing him and letting off a little steam, stopping shy of actually spitting on the church floor.

Luigi turned to see two short women arrive, decked out in such elaborate mourning regalia it was as if they were spoofing classic funerary attire. They looked like two stocky funeral barges.

"Uh-oh, here they come," Raphielli sighed.

"You don't have to speak to them," Alphonso said reassuringly. "They won't make a scene in a church."

Luigi asked, "Who are they? Distant Scortini relatives?"

"My mama *et nonna*. We're estranged."

"She calls them the Dour Doublet," Zelph said to provide color.

The women ignored Luigi and gave the stink eye to the Vitalis as they butted their way over to Raphielli.

"What are you doing, practically naked at your own husband's funeral?" They gestured at her ankles in black stockings, which were visible below her tasteful calf-length dress. "You look like a cheap piece of goods. Where's your mantilla?"

Raphielli ignored them and moved off to greet Marco Falconetti.

The *nonna* squinted at Luigi and treated him like an usher. "We are the head of the family now, where does the family sit?" Up close, she was quite hairy, and her face was as wobbly as gelatin *panna cotta*. Luigi found this interesting. Raphielli had Cardinal Negrali and two old battle-axes who all considered themselves the head of her household. He wondered if any of them had said as much to her. He wondered if this pair could steam roll over Negrali.

Alphonso extended a hand to the Dour Doublet. "Let me show you your place." He walked them to the center of the front pew where they sat down, and Luigi could see they instantly regretted it because they were forced to stare at the dead man everyone hated and everyone else was arriving behind their backs. The builders, who now had spotted Raphielli, were paying respects to her. Luigi listened to the streams of condolences: "I'm here for you", "If there's anything you need", and a couple of "You're better off now he's really dead" comments.

The Dour Doublet almost abandoned their places to come hobnob with Mayor Massimo and Elene Buonocore. Then Domina, the *prima ultima* interior designer appeared, turning heads as she shook the rain off her silver raincoat like she was in the movie Flash Dance. Domina was accompanied by an A-list movie star who stood talking to Raphielli and the Vitalis just long enough to make the Dour Doublet grip the back of their pews like children forced to sit in a time-out.

When reporters arrived, the two old monsignors appeared from the shadows and ejected them.

Luigi signaled to get Alphonso's attention. "Can we talk for a moment?"

"*Certamente.*"

They walked slowly along the wall as he said, "Alphonso, I'm gonna solve these murders, and you're gonna help me."

"Of course."

"At this point, you're either with me or against me."

"I'm with you." Alphonso's big brown eyes widened. "I'm just here to keep Raphielli safe. You're the one who told us she's still in danger."

"She is. She really is. Why won't you tell me what happened at the palazzo?"

Just then, Cardinal Negrali ascended the steps high above the pews. A crack of lightning illuminated the windows, and a muffled roar of thunder came from outside as the lights in the old electric sconces flickered, momentarily leaving the place in gloomy candlelight.

"We'll speak later," Alphonso said and went to lead Raphielli to her seat up front. Luigi and Zelph followed.

Raphielli turned around, scanning the church, and then gave a strangled yelp. Pointing at the door, she screamed, "Stop that man! That man in black!"

There was a flash, another tremendous boom of thunder, and the lights went out. Zelph clutched Raphielli to his massive chest as Alphonso raced down the candlelit aisle. Luigi ran, too. By the time they burst through the door onto the storm-swept *campo*, the man had disappeared. The press had gone off to write their articles somewhere indoors, and turning in all directions, Luigi and Alphonso found they were alone in the downpour. Whoever Raphielli had seen was gone. Luigi and Alphonso splashed across the *campo* to check out a dark underpass that someone fast could have made it to but found it empty.

"We just chased a man in black from a funeral." Luigi was shaking his head. "Don't tell anyone we just did that. They'll assume we're idiots."

Alphonso scanned the shadows. "She's been seeing men in black for weeks now. Ever since Salvio attacked her this fall she's suffered from post-traumatic night terrors and paranoia."

"You saying she's suffering from PTSD?"

"I am, but she'll get over it. She's more resilient than she looks."

"I don't believe she's paranoid, she's in real danger. She and the Veronas are still being hunted by whoever Salvio hired...and they wear black...and they hate Catholics."

———·◈·———

Giselle was on the phone with Fauve catching up on local gossip in Gernelle and Aiglemont when Fauve got practical. "We've completely lost track of Spratman, so you two'll be at the abbey for a while. What are you gonna do for fun? Carolette asked me to see if you need her to send the honey wand."

Giselle rolled her eyes. "No need for that. But can you have Selma pack up my Nyakio skin products and toss my Bunny Balm into a bag? It's dry and windy here, my skin and lips are chapping. I'll coordinate Daniel getting the bag from you. Oh! And will you or Selma find my science fair notebook? I want to make some solar panels to lower the monk's electric bills here."

"No problem. Guess they won't let you make one of your dangerous sculptures there."

"You guessed right."

"What about the one you were working on? Is that benign enough? I could bring those supplies."

Giselle felt cold as she pictured her last sculpture. "*Mon Dieu!* No!"

"Okay, okay, just asking."

"I mean, holy shit! *Immure to Madness* was a vision I had

of someone flailing while drowning inside bars."

There was a big intake of breath before Fauve's spooked voice came back. "Gabrieli? Impossible! You had that vision years ago." She gasped again. "You can see the future!"

"I certainly don't want *that* to be true."

"Well, hey, you were building a cage and Gabrieli didn't drown in a cage."

"The whole underside of Verdu Mer is a metal grid work. He was surrounded by underwater pilings when he drowned...was murdered."

"*Merde,* that's eerie."

They sat in silence for a moment or two, both thinking, then Fauve said, "I can have Selma pack up Markus' box of supplies and bring that as well. He must need something artistic to do, too."

"That'd be great. Those ornaments he makes would make lovely Christmas gifts for the chapel here. Can you deliver everything to that warehouse Daniel told you about in Brussels? He can pick the boxes up."

"Will do. Does Yvania need us to bring anything?"

"Nah, she's blissed out working on the cookbook she's co-writing with Juliette. The ingredients here are rocking her world."

<hr />

Hiero Karno sat at his desk making notes. Funeral attendees were ripe for pumping after a good cathartic cry. He'd avoided touching Vincenzo, just as he'd always avoided touching Gabrieli. In the past, when Ecclesia Dei operatives had come into contact with the late count, plans had been ruined and campaigns that took years to set up unraveled in minutes.

Hiero thought about the girl at Juliette's side, Gina. He was a sucker for pearly white teeth and exquisitely cut clothes. That one had a knife-edge to her seams, hem, and her hair. Even her body seemed to follow the same line. The way she smelled aroused him on a primal level.

He pushed aside the fantasy that threatened to unfurl and reached for one of the scrolls on Marcion of Sinope. The cat and mouse chase that the church had played with the Alithiníans was quite a romp through history. They'd almost exterminated this Venetian nest of Alithinían water vipers back in 1355. For the first time, Ecclesia Dei operatives had suspected the Scortini family of being Alithinían, along with Filippo Calendario, one of the Scortini's architects, who was working on the Doge's Palace. Apparently, the new governor of the islands wanted a palazzo to rival those of the founding family, the Veronas, and the founding builders, the Scortinis.

Ecclesia Dei operatives had made their move, ordering the Doge to put Calendario to death for treason, a demand he wasn't happy about because it delayed work on his palace. But the rest of the plan went sour because that same day the black death struck il Veneto, and for months it swept through the islands killing people in almost every household. Nothing but plague masks and shrouded figures were seen out-of-doors, making it impossible for Ecclesia Dei to track down the Alithiníans. Notes made by the head of Ecclesia Dei surmised that the Alithinians fled when Calendario was seized and had escaped the islands by lying still in boats pretending to be dead bodies. Hiero thought it was as good a guess as any.

He had also found family tragedies in both the Scortini and Verona households. Ships lost carrying branches of one or the other, plane crashes, boat accidents. Then there was the recent strange case of Salvio's parents, Gelsonima and Salvatore. While on their way back from a festival this past summer, a power line near an old bridge collapsed into their gondola, electrocuting them instantly. Hiero used a magnifying glass to examine the photo of a well-dressed couple laying sideways in a gondola festooned with flowers and ribbons, their gondolier bobbing face down in the water next to a bridge so covered with moss it glowed an outrageous emerald color, a verdant pastoral backdrop to the death amidst masses of flowers.

The couple appeared to have dressed for their own funeral. Salvatore was in a smart black suit with a yellow flower in his lapel, and Gelsonima was in full-length crinolines looking like a stout ballerina who'd collapsed in her black tutu. She was holding a bouquet with one hand and Salvatore's hand with the other. Visible on his hand was a big gold ring which Hiero knew to be the Scortini family symbols, a horse and boat. While other Venetian family crests had boats, none had horses. Hiero reasoned it was because the beasts were too wide to move easily through the narrow *calles* alongside pedestrians, and the danger of the horse slipping off a slick *fondamenta* into the drink would be constant.

He closed the file and Salvio's dead parents disappeared. Their deaths last summer had left the Venetian builders in turmoil because Salvatore had been their powerful benefactor and generous de facto ruler. He was the glue that held the Venetian builders together in a trial against the most ruthless Mafioso out of Sicily, don Giancarlo Petrosino. Then just after the jury was empaneled, Salvatore was dead and Salvio was the sole surviving Scortini until someone shot him. Bang, end of the family line. Hiero surmised Salvio had been rejected by the brotherhood of builders because he was a greedy, pompous asshole. The pope had certainly never considered putting him in charge of the Vatican's sweeping re-gentrification of Verdu Mer, and instead had tapped Count Gabrieli Verona to helm the project.

Hiero opened a file on the Verona family. Juliette was their weak link. After repeated miscarriages late in pregnancy and a stillborn son, Vincenzo survived a grueling labor and was the last living Verona until he'd gotten his wife, Giselle, pregnant. Intelligence reports had no idea of her current location. Recently her traveling companion was Markus Shevchenko, a Ukrainian national, and she'd frequently been seen with an old couple, Ivar and Yvania Czerney. Ivar had just been in Rome for Gabrieli's funeral, but Yvania's whereabouts were unknown. She'd been celebrated earlier in the fall after conking Salvio on the head during his first rampage. Papers had uncovered her background as Chechen. Interesting.

Raphielli woke to the rumble of thunder. The storms that had been rolling through Venice for over a month showed no sign of letting up. She was tucked against Alphonso, his arm cradling her head. He lay on his back, as serene as the men she'd seen sunbathing on travel posters for the Italian Riviera. Last night had ended with him making passionate love to her. It was a release that left her relaxed and happy until she started comparing her two lovers. In the weeks since Salvio's funeral, she'd been in Gio's bed more than a few times, and he was masterful. Alphonso still only knew the one trick that Markus had taught him. She had dropped off to sleep feeling guilty.

Now she pressed herself against Alphonso's body and kissed his shoulder. His eyes opened and he looked out at her from beneath his black lashes. Feeling amorous, she slid a leg over his thigh. Her pulse quickened as he lifted her onto his hips then felt under her nightgown, seeking out her breasts and slowly stroking his thumbs across her nipples as he stiffened beneath her and whispered, "*Ah, mia bella Raphielli.*"

By the time they had come back to their senses, she was running late and had to hurry through her morning routine, with her elderly maid Rosa doing her best to keep up.

"There is no need to hurry. You are a great woman of a great palazzo. You are expected to keep people waiting."

"I was taught that it's disrespectful." She got her arms through the sleeves while Rosa smoothed the sweater into place and zipped it. On the way to claim her shoes, she caught sight of her figure in the trifold mirror. Maybe one day she'd see what her lovers and her French friends saw, but right now all she could see was a pudgy hourglass. "Paloma will think I've abandoned her, and I've got to get some breakfast into me."

"Paloma has been up for hours. She and Signor Zelph went up inside the fireplace rafters, if you can imagine. When Zelph came down he was a blackened mess, but that Paloma knows how to stay clean inside a chimney."

Over the past few weeks, the little bits of information that Rosa offered about the household were increasing. Discovering Rosa's taste for informing was a welcome new side to the normally monosyllabic woman who had been her maid for two years. It made Raphielli feel less like a child being kept in the dark, and more like the woman who owned these endless dark halls and rooms. She guessed Rosa wouldn't have dared gossip while Salvio's parents were alive, and since their deaths there hadn't been anything to tell.

Having Paloma and workers here—and soon other women—would do her old maid good.

Rosa started toward the bathroom. "We have time to put your hair into a bun."

Raphielli felt her curls, still damp from the shower and slippery from the product she'd used. "No, I'll go to work like this." She ignored her maid's lip as it disappeared behind her teeth, as if her wild hair was a silent cry, *I'm a wanton woman!* "It's okay, Rosa, I promise."

When she arrived in the breakfast room, Zelph and Paloma stopped eating and Alphonso jumped up.

"*Buongiorno.* Somehow, I'm running late," she said.

"*Buongiorno,*" Paloma said while giving her a sly look of admiration that communicated, *I know why you're late.*

Alphonso held her chair out for her. "You have time to eat, don't you?"

"A quick bite." She sat down and selected a bite-sized egg salad sandwich from a tray. "How'd you get so dirty, Zelph?"

"Oh!" He threw his arms up and pointed willy-nilly at the ceiling. "You have a veritable highway in your ceilings! Paloma took me up."

"How was that possible with fires going this morning? How did you breathe?"

"Are you kidding?" Paloma flipped her hand dismissively. "You have hundreds and hundreds of rooms. You don't use a fraction of your fireplaces, and judging from one wing, there are maybe twelve hundred of them. You only have, like, five fires burning at any given time, and your palace has the most impressive vents—super powerful—so the smoke draws up with real *oomph*. It rises in perfect columns. You can walk through the airways and easily avoid walking through a column. Of course, if you had a huge fire, like to cook a cow for a dinner party, you'd want to avoid that tunnel for the heat. But *your* fires don't even warm the airways up."

"They barely heat the space down here," Raphielli grumbled.

"Come on now," Paloma said, standing up. "Dr. Risinger is starting a new therapy topic about stress and the holidays. I don't want to miss it."

Zelph stood up, too. "I've got to meet with Ghost and Mister Fox."

"*Ah HA!* There *are* ghosts here!" Paloma smacked the table.

"Nah," he replied. "My audio and visual security team. They've been in and out of here for about a month now. You wouldn't notice them, they're very discrete."

Raphielli got up as well. "Thank them for me. I prefer not to notice the workers if they're in this wing. I'm relieved Tosca convinced me to put the shelter in that music wing."

"Ghost and Mister Fox are the best, and their clients never even see them while their homes are being wired for technology."

At the shelter, Raphielli visited Benny for a while, then had a meeting with Kate and Mia on the women's progress and status of their cases in family court. By the time the meeting concluded, Raphielli felt a little stir crazy. It had stopped raining, so she decided to get a breath of fresh air.

Just over the little bridge outside, her eyes fell on the spire of a church she'd never visited, and she got an idea. Pulling her big scarf up around her head *nonna* style, she splashed through the *calles* and found the entrance. She fished a bill out of her purse, stuffed it into the donation box, and pressed the button requesting a confession. When the light above the confessional blinked green, she made sure to shroud her face with the scarf and went inside. She needed spiritual counseling that wasn't influenced by who she was.

"Bless me, *padre,* for I have sinned."

"What have you to confess?"

"I need advice on an annulment."

"Annulment? Have you discussed your marital problems with your priest?"

"I'd like to know what you tell your parishioners when the subject comes up."

"Well, a decree of nullity must be entered into with grave forethought and should only be considered if you believe the marriage was invalidly contracted or that ordination was invalidly conferred."

"What if it was an arranged marriage? Against my will?"

He cleared his throat but said nothing.

"*Padre?*"

"That is a grave matter. Who forced you into the marriage?"

"My mama and *nonna.*"

He sighed, and she saw the silhouette behind the screen drop his head, hands holding his rosary raised to heaven in a gesture of supplication. "My dearest child...your immortal soul is at stake. You should request an annulment and purge that unholy contract from your life once and for all. You must reject that evil bastardization of God's holy marriage sacrament. Atone, ask forgiveness, and perform a perfect act of contrition to be restored to grace."

"*Grazie, padre.*"

She stood up, and as she left the booth she heard him say, "*Che Dio ti guidi in questa faccenda.*"

She left the church feeling that she was restless because she'd fallen away from her faith. It started to rain again, and she hurried back to the shelter where she buried herself in paperwork.

Hours later, her phone rang. Seeing that it was Carolette made her smile. "*Pronto.*"

"Elli! I've got Fauve on the line with us."

"*B'jour*, Elli! What's new with you?"

"I'm in a funk."

"Out with it."

"Let's have it."

She knew that no subject was taboo with them, so she blurted out everything. Sex with don Giancarlo Petrosino, Alphonso suffocating her, and her father confessor being pushy and not granting her an annulment. When she was done, she heard them let loose a torrent of French, but with their heavy northeastern accents and local jargon, she didn't catch it all.

Carolette said, "Yum! You're having it off with a Sicilian Mafioso? Hooo!"

"*Tais-toi*, Carolette!" Fauve snapped.

"Don't tell me to shut up."

"I mean it! Are you fucking kidding me?" Fauve sounded horrified. "Elli Scortini! Get your head out of that shapely ass of yours!"

Raphielli almost dropped the phone. "What the..."

"Listen to me, girl! You can't get into bed with the Mafia, they're vicious killers who steal money from hardworking people! They're parasites! As for Alphonso, you should be ashamed of yourself. He was your only friend. He and Zelph have stood by you, done their best to protect you, and he's madly in love with you!"

Carolette added, "And he's a gorgeous stud."

"Zip it, Coco! I'm not done!" Fauve continued, "Elli, you sound completely unstable. You go from a convent girl to..."

"It was an abbey..." Carolette corrected.

"I don't care if it was an ashram! You've gone from being virtuous to being don Petrosino's moll. Get away from him! And as for an annulment, you can't do that! You went through unmitigated hell as Salvio's wife. Now you're the last Scortini and all that money and property are legally *yours.* If you go erasing that marriage contract, you can kiss it all goodbye. Forget making shelters for abused women, you'll be hoping to get a job copying musty old books or whatever you said you did when you were at school!"

"I hadn't thought about that."

"That's why you have us, you slutty bunny. Petrosino'll lure you in, he'll take over your life, take what's yours, and then he'll discard you!" Fauve's tone became softer. "Honestly, I don't mean to yell at you, but suddenly I'm scared shitless for you. I was under the false impression that

Alphonso was acting as a bodyguard and that Detective Lampani was shadowing you, keeping those hit men that Salvio hired at bay. Now you tell me you've been sneaking off to have trysts with the head of the Sicilian Mafia. Honey, can't you just disappear for a while? Like Gigi?"

"I can't just tell Gio it's over...he killed Salvio for me."

There was silence on the other end of the line, and then she heard a shaken Carolette breathe, "Oh, this is really, really bad."

Fauve's voice quavered, "Where's that cognac? I need a drink."

Giselle was in an excellent mood as she climbed the hill from the barns. She'd spoken to Vincenzo and Juliette, and both were holding up well. V had done his baby-making duties, and when she cautioned that Gina would fall in love with him, he'd chuckled and replied, "No, it's you she wants."

Giselle was just putting her phone back in her pocket, recalling that Gina had in fact always blushed in her presence, when she received a text.

SPRATMAN DRIVING FAST IN DAMOUZY
ALMOST HIT AUGUSTE ON HIS BIKE!
DRIVING SAME RENTAL CAR!

Laetitia and her twin brothers, Robert and Auguste, lived in Damouzy. Spratman must be the most frustrated stalker in history.

Yvania presented lunch, which smelled like browned cheese and something dark green, like kale. Daniel said a blessing over the food. Then Yvania said proudly, "Thees is somethink I am working on for the cookbook. Is cod braised in butter, then I covered with a gratin of sour cabbage, bitter greens, and the cheese and cream are from Monkey."

"How have I missed *that* enclosure?" Markus squinted at the food on his plate. "Surely you did not milk a monkey."

Daniel laughed. "Monkey is the name of one of our female goats. She likes to climb trees."

Giselle dipped her fork into the layers and blew on it so she wouldn't scald her tongue. The fish tasted like browned butter mashed potatoes, and the other layers were a wonderful contrast of flavors and textures. They all ate enthusiastically and reached for extra slices of Yvania's bread. The light flakiness of the crust speckled with a dusting of sea salt gave way to the bouncy texture of the best bread Giselle had ever eaten.

She said, "Spratman's still hunting me."

"I know, I saw the text your friend sent," Daniel said. "You're protected here within the keep."

"Wait, I...the keep? I thought it was an abbey."

"*Oui*, the abbey is the next building over. We're sitting in an ancient keep. A secret fortress."

"With dungeons?" Yvania asked.

"Of course. What good is capturing a bad guy if you have no secure place to hold him?"

"This gives me ideas," she said softly to herself.

Giselle saw Daniel give Markus a questioning look and he said, "Markus, should I be worried about her?"

Markus shrugged. "You have no idea. Best not to ask."

———※◎※———

Mateo was glued to his computer, watching a live feed of a tabloid show where Benedetta's parents were begging for news of their daughter. He had to consciously unclench his hands as the couple started speculating that in the four weeks since her disappearance she may have been taken to Rome, that they had reason to believe she could have been taken somewhere near the Vatican, and asking people near or working in the Vatican to keep their eyes open for her. They were practically accusing the pope of kidnapping her!

Mateo's phone buzzed and he was relieved to see it was Benjamin. He lowered the volume on his computer.

"*Prego.*"

"I've driven every country road in this part of France and can't get a bead on Giselle's location."

"Could she be holed up in that big place of hers in Gernelle?"

"I can't get onto the property, she has guard dogs on constant patrol. I bought a telescope and did surveillance from the other side of the fence. Two women, one older and one younger, come and go but they appear to be tenants or caretakers. I've been sticking around the area keeping my eyes peeled and my ears open, waiting for somebody to say something about her. They're wary of outsiders, but I'm careful not to tip my hand."

"No one's given you anything to go on?"

"I got someone to give me Giselle's art agent's number."

"How'd that go?"

"My hopes were high when Fiamina answered her own phone. She was even nice when she thought I wanted to spend millions on one of Giselle's sculptures. But I couldn't get her to say one word about Giselle herself or her current whereabouts."

"Millions? Plural?" Mateo couldn't imagine someone spending that much on modern art.

"Apparently her prices keep climbing the more dangerous and bizarre her works are. They'll go into the stratosphere when we kill her."

"Unbelievable. I could get banned from a museum for showering patrons with broken glass—or whatever her piece did in that London museum—and I wouldn't get rich, I'd get a rap sheet for assault. Forget whatever substance she studded that piece with that Miguel ran into on her property."

"I wonder why a young woman who looks like a delicate cover girl would create violent art," Benjamin said.

"Something Freudian. She had a big adoring family, and every last one of them was blown to bits when she was in high school. Now she's trying to kill her adoring patrons."

"Don't make me feel sorry for her, okay?" Benjamin sounded uncomfortable. "Have you heard anything on the French legal front?"

"Nothing good. The judge refused Bernardo bail for the second time."

"I'll drive down to Paris, check to see if Giselle's staying at her home there. She and Vincenzo have a mansion on Île Saint Luis. While I'm there maybe I can get in to see Bernardo. I'm his brother, the police should let me talk to him."

"Just be careful."

"I will. And speaking of 'nothing good,' I've had two calls from the Amendolas. They keep talking to the media."

"I was just watching them on a tabloid show when you called."

"They want to sell their story for a book deal and a movie option."

"What? They don't have a story they can tell!"

"They want to make one up, get a fat check, and pay off some bills."

"Oh, my..." Mateo bit off his next words and swallowed them with real effort. Once he felt in control he said, "I swear, I'm ready to take care of them, too."

"It may come to that, but let's stay focused," Benjamin said. "The good news is that Rome didn't send a death squad straight to Venice to kill us. It's been weeks, and we haven't had to send Nejla away for safekeeping."

"Right. We can't worship without our orator," Mateo acknowledged.

"She's a master at staying under the radar, and she's had more training than most of us. Even if the Vatican's Ecclesia Dei caught her, they'd never get a word out of her."

"She's the repository of all our knowledge. Perhaps I should send her to Nautilus just to be safe."

Benjamin said, "The Vatican is up to their eyeballs in scandals, and yet all the pope talks about is the youth of the world."

"I wonder how out of touch the pope really is. He's busy playing scout leader."

"It's gross the way news agencies cover Leopold's youth campaigns like they're getting the scoop of the century. Where've they been for the last two thousand years?" Benjamin said. "So, what are you up to?"

"It's been long enough since our last attempt to get into Porto delle Donne. I'm trying to get someone on the inside in case Benedetta is hiding there. I've also heard that Raphielli's planning to open part of her palazzo to women and that they're looking to hire staff."

"Now we're talking! We could get Paul's ring back! We could have access to the temple! Great news!"

"After our last church service, we all had a meeting and brainstormed any skills our worshippers had that could look good on a shelter resume."

"All of you? Even the ones who haven't been willing to get blood on their hands?"

"*Sì*, all of us. All of the faithful are willing to spy. We've gotten some chloroform to knock Benedetta out, but now there's only the three of us who have what it takes to kill for our cause: you, me, and Doctor G. Now that the pope had Salvio killed, our little congregation has come to understand the urgency of getting his unborn child back."

"Well, how far are they willing to go?"

"They've agreed to use any skill they have, take any job that will get them into Raphielli's buildings, but most of them still aren't willing to admit that bloodshed may be called for. They're secure in their faith that God will take care of everything."

"Any word from Lydia on what the Venice police are doing? Has Lampani closed the Salvio investigation?"

"She says he's been looking pretty ragged, but he's still on the case."

"I don't like the idea of that detective working so hard to smear Salvio's name. Venice should erect a statue to him, not paint him as some crazed killer."

———✦———

Gina looked at the calendar, which now dictated so much more than school and flower shop shifts. It had taken the boys about a week to get over their disappointment when her period arrived, and now they were looking forward to starting more attempts on Christmas day. Juliette had increased the frequency of their vitamin clinic appointments, and while Gina didn't notice any benefits personally, Juliette was looking more lustrous every day. Maybe Gina could ask her technician to swap out the fertility formula for some of what the contessa was getting. And maybe she should inquire about fewer colonics. She must have the cleanest, most vitamin-rich colon in the Mediterranean by now.

So far it had been a busy day for Gina. She was up at four, and it had rained freezing buckets during her commute to the flower shop, but her shift had flown by. School had been a series of ups and downs. On the upside, she'd whizzed through her scientific classes. On the downside, she'd struggled in math class. This was problematic because formulations were mathematical, so she really needed to find a way to improve her ability to use math for calculations.

Another down happened in business class when she made the mistake of raising her hand and asking a question about calculating net averages that revealed her fundamental ignorance of the topic. Beatrix was in that class and had gotten quite a bit of mileage out of mimicking her for the rest of the day. "Uh, I have a question. Vat is the difference between supply and demand?" But Diego had defended her, which had made her feel good. Upside.

Her classes ended early, and she had almost two hours before her closing shift at the flower shop, so on a whim, she called Vincenzo.

"*Pronto,* Gina," he panted.

"You're out of breath. What are you doing?"

"Leonardo and I are sculling."

"You stopped rowing to take my call? He must be furious. Are you going in circles?"

"We don't sit side-by side, we're stacked and both have a set of oars." He laughed, and she liked the sound of it. Vincenzo was so genuine when he laughed, it sounded as if he didn't have a care in the world, one of the many reasons people were drawn to him. "He's retaping his handle grip, so we're just floating by Giardini delle Biennale."

"That's not far from my apartment. Want to meet me for lunch at Al Leon Bianco?"

"In Campo dell'Arsenale?"

"*Sì,* my friend Diego's family owns the cafe."

"*Perfetto.*"

Fifteen minutes later, Diego had just waved her to a table for three along the back wall of the little cafe when she looked out the window and saw the boys mounting the stone steps of Canal Arsenal. They propped their shell against the wall and came inside. Both were wearing heavy athletic rain gear. While the rain had held off for a few hours, the sky looked ominous again.

"Don't you two switch sports in winter? These storms are fierce. You don't want to be caught on the water."

Leonardo swooped in first to kiss her cheek. "It's not like we go out to sea. We stay in the canals and lagoon."

Vincenzo waved Diego over and then leaned in to give her cheek a little peck, too. "I can't get enough fresh air. I couldn't sit on a rowing machine in a stale gym. What's a little wet? I'm Venetian. I belong out on the water with the wind in my face."

Over sandwiches and potato chips, they talked about her school day and she confessed her trouble with math.

"Why don't you bring your books over after you're done at the shop today?" Leonardo asked.

"I'm sure we can bring mathematics alive for you," Vincenzo said.

After lunch, she watched the boys row away and then hurried in the opposite direction to the flower shop. Mercifully, the only math she had to do at work was simple addition. Once she closed the shop, she went home for a shower. While dressing, she'd glanced at the sex potion, but only for a moment. Its sole purpose was to help the boys find her more interesting...in that way...for the purpose of pregnancy. She was emphatically not trying to be tricky and make them think they loved her.

Grabbing her textbook, she headed to their apartment where, to her surprise, they taught her easy, practical ways to grasp math. Then they went to the Verona palazzo for dinner.

There they found Juliette and Ivar in the parlor talking animatedly and laughing. Juliette looked up at their arrival. These past weeks, Gina felt more like a member of the family. The era of her being announced by servants was long past.

"Ah! The Holy Father has just beaten you home and is changing. Dinner will be served when he joins us," Juliette said.

Just then, the pope appeared and dinner was announced.

Gina asked, "Juliette, how was your day?"

The contessa walked with Ivar into the dining room and patted his back. "Ivar and I are a great team. Verdu Mer is running smoothly."

As plates were placed before them, Vincenzo turned to the pope, who had taken his usual place at the head of the table. "What's happening in Rome?"

"For the moment, Cardinal Negrali is assisting me with some of the scandals. He is conservative, but he is using his considerable influence to stop the mad rumor that Arguelles' and Klerk's actions were directed by me."

"You?" Juliette gasped.

"*Sì*, it is despicable! Someone has printed a poster titled 'Pope Masterminded Baby Thefts!' with twisted quotes of mine. Anyone who read it would believe I ordered the Church to take children born into poverty and find them new homes."

"*Dio mio!*"

Ivar said, "People have been twisting words to suit their causes since man began communicating verbally."

"And speaking of child thefts, has anyone heard anything about the missing girl, Benedetta Amendola?" Juliette asked. "That is so close to home."

"Only what the news says. I pray she returns to her parents soon," the pope said as he accepted a plate. "Although why they have intimated that someone at the Vatican is involved is beyond me. I offered to meet with them, but they declined."

Gina folded her hands as His Holiness blessed the food, and afterward, he pointed to the top of his glass as a servant poured his wine. She'd never seen him do that before, and could see he was stressed, just like any world leader would be when facing lies and scandal. But he was a spiritual leader, so the pressure to be seen as perfect must be unreal.

His eyes met hers. "So, you and the boys are back to attempts for a child soon?"

"*Sì*, in a few days, right before Christmas."

"Speaking of children," Juliette said to the pope. "I hear a group of children that you spoke to was so inspired by your message that they cleaned an entire field of trash next to a favela in Rio de Janeiro."

Gina jumped at the opportunity to join in the positive news. "*Sì*, and another group formed a flash mob and stormed a sweatshop in São Paulo. They liberated the children and took them to a mission where they're getting schooling half the day and helping rebuild the community."

"I saw a report where one of your youth groups came up with a plan to rebuild their favela by using surplus shipping containers from an abandoned harbor nearby," Ivar said. "Sort of Verdu Mer without the expensive foundations."

"Good for them," Leonardo said.

"Until I heard the news reports, I had no idea that some favelas have a population of over six hundred thousand people living in hovels made of stolen materials on squatted land," Vincenzo said.

Ivar spoke up. "Man has overpopulated our Mother Earth. Where are they to go?"

The pope's face lost more of its color, and he reached for his wine.

Gina said, "I'm thrilled you're speaking to people my age—and younger—like we matter. It's time we stop being sold 'things' and be urged to *act*. I watched some of the South American speech you gave."

"How did you see that? I delivered it to the stadium on a closed feed."

"I go to school with a hacker who's a big fan of yours. He put it up on all the screens at the university for about five minutes. You got cheers when you spoke about procreation."

"Cheers? What part?"

"The part about parents needing to be settled and ready to give themselves to their children the same way single people should be settled and ready to give themselves for life to a spouse. I knew you weren't counting me, of course. The child I make with Vincenzo won't need me."

"Your child will need you," Juliette said. "Your baby will be raised by all of us."

It was a lovely sentiment, but as Gina began eating she felt a little pang and wished Juliette had said something like, "You are my daughter now, you *are* a Verona, and will be part of everything that Giselle would have been." Then as the dinner continued and Ivar shared the Verdu Mer updates, Gina felt ashamed because she already had a perfectly good family. Why did she crave belonging in this one? Certainly, she was more than just a groupie. They loved her, too. Didn't they? The food had lost its flavor, muted as it was by shame and confusion.

The homicide department was deserted, and Luigi was nursing a headache as he reread his secret Benedetta and Salvio files by the light of his desk lamp. The Torre dell'Orologio struck midnight just outside the window. On the Piazza San Marco, the holiday decorations were already strung in celebration of Christmas. He didn't feel like celebrating anything. He felt miserable.

It had been an exhausting couple of weeks. His head had been splitting and his wife had started urging him to take sick leave, about the time he'd learned Giancarlo Petrosino was back in Venice and staying at the Aman. Luigi had expended a lot of time and called in a lot of favors trying to figure out what had brought that Mafia don back to il Veneto, but he'd been given a sound education in the ironclad silence that gripped people when the subject of La Cosa Nostra was broached. He'd learned exactly *nada.*

Today he had hoped to do some Christmas shopping on his lunch break and start to ease up on his workload, but he'd overheard that Benedetta's parents had filed a request for a court order to search Porto delle Donne. Instead of shopping, he'd gone straight to Kate and Benedetta and warned them. Neither seemed surprised, and he found himself more protective of Benedetta than ever. The poor kid had two sadistic nut cases for parents.

"Look, Benny sweetheart, your parents can request a warrant, but I'm going to do everything I can to prevent a judge from granting them a search of this shelter."

"*Grazie,*" she said, and then her expression changed. "Pardon my saying, but you look like shit."

"Pardon granted. My wife wants me to get a brain scan."

"How about you start with some sleep? You look like you're going to fall over."

"Now isn't the time to sleep. I need to get back to work."

She put a hand on his arm when he tried to get up. He felt as if she was going to tell him something important.

"What is it?" he asked.

She shook her head and withdrew her hand. "You're too stubborn for your own health."

"It's what makes me a good detective."

"Or it could make you an old man grumbling about this case in your retirement, and find your wife left you for someone less stubborn."

"Woo! You've got a grim side to you."

"I'm a teenager. We're the grim generation."

"Gladys would never leave me," he said as he stood up.

"What would you like for Christmas?" she asked.

"More than anything, I'd like some Pocket Coffee candy."

"The chocolates with the sweetened espresso inside?"

"Sì! They're my favorite, and for some reason they're all sold out wherever I look. But, you don't have to get me anything, kiddo."

"I have to focus on something. I mean this place is great, but I'm kind of imprisoned at the moment."

"It's to keep you safe until we can figure out what to do with you."

"My parents won't give up. Especially when they...I mean when I don't know what I want to do with my life or where I want to go."

She'd caught herself about to say something she didn't want to. Her secrecy and self-editing were infuriating. He'd been visiting her any chance Kate would allow and he thought they were becoming friends, but she had a real issue with trust. "Give it some thought. A smart girl like you can do anything she sets her mind to." He got up and gave her a hug before going down the back hall past the kitchen to Kate's office to let her know he was leaving.

He went straight back to work tracking down the court order paperwork. He couldn't turn his mind off. The

Amendolas must have sold their story to that tabloid news show, because the lawyer representing them had a list of past clients who'd all featured heavily on that trashy tabloid show. Strictly fodder-of-the-month. He figured the tabloid reporter had probably duped Benedetta's parents into signing an exclusive with her and the show was paying for the ambulance-chasing attorney to keep the "Missing Girl" story going.

Luigi would try to delay the judge's ruling on the search warrant until after Christmas. He'd just have to do it with enough finesse that the lawyer didn't get wise and request another judge. Of the six judges in Venice's Family Court Division, the one whose desk their request had landed on was by far the most police-friendly. So, he'd have to maneuver in secrecy and pretend to be oblivious about the Amendola case. He hoped that shyster lawyer would get a juicier tabloid case soon and abandon the effort to get into Porto delle Donne.

Now he was the last person in the homicide department, and his head felt strange, like it was bruised on the inside. He had to go home for some proper sleep.

The clock was finishing the final midnight toll when Luigi locked the reports in his desk drawer. He got to his feet and felt unsteady. His legs were a bit rubbery as he plodded down halls and stairs, and then out over the raised boards crisscrossing Piazza San Marco. Looking down, he wondered if he was hallucinating. He could see the shadow of small fish darting across the white lines of the marble beneath the water. The place was deserted and, while no rain was currently falling, the frosty night air was so heavy with moisture that everything dripped and fog halos formed around the street lamps.

On his way home, Luigi thought the city looked nice with the Christmas decorations everywhere. All the graffiti seemed to be missing.

5

L uigi was standing at the counter of his favorite *caffè* bar, watching the news coverage of one of the pope's youth celebrations while he waited for his drink.

On the TV, the field reporter was saying, "Pope Leopold the Fourteenth has asked other religious leaders to join him in urging young people to undertake environmental causes, and he's handed out these little cups and bento-style lunch boxes. Aren't they great?" She held up a compact metal mess kit. "Part of the pope's 'Say NO to Disposable' campaign. Kids are vowing to ask fast-food vendors to place their food and beverages in these personal reusable serving vessels."

"I see the Vatican missed an opportunity to put the pope's image on those giveaways," the studio anchor chuckled.

"Right, they feature a planet earth logo. And they didn't make nearly enough. The crowds here, mostly of people under twenty, have spilled far outside the stadium, filled the grounds, and even taken over surrounding parks and parking lots."

"They must be disappointed."

"Not that I can see. They're all watching his speech on their phones and seem very enthusiastic."

"Luigi, you look awful."

Luigi turned to the voice at his elbow and saw Marco Falconetti. "Do I?"

"What're you up to?"

"On your son's case? Actually, I have good news. I got close-up enhancements on the footage from Leah and Sarah's camera—the gallery assistants who were photographing art on a balcony overlooking where Reynaldo and Salvio went into the alley."

"Really?" He grasped Luigi's elbow. "What does it show?"

"What we suspected. Salvio did it. The digital enhancements are crystal clear. Salvio walking into the alley, Reynaldo running in behind him trying to catch up. Just eighty-five seconds later Salvio comes stumbling out looking wildly around for possible witnesses and wiping something like blood off his right hand. Reynaldo didn't come out."

"Amazing what technology can do these days. Too bad it can't show what happened in those seconds—what my son could have done to make Salvio kill him. And there's nothing you can do with that footage now that Salvio's dead."

The barista was setting Luigi's espresso cup in front of him when his phone buzzed. It was his friend, the judge's clerk. He didn't want anyone to know he was trying to interfere with the court docket, so he said, "Marco, go ahead and get your coffee. I gotta take this."

Luigi moved to the far side of the bar with his cup as he answered the call. "*Pronto.*"

"I've been keeping my eyes open like you asked," the clerk said. "The Amendola's private citizen's request for a court order to grant a search warrant just arrived in court. My court."

Luigi felt panic rising. He couldn't let the Amendolas take Benedetta back, even though they had every legal right to. "Can you stall? Delay it getting on the docket?"

"It's on the docket. That's why I'm calling you. It got past me."

"Shit! Do anything you can to derail it."

"I'll give it my all."

"I'll owe you."

"Are you kidding? After everything you've done for me?"

Luigi downed his espresso, waved to Marco, who was talking to someone, and decided to take a walk around Parco Savorgnan. It wasn't his case and he was keeping it off the radar, but Benedetta couldn't have been that far off the direction she'd run the night she'd escaped from Salvio's hiding spot. Her naked and bloody body flashed before his mind and he felt he'd do anything to make her parents and Salvio's conspirators pay for what they'd done to her. Then he thought of what Raphielli's neck had looked like after Salvio hung her and felt the beginnings of a headache. Fucking Salvio and his savagery.

——◦⦿◦——

Raphielli and Paloma were relaxing over tea when she heard Dante clear his throat.

"Signora, Cardinal Negrali is here to see you. I put him in the receiving room."

Feeling perturbed, Raphielli went off to see her father confessor. She'd started keeping more and more from him, and it was becoming uncomfortable acting innocent and making up negligible sins to tell him. How many uncharitable thoughts could she invent?

She was hurrying down a long corridor when she heard Negrali say, "Are these by Caravaggio?" The voice came from her late father-in-law's library.

Startled because she was unaccustomed to anyone walking around her home uninvited, she did an about-face and looked in Salvatore's library. Negrali was talking on the phone, looking at paintings. He said, "The connection is terrible in here, but the first one looks like *The Denial of Saint Peter*, and the second one looks like *The Conversion of Saint Paul*. But they're different...bigger."

"*Padre*, I thought Dante showed you to the receiving parlor."

He startled and shoved his phone deep into a pocket in his vestments. "Oh! My dear! You don't want to sneak up on a man as old as I am! Why, I came looking for you. I've got a very busy schedule today—calamities worldwide."

"Oh?"

"Nothing that can't be fixed by returning to strict conservatism. Do you know how the Scortinis came into possession of these paintings?"

"Salvatore told me all the paintings in here were commissioned by his family from the artists themselves."

"Ah, they could use some restoration. Probably haven't been cared for since the late fifteen hundreds."

"They're fine."

"We have the best restorers at the Vatican. I can take them for cleaning."

"Do you have any news for me?" she asked.

"News? Well, no. But I understand that you do. Planning to expand your Porto delle Donne endeavor here at the palazzo."

"That's correct."

"I'll help you."

"You?"

"*Sì,* help you with the management and oversight of the project. Take care of the hassles for you."

"I did fine last time. I actually enjoyed it."

He gave her a look of pious concern. "I was remiss in supporting you when you created that little shelter. And now that you're a widow, who has suffered such calamity, you need someone to fight the daily battles with the builders. They can be so..."

"My builders have exceeded all my expectations."

"Ah, but as a mere girl, your expectations must be very low. The permits alone could hold up any changes to an historic landmark of this pedigree."

Inwardly she bristled, but she kept her tone respectful. "I didn't know you were in construction."

"Oh, certainly. The project of restoring Chiesa di Santa Maria dei Miracoli took years, and...oh! The logistics! Also, I'm going to assist at the helm of Verdu Mer."

She didn't like the sound of that. It seemed too much like Salvio's predatory interest in Verdu Mer. "*Padre*, I'm not feeling well. I hope we can postpone my confession."

He brightened. "Of course! Most certainly! You go lie down. You should take it easy. You push yourself too hard. I can handle everything if you'd just assign me authority..."

She pretended not to hear him and walked off, leaving him staring at a painting of a pregnant woman in a boat by Titian. Dante was waiting in the hallway, and she asked him to show the cardinal out.

An hour later, Raphielli sat astride Gio, who was looking up at her with a peaceful expression. She asked, "Will you always be honest with me?"

He wrapped his arms around her. "Always."

"Are you a bad man?"

"I'm a businessman."

"A businessman with a gun."

"A businessman who does business with men who carry guns, and doesn't carry one himself, doesn't stay in business for long—or alive, for that matter."

"You men...of La Cosa Nostra...you all carry guns to level the playing field?"

His brows lowered. "What are you talking...nobody says that name."

"How did the Sicilians get the reputation for being violent?"

"Our reputation as happy-go-lucky fishermen got us conquered by the Greeks, the Normans, the Moors, the Germanic Vandals, you name it."

"How did La Co...er...your association come to be?"

"At first, they were smart business people, good politicians who unified Sicily and made us a force to be reckoned with. But by the time I was a kid, they were all corrupt. Obsessed with money, drugs, and sex."

She clenched her loins, causing him to groan.

"They didn't have what you and I have." He stroked her thigh admiring her.

"What kind of sex?"

"Prostitution. They forced pretty much everyone they could into selling it, they took over buildings and turned them into brothels, they forced the sex slaves to sell drugs. It was ripping Palermo apart when I was a kid."

"Is it still like that?"

"What? No. You'd love it. Blue sea, fresh food, clean air, and good people."

"How'd it change?"

"I took over."

"As a kid?"

"Pretty much."

"How?"

"It started when an animal named Meagri killed my father. My pop had been a quiet man, a fisherman who owned his own boat. Meagri wanted him to run some cargo and he refused. We found my pop dead on the beach. When I started fishing to support my family, Meagri told me to run cargo. I couldn't refuse, so I agreed."

"What was the cargo?"

"Kids."

"Kids?"

"Ah, you're so innocent, Raphielli. The sex trade was just as big then as it is now, just not in Palermo where I've put a stop to it. If you see a poster for a missing kid anywhere else in the world, they're probably somewhere on the sex-trade route."

"It makes me sick."

"Me too. So, I picked up the cargo. Eight kids between six and ten years old. I sailed in the direction of Alicudi Porto until I got to the coordinates I'd been given out on the open water. Meagri's guy was waiting on his fishing boat. He was a big guy, but he was alone. I acted friendly and not too bright. He relaxed when he thought he had me intimidated and bragged that he was gonna try one or two of them out before he set sail. He said I could use one before I headed back to Palermo. We could have a little party to test the merchandise.

"I came up behind him, and when he reached for a kid, I took the gun off his hip and killed him. Then I tied him to a heavy toolbox and the kids helped me shove him overboard. I put the kids back on my boat, except one. I tied a rope around his waist. I rigged the steering wheel of the pervert's boat to point into the middle of the ocean, and I had the kid pull the throttle all the way back, then go sit on the side of the boat. When the rope played out to the end, he dropped into the water and all the kids cheered as we pulled him aboard my boat."

"Did Meagri ever find the man or his boat?"

"No, and everyone assumed he ran off with the kids."

"What did you do with them?"

"I took 'em to my grandmother on Isola delle Femmine."

"What did she do with them?"

"They'd have been caught if they went back to their families, so she saved 'em."

"Saved them?"

"You ask a lot of questions for a woman who has me inside her."

She stroked her hands along his stomach, feeling his hard muscles. "How'd you get so powerful?"

"Every monster who tried to use me ended up dead."

"Oh."

"Even Salvio." He paused for a moment and seemed mesmerized by her breasts as he stroked his thumb across the areas above her nipples and hefted them gently in his hands, feeling the weight of them. "But my real business started when a nice old guy asked me to save his building from becoming a brothel. A drug kingpin had his eye on it. The old guy signed his building over to me as owner. I kept the place clean till the day the old guy died. I started buying old buildings and fixing them up. I paid my construction crews fairly and on time from the money I was earning on my boat taking tourists out to the best fishing spots. By then the old-guard kingpins were killing each other off in a drug-fueled wave of paranoia. I put the word out that I'd run for local president."

"President?"

"A euphemism."

"Ah, oh, *sì*."

"Residents all showed up with tributes they'd given to the other bosses, but I refused 'em. Told them to clean up our city and our coast, keep their noses clean. They did.

When someone was trying to get strong over someone else, I let 'em know preying on someone weaker wouldn't be tolerated in Palermo."

"You're more than a local power now."

"I met with Italy's president about some laws affecting Sicily. He and I got along, he took me to the United Nations, and I've been a representative there ever since."

"So, you still need to carry a gun, even though you're legitimate?"

"What a word...*legitimate*. I need to keep my guard up now more than ever. People want to break apart what I've created."

"Why? If it's good for Sicily, for Italy?"

"People are easy to victimize when they're alone, not connected. And these days all the greedy bastards want victims."

"So, you're a hero?"

"I'm just a man." He rolled her onto her side, and she gave herself to him.

⸺◈⸺

Hiero saw a message at the bottom of his computer screen.

NEGRALI IS HERE

He'd have to put a stop to this, Negrali feeling welcome to pop over for a chat. He typed:

I'LL GIVE HIM 4 MINUTES THEN COME GET HIM

When Hiero pressed the button that unlocked his office door, Negrali yanked it open and sailed through leading with his hawkish nose, his expensive crimson material hissing all around him, embroidered skull cap perched on his head, and massive cross glowing ostentatiously.

"Waiting with your hand on my door handle?"

"I'm a man in a hurry."

"You should read Proverbs 19:2."

"Haste makes waste? Or are you calling me an ignorant zealot?"

"Take your pick. What are you doing here?"

"I've identified two paintings at the Scortini palace, both incredible works and, as far as I know, never before seen by the public."

"Oh? You have three minutes to entice me."

"The paintings are on the wall of Salvatore's private library and appear to be versions of *The Conversion of Saint Paul* and *The Denial of Saint Peter*, both by Caravaggio!"

"What condition are they in?"

"It's a remarkably dry room for being in Venice and the light is filtered, so from what I can see they're masterpieces in exquisite condition."

Hiero considered rejecting the offer as Negrali kept talking, but he liked the idea of owning masterpieces.

"I've got to work on Raphielli. The idiot girl asked me to grant her an annulment, of all things. I'll keep her in place as head of that household so I can manage the estate. I'm confident I can have them to you by spring."

"After you hand over the paintings, I'll get to work on what we discussed."

"Wait that long? You have to consider how delicate my work regarding Raphielli is!"

"Delicate? You just called her an idiot. Lost your touch, have you?"

"Certainly not. But I need the Verona situation handled before spring if I'm to get Verdu Mer."

"You were at Gabrieli's funeral. You saw that tidal wave of grief. The grip that family has on the emotions of everyone in power is nothing short of witchcraft. It's grotesque, and my team will need to move with extreme caution. Every time Gabrieli came into contact with one of my operatives, he'd unravel logistics it'd taken years to put together."

"Well, I want you to move *now* and consider it a promise that I'll get you both Caravaggio's in return."

"I don't care about your promises."

"At least send someone to France to deal with Giselle."

"There's nothing her unborn child can do to you at the moment. Get back to work on Raphielli."

His operative was standing at the door to show the cardinal out. When Hiero was alone, he allowed himself to contemplate sitting with a couple of masterpieces to keep him company. He wanted to be rid of the Veronas as much as Negrali did, but he wasn't going to let that greedy bastard know it.

Giselle was hard at work making solar panels and letting her mind wander while her hands moved. As they counted down the days to Christmas, Giselle found herself enjoying country life. The abbey's dray horses pulled sleighs and tourists came from all around to drink spiced cider and go for rides. The enormous Ardennes and Belgians were energetic beasts whose winter bell harnesses jingled as they pranced down snowy tracks across fields and into the forest.

While she still couldn't mix with any of the visitors, when the tourists were gone, she and Markus had been allowed to take moonlight rides through the countryside. They cuddled under woolen blankets and warmed in each other's arms as she listened to stories about his childhood. She shared hers, and together they planned how they would raise their family. She felt no danger during these moments and more than a twinge of guilt that the Veronas were still in open danger while Juliette had arranged for her to enjoy what felt like a pristine vacation with Markus and Yvania.

And then there was Daniel. What a great friend he had turned into. His ties to Juliette made him feel like family and he was completely devoted to her safety. Although, what could a monk do if a couple of men came racing onto the property like they'd done in Gernelle? That had been a close call even though she and Markus had gotten a warning from Fauve. Even with the head start, they'd still ended up sprinting for their lives with two armed killers just steps behind them.

Life in hiding was lived at a sedate pace. On mornings when Yvania was engrossed in her cooking experiments and writing letters to Juliette, Daniel took Giselle and Markus into the surrounding forest. The experience was like crossing into another time or dimension. Once they passed the first line of trees, the atmosphere became otherworldly and nature took over. Dense brambles of dormant berry bushes served as homes for woodland creatures, and the rich scents changed depending on what they were treading on or what wood was used to make the hearth smoke that was carried on the wind.

These walks took Giselle back to her childhood, and Markus had spent much of his own boyhood playing in the woodlands of Zalishchyky in Ukraine. Daniel's knowledge of the local area's history was encyclopedic, and wherever they walked he was able to bring them back to a particular time when a persecuted group sought refuge or a battle was fought. He brought history into the here and now...literally the *here*...standing where so much life force was expended in survival or cruelly lost, bleeding or decomposing into the very rich soil that was now on their muddy boots. She had no desire to wander off the beaten path because of the risk of gas-filled UXOs from as far back as World War One.

Late one morning, they were sitting on a big fallen tree where the sun had melted the snow, enjoying shortbread and *goût du ciel* washed down with berry cider, when Giselle noticed Daniel eyeing an old water pump near a clearing.

"Do you want to add some water to the cider?" she asked as she hopped down, thermos in hand. "It's a bit tart."

"No." Daniel put a leg out, preventing her from walking past, and then clamped his hand on her shoulder. "Don't ruin the cider." He surprised her by the physicality of his move—restraining her.

Markus slid off the log to stand next to her.

"What is over there?" he asked.

"A trap," Daniel said in a neutral tone and then pointed in another direction. "Let's go past that ridge and you'll see the bridge where—"

She shrugged his hand off, dodged his outstretched leg, and followed Markus, who was already moving cautiously in the direction of the pump. They stopped before getting to the clearing, and both she and Markus eyed the nearby branches for snares or ropes.

"It's not a trap like that," Daniel said as he came to stand next to them.

"Show us," she said.

Daniel looked around, picked up a big rock, and using a sort of discus spin move, he chucked it into the clearing by the pump. It sent a flurry of powdery snow into the air as it disappeared into the ground. "See? A pit."

They approached the edge of a square pit that had opened up, and Giselle saw a torn web of material. "How often do you restring that webbing?" she asked.

"We patrol the pits around the abbey several times each day. They're placed in areas free of berries or any tasty greens and they're not in the natural animal paths to a water source, so it isn't often that animals land in the pits."

"The pump is fake?" Markus asked.

"Right, just fake."

She stepped over to the edge. "Impressive. So deep! The sides are smooth and hard, and the ground looks squishy with soft matter, so no broken legs."

Markus looked into the pit, his blue eyes missing nothing. "I see you have nuts scattered for small creatures who may fall in, but where is the ramp you place inside for the larger creatures to climb out?"

"Ramp?" Daniel was looking at him with interest.

"The one that goes here." Markus walked to the far edge and pointed to a set of indentations high up in the wall.

"Very good." Daniel clapped his hands. "Here." He beckoned them to follow and walked behind some trees where he revealed pieces of a wooden ramp that could be assembled and dropped down to allow anything from a fox to an elk to walk out to freedom.

"What happens when you catch an enemy?"

"Then we use the tranquilizer darts or a spear with a stun-tip. They sleep as we haul them out and take them to the dungeon."

"Makes good sense. Why are the pits still in use?" she asked.

"We do things the old way here. Let's call it a tradition and leave it at that," he said enigmatically.

"Do you have other pits you can show us?"

"There's a whole network, all like this one. See one, you've seen them all. The important thing is to know how to avoid them. They're all marked by these water pump decoys. The pumps look real, and if someone is on the run they'd be on the lookout for fresh water. They take out their flask, approach the pump, and down they go. When we find them, we put 'em to sleep and drop them down the oubliette behind the cider house.

"Behind the abbey?" she asked. "Is that safe?"

"Sure, it's behind the crumbling stone wall."

"An oubliette?" Markus sounded uncertain.

"You know, a concealed mouth to a slide that drops a person down into a jail."

"Ah! The intruder trap. I have seen those in castles my father and I worked on back home."

"Every castle made around the middle ages has one, though current owners may not be aware of them," Daniel said.

By late afternoon, Giselle had completed another solar panel and it was fully dark when she went in search of Yvania in the kitchens on the far side of the property. Coming into the deserted kitchens through a side door, she'd just found her and was about to offer a greeting when Yvania spun around with her finger to her lips signaling Giselle to be quiet. Yvania then picked up an exceedingly long knife, and the look on her face was total concentration.

Had she detected a hit man's presence? Giselle's heart began to pound as the old woman slipped out of her clogs and, gripping the saber, snuck down the access to the pantry near the back door. Giselle grabbed a rolling pin the size of a bat and followed close behind on tiptoe. Then Giselle could hear what Yvania had heard: raspy breathing and muttering.

Over the top of Yvania's shoulder, she saw a big man pulling his pants down while holding a bare-assed youth's legs apart with his knees. The child's entire head was wedged between big sacks of flour. The instant the man's pants dropped, Yvania moved forward like a fencer, stuck the tip of her knife between the man's butt cheeks and growled, "*Stiy!* Stop!" A trickle of blood ran down the pale white of the man's inner thigh, and Yvania lifted her blade a fraction causing the man to rise onto his toes, his hands raised over his head in surrender.

Yvania commanded, "Let the boy up." She used the same calm, deadly tone that Giselle had heard Markus use when he was on top of her stalker.

The child wriggled free, gasping for air and dragging his pants up. It was the dishwashing boy.

The man's head was bowed over the flour sacks as he begged in another language and then babbled, "Please, my Russian isn't good. Please!"

Giselle reached for the boy's hand, but he shrank away behind some shelves to fasten his pants. Yvania spit on the assailant's back and said, "I am not Russian, you pig! The Russians did to my village what you were just doing!" With a neat step, she advanced, hooked her foot in the crotch of his lowered pants, and jerked his feet out from under him. He screamed as he fell and the tip of her knife sliced the thin skin of his tailbone. Then in the blink of an eye, she cut an X into the back of his left hand.

"Now you bear the mark of rapist. Courts never make justice for men like you. But if you ever do this again, I will come for you. I will cut an X into your chest and take out your heart."

Giselle had a hard time understanding the words. Yvania's

pronunciation was challenging on a good day, but when provoked, her words were only approximated sounds.

"Puh-*lease*..." the man moaned.

It sounded like the man was begging for the police. Maybe he was more afraid of the little old lady with the long butcher's blade than facing charges.

"Get out! Never come back here!" Yvania yelled.

He dragged his pants up and ran out the back door as monks and the cook came running. "What happened?"

"Who was that man?"

"I've never seen him before," the boy said. "He just delivered the beet sugar from town."

6

Luigi joined the morning commuters moving beneath festive Christmas displays when his phone rang from inside his coat pocket. By the time he got it to his ear, the call had gone to voice mail. It was the judicial clerk asking him to drop everything and come to the courthouse. He did an about-face and hurried to the courthouse where he waited at the back of the courtroom until a fifteen-minute break was called. The clerk beckoned Luigi to approach and slid a file onto the desk.

"That the request?"

"Uh-huh. Crap job. Missing information, typos. Somebody without legal training wrote it."

"Were you able to delay it?"

"*Certamente.* The judge hates this kind of thing. I told him it was missing crucial information. He struck it from his docket, and I stamped it "Rejected: Incomplete." I'll bury it till their lawyer comes looking for it then hand it over and give them a lecture about the importance of paralegals."

"How long do you think that'll be?" Luigi asked while silently praying the ambulance-chasing lawyer was already onto their next scandal and would forget this case for a while.

"No idea. But the courtrooms will all go dark in the next couple of days—adjourned for Christmas."

"You're buying me important time. I can't tell you why right now."

"I trust you."

Luigi headed back to police headquarters feeling bleak. He didn't know how he was going to save a girl from her own parents, and he'd gotten all the way back to the station before realizing he'd been gritting his teeth because of a headache. This one was coming from the bridge of his nose, across the back of his eyes, and radiating through his jaw. He fished two aspirin tablets out of the little tin in his pocket and swallowed them dry. Instead of his usual disappointing pilgrimage to the vending machine in a vain search for Pocket Coffee, he headed straight for the homicide department. Once at his desk, he had just unlocked the drawer to make notes in his Benedetta file when he saw a DHL courier package sitting in his inbox.

"Hey!" he called to the room at large. "Who brought this up from the mail room? Who signed for it?"

"Me," called Bruno, a detective on loan from the drug enforcement division. "It came from France. It's been sitting in the mail room for weeks."

Luigi pulled the sealed tab, tipped the padded plastic

pouch, and felt a little flutter of excitement as a phone slid into his hand.

"I didn't know it was your birthday, Lampani," Lydia said as she walked past with her own phone pressed to her ear and her hand over the mouthpiece. "What d'ya get?"

He palmed the phone and put his hand into his pocket. "A Christmas present for my wife."

Her eyes went to the courier label, but he opened his desk drawer and swept it in before she could read it. "What is it?"

"You're not very curious, are you?" He gave her a look that said, *Keep moving.*

She moved off, picking up the thread of what she was saying into her phone. When she was gone, he looked around to make sure no one was watching him, then he opened the drawer and retrieved a note from the pouch.

Ciao Detective Lampani,

After my wife and I subdued Bernardo, we had access to his phone. I sent everything I could find on it to myself at my phone number. Here's my phone and charger. My passcode is 36020. Giselle asked me to send it to you for your investigation. We hope it helps you nail Salvio Scortini.

Sincerely,
Henri Malreaux

P.S. If you need to reach me or my wife, Fauve, we run Chez Nuage Bleu Hôtel in Aiglemont, France

He could kiss this Henri! French police had Bernardo and his phone, and they weren't parting with either anytime soon. Luigi had a whole new respect for Giselle Verona. She was smart and fast thinking in addition to being an artistic power player with phenomenal good looks. Apparently, her friends were no slouches either. Fauve and Henri had figured out the man in their hotel was up to no good and subdued him.

French police had forbidden Italian police from questioning any of their material witnesses in the case, but this was an express invitation in writing from a material witness. Luigi looked up the number for the hotel in Aiglemont and dialed it. A man with a smoky Gauliose accent straight out of Central Casting answered. *"Chez Nuage Bleu. Comment puis-je vous aider?"* It was all strung together in a slur.

"Henri Malreaux?"

"Oui."

"It's detective Lampani in Venice—"

Before he could finish, the Frenchman let out a string of happy sounds, something like, *"Oh! Boh! La! Eh! Fauve! Viens!"* Then back into the phone he said, *"Ciao!* Has my phone been any help?" To someone else, he said, "It's Lampani!"

"It got waylaid, I'm just getting it now. Quick thinking on your part. And judging from what your police over there tell me, your wife's quite daring with a hypodermic syringe."

"You heard right," a woman's voice answered. He pictured Fauve, the wife, pressing her ear to the phone, too.

"Fauve, is that you?"

"I'm here," she answered. "We thought we'd hear from you sooner."

"Well, the police in Paris asked me to stay out of their case, and specifically told me to leave their star witnesses—namely you two—to them."

"Who we talk to is none of their business. We won't tell if you don't."

"Great. And since you sent me this phone, I say the less we admit to your authorities the better. I haven't gone through what's on it yet, but I was hoping you could tell me if the hit man, Bernardo, said anything."

"Not a thing. Nothing of use."

"All right, then can you put me in touch with Giselle?"

"Sorry, she's in hiding," Fauve said.

"I know she's in hiding."

"Sorry."

"It's important."

"No can do."

"She's still in danger," he pleaded.

"We know."

"Oh really? How?" He could hear them struggling to shut each other up on the other end of the phone. *Dammit! They're holding back!* Not wanting to alienate them, he softened his tone and said, "I believe she'll want to speak to me. Will you please give me her number?"

"We'll give your number to her if she calls," Henri said helpfully.

"You two wouldn't happen to be the ones hiding her, would you?"

"No."

"My French police contact says she's got a tight group of friends…"

"*Oui*, we all grew up together."

"Do her other friends have her?"

"No. Her mother-in-law found her a place."

"Juliette's head is in the sand!" he raised his voice and then glanced around the office self-consciously, but no one seemed to notice his outburst.

"We don't judge family, what can we say to that? Look, we want to help you. So does Giselle."

"Who's watching Giselle's home?"

"Château."

"Château?"

"*Oui*. Selma and her mother, Veronique, watch the property."

"Can I call Selma?"

"Got a pen?"

"I do." He wrote the number down, and after the couple wished him *Joyeaux Noel* he hung up and called Selma. She didn't answer, so he left a message asking her to call him. He'd bet Fauve was already on the phone with Selma warning her of his interest.

When Selma called, they had an interesting exchange.

"How can I help?" she asked with the same accent as Fauve and Henri.

"What do you know of Salvio Scortini's interest in Giselle?"

"Interest? Other than he was here spying on her at the end of summer?"

"What? Salvio went to France?"

"*Boh, oais!* Or he had a hit man out here.*"

"Fuck me!" He completely lost his cool and dropped the pen he was using to take notes. He leaned over and felt around under his desk for it.

"I'm in a relationship." He could hear the smile in her voice. "But you do sound cute."

"I'm happily married."

"What movie star do you look like?"

"Mmm...De Niro."

"Taxi Driver, God Father Two, or The Intern?"

"God Father Two."

"*Oh la!*"

"Selma, I need Giselle's number."

"I can't give it to you."

"Then give her mine and ask her to call me."

"Will do."

He was getting little bits and pieces of truth from everybody, but at some point he'd have all the pieces. He pinched the bridge of his nose trying to squeeze the life out of his headache.

He powered up Henri's phone, keyed in the passcode, and started scrolling through screenshots, text messages, and files emailed from Bernardo's number. They'd all been sent in rapid succession beginning just after five o'clock the night the French hit men died, which must've been the window of time before the police arrived at Chez Nuage Bleu to take Bernardo—and his phone—into custody.

Luigi sat back in his chair, riveted by what he was reading, and didn't even look up when Lydia dropped a *panino* on his desk. He was too busy reading texts between Bernardo Vitti, and Felix Montand and Miguel Turrion, the two hit men found dead on Giselle's property in Gernelle a short drive from Henri and Fauve's hotel.

The texts laid out their plan to kill Giselle and a Russian male, probably Markus Shevchenko, who Luigi knew was actually Ukrainian. The plan was to shoot Markus, but bizarrely, they had specific instructions to drown Giselle in a lake on her property. There was even a screenshot of a map showing the route to access the private lake.

He thought about how Count Gabrieli Verona had been drowned that same day here in Venice and wondered what Salvio's preoccupation with drowning was about—it was an extremely rare mode of murder. He came upon a string of messages between the hit men that spelled out how Giselle's left ankle was to be tethered with a length of vintage amber-colored nautical rope that was sent from Italy.

Luigi came forward, sitting bolt upright with a start. Gabrieli had drowned because his left ankle had been tethered with rope that held him far below the water's surface. It was an amber-colored rope that no one at Verdu Mer was familiar with. What on earth was that about? Nothing on the phone was sent by or to Salvio, his name wasn't even mentioned. There were also two murderous directives initiated by two people, someone named Mateo and Bernardo's brother or someone who called him '*Fra.*' Luigi called out to the room at large, "*Eh!* Anyone know if the hit man the French have in custody..."

"Bernardo Vitti," a voice yelled.

"...has a brother?" he finished.

"*Sì*, Benjamin. The Vittis are from here, they live over on Murano."

"Anyone talk to Benjamin yet?"

"Don't know about that. Don't think so. His address is in one of the files marked 'French Case.'"

"*Grazie.*" Luigi started shuffling through the files on his desk.

"*Prego.*"

"Who did the work on the Vitti brothers?" he called out to the room.

"I did." Bruno again.

"Run a search, get me his phone number."

"It's in the file."

Luigi's excitement built as he found the file and pushed the others back into a stack. "You're a beautiful man, Bruno. Maybe we'll keep you over here in homicide after things settle down."

"Remember that when commendations come out. You're the one with the Chief Inspector's ear."

"Plan on it."

"I will."

Picking up his phone, Luigi dialed Benjamin's number and got a message that the voicemail was full.

He clicked off the call and continued scrolling through Henri's phone. He found the number he'd just dialed, proof that the brothers had spoken the day Bernardo was sidelined by Fauve. He wouldn't fall for "I haven't spoken to him in a long time" when he finally got to question Benjamin. In fact, he now had enough evidence to bring

Benjamin in for questioning. And then Luigi's breath caught. Henri had taken a screenshot of Bernardo's recent calls! Fucking brilliant!

Bernardo had called Benjamin nine times for varying durations on the day in question. Luigi found a text that had been sent a month prior from Benjamin to his brother about a phone bill that included an attachment of the bill. It showed an address on Fondamenta Savorgnan. Turning to his computer, he searched the address and found a house two *calles* over from where Benedetta had sent him the night she broke out of captivity.

Two big puzzle pieces snapped into place that he felt certain would lead to the critical pieces he'd been waiting months for. He was filled with gratitude for Giselle's friend Henri. He pictured him as a scruffy Gérard Depardieu-looking man with a home-rolled cigarette dangling from his mouth as he coolly stood over a drugged hit man scavenging his phone. He pictured Fauve as Brigitte Bardot in "...And God Created Woman" wearing a black ballet top, wrap-skirt and bare feet, stashing her hypodermic needle and then stepping over Bernardo to go check someone into their hotel with a sultry look.

Luigi got up, pulled on his raincoat, grabbed his cellophane-wrapped *panino*, dropped both phones into his pocket, and headed off to visit the address on Fondamenta Savorgnan where hit men get phone bills and virgins were taken by their parents to be raped by Salvio Scortini.

The rain had just stopped when he knocked on the door of a two-story whitewashed home kept neat with healthy winter greenery in the window boxes. A man with an immaculately clean-shaven head answered the door. He was dressed somberly, all in black with glossy black shoes. Bingo!

"*Sì? Che cosa?*"

"I'm Detective Lampani, Venice police." He flashed his badge. "I need to ask you a few questions."

"Okay."

"Do you live here?"

"*Sì.*" He didn't appear nervous.

"What's your name?"

"Mateo."

Gotcha! Keeping his expression neutral, he asked, "Are you familiar with Felix Montand, Miguel Turrion, or Bernardo Vitti?"

"I know *Benjamin* Vitti, and I've heard of his brother Bernardo. The others, no."

"Ever met Bernardo?"

"*Sì.*"

"What's your opinion of him?"

"I don't know enough about him to form an opinion. Benjamin doesn't speak highly of him, so..."

"But the brothers live together, right?"

"No."

"They don't live in an apartment..." He consulted his notebook and found the address from Bruno's report. "...in Murano on Calle Brussa?"

"Benjamin lives there, Bernardo doesn't. Is this about Bernardo getting mixed up with some *pazzi* trying to pull off a robbery in France last month?"

Luigi ignored the attempt to mislead him. "I'm looking into Bernardo's involvement with the Veronas."

"The Veronas? He has no involvement, as far as I know."

Luigi figured he'd shake this liar up since he'd seen the texts both he and Benjamin had sent to Bernardo. "Bernardo was in France trying to kill one of the Veronas."

"No way. You've got the wrong guy. Neither brother knows anything about the Veronas. It was an attempted robbery of some French château."

"You sound like you know what happened."

"No, just what was on the news."

"Uh-huh. Do you know where Benjamin is right now?"

"No."

"Does Bernardo get mail delivered here?"

"No."

Luigi looked past him to a gleamingly clean entryway and beyond to a pleasant sitting room filled with similarly gleaming antique furniture. Apparently, this bald man was fond of polishing things: his furniture, his head, his shoes. "Nice place you have here."

"*Grazie.*"

"Are you a decorator?"

"No."

"You've got excellent taste from what I can see." Luigi gestured toward what looked like furnishings circa seventeen hundred.

"My furniture was passed down from my great-grandparents—sturdy old pieces. Why give them up, right?"

"There must have been real money in your family."

"Nah, they worked in service of one of the great palazzos and were given old furnishings."

"Oh? Which great palazzo?" *Please say Scortini! Please say Scortini!*

"I don't recall."

"Right. Okay then, I'll be on my way." Luigi walked away with the knowledge that Mateo was protecting Bernardo, he'd likely held Benedetta against her will, probably sheltered Salvio here while the entire police department had been hunting him, and was possibly involved with Gabrielli's murder as well as the ongoing effort to kill Raphielli Scortini. Despite being unable to discuss his new evidence with anyone, he felt like things were finally coming together.

He walked carefully to avoid the ice that was forming everywhere as the sun set. It was even floating in chunks along the canals. He ducked inside a *tabaccheria* as much to get out of the cold as to search for Pocket Coffee. They had none, so he bought a Mangini hard coffee candy and some aspirin. Opening both, he chewed two aspirin and popped the Mangini in his mouth. He did his best to pretend it was dark chocolate and sugary espresso. He failed miserably.

Luigi was supposed to be ramping down from work for the holidays. He was scheduled to take the next two days off and was looking forward to some quiet time with Gladys. He used to love Christmas with his parents and uncles and cousins. But after a steady family exodus, he and Gladys were the only Lampanis who hadn't moved to Sorrento for a slower-paced life. Now, there were so many of his relatives in Sorrento that when he and Gladys visited, the locals said, "Oh! No more Lampanis! We know you're going to change the name of our little town to

Lampanirento!" It was said in jest. His family had been warmly embraced there.

Since being stymied by the Scortini case, Gladys had been putting pressure on him to retire early and move. He hadn't had time to consider it, but he was in love with two wives: Gladys and La Serenissima.

Mateo didn't want to do what had to come next, but Nejla had to go. Lately, he'd had to do a lot of things he didn't want to do, but the Alithiní faithful had survived this long through secrecy, abundant caution, and when threatened, moving fast to escape the pope's thugs. They worshipped listening to Jesus's teachings as given to him directly from God, and Nejla, their orator, was the repository of their divine spoken tradition. Nothing, absolutely nothing, was written down. It was too dangerous for Nejla to remain in Venice. Mateo placed a call to her.

"*Pronto.*"

"Nejla, our anonymity has been broken."

"How bad is it?"

"I've just had the authorities at the house. If the dull-witted police have found us, we can't risk the Vatican finding us, too."

"You're sending me to Castine?"

"*Sì.* Pack a small bag, nothing anyone would notice. Make it look like a day trip. I'll get in contact with our people on Nautilus Island and get you on a flight to New York tomorrow.

"New York? Aren't I going to Castine, Maine?"

"I'll book you a connection to Portland, don't you worry about anything. One of our people will meet you and say the code word 'sinope.' They'll drive you to Penobscot Bay and then sneak you out to Nautilus Island where you'll stay with the first North American congregation until you're called back here. Call your niece and tell her she'll be leading services in your absence."

He ended their call and started making preparations. He didn't like the idea that Nejla's niece would be their substitute orator, but it couldn't be helped. She had memorized everything perfectly, she just didn't deliver the lessons with anything approaching Nejla's power.

It was getting late and the sun was gone by the time he'd made the arrangements. He paid cash at a travel agency run by one of their Alithinían brethren. He'd just left the agency when one of his neighbors bumped into him in the cramped alley.

"Eh! Mateo! Where's the fire?" It was an old man who rented a room in a home near the safe house. He was always hanging out in Parco Savorgnan and seemed to never go inside in the summer no matter how bad the mosquitos got. He'd just sit in the park, like a fixture, either watching the children play on the playground, looking dreamily up into the trees, or dozing. No one in the neighborhood could avoid conversing with him if they were in the park.

"Oh, no fire. Just trying to stay warm."

Ignoring his reply, the old man continued, "Everyone's in such a hurry this time of year. It's almost Christmas. Are you off to visit your relatives in...where are they again? Emilia Romagna?"

"*Sì*, San Lazzaro. You have a good memory."

"Well, if I don't see you before your trip, *Buon Natale*."

"*Buon Natale*," he said and hurried off in the opposite direction of his neighbor.

When Mateo reached the promenade at the edge of the Grand Canal, he could hear a low rumbling and occasional screeching sound. The ice was clacking together out on the waves, and the sound of heavy ice being tumbled about by the powerful motion of the lagoon was other-worldly.

He walked to the *vaporetto* pier feeling secure in the Alithinían custom of always pretending to be somewhere visiting far-off relatives during Christmas. It provided an excuse to avoid celebrating the holiday mass that even the most lapsed Catholics observed, showing up and faking their way through a charade.

For Alithiníans, Christmas meant nothing. They didn't celebrate Christ's birth on some arbitrary day by engaging in gross consumerism and then gorging themselves like Roman emperors. They celebrated their High Holy Day in the spring when God's natural bounteous gifts were bursting forth in all their glory. Italian Alithiníans tended to celebrate by snorkeling where there were still underwater wonders in areas like the Cyclops' Sea, Aci Trezza, or Taormina. That was the ultimate Alithinían religious experience!

It was still dark when Gina woke up. She moved about her little apartment, grateful that her landlord had fixed the radiator. But now it was beyond cozy, in fact it was a bit stuffy. She went to the window overlooking the Campo San Martino and lifted the sash a crack, grateful that it wasn't raining. The cold air felt refreshing on her bare legs.

Down on the street, she saw a man in black standing in front of the locked church door looking up at her. She sprang away from the window, pressed herself against the wall, then peeked out again, careful not to be seen. She watched him move to the adjacent shuttered grocery store. He pretended he hadn't been looking at her window and looked down at his watch. She stood pressed against the wall wondering if she should drop to the floor and crawl to her phone. Who should she call? She peeked out again at the man, unable to move. All this intrigue with the Veronas was making her jumpy.

A woman joined the man on the well-lit *campo*. She was wearing sweatpants, a heavy jacket, scarf, and hat, all bought no doubt at the Grand Canal kiosks for extravagant prices. She was pulling a shopping bag on wheels bearing the outline of a gondolier. These weren't spies. They were tourists. After hooking her arm through his, the woman propelled the man toward what must be another day of spending money.

Gina put the couple out of her mind and went through her morning routine getting ready for work. Half an hour later, she closed the window, locked the apartment, and moved cautiously down the *calle* to her favorite café across from the Arsenale, careful to walk on the side where ash had been spread and the ice was turning to slush.

With a quick rap on the door of Al Leon Bianco, she summoned Diego and his head appeared from behind the kitchen curtain. He came out grinning as he eased himself around the big espresso machine and came to unlock the door.

"*Ciao,* Gina. On your way to the shop?"

"*Sì,* but I need…"

"Espresso coming up."

"No, *cioccolata calda.* A big one, to go."

"You got it. Let me see, my dad put some big paper cups in back."

She eyed the pastries in the glass case and the biscotti in the glass jars at eye level. "And I'll take a biscotto with chocolate and almonds."

"*Sì,* okay. Those are from yesterday, I haven't replaced them yet. Just take one."

"And a *sfogliatella.*"

"Those just came, they're still sticky. I'll wrap it."

While making her hot chocolate, he asked, "Doing anything special for Christmas?"

"Maybe a quick trip to Rome for the pope's Christmas Eve mass."

"Hey, that's special."

"You?"

"We're going to see my aunt, taking our boat down to Pescara to see her and my cousins."

"Will your brother be there?" She thought about the evening she'd had with him.

"He'll be there."

"Give him my regards."

She watched as Diego took extra care securing the cup's lid before sliding her pastries into a bag. He handed both over before giving each of her cheeks a little peck.

Forty minutes later at the flower shop, she'd finished her breakfast and her morning duties when Horace, the owner, came banging through the front door, sending the bell almost flying off its mount.

"*Buongiorno,* Gina! Look what I bought to make our holiday arrangements extra special!" He reached behind him for the handle of a red wagon and hauled in what looked like a sleigh-load of wonders. Then he flipped the sign on the door to *Aperto.*

"Look!" he gushed. "The most gorgeous stained glass mosaic vases, hand-painted ribbons, and opalescent cellophane. And wait till you see these sparkly curlicue ornaments we can stick in the bouquets!"

"Very pretty," she said. "But we're already the most expensive flower shop in Venice. How much will these increase our arrangement prices?"

"We're the most *exclusive,* honey. *Exclusive* is the word. They'll never complain when they're getting something like this!" He produced a golden blown glass partridge perched on a glittering pear tree bough and waved his hand beneath it like a prize lady on a game show.

Horace continued, "Hey, did you know some kids are planting a big winter garden by the wholesale mart? Some world youth project the pope is encouraging. Anyhow, they actually came up to me and told me that this beautiful treasure trove was destined for a landfill." He pointed to his goodies. "They called me 'ecologically irresponsible.'

Bah humbug, eh? Who could disapprove of anything so festive?" He waved one of his glittery curlicue sticks like a Christmas fairy and started to quietly sing "Santa Baby" in English to himself while he began adding ornamentation to the bouquets Gina had just made.

She was busy organizing the new supplies back in the wrapping station when the bell above the door rang and Juliette, Vincenzo, and Leonardo came in. They'd just gotten inside when Raphielli set the bell jangling again as she came in with a woman Gina had seen at the women's shelter. Then Alphonso came in with another extraordinarily well-built, big, longhaired man—apparently his twin brother. This was the second time Alphonso had been in this morning. He'd already come to claim the arrangement she made every morning for Raphielli. His eyes found hers and he gave her a little chin acknowledgment.

"*Ciao di nuovo,*" he said with a grin.

The place was suddenly full. Behind the counter, Horace reached into a refrigerated case and retrieved the hibiscus bouquet Gina had just created for Juliette.

"*Grazie,* Horace. *Buongiorno,* Gina," Juliette called. Then she pivoted to Raphielli. "My dear, come to lunch today. I will bring Ivar and he can talk to you about using his skylights in your renovations. Your palazzo needs some sunlight."

"That'd be wonderful!"

The contessa leaned over the counter to kiss Horace's cheeks as she accepted her bouquet and, after asking how he was, she waved to Gina. "Come have lunch with Ivar, Raphielli, and me. We will take a table over at Caffè Florian, eh? Ippy will call both of you with the time."

"I'd love to." Gina was excited to do lunch with Raphielli.

With a nod and a wave, Juliette was out the door. Horace now turned his attention to Raphielli, who said, "I'm looking for a holiday bouquet. Something good-sized."

Alphonso's twin pointed at the large offerings in the refrigerated case.

Horace picked up a wide urn containing crimson alstroemeria, blood-red snapdragons, and little red roses springing from between white birch branches and evergreen boughs. "What about this?"

"Ooh! Lovely!" Raphielli said.

"I'll have it delivered this morning. Just jot down where it's going. And I'll add this." He inserted a little glass sleigh ornament then reached for a roll of his new hand-painted ribbon. "And this!"

Alphonso bent over the pad of paper and began writing.

The shop bell jangled once again, and a dashing wolf of a man in an immaculately tailored suit and overcoat walked in. "*Buongiorno,* everyone." His accent was Sicilian. He looked at Raphielli and said, "I was just walking by when I saw you in here. I wanted to wish you good luck at the City Permit Office."

She looked pleased. "*Grazie,* but it's just a formality. Tosca's gotten all my renovations green lit."

He smiled at her, and Gina noticed a little dimple to the left of his full mouth. Then he gave the rest of them a subtle nod and waved before backing out the door to rejoin a young man outside.

Horace raised his brows and looked over his half glasses at Raphielli. "Excuse me? Did the Mafia just give you a

Siciliano version of "toodle-oo?" He tossed his scarf over his shoulder and threw his hand up with theatrical mock outrage. Then he refocused on tying the ribbon around Raphielli's arrangement.

———※◎※———

That afternoon Raphielli sat at lunch with Juliette and Gina and tried to focus on the charming Ukrainian man sitting opposite her. He spoke passionately about the special skylights he could put in the sections of her palazzo that were being renovated.

Juliette was excited by the prospect. "Ivar, you have no idea how dark and gloomy it is inside the Scortini palazzo. Raphielli wants to make the place warm and inviting for her residents. If you could bring some light in, it would change the place completely."

Raphielli nodded, but she felt unhinged. She kept reliving the conversation she'd had with Zelph outside the flower shop this morning while Alphonso was inside talking to Horace about the delivery details. Zelph had surprised her by asking Paloma to give them some privacy. He'd kept his voice very quiet and his tone was respectful, but his words had hit right her between the eyes.

"I can't believe you, Raphielli," he whispered while leaning over her. "I thought you were the kind of girl who might break my cousin's heart, but here you're gonna get him killed!"

"What do you mean?"

"I know what I just saw," he said through tight lips.

"Don't lie to me. You're two-timing Al with Petrosino. What's happened to you? When did you become so fast and loose?"

She'd wanted to slap him, but he was just speaking the truth. She couldn't meet his eyes and stared at the ground.

"You don't gotta admit anything to me, but Alphonso is madly in love with you so he's not seeing what's right in front of his face. This isn't a game! You need to figure out a way to keep him from falling off a boat with cement boots, and fast!"

"Gio wouldn't..."

"Wake up!" he snapped. "Your secret boyfriend is the most vicious killer in Europe, and he doesn't share. Sure as shit not his *goomah*."

"I'm not a..."

Zelph's big brown eyes searched her face. "Nah, I can see he's in love, and his son looks at you like you belong to his pop."

She came back to the present moment as Juliette and Ivar were exclaiming over a new recipe Yvania had sent from wherever she was hiding with Giselle and Markus.

"The complex flavor she packs into simple dishes is astonishing!" Juliette was saying. "I am making her lentils with bay and carrots tonight and simply cannot wait to experience it. Where does she think of these things? Muddling bay leaf into brown sugar?"

Raphielli rejoined the conversation. "I hear assurances from Giselle's...well, now, my friends, Fauve and Carolette, that Giselle's safe, but they won't tell me anything. How are she and Markus doing? And Yvania, of course."

Juliette reached over and patted her hand. "They are quite safe. Enjoying a holiday with a dear old friend."

"But the attempts on her life have been such close calls, and Detective Lampani believes the French police should be trying to catch more hit men in France. How can you feel so confident?"

"Oh," Ivar said with a little smile, "my wife is uniquely capable of guarding her, her unborn child, and even Markus if it comes to that."

On Christmas Eve, Luigi woke up and reached for his wife, but her side of the bed was empty. He searched for his phone on the nightstand, and it was missing as well.

"Gladys?" he called.

Momentarily she appeared in the bedroom doorway wearing a slip, one of his old cardigans as a robe, and holding a mascara wand in her hand. "I was trying to help you sleep in. I even took that damned phone of yours."

"You shouldn't do that. What if Laszlo called me in?"

She put her hand in the sweater pocket and produced his phone. "I'd have jumped on that bed and bounced you to your feet."

"Come here and try it," he laughed. Their mattress was old and the springs were out of control. He kept meaning to buy them a new one, but the prices were outrageous.

She joined him in bed for a quasi-dangerous quickie. It was like having sex on a trampoline.

Afterward, Gladys looked sated as she said, "How about I make you breakfast, and then we go buy each other presents? I've got my eye on something pretty."

"Something tells me we're going to Tommasi's over on Murano."

"Such a good detective," she said with a laugh.

He didn't want her to cook. He wanted his usual espresso and biscotti from the corner cafe. What he really longed for was a handful of Pocket Coffees. But come to think of it, he might find Pocket Coffees on the glass island, so he said, "Come on, I'll take you to breakfast on our way to Murano."

"No, let's not go out for breakfast. We're going out to dinner. I made reservations at Osteria Trefanti."

"We can do both. Hey, how about this afternoon I take you to meet Benedetta."

Her face lit up. "I'd like that! You talk about her so much, it's like I know her. We can get her a Christmas present, too. Oh! I can change the reservation!" Then she clapped her hand over her mouth. "Right. Sorry, I keep forgetting she's the missing girl." She made air quotes with her fingers.

"Don't forget."

"You haven't told me anything about her case, just that she's missing from everyone but you and Raphielli Scortini. Ooh! Can I meet Raphielli, too?"

"You can if she's at the shelter."

His wife hummed happily as she spent the next half hour getting ready.

Venice looked like a white wonderland as they walked to the pier for *vaporetto* number 4.1. On the ride to the glass island, they sat close together keeping each other warm. Arriving on Murano, they bypassed tourist stores and went straight to Tommasi's where the glass artist who owns the store knew Gladys by name. He helped them choose a heart-shaped pendant for Benedetta and a necklace made of multicolored beads for Gladys that she practically drooled over. She asked for them to be gift-wrapped so she could open her present over dinner at the restaurant tonight. Luigi never could figure out her numerous silly quirks, and these constant little discoveries about his wife kept him deeply in love with her.

They'd just come out of the store and Gladys was in the mood for a snack, so she started in the direction of the little *osteria* that had the best *bacalao crostini*. Luigi was about to follow her when he saw Mateo and his shining bald head go past in a boat. Mateo didn't see him—he was focused on the boat traffic—and had a little old lady with him.

Luigi snagged Gladys by the arm. "We have to follow that boat! Come on!"

He was grateful the sun had melted the recent ice as they sprinted to the transportation pier. He waved to the first *acqua taxi* in line and they jumped aboard. "Police! Follow that boat!" he yelled, pointing at Mateo. "The green cruiser with the white canopy! Don't let him see us!"

The driver's face came alight. "No worries." He clamped his cigarette between yellow teeth as he reached for the rope tethering them to the pier. He gave it a flick like a lion tamer's whip, making it soar through the air and snap back to form a pile in the back of the boat. Simultaneously, he throttled the boat's engine into a moderate belching and they slid out into traffic.

They followed at a safe distance to Marco Polo Airport on the mainland and paused, bobbing behind a tour boat, while they watched Mateo dock and then help the old woman out of the boat. She was dressed in black, so she looked like every other conservative older Italian woman, and she was clutching an old-fashioned carpetbag.

"Driver, let me out at this pier and wait for me." He turned to Gladys. "Stay here. This shouldn't take long."

"What are you going to do?" she asked.

"Nothing dangerous. I just have to see what he's doing."

"It looks like he's taking his mother to the airport."

"Maybe. We'll see. I shook him up recently, and now he may be leaving the country."

"That guy don't got no luggage," the driver interjected, obviously interested in their conversation as he tethered them to the pier. Luigi climbed out of the boat and trailed Mateo and the woman inside. He hid behind tourists and watched the pair go to the Alitalia counter. Luigi readied his phone, and when the woman turned around to check the clock, and he snapped a few full-frontal images of her.

Once the two moved off to the security checkpoint, Luigi approached the ticket agent and held up his badge. "The two people you just assisted, they're persons of interest. What flight are they on?"

"It's just the woman. She's on the next flight to JFK number 1467, New York, then a connection on United to Portland, Maine flight 209."

"What's her name?"

The agent gave him a dubious look. "You don't know your person of interest's name?"

"That man is sneaking her out of the city, and I need to know why."

"They didn't talk in front of me. I can't help you there."

"What's her name?"

"Nejla Brindoli."

"*Grazie*, now how do I find out if she gets on the plane?"

She motioned for the next agent to take care of the people in line who were becoming impatient and turned her full attention to Lampani. "Her New York flight is boarding now, so I can call the gate to verify."

"Okay."

She picked up the phone and talked and talked. Finally, she hung up. "She boarded the plane."

He hurried back to his waiting driver and Gladys. "Police headquarters at San Marco."

Gladys glowered at him.

"It'll only take me an hour. I need to do some quick computer work and upload some photos. How about you go get some lunch."

She crossed her arms and jutted her chin.

"This is important."

"So am I."

"Right."

"You're supposed to be taking some Christmas time with me."

"I am. How about you see if you can get your hair styled while you wait for me?"

She brightened. "Hey, that'll be nice for our dinner tonight, and I might be meeting Raphielli Scortini." She whipped out her phone to call her hairdresser.

Once at his desk, he uploaded the photos of Nejla Brindoli and went through the machinations of getting in touch with the TSA in New York and Portland. He sent them her picture and flight numbers and asked that an agent be assigned to verify that she got off those planes. Both entities sounded intrigued and promised to be at the gate of both disembarkations and call him with the particulars.

He printed out a map of the greater Portland area and looked at it. He wasn't familiar with that part of the world, but there were so many islands it looked like il Veneto. Detectives walking past his desk glanced at what he was doing, so he slipped everything into his Salvio folder and turned his efforts to learning more about Nejla but came up with nothing.

Feeling restless, he pushed back from his computer, locked the Scortini and Benedetta files away in his drawer, and went to claim Gladys. Her hair looked so lovely she refused to wear her hat even though the temperature was dropping. She was swinging a new bag.

"What's in there?"

"The softest stuffed cat for Benedetta. It's *sooo* soft and squishy, I think she'll like sleeping with it."

When they arrived at Porto delle Donne, he greeted Azure, the lone-surviving original guard at the shelter. "*Ciao*, I've come to see my friend. This is my wife, Gladys."

"*Ciao*, Luigi, Gladys. I'll buzz Kate."

A moment later, Kate poked her head out the front door. "The ladies are decorating the tree here up front. I'll meet you around back at the kitchen door."

On their way around the little pastel-colored building, he explained to Gladys that all of the resident women had been battered by men, and whenever possible they kept to a no-men-allowed policy.

"But you come and go all the time."

"Kate makes sure the women are busy in other rooms, and Benedetta stays in a room behind the kitchen that they used to use for the nurse. The new nurse doesn't sleep here."

They entered through the kitchen where the cook was simmering an enormous pot of white bean and kale soup that smelled delicious. Kate shook Gladys' hand and then went back to her office.

Luigi knocked on the door at the end of the hallway and it was opened immediately. Benedetta was glad to see them, took an instant liking to Gladys, and was delighted by her gifts. Lifting her curtain of hair to expose the delicate nape of her neck, she sat petting the stuffed cat as Gladys put the heart pendant on her. She was so young.

If she were his daughter, she'd be going to go see the Nutcracker or something magical tonight with him and Gladys instead of hiding in a shelter for battered women.

Gladys asked, "Will you be getting out to attend a midnight mass?"

Luigi watched a micro-expression flash across Benedetta's face. It was a sneer. He leaped at the chance to exploit the calming effect his wife was having on this critical witness.

"Benny?" he said softly. "You don't like Catholics, do you?"

"What? That's silly. I'm Catholic."

"But your parents don't attend church."

"Of course they did...we...do."

"Not within forty kilometers of here, you don't."

"You checked?"

"I did, because Benny, honey, I think you're caught up in a conspiracy of silence and..." He felt a clap of pain in his head and pressed his palm above his eye. "...it could be dangerous," he said through gritted teeth.

Normally, the pain bloomed at the bridge of his nose, but this felt like a spike had been slammed through his skull over his eye with a sledgehammer. He swooned and panted trying to catch his breath for a scary couple of seconds.

Gladys was at his side in an instant. "Ah, Luigi, this job is killing you. No! *This case is killing you!*"

"I'm close, I don't care if it kills me," he said with grim humor. *Which could be soon if I'm having a massive stroke.* "Before I go, I'm gonna solve the mystery of the Veronas."

Again, he saw a micro-sneer on Benny's face. "Why don't you like the Veronas?"

"What?" She did a poor job of feigning ignorance. "I don't even know them."

He had a flash of brilliance and asked, "Do you know anyone named Nejla Brindoli? Or why she'd go to Maine?"

The girl retreated behind feigned boredom.

"I'm not mad at you, I really care about you, Benny. I need you to take a deep breath and give me your secret. Okay? Do it quick." He leaned in.

"I missed my period."

"What?" He forgot the pain in his head. "You were tested when they admitted you."

"The test musta been wrong, and I don't know why I didn't tell anyone about my missed period a few weeks ago. I pretended I was using feminine napkins...I kept wrapping them up and putting them in the trash can."

"You and your secrets!" He was horrified that Salvio had impregnated her. "Are you kidding me?" He kept a palm pressed to his head as he jumped up and lunged for the door, almost knocking Raphielli over as she came in.

"Oof! Luigi, *Buon Natale.*" She looked at the gift boxes and wrapping on the side table.

"Raphielli, I brought my wife to meet Benny," he said. "This is Gladys. Gladys, Raphielli Scortini."

His wife reached for both of Raphielli's hands. "I'm so happy to finally meet you."

He cut in, "Benny's pregnant."

"What?" Raphielli's eyes went wide and then she called over her shoulder down the hall. "Kate? If you have a Mentos in your mouth, please chew it up and swallow it."

"What are you going to tell me that would make me choke?" came Kate's reply.

"Have Constanza administer another pregnancy test on Benny."

The four of them heard muttered curses and the sound of Kate's heels clacking down the hall.

———※◉※———

On Christmas Eve, Giselle spent all day in the workshop finishing the solar panels for the abbey. Everyone was busy today, Markus inside the church installing his gifts—

delicate glass stars—around the altar, and Yvania in the kitchen preparing a special feast. At breakfast, she'd been so excited about this dinner that Markus said something in Ukrainian to her in a cautioning tone, and then Daniel had made a vague excuse before leading her from the room.

Giselle had eyed the two of them. "What's with her?"

"Very excited about the gifts," Markus said.

This morning when she arrived in the workshop, Giselle had been filled with purpose. But as she completed the final panel, she felt strangely empty. Normally she craved solitude while working, but as this afternoon crawled on she felt a creeping loneliness that built and pressed. Now, with the sun casting long shadows across the floor, Giselle felt bitterly alone. She leaned the panel against the wall and knew should feel proud—these units would save the monks a lot of money—but she felt...off.

As she put her tools away, she thought of recent Christmas Eves with the Veronas, their cheerful palazzo filled with a procession of friends, and Juliette's special dinner before midnight mass. Then came thoughts of her childhood, the château filled with boisterous guests, a mismatched herd of their pets stampeding over furniture and each other, and—according to Forêt tradition—everyone entertaining.

Her parents and grandparents would tote the enormous green velvet bag around to wherever the action was taking place and bestow prizes with a gushing "*Ton prix!*" on anyone who took part in the entertainment. Her sister's ballet across the marble floor of the entrance hall with guests looking on from the grand staircase, her brother's magic tricks, Aunt Tina's heart-breaking rendition of "*J'attendrai*" that never failed to make everyone misty-eyed, only to be remedied by Giselle and her friends' uninhibited musical reviews complete with pratfalls and costume malfunctions.

Everyone in her family was long gone, and Gabrieli Verona gone so recently he still felt near. The memory of his murder brought her violently back to the present, and as she grabbed her coat, the fact that she was still being hunted was suddenly all too real. Giselle wanted to be near Markus.

She hurried out into the frigid silence of the late afternoon, her footsteps echoing through the cloistered courtyard where stones amplified the cold like an elaborate gothic freezer. Emerging from the arches, she looked up at the towering Madonna and child on the front of the church and thought of the baby inside her. Would she be as serene a mother as the haloed Mary? She thought of her own mother's relaxed "*que será, será*" philosophy and her heart ached. She broke into a jog.

The interior of the church smelled of old candles, old cloth, old books, old wood, and the mineral tang of eternal stone. Markus was high up on a ladder at the altar, bathed in the twinkling glow of the delicate stars he was placing. He smiled when he saw her.

"I have just finished," he called. He came down off the ladder and then descended the altar stairs as she admired his work. "What do you think?"

"They're so beautiful, I don't think they'll take them down after Christmas."

The door opened, and Daniel and Yvania rushed in. They both looked excited, and Yvania was clapping her gloved hands either from the cold or approval of something.

"Giselle, your present is arriving! Come outside to receive it," Daniel said and turned to leave again.

She looked at Markus to see if he was in on this surprise, and from the excitement on his face, he certainly was.

"Present?" she asked as Markus propelled her toward the door to follow them.

"More like many presents," Yvania said as she hustled along. "Hurry, you must not miss the arrival."

When they got to the walkway above the farmland, Giselle spotted two sleighs emerging from the forest trail in the twilight. She saw a tall figure stand up and wave. It had to be Laetitia with her impossibly long arms and legs, the braided tassels of her knitted hat flying. Auguste and Robert were holding her steady as their sleigh glided at top speed behind the big Belgian horses. She looked like the prow of a Viking ship.

"They've been traveling all day to avoid being followed," Daniel said. "We invited them for the night."

Giselle felt her heart suddenly full to bursting, and tears rolled down her cheeks.

"Oh! *Merci! Merci!*" She pushed through the gate and tore down the stairs to meet her friends with Markus, Daniel, and Yvania following.

As the sleighs approached the paddock, Selma stood up in the other sleigh and made a move to jump out, but

Carolette hauled her back yelling, "Me first!" and jumped out and into a run straight for Giselle. Selma was right behind her, and then Fauve piled out. Within moments, the foot race turned into an epic snowball fight with Giselle and Markus joining in. Finally, as they all lay in the snow panting, Henri walked past at a dignified pace bearing a case of champagne.

"You must be Daniel and Yvania. I'm Henri, that woman with the wicked snowball arm being held down, is my wife, Fauve. The trio spanking her is Laetitia and her twin brothers, Auguste and Robert. The three energetic snow angels next to them are Selma, Solange, and Carolette."

"Oh! Carolette! She is the blonde with the beeg hair?" Yvania asked.

"*Oui*, the beehive is her signature," he responded.

"Even in spin classes!" Giselle looked up from between her friends. "Yvania, Daniel, meet *mes amis!*"

"I'm the most mature one of the group, but they've been like this since they were all in diapers together," Henri said.

Giselle helped Solange to her feet and asked, "You're sure no one followed you?"

"*Boh!* Not a chance. We split up, some of us went by train from Charleville-Mézières to Paris, then came back via train through Brussels. Some went to Nice, then flew to Lyons and rented cars. Carolette and I drove all over in crazy routes picking up the group, and then we parked in a locked barn way past the forest. Spratman is no match for us."

"I'm sorry it was such a hassle."

"More like an adventure. Something fun to do and now we're all back together. Going back tomorrow morning, we'll just take sleighs back through the forests and pile into the two cars. Simple."

"I'm so glad you guys came!" Giselle said and wrapped her arms around her dear friend.

Everyone followed Daniel to a bunkhouse where they dropped overnight bags, then proceeded to the dining hall where the first course of Yvania's feast was being brought in for the party.

The meal was a big family-style affair. Giselle's friends swept Yvania and Daniel up in their steady stream of local updates that tumbled out in gleeful bursts while each jockeyed to be the one to deliver the punchline. Over dinner, the conversation circled around introduction stories from each of the guests, and then the latest news from the region.

"Did you know there's been a rash of thefts around Gernelle?"

"No!" Giselle gasped. "No one texted me."

"In such a tight community?" Markus looked unbelieving.

"*Mais oui!* It started with some tools from sheds and workshops."

"A wind chime from near Madame Panel's lounge chair."

"The keys for the community playground gate."

"No!" Giselle said. "How strange."

"Jerome lost the velvet curtain from his sun porch along with all the antique brass curtain rings. Then the Picards lost pieces of their silver off their kitchen drying rack!"

"But the gang of thieves has been caught," Fauve jostled into the conversation and then pointed at the whipped sweet potatoes and snapped for Robert to pass them.

"Their lair was discovered," Solange said while taking a spoonful of potatoes from Robert before handing them to Fauve.

"Two days ago, Maurice...you know, Jeneve's uncle from Nevers...well his car wouldn't start, and when he opened the hood all his wires had been chewed and there were pieces of dog food and family photographs all over the engine."

"What?" Yvania said, her eyes narrowing at the clue.

"Wait! And there were photo bits and dog kibble all over the floor of his garage."

"What?" Daniel leaned forward, caught up in the mystery.

"When Maurice climbed into the garage rafters, he found velvet shreds from Jerome's missing curtain."

"The gang was in his garage?" Giselle asked.

"Wait!" Auguste put a hand up. "So, he called the fire department, and on a hunch, they pointed their hoses down inside the cinderblocks of the garage walls, you know those two openings in the blocks? And woosh! Out flew pack rats and all the missing stuff!"

"Pack rats!"

"Pack rats?"

"*Oui!* They'd made a condominium complex inside the cinderblock hollows!"

"They'd been scuttling everywhere, even into people's homes through their dog doors, and taking whatever caught their eye!" Solange announced.

"So…" Carolette casually waved her fork about indicating the walls. "Daniel, like all school children of the region, we've all visited your abbey's cheese shop many times, but what's the story with this place? Tell us about the ghosts, the folklore."

"We are mostly known for our beer, but our most famous story is how Abbaye d'Orval was founded. In 1113 Countess Matilde of Tuscany was visiting this area and lost her wedding ring. She knelt by our stream and prayed for God to return it. Just then a golden trout surfaced and opened its mouth to reveal her ring. After plucking it out she declared, 'Truly this place is a *val d'Or!*' In thanks to God, she founded a monastery on this site, in this golden valley, and named it Abbaye d'Orval."

"Any more of those trout around? I love jewelry!" Fauve said.

"This bread is the best thing I've ever eaten, and that layered dish comes second!"

"What else is going on?"

"Not much. Spratman is our big past time, watching his every move, but he's so erratic."

"I have a plan," Yvania said, which got everyone's attention. "No goot sitting here hiding. We believe Spratman is brother of the hitman Bernardo, who the police have?"

"Absolutely!" Fauve said firmly. "He looks just like him and dresses just like him with those shiny black shoes, too."

"Hokay, so we will trap him," she said as if it were the simplest thing.

"How?" the group asked in unison.

"Make him think he is following Giselle, take him to a place where your friendly police…"

"Luc, Terrance, and Gendarme Evan," Henri supplied helpfully.

"...are waiting, and we take him."

"Take him?" Laetitia asked.

"To question," Yvania said.

"On what grounds?" Henri asked.

"If you are so certain that he is part of the murderers Salvio hired, I am not worried that he would take us to court for questioning him. Then Giselle, Markus, and I can go live in Gernelle in peace."

Giselle felt a spark of hope.

Robert looked dubious. "Um, how would we accomplish that?"

Yvania's expression became even more nonchalant, if that were possible, and she flipped a pudgy hand. "When you next see Spratman, Carolette can pretend to be Giselle—driving Giselle's beeg truck—and get him to follow her."

Giselle's hope deflated. No one could drive that truck but her and some elderly gearheads.

"I'm a good driver," Carolette gave her a knowing look and turned to Yvania to explain. "But that tank has a transmission called 'three-on-the-tree.' No one but Giselle knows how to drive that. I might be able to get it moving, but in a car chase I'd stall it and get murdered by Spratman."

"Oh." Yvania tapped her lip thoughtfully.

"What about the Exagon?" Solange asked.

That brought a round of hoots and "Oohs!" from the group.

"What is an Exagon?" Yvania asked.

"Vincenzo has an outrageously fast electric car called an Exagon Furtive-eGT," Henri said. "It's one of Vincenzo's prized possessions, and of course since he grew up in Venice with no streets, he adores tearing up the French countryside in it. It's metallic gold, unmistakable. Unlike anything on the road. No way Spratman could miss it. It's still parked at Giselle's château."

"Our château," Giselle corrected as she reached out for Markus' hand.

"Right."

"Sounding even better," Yvania said. "When Spratman is seen next, Carolette gets into that Exagon and drives to where he is lurking, and you get the people to point and yell, 'There goes Giselle!' so Spratman follows."

"I can do that," Carolette said. "Where do we spring the trap?"

"Some place your police friends..." she gestured helplessly trying to recall their names.

"Luc, Terrance and Gendarme Evan," Markus said.

"...can hide, and Carolette can run inside and back out without Spratman catching her."

"What about Château de Clavy?"

"It's public."

"Very public, non-stop school tours and tourist groups."

"Right." Carolette continued, "They have a secret passage from the downstairs up into that second floor library."

"Is it in the general area where he has been searching?" Markus asked.

"It's in the area."

"If we make him believe he has intercepted Giselle while she runs an errand, that would work."

"Like dropping off a package at Château de Clavy?" Giselle offered.

"Brilliant!" Laetitia got excited.

"Theenk about it while I go to bring dessert and coffee."

"Got any dessert that goes with that amazing sweet beer your brethren make, Daniel?"

"Of course!" he said proudly and followed Yvania out of the dining hall.

The moment Yvania and Daniel left, Selma turned to Markus. "Is she serious?"

"Yvania is always serious about anything tactical," Markus replied.

"Not what you'd expect from a short pudgy old Russian dumpling with Dame Edna glasses," Fauve said.

"Ukrainian," Selma supplied helpfully.

"Actually, Yvania is Chechen," Markus said.

"Lord! You'll have to give us time to keep this stuff straight," Solange drawled. Markus winked at her, and she fanned herself. "And don't flirt with me, I can't resist those ice blue eyes any more than Gigi can." She grinned and ran her fingers through her chopped platinum hair, making it stand at attention.

Giselle felt herself getting her hopes up at the prospect. "I want to try her plan. I'm sick of just hiding. I'd feel better actually doing something."

"I'm all for it," Carolette said. "Drive V's car, get Spratman to follow me, get far enough in front of him to get a running start into Château de Clavy."

"It's simple, actually." Fauve said. "The rest of us would get locals to point as you drive by, and then we'd get over to Clavy to be on hand in case you need help."

Reaching for her phone, Laetitia said, "Luc, Terrance, and Gendarme Evan would do it in a heartbeat. I'll call Luc,"

"I'll call Terrance," Auguste said.

"I've got Gendarme Evan." Solange was already tapping on her phone.

The dining hall became a flurry of activity as some of them paced around on their phones and others helped clear the big table.

Giselle pulled out her phone. "I'll call Stephan at Château de Clavy, see if he'll let us use the château as a trap sometime in the hopefully near future." She saw that her contacts were missing. "Damn this burner phone. Who has Stephan's number?"

"Here," Henri said as he tapped Stephan's contact and handed his phone to her. It rang a few times, and then Stephan's voice came on. "Henri, *Joyeaux Noël. Qu'est-ce qu'il y a?*"

"*Joyeaux Noël,* Stephan. It's Giselle."

"Ah, *ma chérie!* How are you? Staying safe?"

Yvania reappeared, rolling a cart bearing a *Bûche de Noël* cake, which looked like a perfect log with cocoa sprinkled for realistic bark, a quivering blancmange, and a towering croquembouche contained within a finely spun golden sugar net. Daniel followed, rolling a bar cart tinkling with bottles of dessert beer, the champagne her friends had brought from their vineyards, an urn of fragrant coffee, and assorted cups and glassware.

While dessert was being served, Giselle convinced Stephan to join their plan. She overcame his initial reluctance to any possibility of danger to his visiting public by offering to buy a new pergola for the visitor's restroom area next to the château's parking lot.

They all finished their calls and sat down to dessert. Giselle said, "We can use Château Clavy."

The rest of the group reported that their police buddies were happy to join the plan.

As Yvania served up delicacies, she said, "Of course we must have a Plan B."

"Ooh! Plan B! Can I do something fun in Plan B?" Fauve asked.

Daniel looked unhappy. "I promised Juliette that Giselle would be having a quiet pregnancy here until the hit men are caught. Let's not get too crazy with these plans, Yvania."

"Nothing crazy. But if Spratman gets away from the police boys, Carolette drives to that airstrip near Gernelle, hides the car in a plane garage and a plane takes off. Fauve, you can tell Spratman when he pulls up that, uh-huh Giselle Verona was on that plane, that she is going to Iceland to the home of art collectors named Guðmunds. I theenk Spratman will quick drive to the nearest commercial airport and fly to Iceland to follow her. So, for Plan B we need a plane."

Henri and Robert both said, "Stuart!"

Robert continued, "Our friend Stuart has his Cessna Citation at the Gernelle airstrip. He'd take off in the ruse to help us. Any excuse to fly his jet."

Yvania nodded. "Be sure to say she is going to Kópavogur, Iceland to install one of her sculptures at the home of some collectors named Guðmunds."

Selma looked at Yvania with admiration. "You really think fast, don't you?"

"You have no idea," Markus said. "And it's not just thinking, you should see her in action."

Giselle turned to Yvania. "You think Spratman would fly to Iceland in pursuit?"

"Sure, why not? He has a job to finish. He goes to find you, but I will have a trap for him in Kópavogur. The Guðmunds are my two nephews who live in a big place, very nice, very remote."

"They can handle a hired killer when he arrives at their house?" Giselle asked.

"They were in Special Forces, now are underground cage fighters."

Daniel's fork hit the table as he turned to gape at the sweet rotund grandmother who offered him another serving of cake with a smile.

Giselle handed his fork back to him and said, "Yvania doesn't say much about her life during the struggles against the Russians, but she's more than a little bit scary. Don't you think?"

"Who is wanting more dessert?" Yvania hopped up and her clogs clacked along the floorboards as she went to refill her champagne glass.

"We have some time before midnight mass," Markus said. "What would you like to do?"

That was the magic question that got the gang out of

their seats and performing hilarious versions of "It's the Most Fattening Time of the Year," and "We Wish You Weren't Living with Us" to the tunes of "The Most Wonderful Time of the Year" and "We Wish You a Merry Christmas."

After more drinks and sweets, they went to the church and took part in the Christmas Eve mass with Markus' lovely glass lights twinkling all around the altar, much to the monks' delight. As dawn was blushing the silent forest around the secluded abbey, the guests retired to the cozy bunkhouse.

———⏤⦿⏤———

On Christmas Eve, Gina and the boys had exchanged gifts in their apartment, and she may have used a bit too much fragrance because while they were technically supposed to renew their attempt to get her pregnant tomorrow, they'd had sex before going to the Verona palazzo to pick up Juliette, Ippy, the pope, Ivar, and various security agents for their flight to Rome.

She wondered what could be done about the scent. She was sitting between the boys and while Juliette and Ivar were oblivious—talking on the phone to Yvania, Markus, and Giselle—the boys were exchanging knowing looks and talking about nothing but becoming parents. The fragrance wasn't water-soluble, so no remedy came to Gina's mind.

Upon arrival at the Vatican, Vincenzo's bodyguard and the Swiss Guard melted into inconspicuous rounds. The family went straight to the papal apartments where, unlike what she'd imagined, the meal was a simple affair. The moment the meal concluded, the boys spirited her down the hall to a small door and ushered her through it. Gina found herself inside a dark Frankincense-scented chamber with velvet tapestries on the walls and candles flickering in red votives. She was already pulling her dress up over her head as they ripped their own clothes off and, together, they made an excellent attempt at conception with her laid across a heavy low marble table.

They put themselves back together pretty well afterward, but Gina's purse was in the dining area by Juliette, and she desperately needed her comb. Leaving the boys behind, she snuck into the hall with her bedhead and hadn't gotten more than three strides when she heard, "Ah, you've returned. What a nice surprise."

It was that frightening man. *What had Ippy said his name was? Carnal?*

"Uh, *Buon Natale,*" she stammered as she turned around to face him.

"Taking some time for prayer and reflection before midnight mass?" He looked to the door she'd just come through and then back to her. His mouth was smiling, but his eyes weren't.

"Do you know where la contessa is? I seem to have gotten separated from her."

"She's just through those doors." He pointed in the direction of the papal apartments.

"I'm sorry, I didn't catch your name."

"Hierotymis Karno. And you are Gina."

"You have an excellent memory." She looked up at him and offered a smile she hoped would be disarming.

"I do." His expression was opaque. His eyes were all over her, from her mouth to her hair, and roaming over her body. He made no effort to move, and then his eyes slid to the door she'd just exited.

"Would you accompany me?" she asked out of sheer panic. She hoped to lure him away from the boys. "I've never had a tour of this area. What's that statue over there on the end? Is it a pope?" She began walking toward it.

"There are no tours in this area," he said as he fell into step alongside her. He took her arm and leaned close as he pointed down the hall. "That statue is Papa Gregorio XVI."

The closer they came to the statue, the uglier it revealed itself to be. They stopped in front of a stone figure with a grotesque orb coming out of its robes that looked more like a deformed egg than a head.

"Goodness! He couldn't have been pleased when it was unveiled. It isn't flattering."

"My understanding is that it's a faithful likeness. Apparently, he didn't have a neck. I've seen texts that refer to Gregorio XVI trying out several hairstyles in an effort to obscure the shape of his head, the most successful being the halo that only left the top of his pointed tonsure visible. I believe this statue was better received by Gregorio than when that awful monstrosity of Papa John Paul II was unveiled at Rome's Termini Station."

"The one that looks like Mussolini?"

"The very one." She felt his hand slip around her waist.

They had just cleared the rotunda when Ippy appeared. "There you are! We're ready to take pictures."

She felt his hand slide reluctantly from her waist, across the small of her back, and his fingers trailed off her hip.

He said, "She'll need a comb first."

Gina prayed he'd keep walking in the direction she'd led him, or at least not turn around to see the boys come out of the closet.

———◦◉◦———

Raphielli had been reeling from the impact of Luigi Lampani's news when Benny emerged from the bathroom holding a pregnancy test stick in front of her. The strange look on her face was impossible to read. The girl was an enigma even after a month at Porto delle Donne. Kate, Raphielli, and Constanza pushed forward and they huddled around Benny staring at the test stick. One pink line would appear in the window for negative, and two pink lines for positive.

They watched as one appeared, and then Raphielli's vision started to blur as the second one materialized. She felt faint and realized she was holding her breath. She let it out and blinked. It was two lines. Positive. Then the three women all focused on Benny. The girl was swooning with her eyes closed, fingertips of her left hand pressing her eyelids. Then she opened them again and brought the stick practically up to her nose.

Kate and Constanza plucked the stick out of Benny's hand and launched into a debate about the efficacy of tests, while Benny reached out and took Raphielli's hand. There was a light in the girl's eyes and she was shivering minutely.

Raphielli drew her over to the little bed, sat her down, and put an arm around her.

Benny breathed, "I'm carrying the most important baby in the world."

Raphielli squeezed her and thought about how Salvio had believed he was God's son, sort of like Jesus' brother. What had he told his followers? She wondered exactly what Benny believed. "We'll take good care of you and your baby. Everything's going to work out."

"Now more than ever...we absolutely can't let my parents get a hold of me. Before, I was just...me...but now...they'd lock me up somewhere and give my baby away to...*them*."

"We'll protect you." She thought about the baby being a Scortini. *What part of the estate should I set aside as this baby's inheritance? What is appropriate? Who should I ask?*

Benny sat staring at the glossy black trainers on her feet which she'd had Kate order for her. "Luigi's gonna put my parents in jail for what they did."

"He might. He's very good."

"He'll keep them away from me, right?"

"He'll try."

"I wish *he* was my dad." She reached up and grasped her new pendant, a clear glass heart with flecks of red and gold suspended inside like sparks.

"You mean a lot to him, too."

There was a knock at the door and Paloma stuck her head inside. "Come on ladies! It's *Vigilia di Natale!* Time to eat and open presents. The promise that the kids don't have to wait for *Befana* has them freaking out."

Kate's aunt had created a homey feast from the sea. Conversation was lively until Ottavia and Nanda began arguing whether octopi were fish. Nanda insisted octopi were mollusks, which she asserted was a fish, while Ottavia swore octopi were cephalopods, not fish. Then everyone joined in offering knowledge, such as octopi are intelligent and can work puzzles and have no bones whereas squid have a "pen" backbone of cartilage and only use two arms to capture prey.

Leona ended the debate with, "I don't care if you say it's a fruit, I'd like another helping before the kids down at that end eat it all. Pass it back up this way."

After dinner the women, children, and staff gathered at the tree to open the gifts Raphielli had bought with each person in mind. By now they all knew she was the founder and benefactor of Porto delle Donne, but she avoided any awkwardness about the gifts when she hired a couple of actresses dressed as elves to deliver the presents and sing a jaunty little song entitled "No Peeking at Your Gifts." It was a racier performance than she'd expected, but the women and their children loved it. Kate had kept Benedetta out of sight on the chance the actresses might recognize her.

The children ripped open their presents and played with their games and stuffed animals. All the women *ooh*-ed and *ahh*-ed over their boxes of flannel pajamas, new slippers, and body lotions. By the time the guard buzzed to announce that Alphonso had arrived to walk Raphielli and

Paloma home, the ladies were relaxing in front of a fire nibbling cookies and sipping spiced hot tea.

"My family's excited to meet you," Alphonso said as they headed down the *fondimenta.*

"Me, too. It'll be good to meet the Vitali clan." She lost her footing on a patch of ice and grasped the metal bars on a nearby window to keep from falling. "*Woops!*"

Alphonso took hold of her as they moved on and she continued, "I know Cardinal Negrali's assuming I'll attend his mass..."

"You see him every day and you didn't tell him?"

"I chickened out. I don't want the hassle of getting his blessing, and frankly, lately whenever I'm at the Little Church, he shows me off like a trophy. It's embarrassing. I don't want to go through that tonight. And I really want to be with your family, so I didn't say anything."

"Well, you'll like Chiesa di San Zaccaria. All of our family is baptized, married, and mourned there."

Paloma said, "I went to a wedding there when I was a teenager. The paintings are incredible. Hey, there's a secret marble swimming pool under the church."

Raphielli's knees buckled for a scary second and she felt Alphonso falter beside her.

"Jeeze, you two should walk over here where the ash was spread. You're gonna end up in the canal if you stay on the slick side of the *calle.*"

Raphielli's mouth wouldn't form words, and her mind spun loose in its moorings as Alphonso said casually, "A marble swimming pool? I've never seen it, and I've been going there my whole life."

"I bet nobody knows about it. But a boy I was dating, he was bored and looking for a place to fool around and smoke a little weed, so we went way down under the church."

"Just like that?"

"He broke a few locks," she admitted, sounding contrite. "The padlocks were so old and rusted, he just kicked 'em a few times and they broke. But before we went back upstairs, we fixed everything to look like we hadn't been there."

Raphielli looked up at Alphonso, and his expression told her they'd be sneaking around under the church during midnight mass.

The three arrived back at the palazzo with enough time to take naps before dressing for church.

It was five minutes to midnight when Zelph, Paloma, Raphielli, and Alphonso came out of the cold into the warmth of Chiesa di San Zaccaria. Raphielli looked above the heads of the milling crowd and eyed the paintings around the narthex. Paloma was right, they were incredible. A crowd of Vitalis enveloped the big cousins, all talking at once. "Boys, over here! Where ya gonna sit? We all saved you seats!" It was pandemonium in different pews as everyone started pointing at once, people moved coats all over the place, and other families were asked to shift and make room.

Before they'd decided where to sit, the organ music swelled to a crescendo so loud it silenced everyone, then the lights blinked to signal the mass was about to begin. The four of them snuck away when the lights went low, and they hustled along following Paloma, who was speed-walking down a side aisle. Ready with a story that they were looking for the bathroom, they ducked into a side passage, through a back door, and then down a series of corridors. They didn't encounter anyone, and finally they were in a dark alcove standing in front of a gate covered with flakes of black paint and rust.

"He broke that lock. We just pulled the gate into place."

Zelph pulled, but it didn't budge. "It's wedged against the stone floor. Here, Al, help me lift it a bit."

The boys opened it, revealing eroded stone stairs.

As they descended, the air quality changed, becoming warmer and more humid. Raphielli felt tingles of anticipation and looked around for Alithinían symbols, but there were none. They stood at a metal door that had bars welded where the handle should be, and a chain with a padlock wound around it.

"Twist it, it's not locked," Paloma said with certainty.

She was right.

They removed the lock and chain, and when they crowded through they were standing on a landing above a medieval cistern with an arched ceiling. It was nothing like an Alithinían temple.

"Cool, *riiight?*" Paloma grinned and swept her arms like a tour guide. She noticed the looks of disappointment on their faces. "Fu-- I mean wow! You guys are hard to impress."

They put the doors back into place, snuck into pews, and finished the mass like good Catholics.

After the service, they went to Zelph's parent's home for

a big noisy crowded family meal. Raphielli had never experienced anything close to this at home when it had just been her parents and *nonna* before her father had died. Then at the abbey they ate in silence. Here, people talked a blue streak as they ate at every surface, and their tented back courtyard was set up with tables mounded high with a feast for an army. Raphielli felt Alphonso watching her, trying to discern if his family was getting on her nerves with all their laughter, cheek pinching, and hugging. But she loved every minute of it.

A cousin's *nonna* brought up the fact that Alphonso's parents had been gone since he was a baby, but then made animated sweeping motions with her hands before brushing them together to show that topic was done. While Raphielli was squished between two of the boys' vivacious-yet-maternal great-aunts, she formed the opinion that Al had ended up in a family she'd have loved to have been raised in.

On Christmas morning, Luigi and Gladys had a breakfast they used to enjoy when they were dating. They sipped mugs of steamed milk with chocolate syrup, and while he stood at the cast iron pan in their little kitchen frying panettone cake in brown butter, Gladys wrapped her arms around his waist and kissed the back of his neck.

"You're gonna get burned with this butter splatter. Eh? I'm frying here." He bent at the hips and pushed her back with his butt.

"She never answered your question," Gladys said without preamble. Benedetta had been on both of their minds.

"I know."

Gladys came around to stand next to him. "She threw you a big red herring."

"Apparently not a red herring. She's really pregnant."

"Ow!" Gladys jumped away as she wiped a splatter of butter off her cheek with the back of her hand. "She also showed us that a severe shock can cure one of your headaches."

"Mmm-hmm. Didn't cure it, just made me forget it momentarily. This development complicates the Scortini estate."

"Why's that?"

He turned to look at her as he dropped the bombshell. "She's carrying Salvio Scortini's baby."

She stood stunned, so he gave her something to do. "Get us some plates."

While eating the browned buttery cake, she asked, "She was raped? Do you think she'll demand Raphielli give her baby half the Scortini estate?"

"She was, and I don't think she'll have to ask. Raphielli's a good girl. She'll do what's right. She's got more money than she could ever spend."

"Benny'll need her parents' help with the baby. Why are you hiding her from them? They're all over the news looking for her."

"You can't tell a soul."

She looked hurt. "I've never spilled one word of what you've shared with me."

"Her parents sold her to Salvio, or something like that. They were trying to get her pregnant, maybe to get part of the estate. But there's some bizarre religious twist to the whole Salvio murder case that I can't get a handle on. I think Benny can help me, but she doesn't trust me...yet."

"That's why you were trying to get her to admit that she's not Catholic?"

"Not just that, I think she's *Anti*-Catholic."

"Who are you? Torquemada?"

"Torka-who?"

"The grand inquisitor in the Spanish Inquisition. There was more than one Inquisition."

He shook his head.

"Come on Luigi, you don't have to study religion. Even social studies teaches how the Catholics oppressed, tortured, or even killed anyone they felt was undermining the Catholic Church."

"Well, I know the Catholic Church has warred against the Muslims for the holy land throughout history, but I don't think Benny's a secret Muslim."

"Also, Protestants, Jews, scientists, even doctors. She doesn't look like she practices witchcraft, but the Catholics hunted them, too."

Luigi started on his second piece of cake and could feel the sugar doing him good. "I don't want to hand her over to her parents. They bartered her virginity—her body—*her womb*—away to a monster. They should be in jail. She needs a fresh start with parents who'll protect her."

"Okay," she said as if he'd asked her for a favor. "She can live with us."

He stared at his wife, a little woman with a trace of last night's mascara that her night cream failed to remove shadowing under her lashes, crow's feet beginning at the side of her eyes, and he wondered what he looked like to her. They knew each other so well.

"Only if she wants to," he said. "Do you want to be a mother?"

"An instant mother and grandmother." She gave it some thought and then just said, "I can see she's very special."

"She's quite a girl."

"What was Salvio Scortini like? I mean, Raphielli seems sweet. He couldn't have been as bad as they say in the news. Did he really kill all those people? Like Count Verona? How'd he get past the bodyguard?"

Oh boy, I've unleashed a badger. "It's an ongoing investigation."

"Salvio's dead. You can tell me some of it."

"You already know I think Salvio is guilty of several murders, including Count Gabrieli Verona. Salvio was vicious, cunning, and lightning fast. That's how he got past people's defenses."

"But what was he like?" she persisted.

"Here's something to chew on. Raphielli told me she'd never seen him naked."

"She was married to him for a couple of years! Not even in bed?"

"Nope. Couldn't tell me if he had any birthmarks, scars, or tattoos."

"What goes on in those spooky old palazzos?"

"And there's none spookier than the Scortini Palazzo," he said as he got up to refill his mug.

Luigi thought about the little old lady, Nejla, and wondered what her connection to Salvio was. No way she was a hit man or still fertile enough to be carrying one of his babies. The TSA verified that she'd gotten off flights at JFK and Portland. The agent had strolled behind her as she walked out of the Portland airport and was picked up by someone who'd approached her. She seemed relaxed, or maybe just tired as she climbed into a reddish Ford 4-wheel drive pickup with big tires. The license plate was obscured by snow and they'd driven off down Westbrook Street, disappearing into Portland holiday traffic.

"What do you want for Christmas, Luigi?" His wife had taken their plates and was heading to the sink to wash them.

"Other than Pocket Coffees? A new mattress."

"Ooh! Are you getting a bonus from Inspector Laszlo?"

"No, we'll dig into savings. We deserve a nice bed."

"I agree. But stores are closed and you need to rest up, maybe take a long nap. How about we sprawl on the couch and watch an old movie? I've got some gnocchi in the fridge and I can make a Gorgonzola cream sauce for dinner."

The thought of her one excellent dish of melting butter, heavy cream, and blue cheese made him get on board with her plan. "You got it. Maybe I'll take a hot bath later."

"*Bene, bene,* you go get on the couch and find a black and white movie. I'll bring you the blankets from the bedroom."

He went and lowered himself onto the couch and put his feet up. He hadn't done this during the day since he'd been young—waiting to hear if he'd been hired by the police department. What was it? Twenty-five years ago? He thought about his parents. His father had worked himself almost to an early grave and then retired to a quiet seaside life. He seemed to be pulling a Benjamin Button and getting more youthful every time they went down for a weekend. He'd started out just sitting and admiring the sea, then watching bocce in the square, then playing the game, and now he was whipping little wicker balls around on a jai alai court. Luigi couldn't imagine where his father was getting his energy as he laid his pulsing head on the sofa pillow, gratefully accepted blankets, and pulled them up to his chin.

Raphielli and Paloma eyed the array of cold breakfast offerings that had been set out for them, buffet style in the breakfast room. The two women were left on their own for Christmas breakfast while Alphonso and Zelph celebrated with their family, and Dante, Rosa and the part-time cook spent the morning with their loved ones.

The two were bundled up in warm robes and booty slippers while they perused the buffet. Paloma started stacking her plate with little bites. "I don't know if any of this should be eaten together, but I'm having a berry blintz, some lox and cucumber with some of that white stuff with the green stuff, and ooh, the cold shrimp with the cocktail sauce, and what is this? Sweet rice pudding? And pastries?"

Raphielli poured them coffee and added heaping spoons of whipped cream from a silver bowl that was resting in a block of ice, then she took her plate to the buffet. But staring at the outrageous mixture of flavors, she selected only a small bowl of pudding and a bran muffin.

They'd just sat down to the table with an air of girls having a tea party when Raphielli's phone played dramatic organ chords.

"Fu-- I mean woah!" Paloma startled. "That's some ring-er! I almost dropped my coffee!"

"Ugh. Cardinal Negrali," she said. "Let's ignore it."

"Do you dare? Can't he send people directly to Hell?"

The phone stopped ringing, and they'd just started on their breakfast when her phone emitted the dramatic organ chords again.

"Oh, for the love of Christ! I don't think he's used to getting voice mail," Paloma said.

Raphielli hit the answer button. *"Pronto, padre."*

"Raphielli! You missed mass last night! What happened?" He sounded both exasperated and offended.

"I went with some friends."

"We would have welcomed them. You're like my own daughter and...how do you think it made me look?"

"What?" It came out sounding angry, and she pulled the phone away from her ear to glare at it.

"I mean, everyone could tell I was worried sick. You didn't call...to tell me you would miss the service. You belong in your own house of worship for services like that."

She felt a stab of chagrin at her thoughtlessness. But the next second, she felt he was deliberately trying to make her feel small and she resented it. "I know you don't like me being on my own. I'm trying to make some solid friendships, surround myself with good people I can trust, and I had a lovely time at their church."

"Er, oh, as long as you're all right. So, I'll come over and hear your confession in about an hour..."

"That won't work for me. I've got other commitments today, being Christmas and all. I'll see you tomorrow morning at my office."

By the time she terminated the call, Paloma had almost

finished her plate. "So, onto a completely non-spiritual topic, did I hear right that Tosca thinks you can have some women move in here before the end of March?"

"You did. Apparently, the dorm rooms and the common rooms, even the kitchen in that wing just needed some reconfiguring. It's really making the new shelter entrance, upgrading the lighting, and Ivar's skylights that's taking the most time and labor. The second location of Porto delle Donne will be open before too much longer."

"Can I help with staffing?"

"Do you want to?"

"I need a job, and although I've never had a fancy job like this, I'm organized, and I'm thorough. Kate has a lot on her plate with evaluating the women who you'll accept as residents, so maybe she could use my help to find staff for this location. I promise never to swear on the job."

"I'm mostly the silent partner so I'll check with her, okay?"

"Deal," Paloma said. "Hey, Dante's in charge of the house staff here. Will he be helping Kate?"

"I hadn't thought of that. I don't want to make him feel ignored. Maybe the final shelter staff candidates can be interviewed by him...as a courtesy."

Raphielli eyed Paloma's damaged hair. "Speaking of fancy jobs, I got some advice from Tosca once...that I needed to look more professional. I took it. Now I'll pass it on. You'll need some good clothes."

"Tosca told you that?"

"I was mortified, but it wasn't just him, it was also Juliette and Kate. But who's counting? Anyway, when Kate gives her approval, how about I give you a signing bonus for the new job, and you can get some clothes to wear while interviewing applicants. And maybe the Lombardi Salon can fix your hair."

Paloma gave her a deadpan look. "What? My Johnny Rotten style won't work?"

"I'm sure it looked great when you did it, but it needs to be freshened up and perhaps re-styled."

"Couldn't agree more."

Raphielli went over to the buffet and thought about Gio, who was back in Palermo until tomorrow. She wished she was having one of their leisurely breakfasts in bed at the Aman.

Christmas day started off early with a bang for Gina and the boys, literally. Then they all flew back to Venice where Juliette hurried off to prepare breakfast and distribute gifts to the residents and staff of her homeless shelter, Rifugia della Dignità. Gina and the boys were on their own for the morning. They had a good feeling that they were pregnant and felt like celebrating, so the boys took her out for a decadent Christmas breakfast at Caffè Florian on Piazza San Marco. Vincenzo's bodyguard sat at a table with an unobstructed view of the restaurant and the piazza, and as always, unless anyone knew better, no one would guess he was with them.

She and the boys were seated under the arcade bundled in warm coats and boots. Anna Rita, the floor manager, had provided a faux fur lap blanket for Gina, and the waiters brought out gleaming tiered trays of food that were works of art. She felt as if she were part of the family she'd admired for so long—maybe it was their silly declaration of success. Sitting between the boys, anyone looking at them could tell they were close, but nothing about their manner suggested sexuality. The boys were very good at projecting wholesomeness. She gave them permission to surprise her with dessert and excused herself to go to the restroom. She was washing her hands when she heard a familiar voice speaking in German, and in walked Beatrix.

Pocketing her phone, she stared at Gina. "Look. Who. It. Iss. Gzzh-een-ah. You are delivering flowers to the toilet?" She had a darker spray tan than usual, and after checking her reflection in the mirror, she started petting the fur collar on her coat.

"No, Horace's is closed for the holiday. I'm here with friends."

"Pretty steep prices for Diego, unless perhaps he has snuck in some of his father's potato chips. That *is* what they serve at his Vhite Lion?"

"Diego is out of town. I'm here with the Veronas."

"Of course you are," she said slowly with wide innocent eyes as if she was speaking to a delusional mental patient.

Just then Gina's pocket vibrated, and she pulled out her phone. It was Juliette on FaceTime. "*Pronto,* Juliette."

"My darling, we are home now. Casimir and I are in the kitchen. Do you prefer spinach or chard in the strata?"

"I'm sure either would be good."

Beatrix leaned in and peered at the phone screen as the

pope waved a bunch of leafy greens in each hand. "No, we want *your* favorite. If you like kale, we have some of that," the holy father said.

"The chard in your right hand looks perfect," Gina said.

"We agree. Now, come home. We have gifts to open," the pope and Juliette said in unison.

"*Sì, grazie, ti amo,*" Gina replied and then disconnected the call.

"That was ze pope!" Beatrix gawped.

Without saying another word, Gina pocketed her phone, pushed the door open, and fled back to the table. The Caffè Florian orchestra had begun to play "White Christmas," and waiters served her an extravagant hot chocolate mounded with ice cream. On the table was a tiered silver tray bearing Sacher Florian cake sheathed in layers of dark chocolate alongside flights of macarons in every color. The boys were served something hot and alcoholic, and just as they raised their glasses in a toast, Beatrix appeared in front of their table, blocking their view of the orchestra.

"*Ciao!* Gzzh-een-ah said she vas here with friends. I am Beatrix Knudsdatter. I have several classes with Gzzh-een-ah."

In the past, Gina had mentioned how nasty Beatrix could be, and the boys leaned in closer to her.

"Vincenzo," he said while offering a curt nod.

"Leonardo," he said without bothering to smile.

Unperturbed, Beatrix continued, "I am about to catch a flight to Berlin, but we should get drinks together when I return."

Gina knew it would be rude for the boys to reject that

offer and felt her shoulders slump. But the boys just went back to their drinks and ignored Beatrix until she left. After she was out of sight, Leonardo turned to Gina. "Hey, that mean girl really upsets you. What is it?"

"She called me a..." she felt humiliated at the recollection.

"What? Could it be so bad?"

"...a Verona groupie....in front of a classroom full of people."

"Ah, she's very good at the attack," Vincenzo said. "She's taken away your legitimacy as a part of our household by labeling you a hanger-on."

"What an awful person," Leonardo muttered.

"And it couldn't be further from the truth." Vincenzo looked deep into her eyes. "Gina, you are family, you're helping make our family, and somehow we'll find a way to claim you."

———⚭———

On Christmas morning, Hiero hadn't heard anything from Negrali, which he took to mean the old cardinal had failed to get Raphielli under control and therefore was no closer to handing over the paintings. The top cardinal must have his scarlet undergarments in a twist because he was no closer to wresting the helmsmanship of Verdu Mer away from Contessa Juliette Verona, either. In fact, just this morning the pope had put out a press release on Verdu Mer's progress, and it was a real knock out. Apparently, Juliette and her Ukrainian buddy, Ivar Czerney, had just completed the underwater infrastructure for one whole section and were ready to begin demolition of the final streets so the last of the underwater renovation could begin. The model home that represented the housing being built throughout Verdu Mer was racking up more architectural and engineering accolades than any other home in Italian history. Negrali'd better get his coup in gear and replace Juliette, or her place at the top of Verdu Mer would be cemented and no amount of lobbying would pry her fingers off the project.

Hiero thought about Venice and the Veronas. The pope's movements were always kept secret. He traveled with a personal contingent of the Swiss Guard headed by Alberto, his personal head of security. But Ecclesia Dei was aware that this pope, like those before him, spent a lot of time in il Veneto living at the Verona's palazzo.

In anticipation of Negrali repeating his request to kill Juliette, Hiero decided to sneak into the papal archives to see what the pope's private documents would reveal. He left the Central Administration Office building and took some evasive measures until he gained access to the papal office. With the Holy Father away at a Christmas Day youth convention, Hiero took the keys out of the pope's desk and headed down a back staircase to the pontiff's private vault. Inside the vault, Hiero saw a painting labeled *Saint Callixtus traveling with the Verona from the Iberian Peninsula to Rome for his inauguration.*

He paused and thought about the mind-bending quality of that family. Had they been at the side of every pope from the very beginning? That would mean that while popes were elected from all over the world, there was always the same family at their side. The Verona bloodline would be...an anthropological anomaly. He didn't know if they were marrying their siblings or exactly how a family could survive a couple of thousand years, but suddenly he wanted to kill off that lineage whether he got his gifts from Negrali or not. Just on principle. Of course, he wouldn't tell Negrali that.

Carolette could have used a few more hours sleep when the gang got up on Christmas morning. Yvania miraculously presented them with a breakfast spread in the dining hall, so she either didn't need sleep or had prepared it in advance. They all tucked into the feast of breakfast casseroles, fluffy egg dishes, and a savory bread pudding made with that insane bread. Everyone had several cups of coffee to fortify their energy and soon, it was time to return across the border to France. Before they headed out to the sleighs, they handed over the gifts they'd brought for Markus and Giselle.

Selma grinned as she handed a beautifully wrapped box to Giselle. "I was fishing for ideas when I asked you what you wished you could give to Markus. Here, it's from you to him."

Giselle hugged her tight and then presented Markus with her late father's watch, which he'd worn almost every day of his adult life. It survived because on the day of his death he'd worn his dress watch.

Laetitia had tears in her eyes as she handed a box to Markus. He got on one knee before Giselle and presented it to her. She opened it to reveal an elegant ring, a sparkling oval peridot with one trillion-cut diamond on each side.

"Will you marry me, Giselle? Be my wife."

"*Oui!* It's beautiful!"

"It was my mother's."

Yvania said, "I sent Laetitia my key to our Paris home when she offered to get the ring for Markus."

Laetitia was wiping her eyes. "It was nothing. I was just going to see Pierre for a weekend, you know."

They all got teary-eyed as Giselle and Markus hugged and kissed.

Then Carolette handed a box each to Giselle and Markus. "And from me because I know you two can't get enough."

Giselle opened hers to find a full array of Nyakio skin care products, and Markus opened his to reveal a honey pot and wand. Giselle was grateful for her gift, and Markus rolled his eyes at his.

After breakfast, Carolette piled into a sleigh along with the others, and Giselle looked like she had a new lease on life...along with an engagement ring that sparkled when she waved as they rode off toward their cars on the other side of the forest. Forty minutes later Carolette felt wired from too much coffee as she drove behind Solange's car on their way home. They were making good time due to light Christmas Day traffic, when she saw Solange put on her turn signal and take the exit for Clémency.

"We've only been driving for fifteen minutes," Robert grumbled.

"Must be Selma's tiny bladder," Auguste sighed.

"My legs could use a stretch," Laetitia said, and it was no wonder since she was folded up in the back seat.

"*Oh putain! C'est Spratman! Là bas!*" Robert gasped.

Carolette spotted him getting out of his rental car. "Holy shit!"

"Don't look!" Laetitia cautioned.

Spratman was oblivious as he walked toward the center of town.

Carolette eased her car down the street and parked behind Solange's Citroën Cactus. The doors flew open, and Henri, Fauve, Selma, and Solange came speed-walking to her car.

Carolette rolled her window down and they huddled together as Spratman entered the Chouettes Jumelles Hotel in the distance.

"Who volunteers to keep an eye on him?"

"I will," Laetitia said as she jumped out of the car.

"I'll stay with her." Robert climbed out after her.

"Don't speak to him! We'll text each other updates."

With a nod, he was off and hurrying to catch up with his sister's long stride. She was already halfway to the hotel.

Carolette called Giselle and put her on speaker.

Giselle answered with a breezy, "You just left. Miss me already?"

Fauve crowed, "We found Spratman!"

"Where are you?" Giselle asked, sounding instantly excited.

"Clémency."

"Let's trap him! I mean unless you guys are too tired. You all didn't get much sleep."

"Are you kidding? This is war!" Carolette declared.

"Okay, let's do this! Henri and Fauve, get Stuart and his plane ready for Plan B. I'll call Stephen and tell him you're heading for Château de Clavy."

"Make sure he unlocks the secret passageway I'll be using," Carolette urged.

"I'll make sure to remind him. Selma, you call your mother and have her pull the Exagon out of the garage."

"Right! I'll have her pull out one of your dresses, too," Selma said while grabbing her own phone.

"Fauve and Solange, call Luc, Terrance, and Gendarme Evan and tell them to get right over to Château de Clavy. It'll be a great Christmas gift for them to question one of the hit men!"

Carolette saw group texts popping up on her friends' phones. "Gigi, the locals have spotted him." She looked at the group text on Auguste's phone, which he was pushing toward her.

SPRATMAN ORDERING BREAKFAST IN
CHOUETTES JUMELLES HOTEL CLÉMENCY

Solange said, "We're all covered on this end, Gigi, don't worry. Carolette will drive her car to your château. Henri and Fauve can take my car straight to the airstrip to set up Plan B. Robert can stay here to keep an eye on Spratman. I have a friend here in Clémency who can help us. He's got a big SUV and can take me, Laetitia, and Selma to Château de Clavy to help monitor the trap."

They all flew into action, and Carolette couldn't remember a better Christmas as she and Auguste roared off down the road. She was getting to borrow one of Giselle's dresses, drive Vincenzo's Exagon Furtive-eGT, lead Spratman on a merry chase, and after his arrest, Giselle, Markus, and Yvania could come out of hiding. They'd be back home by dinnertime.

It was almost no time before she reached the turnoff to Giselle's property in Gernelle.

"Damn, woman!" Auguste almost dropped his phone as he put up hands to brace himself when she banked off the country road and onto the château's long white gravel drive. "Selma just texted. Veronique has pulled the car out front and is waiting with your disguise."

"Right, we'll be heading back to Clémency within ten minutes."

"Spratman may move on. Can you get us back on the road in under five?"

"That depends on whether or not I can fit into Giselle's clothes. I've got a bit more...of everything than she does."

As they reached the château's grand courtyard, Veronique was standing next to Vincenzo's gleaming metallic gold electric car, which was parked at the ready with the doors open.

Carolette put her car in park and jumped out with Auguste right behind her lugging her purse.

Veronique gestured for him to toss the purse into the Exagon. "I put a package in there as Selma asked. Drop it somewhere before you exit Clavy just in case Spratman hasn't followed you inside. It'll look like you dropped something off. But then run like hell back to your car so he can't catch you. Luc and the boys, plus Selma and others will be outside to help keep you safe. Here, put on Giselle's red dress. It's elastic so you just pull it on. Cover your hair with this red scarf. You'll be easy to spot."

Carolette felt giddy at the prospect of wearing that dress. Giselle had worn it to the opening of her show at New York's Metropolitan Museum of Art.

"It's certainly an eye-popping color, especially with the scarf. There's no way Spratman could miss me unless he's color blind. Oh! Could he be?"

"Perish the thought Auguste!" Veronique moaned.

"I think that's green they can't see. But even if he is, he won't be able to miss your figure," Auguste said.

Carolette let Veronique and Auguste yank her boots off, while she stripped her clothes off right there on the flagstone driveway of the regal old estate.

"No bra?" Veronique queried in motherly consternation. "Lift your arms."

With Auguste's help, Carolette shimmied into the clingy dress and dragged it into place.

Veronique knelt at her feet. "*Dépêche toi!* Put your boots back on, your feet are too big for Giselle's shoes."

Carolette accepted their help getting her feet back into her boots and tried not to fall down as she did a quick new hairstyle that was more like Giselle's, then topped it with the scarf and tied it neatly under her chin.

Auguste's phone rang. "It's Robert," he said. He answered

with, "Is Spratman still in town?" while zipping her left boot with his other hand. He listened to Robert while Veronique zipped Carolette's other boot and then smacked her derrière as a dismissal.

He said, "Glad he's such a thorough hunter, it makes him slower. We're driving back now. Gotta go!" He ended the call and they hurried to the car.

Veronique yelled, "Just put it in gear and start slow! That's a racing car that hits ninety-six kilometers an hour in under five seconds!"

Carolette found that getting into V's car wasn't easy. It was so low to the ground, there was no way to do it like a lady, and she was grateful to be wearing underpants. Veronique already thought she was a slut without giving the poor woman a gynecological view. But once inside the car, it was pure luxury! She secured her belt, stroked her hands over the curving dashboard, and ran her fingers down the gauges, controls, and electronic screen before putting it into gear and taking a firm hold of the steering wheel.

"Ready?" she asked Auguste, who was on his phone calling Robert back.

He nodded. "Let's get that hit man!"

Carolette pressed down on the accelerator and the custom tires screamed, leaving rubber on the flagstones as the heavy machine roared forward. The instant they reached the gravel drive, the car fishtailed and shot twin geysers of white pebbles high into the air. For a scary second, she grappled with their velocity and direction before regaining control.

"Wee! I'm a Bond girl!"

It didn't take long for her to get the feel of the car. She knew this part of France like the back of her hand and racing along the quirky local arteries in a car this responsive was a thrill she would have gladly paid for.

"Ask him what Spratman's doing now."

Auguste did, and after listening he said, "Robert is strolling behind him. He's going into every open door in Clémency as if expecting Giselle to be hiding inside. He just went into a bookstore."

With no traffic on the A34, Carolette had them back to Clémency in under fifteen minutes and Auguste told Robert to be ready to yell, "There goes Giselle Verona in that gold car!" As they entered the small town, Auguste slumped so low he was practically on the floor so Spratman would think Giselle was alone.

Driving slowly down Grande Rue, she spotted Robert, who gave her a little nod before going into the bookstore. He immediately came back outside, held the bookstore's door open, and pointed dramatically after her, saying his line, "Hey! There goes Giselle in her fancy car!"

"Oh!" Carolette felt a thrill. "Auguste, there he is! Here comes Spratman!" They watched him shove past Robert and run to his Sprat-mobile.

As she rolled slowly to give him enough time to start his car, Carolette saw another man burst out of the bookstore. He was a big bear of a man wearing a blazing orange Izod shirt and a shocking blue wool blazer, and he was followed by an expensively maintained woman in an ivory cashmere coat with frosted hair from the Dynasty era. Carolette rolled the window down and could hear him hollering, "Giselle! It's me! Hank Taft!"

What the hell? Then she saw the hitman's silver Peugeot coming toward her.

"Ooh! Here we go!" Carolette goosed the accelerator, leaving Spratman in the dust.

"Okay Coco, now don't lose him on the way to Clavy."

"Don't you worry about me. Call Laetitia, tell her we're on our way. Let's see what that little rental car of his can do... Château de Clavy here we come!"

She roared onto the A34, where she and Spratman practically had the road to themselves. In traffic, it would take just over forty minutes to get from Clémency to Château de Clavy, but at this rate of speed, they'd be there in no time. She slowed down a touch so he wouldn't think she knew she was being followed—just out running errands in her fast car. But as she approached Clavy, she put some distance between them so he would be able to see her go into the château but couldn't grab her. Auguste started fidgeting nervously beside her.

"Are you worried for me?"

He blustered and tried to act calm. "Me? Not at all."

Carolette swung into the château's parking lot and pulled into a spot next to a tour bus. She saw Selma standing out front holding a map, and Laetitia was taking photos near a bunch of tourists. Auguste handed her the package. "Go!"

She scrambled from the car and tugged the clingy dress down over her bottom before trotting across the courtyard and up the steps of the château as if she were in a hurry, but not running a race. Inside she was surprised to find the place was mobbed, so she had to dodge tourists who thronged the merrily decorated entryway and halls. Even Christmas Day didn't stop the tourists. She couldn't wait for the place to clear, so she plunged forward.

Carolette bolted down the hall toward the secret passage—which all the local kids knew about but was strictly off limits—yanked the curtain aside and disappeared into the darkness. She knew plenty of people had seen her, but it couldn't be helped. When Spratman asked people where the woman in red had gone, they'd point to the curtains. The darkness smelled the same as it had when on a dare she'd let Gustave Moreau kiss her in these secluded confines back in the fifth grade.

She bounded to the top of the stairs and had a scary moment of doubt. *What if the door was locked?* She'd be killed by Spratman coming in behind her. As she tripped to a stop at the top of the stairs, she started pawing the door for a knob, but nothing! *Don't panic! Terrance, Luc, and Gendarme Evan may have him by now. Of course, the doorknob is here.* She swept her hand lower and grasped a handle with a little thumb lever. It clicked easily, and she burst through the door into an empty library. She tossed the package to the side, ran through the room, down the upstairs hallway, over to the main stairs, and then took them two at a time back to the front door. Thank goodness she hadn't insisted on cramming her feet into Giselle's heels.

Once outside she flew down the big stone steps and didn't care if she looked like she was running a race or not. She dodged more tour buses as they arrived, yanked open the car door, and did an impressive modern dance move to dive inside without skinning her knees.

"Whew!" she said as her butt landed in the seat and she put the car back into gear. "Who are you on the phone with?"

"Gigi," Auguste said and showed her the video call in progress. Carolette could see Giselle, Markus, Yvania, and Daniel all hunched around the phone.

"Inside the secret passage, it really hit me that these guys murdered Elli's staff." She shuddered and made a face of terror at Auguste's phone camera, then shook herself.

"We should have word any moment about Spratman's capture. Hang on, Coco," Giselle said. "Markus is waiting for Terrance or Gendarme Evan to call him with an update."

"Okay, I just need to get out of this spot. A bus is about to block me in, and if the boys miss Spratman, I don't want to be murdered here in Vincenzo's car." She eased to the edge of the lot as Auguste kept his phone pointed at the front of the château for Giselle to see.

They heard Markus' phone ring, and he put it on speaker so everyone could hear.

"We don't see him." It was Luc, and he sounded angry. "He must have blended in with the tour that's going through the main rooms. Terrance is going around the side. Where's Carolette?"

Giselle replied, "She's back in the car. It's okay, we'll move to Plan B at the airstrip."

"He's a slippery fucker," Luc said in exasperation.

"We know."

Just then, Carolette saw Spratman bounding down the steps two at a time. He'd spotted her car. She dropped the accelerator, and in the rear-view mirror, she saw him reach his car.

"Carolette, they missed him!" Markus and Giselle said in unison.

"I noticed," Carolette said. "He's back on my tail."

"Get to the airstrip."

"On my way. Woo, now he's driving like a maniac," she said as he took a shortcut going against oncoming cars and onto the county road via the entrance instead of taking the long way to the exit.

"Luc, do not to chase the Spratman!" Yvania yelped. "Will spoil the next part! The Plan B!"

"Luc, we've got it from here," Giselle said. "Thank Terrance and Gendarme Evan for me, *d'accord?*"

"*Oui, d'accord.* Sorry, Gigi," Luc said before he disconnected.

Carolette opened up the engine and zoomed down the almost vacant D34 with the silver Peugeot not far behind. He must have the gas pedal to the floor.

The chase continued toward Aiglemont's little airport, and as Carolette approached the airstrip, she took advantage of the car's power and put more distance between her and Spratman through the flat farmland. On the open phone line, they heard Markus call Fauve and put her on speaker.

"Fauve, Coco's coming fast. Are you in position?"

"*Oui*, Henri's ready to close and lock the hanger when she's inside. I'm standing next to Stuart's jet, and he's ready for takeoff. *Mon Dieu,* it's cold out here!"

As Carolette pulled onto the tarmac, she saw Henri and Fauve bundled up in ground crew jackets. Fauve stood near the plane, and Henri was at the wide-open hanger that Carolette aimed straight for. She braked hard inside the empty hanger and put the car in park. All was silent as Henri slammed and bolted the door.

"I don't like being locked in here. What if he kills Fauve and Henri? We're sitting ducks," Auguste groaned.

"Maybe this car is bulletproof?" she squeaked under the roar of the Cessna's takeoff outside.

They held hands and stared at Auguste's phone, watching and listening to not only Giselle's group, but listening to her conversation with Fauve.

"Spratman is here!" Fauve exclaimed. "Heading straight for me. Yikes! I hope his brakes are good."

There was a pause, and then they all heard a man's voice near Fauve shout, "Hey, I was supposed to meet Giselle Verona here. Where is she?"

"Just missed her, she was on that plane." Fauve's voice sounded cool, and efficient.

"What? I...uh...have something for her!"

"You'll have to send it to Iceland. She said she'd be there for a while."

"Iceland?" the man sounded upset.

"*Ouais*, said she's going to Kópavogur to install one of her sculptures at the home of some collectors. Do you remember the name she said?" Fauve must be talking to Henri now.

"Name of Guðmunds," came Henri's voice.

"Do you have an address?" Spratman sounded hopeful.

"No."

"Okay, thanks." He sounded far off now.

Then Fauve was back on the line. "And there he goes. Think he'll stalk you to Iceland, Gigi?"

"Let's all hope so," Giselle sighed. "With any luck, he's heading for the airport in Reims or Paris."

"I will call my nephews," Yvania said. "If he knocks on their door, he will not be leaving unless we say so. So, we wait to hear news from Iceland."

The day after Christmas, Mateo's patience was stretched to the limit. He'd called the faithful to the basement chamber of the safe house in an effort to galvanize them to the immediate goal of getting some of them hired on at Raphielli's soon-to-be-opened shelter, and thus gain access to the Scortini Palazzo. But it had been almost impossible to keep the group on topic. The Amendolas vacillated between unhelpful outbursts and bouts of disapproving silence during which they sat glaring at him.

"We still need to discuss a plan to get our daughter and her...*Salvio's* unborn child! Where's the chloroform you ordered?"

"On a shelf in the water garage."

"We didn't see it when we came in."

"It's there, inside a big box labeled 'cleaning solvent' where it'll be safe until we need it. Now back to everyone's resumes..."

"There's not enough being done to get Benedetta back! We're doing everything we can to…"

"What? Stay on television?" snapped Dr. Gugliemoni, who was losing patience with the Amendolas. He glared at the couple. "We've noticed."

Signora Amendola whirled on the physician and snarled, "You can zip it! *You* have no idea! It wasn't *your* daughter who was kidnapped by Catholics!"

Lydia waded into the fray. "Can you and your husband shut up and let us get on with the business at hand? It's bad enough that the police are now suspicious of you and your inconsistent statements."

Mateo held a hand up. "Okay now, we need to stick to the agenda. This entire meeting is about getting your daughter back." Then he looked around the room. "Whose resume have we missed?"

"You don't need mine, I'll continue as always." The doctor waved his hand.

"And I can't try for a position," Lydia said.

Greta waved a paper in the air. "Mine."

"What'd you come up with?" Mateo asked her.

"I think it looks very professional. I'm using my childhood friend Miriam's work history. She was a nanny for an orphanage in Switzerland."

"Do you know anything about babies?"

"I've looked after my baby sister, so I think I can pass an interview."

"Does your friend Miriam know you're borrowing her work history?"

"No. I know the dates she worked there, and I'm familiar

with some of the staff because I visited her a couple of times. I look a bit like her."

"What contact information did you use? It needs to be untraceable."

"The number is for my new burner phone, and I listed the mailing address of an empty duplex next door to my house. It'll be easy for me to check the mail every day."

Another parishioner asked, "Can you ace an interview about child care?"

"It's the best I could do for a fake identity. I'm an insurance actuator, and the new shelter doesn't need one of those."

"You did good Greta...I mean, Miriam," Mateo said. "Submit it and surf medical sites for things like what to do if a baby has a fever."

"I'll get right on it," she said.

Mateo stood up as people moved to leave. "Good work, everyone."

"But..." came the outcry from the Amendolas.

"Just stop talking, you two!" Mateo raised his voice to be heard over the couple. "You're already seeking a court order to get into Porto delle Donne, and we're all keeping our eyes open. Now, let's just focus on getting someone hired at the new shelter."

"Where are you getting this information on her building progress?" Lydia asked.

"Me," another parishioner spoke up. "The city transferred me. I'm now a file clerk with city planning. Genero Tosca is project manager for the Scortini Palazzo renovation, and he thinks the place can start taking in women in March."

As always, for secrecy, the exodus from the safe house was slow. The faithful left in ones and twos from front and back doors as well as the water garage so neighbors wouldn't see an entire group leaving the quiet house. When the last person had departed, Mateo locked up the lower chamber and climbed the stairs to call Benjamin. He took his phone out and watched it do a quick update as he moved above ground within range of a signal. Four voice mails appeared in his inbox, and before he tapped the icon, Benjamin called.

"I almost had Giselle!" The connection was bad, but he sounded excited. "She was driving some futuristic car. You should have seen it. It's really cool and incredibly fast."

"How'd you know it was her?"

"I was canvassing a small town, and people who knew her pointed her out as she drove past. Some flashy guy and his wife were even calling after her by name."

"Where is Giselle now?"

"She hopped on a jet to Iceland."

"This connection is bad, it sounded like you said *Iceland.*"

"I did. You were right. They don't call the Veronas jet setters for nothing."

"How do you know she's not bound for Venice?"

"Airport employees told me."

"A stroke of luck!"

"I struck gold! They told me the town and the names of the art collectors who just bought one of her sculptures. She's on her way there to install it."

"Follow her!"

"I'm at the Reims airport returning the car. I'll get on the next flight to Paris, then connect to an Icelandair flight to Reykjavik."

"Stay on her."

"Will do."

"Do you need money?"

"No. I used our debit card for the tickets and hit the ATM. I've got plenty of cash, although when you get the bill for this car you'll need to sit down."

"No worries on money. Did she have the Russian skinhead with her?"

"I didn't see him."

"Better and better! You'll have one less person to kill in Iceland."

⸺⸺⸺◉⸺⸺⸺

Luigi arrived at headquarters feeling refreshed after a relaxing day at home with Gladys. Maybe there really was something to slowing down and letting the woman he loved pamper him occasionally. The criminal department was crowded. On his way past Bruno's desk, he was greeted with a friendly, "Eh, Luigi, take a cookie. Home-made."

"*Grazie.* I thought the place would be empty for a few days. What're you doing at work?" Luigi asked as he took a cookie.

"Same as everybody else. I needed a break from the family. They're all in town, and it'll be quiet here. The city should be quiet until New Year's Eve."

Luigi unlocked his desk drawer, took out his secret files on the Scortini murders and Benedetta's case, and began adding new information in code about Nejla landing in Maine and Benny's pregnancy. He'd returned the files to his desk and was in the process of writing a list of things to follow up on when he heard Inspector Laszlo bellow, "Lampani!"

He found the big man sitting in his hotbox of an office and, without asking, dragged one of the old wooden chairs over to the window that was open a crack, but not nearly enough to make the choking heat bearable.

"Mind if I open this a bit more?"

"Please do. The heat's been on all morning."

"You should ask maintenance to check your thermostat settings."

Laszlo's black eyes were intimidating, but the corners of his mouth twitched in an effort to avoid smiling. "Always subtext with you. You're saying...what? Someone's purposely over-heating my office?"

"I've suspected it for some time now. Someone's trying to cook you."

"Murder by roasting me where I sit, eh? Who knows, maybe it's the same person who's trying to send you to rehab by cutting off your Pocket Coffee habit." The smile came and Luigi could see the big man was in a good mood.

"Anyway, here," Laszlo said as he pushed a brightly colored gift bag across the desk. "A little something I thought you'd like."

Luigi was touched. They'd never exchanged gifts. From the bag, he pulled out a packet of caramel coffee candies.

"Go ahead, get addicted to these. And they're sugar-free so you can keep your welterweight classification."

"I don't box anymore."

"I thought you still sparred down at the gym."

"Grazie, this is very thoughtful."

"But now that I look at you, you could stand to put on some weight. You're looking a little skinny these days."

"The damned headaches kill my appetite."

"Still having them?"

"With depressing regularity." He unwrapped a candy, popped it into his mouth and bit down. Instead of offering sweet espresso, it instantly clung to his teeth and filled his mouth with the medicinal tang of saccharin. He wanted to spit it out, but it was welded to his molars. He offered one to Laszlo, who waved it off and turned to his computer screen.

"Speaking of depressing, the French police are going to announce today that they have enough evidence to charge Bernardo Vitti with conspiracy to murder Giselle Verona and her 'art teacher.' That'd be Markus Shevchenko."

"Conspiracy? That's a pretty weak case, and even if it sticks, he'll just get a slap on the wrist. They've already had him in custody for over a month. Any lawyer could get him off with time served."

"Apparently they got some evidence on a cell phone."

Luigi didn't say a word but raised his brows.

"They recovered the phone from the hit man who was found dead in the barn, Miguel Turrion. And my contact says the girlfriend knew his phone password. The jealous type, she checked his messages whenever she could get away with it. They promised to tell her if he'd sent any recent messages to another girl, so she supplied his password. They found a plan for murder laid out in great detail between Bernardo, Miguel, and the dead hit man who shot himself... Felix Montand."

"Enough detail to nail Bernardo—who was at a café in the next town—with conspiracy?"

"The French officials feel confident. Giselle's from an old and well-respected family, and they don't want to be accused of looking the other way when hit men try to bump off the country's aristocracy."

"Uh-huh," Luigi said.

"I know you'd like to extradite Bernardo, but they're prosecuting him now, and the other two are dead. They score points in the court of public opinion just by charging him."

Luigi got up. "Thanks for keeping me informed."

"I figured you'd go ballistic when you found out about the information on that phone."

"I'm light years beyond that."

"I'm not going to ask how."

Luigi gave him a little wave with his bag of saccharine rubber cement and headed back to his desk to do some research on Nejla. He sat down, unlocked his drawer, and found his Benedetta file missing. Only the Salvio file was still there. He slid the drawer closed again with a casual sleight of hand and locked it. Everyone was going about their usual business, and unless someone was standing next to his desk, they wouldn't have seen him open and close the drawer. He felt the flower of a headache bloom behind the bridge of his nose.

He thought fast. The person who took that file was either off reading it or making a copy while he was in with Laszlo. *Good luck deciphering my code for numbers, names, verbs, and nouns* he thought. He was betting that they wouldn't risk keeping it, but he'd come back sooner than they'd anticipated. He snatched up the candy bag, went straight to the hall, down the steps, and to the main reception desk where he emptied the caramels into their candy dish and made small talk with the desk sergeants about their holiday. He fished in his pocket for his tin of aspirin tablets and chewed a couple.

After five minutes, he went to the restroom. Then, wanting to give the mole more time to get the files back into his desk without anyone seeing, he walked down to the vending machine, bought a cup of coffee, and joined a conversation about the frigid, soggy weather and global warming while the machine spurted premeasured non-dairy creamer, hot water, and instant coffee syrup into a fragile Styrofoam cup. He noticed a tasteful sticker someone had stuck on the front of the vending machine that showed the earth buried in cups and read "Enjoy drinks from something you don't throw away". Then he noticed the ceramic cups on a hotel tray next to the trash can and wondered if this was the work of some of the pope's youth brigade? He felt guilty when he reached for his Styrofoam cup.

When he finally returned to his desk, he set his coffee down and unlocked the drawer. Benny's file had reappeared. He'd just settled back into his chair to ponder who within his ranks was an anti-Catholic Scortini-loving

Amendola conspirator when his cell phone rang. He glanced down at the display. It was the court clerk.

"*Pronto,*" he answered.

"Bad news. The Amendola's attorney showed up in court and she had a child welfare advocate with her. I don't know how, but that lawyer has got some sort of clout. She got the judge to approve the court order. She and the advocate just left here on their way to police headquarters. I heard them say they plan to be inside Porto delle Donne this afternoon."

"I appreciate the warning," Luigi said, pushing his chair back. He heard, "Sorry I couldn't do more" as he clicked off the call, reached under his desk, pulled out a battered nylon file bag, and shoved his Scortini and Benedetta files inside. Then he relocked his drawer and left headquarters.

The instant he was outside on Piazza San Marco, he called Kate on her personal number and stood bracing himself against a frosty gust that promised rain.

"*Pronto*, Luigi." She sounded perturbed.

"I'm on my way over to get Benny. Her parent's lawyer..."

"I know," she said. "I just got a call from their child welfare advocate. They're on their way with the police to serve a warrant and search the shelter from top to bottom."

"Goddamned slow day! There's nothing doing in this city today, so the cops are available. *Goddamn!*"

"Don't worry about it. I'd anticipated something like this and have been creating a duplicate of my daily records listing Paloma still in residence. We can take care of ourselves."

Luigi thought of what these women had done in self-defense when Salvio's hit men had started killing their staff and said, "I don't doubt it. I can't be seen there, it's not my case, but maybe you can dial me when you answer the door and let me hear what's happening."

"I'll do that. But if they get suspicious, I'll hang up."

"Deal." He needed to get into a quiet place where he'd be left in peace, so he high-tailed it across Piazza San Marco to Caffé Florian and waved to Anna Rita, who nodded permission as he ducked into one of the elegant velvet salons that was roped off. At least here he could wait and listen in while savoring some of the best coffee in Venice.

———— ◉ ————

It had been a busy morning for Raphielli. Before breakfast, she met with Tosca in the wing of her home that was under construction. Then a quick meal with Paloma, Alphonso, and Zelph before Alphonso walked her and Paloma to the shelter. Then she slipped over to the Aman. Gio had been in Palermo for Christmas but had flown right back to Venice to continue hunting whoever was hunting her. Or at least that's what he said. She wondered if perhaps the danger was past and he was just keeping it alive so he could be near her.

He surprised her with a velvet gift box, and Fauve's strident voice came back to her unbidden. *He'll lure you in...and discard you!*

When she saw the diamond ring inside, it looked like the most beautiful lure in the world, so she closed the box and handed it back. "I can't accept this."

"Of course you can, and I want you to have it. I enjoy giving, and I'd like to spoil you a little. It's your Christmas present."

"How about you give me a back rub and tell me a story," she said as she stripped her clothes off. "That's what I really want."

Gio complied, and she spent a leisurely two hours listening to his stories and being worshipped by him before eating a decadent naked lunch in bed. Then, because there's no rest for the wicked, it wasn't long before she was sitting in a boat with Primo while their driver, Drea, piloted her back to work, without the diamond. It was then that she got a call from Elene Buonocore, the mayor's wife.

"*Pronto*, Elene!"

"Ah, my dear! I trust you had a lovely Christmas."

"Oh, *sì*."

"*Bene, bene*. I'm sending out invitations to our New Year's Eve party. I know you'll be inundated with invitations, but you must at least stop by."

"I'd love to," she said, and meant it.

"Excellent. Now, the real reason I'm calling. Carnevale season is approaching, and I haven't heard a word about the costume ball you'll be throwing."

"The what?"

"You're expected to throw a ball—a proper masquerade—and you'll need a *carri di carnevale*. I'll loan you our boat decorators, or I'm sure Contessa Verona will loan you hers."

"But..."

"No buts," Elene said with finality. "We've talked about

this. I know Salvio never would have allowed it, but now you're the grand lady of Casa Scortini and there's no more waiting. Make it happen on February thirteenth. I've spoken with the other hostesses, and we're all holding that date. I'll send you a list of who to invite. Only fun people that you'll like."

That made her feel better, but she wasn't sold. "I..."

"My other line is ringing. Call me with any questions. Come to dinner before New Year's if you can. Feel free to bring Cardinal Negrali again if you'd like."

And then she was gone. Raphielli called Fauve and told her about Elene's demand.

"*Mais bien sur*, Elli!" Fauve sounded thrilled. "Do it! Invite me and the whole gang!"

"Okay, I'll have Dante prepare some rooms for you guys to come stay."

"Maybe Gigi and Markus will be out of hiding by then."

"But I don't know how to throw a big fancy costume masquerade ball." She hated the sound of her own whining.

"You don't have to. You know the right people and that's all you need."

"I do?"

"You're friends with a famous designer, an incredible interior decorator, and according to Giselle, your party planner is the toast of Europe. Plus, you're rich. Throw a real barn burner!"

"A what?"

"Never mind, you're not from the country. Hang up with me and call all three of them."

"Okay, but I'm drawing the line at a *carri di carnevale*. My in-laws were killed riding in one this past summer, and I'd feel ghoulish creating a Carnevale party boat."

When she hung up, she placed the calls, and all three women had accepted the jobs by the time Drea pulled to a stop in an out-of-the-way inlet only a few *calles* from Porto delle Donne. As Primo held out a hand to help her up, he said, "Raphielli, you need to work on your self-confidence."

"Sometimes it escapes me."

"During those times, fake it," he said, and his eyes looked like his father's. She half expected a wink, but Primo was too serious with her for that kind of roguishness. "I don't want to hear you whine again. And you'd better never let my father hear that."

She nodded and hurried to get away from the boat without being seen. When she arrived at the bridge in front of the shelter, Azure gave her a frantic wave from his guard post and hit the buzzer. Within moments, Kate's head and shoulders appeared through the opened door, and the look on her face made Raphielli run to her.

"What?" she demanded.

"Get in here. I've just heard, the Amendolas and their lawyer have a court order. The police'll be here any second."

"No!"

Raphielli ran inside following Kate. She pulled off her coat and threw it at the coat tree in the foyer as they ran to Benedetta's room behind the kitchen. Inside, Paloma was grabbing up anything of Benny's and putting it all in a bag, while Nanda was wiping down every surface with a rag.

Raphielli asked, "What's going on here?"

Nanda was a blur as she said, "They might dust for fingerprints."

Paloma said, "We're turning the room back into the nurse's quarters and removing anything with her handwriting." She spotted Benny's stuffed cat and, because the bag was full, she shoved it down inside her sweatshirt.

Margarita and Benny came out of the bathroom with Benny dressed like an old woman, wearing baggy woolen tights concealing her youthful legs and scuffed old shoes on her feet. Raphielli realized she was wearing the cook's clothes. Paloma shoved the bulging bag into Benny's arms. "Take this and come on!"

When they'd reached the kitchen, Leona was by the back door urging, "*Come on!*"

They heard Azure's voice from the intercom in the office, "Kate, I have the police here with a search warrant."

The women froze for a beat, and then Azure's voice was louder. "Hey! You can't go around back! They'll buzz you in through the main door!"

Leona wrapped the cook's shawl up over Benny's head, wrenched open the door, and shoved her outside into the rain that had started to fall. Benny raced straight across the alley where an aproned Juliette swept Benny into her shelter's kitchen door and shut it. Raphielli was almost knocked to the floor as Paloma, Leona, and Margarita raced out of the kitchen, then stampeded in different directions for the dayroom and up the main staircase. Raphielli saw Kate press a button on her phone, put it in her front pocket, and head toward the front door as Nanda zipped around her and disappeared into the dayroom.

Raphielli looked out the back door again and saw two uniformed police splashing around the corner through the icy rain. They were being yelled at by Benny's mother looked just like she did on television, except with wet, bedraggled hair.

"Let me by you! You're walking too slow! We need the element of surprise!"

"This is a police event now, and we have procedures," one cop said with irritation.

"Are you taking a tone with me?" She grabbed him by the coat. "Are you kidding me? You haven't even gotten me inside, and you're acting like you're out of patience with me? *I've LOST my DAUGHTER!*" she yelled full into the officer's face.

The cops exchanged looks and then noticed Raphielli. "*Ciao*, Signora Scortini, we're here to serve a..."

Raphielli swept her arm in a welcoming gesture. "Come in out of the storm."

They looked at her with gratitude, and as they passed her one said to the other, "Too bad we can't leave the shrew outside."

"Can I offer you a hot cup of coffee?" she asked.

"Coffee'd be great, *grazie*."

The cook, who was now wearing one of the resident's sweat suits—which was a bit snug across her backside—was already pouring them cups of Mia's addictive brew.

"I don't want coffee! How can you drink coffee at a time like this? I'm reporting you two!" Signora Amendola bellowed. Then she did a double take at Raphielli and the strangest look came over her face. The woman seemed to be judging her as if she'd failed at something. *Oh, right, she knows I'm infertile, which is why she offered her daughter to have Salvio's baby. Screw you, you loudmouth. You're just like the Dour Doublet.*

The officers gratefully took the cups and sipped. "Enough outta you. If your daughter's here, she's not going to flush herself down a toilet. You stay outta the way until the paperwork has been presented, and then *we'll* be doing the search, not *you*."

Raphielli said, "I hope you understand that, first and foremost, this is a safe haven for women who have suffered unspeakable violence." She led the way to the front entry where Kate was reading the legal document. She stood flanked by police and two women in dripping wet suits.

"Everything seems to be in order," Kate was saying. "Be as thorough as you need to be, but these women have varying degrees of residual anxiety, so I'll ask you to go about your business as quickly and quietly as possible."

One of the women stepped around the officers. "While the police search, I'd like to see your records. Access to those documents was included in the warrant."

"And you are?" Kate asked.

"The Amendola's attorney."

"I want to see those files!" a man bellowed, and the boom of his voice made everyone jump.

"Signor Amendola, that can't happen," the lawyer said. "And please keep your voice down."

"Don't tell us we can't see the files!" Benny's mother charged forward. "What do you think we're here for? To stand around and drink coffee?" She jabbed her thumb at the cops she'd followed around back. "*They're* telling us we can't be part of the search, and *you're* telling us we can't see the records? What..." she stammered, and her husband joined his voice to hers.

"We didn't come all this way to stand around!" He approached the other woman in a suit and said, "You're our advocate! *Do something!*"

"Not so loud," the advocate said.

"Don't seem to have inside voices, do they?" one cop said quietly to his buddy, and they both took another sip of their coffee.

"Let me be clear," the advocate was saying, "I've been appointed as Benedetta's advocate by the judge, and your presence during a search is highly irregular. Now, if you would keep your voices down, this is a shelter for abused women, and we need to respect their space. You and your husband should stay here at the front door...to, um...stand guard."

That seemed to give them a purpose, and they moved closer to the door as if Benedetta might materialize from behind a curtain and make a break for it.

Raphielli watched as the attorney and advocate accompanied Kate to the office, and an officer opened the door to the dayroom. The women waved shy greetings, and when Nanda noticed she was still clutching the dust cloth, she blew her nose into it and tossed it into a trashcan next to the sofa.

One of the cops with the coffee said, "Signora Scortini, it would be best if you could show us around."

"*Certamente.*" She walked them from floor to floor and room to room. The final room was the dormitory where Paloma used to sleep. Her bed was stripped bare because it hadn't been used since she left. That didn't look good. They'd abided by the legal limit of residents but had Benny stay behind the kitchen so Luigi could visit her without disturbing the "no men" policy.

The officers entered the dorm and gave polite nods to Shanti and Jasmine, who were stretched out on their beds reading.

The cop's eyes were everywhere and with a few "I'm gonna take a quick look in here's" and "I hope you don't minds," they looked in drawers and cubbies where the women's personal items were stored. They came to the stripped bed.

"How many vacancies do you have?"

Paloma appeared at the door and threw herself onto the bed. "None, this one's mine. I had a little bed-wetting episode last night, had to strip the sheets. I didn't used to be incontinent, but I took quite a beating to my bladder region from my old man. That's why I'm here. My old man tried to kill me."

The police looked uncomfortable, and Paloma prattled on. "Peeing never used to be a problem, but a couple of well-placed kicks with a steel-toed work boot will change ya for life. Luckily, they make good adult diapers nowadays. Almost look like regular underpants."

The cop's eyes went to the stuffed animal that had popped out of her shirt when she rolled over to pull on the waistband of her underpants. She snatched it up and started stroking it. "My cat helps my mood. I keep her in my shirt. Hey, lemme ask you, do you consider calamari to be a fish?"

They shrugged and turned to Raphielli. "We'll let these women have their privacy now. You can take us back downstairs."

As she left, Raphielli cast a glance over her shoulder at Paloma, who looked quite proud of herself.

When they'd descended to the second-floor landing, they could hear the Amendolas grousing, and the cop next to her said quietly, "This search is stupid. You only have to meet Benedetta's parents to know she got as far away from those two assholes as possible. I bet she's saved up some cash and moved to New Zealand."

As they reached the entryway, Mia and Dr. Risinger were just coming out of the therapy room with Grace. Raphielli answered their questioning looks by saying, "We've been cooperating with the authorities in their search for that missing girl."

"*Grazie,* Signora Scortini, for being so nice...and cooperative," the lead officer said.

"And for the excellent coffee. What kind is it?"

Mia smiled and answered, "Passero's from Philadelphia, America. Also, I add a wisp of cinnamon and a little grate of nutmeg."

The other group was coming from the back hall saying, "You keep excellent records, Kate."

"What?" Signora Amendola screeched. "Are you going to believe anything written down by this woman? She's kept us out of here because she's keeping our daughter here against her will! Kate's obviously lying and has faked any records she showed you!"

Signor Amendola got down on one knee and rapped the floor with his knuckles. "We should tear up the floors and see what's under there! They could have Benedetta stashed in a crawlspace."

The officer next to Raphielli whispered, "This is Venice. We don't have crawlspaces."

One of the police officers held up a hand. "I'm in charge here and I've had enough of you two. I don't want to hear another word, and if Kate wants to press slander charges, I'll be the first witness against you. We're not tearing up one thing in this building. You already made a mess throwing things around in their nurse's dispensary when you weren't supposed to leave the front door."

"We were searching!"

"Be quiet," the red-faced officer said and turned to the two that'd been upstairs with Raphielli. "Anything upstairs that would indicate the girl..."

"Benedetta!"

"*Stop talking!* That's it! You two and your lawyer, *out!*"

"But it's raining!" Benny's mother wailed.

"Too bad." He opened the door, and the officer next to him ushered them, their attorney, and the advocate outside. He turned his attention back to his officers. "Anything?"

"We looked in every shower stall and closet. She's not here."

The lead officer turned to Kate, Mia, Dr. Risinger, and Raphielli. "I apologize for my outburst. As a Venetian, I'd like to thank you for the important service you provide. We'll get out of your shelter now."

When the door was closed, Kate took the phone out of her pocket and put it to her ear. "Did you hear any of that?"

Kate answered Raphielli's quizzical look by mouthing, "Lampani," then said into the phone, "Uh-huh, Raphielli's going to go get her from Juliette's shelter right now. She promised to stash Benny in the pantry where no one would see her...no questions asked. No, she never asked the name, said she'd prefer not knowing."

Raphielli had a queasy feeling as she ran to the back door to make sure the coast was clear and reclaim Benny. Life was getting so complicated.

———◦◉◦———

Gina sat comfortably warm in one of the Verona's boats and looked out the window while Juliette talked a mile a minute into her phone, rattling off a dizzying litany of things for Ippy to accomplish while Gina and the contessa were at the vitamin spa. Gina watched the frozen wind-blown city glide past. Venice looked like the north pole. She wouldn't have been surprised to see a polar bear surface between the ice and slush on the waterways.

Her ears pricked up when Juliette said, "Call Massimo Buonocore and ask him to declare a *notte bianca* for next Friday. The city has fallen into a funk and we locals need to shake things up... Mm-hmm, you are right, that will be his argument. But tell him that with social media, we can get the word out the moment he gives his consent, and business owners will jump at the opportunity. *Okay, grazie, ciao.*" The sheer power that the contessa wielded was awe-inspiring.

"I love *notte biancas*," Gina said. "There's always so much art, and music, and food."

"We will keep shops and restaurants and venues open for twenty-four hours and make a party. Venetians have been in the grip of ice and rain for months now—not good for our mental states. We must have some relief from the daily routine."

"Do you think the Cinema Multisala Rossini would do a *notte bianca* festival of Glenn Close movies? Like Jagged Edge, Fatal Attraction, and Dangerous Liaisons?"

"I will have Ippy suggest it to them."

"You're the coolest, Juliette."

"You think me cool?" She looked flattered. "I like to help people."

"And the city loves you for it," Gina said.

"They loved Gabrieli for it, too."

"You miss him terribly."

"*Sì*, but when feelings of loss come, I instead feel grateful that he was my husband for over twenty years...and then I feel happy."

"You're still young. Do you think you'll ever remarry?"

She did a double take and then waved her hand in an elegant way that was glamorous and a bit sexy.

"These vitamin treatments are doing wonders for you," Gina said.

"They are very good. But now that I am a widow, I am

making more time for my *travail d'épée*—a superior workout."

"You're in great shape. All I do is walk around the islands, plus climbing the stairs of my building and at school. I should find some exercise that I like."

When the boat docked, they stepped out of the sumptuously heated interior into an arctic blast. Here on the lee side of the island, the sound of ice clattering and crunching brought to Gina's mind a giant dinosaur toppling fences and devouring herds of large beasts. The edge of the windraked pier was newly decorated with lacy scallops of frozen waves. Juliette seemed unaffected by the gale and walked with her spine erect, and her graceful gait was sure in her elegant waterproof boots.

At the vitamin spa, they were welcomed by the owner, and Gina followed her technician down the hall to the now-familiar treatment room while listening to the woman's admonitions. "I can tell by looking at you that you're eating more than just the raw foods I recommended. Remember, no pasta, no cheese, nothing that is not in season. For instance, you wouldn't eat basil, it's a summer herb. Small portions no larger than the palm of your hand..."

"Uh-huh, right, mm-hmm, um, is there any way we can skip the colonic nutritional saturation today?" Although Gina felt none of these restrictions would increase her fertility, it would be disrespectful to argue and her non-compliance would get back to Juliette, who would be hurt.

Three hours later when Juliette's driver dropped her off at Arsinale near her apartment, she headed to Al Leon

Café instead of going straight home to prepare for another attempt at pregnancy. Prepping for Leo and Vincenzo wouldn't take long, and she'd already showered at the spa, so she'd just have to go upstairs and dab on a bit of scent. Pushing the café door open, she squeezed past the people lined up at the pastry and sandwich case next to the door. Diego waved at her as she moved toward an empty table. "*Ciao! Che pasto vorresti?*"

"A big plate of *spaghetti al pesto* and potato chips as a starter." *Limited diet be damned.*

While waiting for her meal, she munched on the best potato chips in Venice and thought about who might make a good mate for Juliette, which segued into a daydream of who might be a good mate for her. Gina couldn't settle on an ideal.

When the glorious swirl of fragrant pasta arrived, she leaned over the plate and inhaled the heavenly scent of basil and Parmesan cheese before twirling an indecent amount onto her fork and putting it into her mouth. She self-consciously covered her overstuffed mouth with her napkin, but no one in the lively restaurant noticed her. Everyone was talking with their hands and convivially socializing within the steamed-up confines of the little café.

She'd have enough time to finish this and order a pastry before meeting the boys. Although they were still dutifully having sex every day during her fertility window, they all felt sure she was pregnant. Gina stroked her lower abdomen and thought, *You want some more, don't you?* And she took another big bite.

10

In the weeks since Christmas, Giselle found herself going a bit stir crazy and becoming increasingly resentful that, although Spratman was out of the picture, everyone around her still felt that it would be reckless to consider it safe to resume life in Gernelle. After the chase that Carolette had led him on, Spratman had fallen for Plan B and everyone involved had waited on pins and needles. She'd felt out of sorts and even twitchy with nerves until two days later when Yvania got a call from her nephews, Jökull and Bjårki Guðmund.

Apparently, Spratman had headed straight for Iceland but the connecting flight through Frankfurt was delayed by a snowstorm. He finally arrived in Reykjavík, rented a car, and drove straight to Kópavogur. Jökull and Bjårki knew this because his travel logistics were the sum total of what Spratman divulged. He'd showed up on their doorstep looking bleary-eyed and slightly feverish. In a display of relaxed hospitality, they opened their door to him and he naïvely entered, blissfully unaware that he wouldn't make it back out without Yvania Czerney's permission.

While questioning their captive, they'd done everything short of permanently maiming him, but he'd refused to tell them anything beyond how he'd come to Iceland. Their guess was that he'd undergone considerable training on secrecy, the sort of conditioning that high-level spies had access to.

On top of that, two days after becoming their prisoner Spratman came down with a cold that worsened every day until it became evident he was suffering from severe bronchitis. Even in delirium, he'd given them absolutely nothing. So, during the first weeks of January they put his dislocated fingers, shoulder, and elbow back into place and acted like nursemaids to Spratman in their basement storeroom. Yvania had gotten regular updates, but nothing of use—namely who else was in on Salvio's plot and how they could call off the order to kill Giselle.

Giselle pulled the collar of her coat up to shield her neck from the strong winter wind that howled through the forest as she walked down to the livestock area in search of Markus. She found him and Daniel inside the heated goat barn. They gave her questioning looks.

"I didn't want to be alone. I've come to see if you can cheer me up," she said while scuffing the toe of a boot in the sawdust and straw.

Daniel led the smallest kid over to her and smiled when it stood on its hind legs, placing both front hooves on her thighs. "Go ahead," he said. "We've just laid down fresh straw. You know you want to. Get down there and let them roll around with you. It's the only thing that seems to chase your blues away anymore."

Giselle sank down onto her knees and pulled the youngster toward her, giggling when it began nuzzling her ear and trying to climb her. She gave up and laid down, which caused a scramble of kids climbing on her and trying to nuzzle under her shirt in search of milk. The billy from the corner corral made a desultory "Muu-aah" sound then fell silent. He wouldn't start making that odd human screaming sound unless she upset the kids.

Markus stood over Giselle, looking content. "I know it is difficult for you with no dangerous art project, but..."

"Right!" She scooped up the smallest kid to save it from being stepped on by its buddies. "I need more work as a distraction."

"I spoke to Yvania about your blue moods, and she believes that embarking on one of your sculptures may not help you."

"Oh? Is that what she said? Based on what?"

"Yvania says that you are at the mercy of your hormones right now. Prepartum or antenatal depression is quite common."

"Really? Isn't it supposed to be the most contented, blissful time in a woman's life?" she scoffed.

Daniel came down onto his knees next to her and started curry-combing muck off the hindquarters of a black-spotted kid. "I don't know what you're supposed to be feeling during pregnancy, but you're stuck here away from your friends, excluded from Gabrieli's funeral, and shut off temporarily from the Veronas. You haven't been able to proceed with an annulment or get married, and your body must feel strange as it grows new life inside and changes shape on the outside. It's no wonder you're feeling...off."

"Well, when you put it that way, I'm quite a good sport, aren't I?"

Markus lay down next to her and moved a kid out of the way so he could give her a kiss. "You are a good sport and we are not going anywhere until the police have gotten to the bottom of this case."

"Well, maybe I'll start at least dreaming up my next sculpture and sketch some plans for it."

"Great idea," Daniel said. "No one can get hurt from a drawing. I'll get you some nice charcoals and paper next time I'm in town."

"Now that I think of it, I keep seeing something in the same way my other ideas come to me. It's two figures one behind the other locked together being sucked into a dark tunnel," she said as she wrestled free of a kid who'd been standing on her hair. She didn't miss the worried look the men exchanged.

Mateo sat at the kitchen table looking at his phone. He hadn't heard anything from Benjamin since he'd promised to call from Reykjavik. That had been three weeks ago. Things had been so clear last fall when Salvio had struck a blow for the Alithiníans, going for the pope's heart, the Verona family. Mateo, Benjamin, Rajim, Carlos, and the rest of the faithful had gone onto high alert waiting for a signal from Salvio, but he'd preferred to topple the Vatican alone.

Finally, they'd jumped into action and given Salvio shelter. Meeting him for the first time had been electrifying, and the feeling of being so close to the divine son of Sinope had been almost intoxicating. It was their time, they would cure the ills of the world, and nothing could stop them. Or so they'd thought.

Since then, Rome had picked them off one by one, and Mateo had been forced to banish Nejla to Castine for safekeeping. Without their orator, Venice felt eerie now. The faithful still worshipped in the little secret temple under the safe house, but it felt like a version of the Ten Little Indians. *One little Indian went off to Iceland and got himself iced,* he thought.

He got up to make himself some espresso. *I don't need anyone to complete our plan, I can do this.*

———— ◈ ————

Raphielli sat at the breakfast table with Paloma and Alphonso. She felt emotional, so she just nibbled instead of eating with her usual gusto.

Zelph arrived and asked, "Can I join the breakfast club?"

"Of course, you know you're always invited," Raphielli answered. "Paloma, pull that cord next to you."

When Rosa appeared, Raphielli said, "Bring a setting for Zelph and fresh coffee." She turned back to Zelph. "What's the latest on construction?"

"Things are moving along. Ghost and Mister Fox have me up at ungodly hours. I'll eat with you all this week if that's okay." Zelph's eyes lit up as a plate was put before him, and he dug into the cherry crepes and creamed pineapple polenta.

Dante arrived with Genero Tosca on his heels. "Signora, Signor Tosca begs your indulgence."

She stopped pushing the food around on her plate. "What is it?"

Tosca looked upset. "Raphielli, I apologize for barging in. But...we should speak privately."

"There's nothing these people can't hear."

He shrugged before plunging ahead. "The Catholic Church has just frozen every permit I applied for on your behalf. They're threatening to sue my builders for altering an historic structure."

"The Church? Why?" she asked.

Tosca looked uncomfortable and buttoned his lips together.

Alphonso cocked his head. "Do you know why?"

Tosca made a little movement with his fingers, rubbing them together.

"Money?" Paloma guessed.

"I'll pay for my permits," Raphielli said. "That's not why you're so upset, is it?"

Paloma said, "Ooh, let me guess again since I got the last one right. Do they disapprove of her shelter plans? Like they want Raphielli to make a home for nuns instead?"

He shook his head.

Zelph's face became expressionless. "They're asking your office for an unheard-of sum of money," he said flatly.

Tosca's eyes flew open in surprise.

"I'm guessing it's like a hundred thousand euros," Zelph continued.

Tosca scratched his nose pointing his index finger up.

"Five hundred thousand?"

Again, Tosca's nose itched.

"A million?" Zelph's eyes were narrowing.

Again, Tosca's nose itched.

"*This is total bullshit!*" Zelph thundered. "They don't own this property! That's the sole owner." He pointed at Raphielli. "And she can do anything she likes with her home! She could open a museum to house Giselle's sculptures that launch blow darts at visitors if she wants."

Raphielli held up her hand. "I'm not worried. My father confessor has all the power he needs to put a stop to this…"

"Extortion," Alphonso said, putting his napkin down. She could see the muscles in his jaw tensing.

"Cardinal Negrali must be here by now," she said.

Tosca startled, dropped his hat, picked it up, and then ducked behind the door, hiding.

Zelph reached for his coffee. "Well, well, well. Now we see more gangsters circling." He looked at Alphonso. "Remember what the don said to Salvio inside the temple? That he was up against the big baddies. He was looking at Americo Negrali when he said that."

Raphielli got up from the table and went to Tosca. "Dante would never let him in here. He'll put him in the room where we pray together. Now, you don't have a thing to worry about. You didn't say anything to us other than notifying me that my permits are on hold. You can leave with Zelph and Paloma, and I'll talk to you soon."

Paloma and Zelph dropped their napkins and headed out the door after Tosca, who was hightailing it out of sight. Raphielli made her way to the receiving room for her prayer session, and the cardinal rose looking happy to see her. "My dear child. How are you on this stormy day?"

"*Padre,* I'm glad to see you."

Now he was beaming at her.

"There is something you can help me with, I believe," she said.

He leaned forward. "If I can."

"My palazzo renovation permits have hit some beaurocratic snag. Can the church help?"

"Of course. I mean, with the recent scandals involving crimes against vulnerable women and children, the church *should* partner, even manage this endeavor for you. Oversight can be cumbersome, but I would personally manage things for you."

"I won't need that. Overseeing my current shelter's creation gave me a real sense of purpose, and I want to do it again here."

"But this is much bigger," he said with a dark expression. "I'll get this larger project rolling for you. I'll get the permits granted, and you can open a line of credit so I can draw the necessary funds."

"I can meet with Vincenzo today to see what that would entail."

"Oh, surely there's no need to involve him. His expertise is investments, not this sort of thing. Just call one of your banks and grant me authority. Speaking of Vincenzo, I haven't seen much of him...since that night in the temple. What did you make of Salvio referring to him as a 'faggot'?"

She played dumb. "I didn't hear anything like that."

"You know, if Vincenzo has strayed outside his marriage *with a man*, it is a grave sin, one that the Vatican has historically punished by death. We are rolling back those so-called church reforms, so I must know. He would be...condemned."

She felt nauseous. *I can't even pretend to pray with this traitor! Not just after my money, but trying to persecute Vincenzo? I feel so used...so stupid...I feel sick...*

He motioned to the floor in front of her. "Shall we pray?"

"*Padre*, I suddenly feel unwell. I need to lie down, perhaps go back to bed."

"Of course. You are only a girl after all, and these large matters are too much for you. Take to your bed. That'll do you good."

After Dante had escorted the cardinal out, she looked down the hall and called softly, "Alphonso?"

He came out of the shadows. "I heard the whole thing."

"I need to find Vincenzo. But I don't want Cardinal Negrali to see me leave."

"Let's try to find Ghost or Mister Fox...one of them is the video technician."

"Fox is audio." A feminine voice with a heavy Greek accent came from around the corner. "I'm video." A woman wearing a black cap with silver ringlet curls escaping from it stepped out of the shadows.

"Are you Ghost?"

"My real name's Athena, but since I aim for invisibility on the job, everyone calls me Ghost."

"And Fox is a 'Mister' so, American?"

"Yep, through and through. He's from Chicago."

"You already know who we are," Alphonso said.

She nodded and searched Alphonso's face. "If I just looked at you on a security screen, I'd swear you were Zelph. But you're Alphonso, his private-eye cousin. *Si*, I've seen you and Raphielli around the palazzo." A smile drew up one corner of her mouth.

Raphielli said, "Can any of your cameras tell us where Cardinal Negrali just went when he left here?"

Ghost produced a cell phone, swiped her finger and tapped the screen a few times, then held it up for them to see. "He's that red blur moving past the bench on the other side of the canal out front."

"What about Zelph, Paloma, and Tosca?"

Two taps on her phone and she held it up. "They're gone. Here's a replay of them leaving the cloakroom and exiting the front door while you were in with the cardinal."

"Impressive," Raphielli said. She took hold of Alphonso's arm and was about to walk away when she remembered her manners. "Pleased to meet you Gho...er...Athena."

"Ghost is fine."

"You don't have any surveillance hookups in my bed-room suite, do you?"

"No, just a camera in the entryway by the fountain."

"Who monitors those cameras?"

"After hearing that Salvio got inside a while back, I've put my most trusted team on your monitors in shifts. But most of the system won't be up until after the New Year, and a bit later in the new construction zone."

"You've been a big help," Raphielli said and turned to Alphonso. "I've got to talk to Vincenzo right away." They left in search of him.

At the Verona's palazzo they sat down with Juliette and Vincenzo, and Raphielli told them about Negrali, ending with, "What do I do?"

Juliette had been watching her intently and got up, came to Raphielli's side, and brushed a curly lock of hair from Raphielli's eyes. "My dear, no one is going to take advantage of you. You have us. Veronas and Scortinis do not get pushed around, especially when they stick together."

Vincenzo leaned forward. "You're a good friend for keeping my secret. If Tosca's correct and Negrali is trying to use the Catholic Church to extort you, I'm sure Pope Leopold will release your permits."

"Now you must trust us with *your* secret." Juliette put a finger under Raphielli's chin and searched her eyes. "When were you going to tell me that you are expecting?"

Raphielli stared at Juliette thinking she'd misheard, but the expression that met her back was serious. "Expecting what?"

"Your child."

Raphielli didn't know if she should be incensed. "What do you mean?" She threw a panicked look at Alphonso, whose eyes widened.

"You are pregnant. You have the hormonal eyes," Juliette declared.

"No. I'm infertile. I can't and I..." Her mind whirled with possibilities of Gio and Alphonso.

"You are. And Romeo here is the father?"

Alphonso moved closer and took her hand. "I am."

"Ah, Romeo." Juliette looked genuinely pleased and turned back to Raphielli. "He will make you an excellent husband."

"You aren't going to judge me? Us?" Raphielli felt hot embarrassment.

"Maybe a few weeks ago. But now? No."

Vincenzo spoke up. "Mama, when you take Gina to see Doctor Gugliemoni today, can you take Raphielli?"

Raphielli bristled hearing Gina's name, then pushed away the jealous fantasy she'd entertained of Gina as Alphonso's lover. "Gina may be pregnant?"

Juliette smiled. "That is our hope, but too early to show in her eyes yet. I am taking her for a test today. I will bring you, too. My doctor is the best in all of Venice. He fought to save my babies and succeeded in saving Vincenzo."

Raphielli turned to Vincenzo. "Does Leonardo know?"

"He's part of the endeavor and waiting on pins and needles for the test."

Alphonso asked her, "Would you like me to go with you?"

"No, *grazie*. I'll go with them, but I don't need an entourage. Juliette can't be right about me."

A short time later, Raphielli sat in the doctor's office feeling dumpy next to Juliette in all her royal glory and the impossibly chic, upright, and composed Gina as the doctor read the results of their urine tests. "You're both pregnant."

She felt an unfamiliar blend of emotions: pride that her uterus wasn't a dud, fear that it could be Gio's child, strangely in tune with her queasiness, and a shimmery little thrill of motherhood. But the doctor's next words brought her back to reality with a clunk.

"What a blessing that your late husband, Salvio, lives on."

He said it with such genuine warmth that she couldn't tell him the truth. *My baby isn't a Scortini. It'll either have incredible Sicilian eyes or be a giant. I'm a loose woman!*

"I see both of you have left the name of the fathers off your paperwork," he said as he regarded Gina, who nodded with a curt swish of her glossy bob. The doctor looked to Juliette, whose expression of maternal pride was so obvious that his brows slid up to where his hairline would have been if it hadn't receded. "Oh. I see. Juliette, will you be helping her then?"

"Consider Gina a Verona. I will sign paperwork to that effect."

"Very well. There is the matter of a last name for the father."

Juliette patted Gina's hand and said, "Verona."

"I see." He now turned to include Raphieli. "If you will both follow the nurse to the lab for your blood draw and your first shot of prenatal vitamins before we get on with the physical exams and ultrasounds."

Gina straightened up, and Raphielli was surprised her erect posture could get even straighter. "No shots for me, *grazie.*" She looked at Juliette. "My diet is sufficient, and I've been taking those vitamin treatments."

The doctor moved to the door, ushering them to the nurse waiting in the hall. "No one's diet is sufficient nowadays."

"No. No shot." She looked pleadingly at Juliette.

"Just the blood draw for now, *per favore,* Doctor G," Juliette said.

The nurse led Rapheilli to the lab, and the doctor followed along with Gina saying, "The fetus requires large quantities of specific nutrients like folic acid and iron, and I'm certain you're not getting near enough."

"You can draw blood, but that's all today." Gina's voice was firm. This wisp of a flower girl was no pushover.

Raphielli didn't see what all the fuss was about. She sat in a little chair, propped her arm on a desk, rolled up her sleeve, let the nurse tie a rubber band around her forearm, squeezed the foam ball as directed, and looked away as a fat needle attached to a port was inserted into her vein.

Gina gave her a sympathetic look. "I can watch other people give blood, but I can't watch anything that's done to me."

Raphielli tried to think about something other than the sensations caused by the fat needle in her arm as the nurse swapped out full vials and attached empty ones to the port to fill with blood. After four vials, another nurse asked if she wanted her vitamin shot in her arm or hip. "I guess the arm's easiest."

"There's not much fat there, so it'll hurt more, and you may have some weakness in that arm for a day or so."

"Ooh, then let's do my hip. I've got plenty of fat there."

After the port was removed, Raphielli got up to join the other nurse just past the counter at the side of the small space, and Gina took her place in the chair, looking away while the nurse prepped her arm. Raphielli felt Gina watching her as she unzipped the side of her pants and tugged until one haunch was exposed. Raphielli watched as vial after vial of blood was taken from Gina, and then felt a bit woozy, so she looked away to stare at the sign about hand washing. The doctor came in and moved to the cupboards in the back of the small room with a comment. "Good place to have your shot Raphielli, smart girl."

Raphielli hadn't meant to turn around, but when she did, she saw the doctor pop a little vial into Gina's empty port and plunge something into her vein. He popped it out and whisked it away as Gina turned her head accusingly.

"Eh! What was *that?*" she cried.

He gave her an innocent look. "Did I bump you? I can take this out. You look like you're fading." He offered her a distracted but sympathetic smile as he removed her port. "Hold this cotton ball right there."

"What did you just do?" she demanded.

"That was the last one," the nurse said over her shoulder as she labeled a vial of Gina's blood. "Oh, *grazie,* Doctor. Let me just get a Band-Aid and..."

"No, not *you.*" Gina waved her off. "Doctor G, what did *you* just do? Show me what you just did."

He opened his hands and looked surprised. "Nothing. I may have bumped your arm. I'm sorry."

"It's very tight quarters in here with five of us," the other nurse said as she withdrew the long needle from Raphielli's hip and applied a cotton ball. "Here, press on this till I get you a Band-Aid."

Raphielli was about to tell Gina that she was right, but her mind literally yelled, *Shut Up!* She felt her heart begin to gallop, and the voice yelled, *Act calm!*

The doctor was saying, "I just came in to get a box of cervical brushes, we're out in room four." He plucked one from the open shelf then left the room.

"Sorry, Doctor," Gina's nurse called. "I thought I'd stocked the rooms."

"Hey, come back here, Doctor!" Gina raised her voice. "I turned around and saw you taking something out of my thingy!"

The doctor didn't come back, and Raphielli's nurse said soothingly, "After a blood draw, you're both bound to be woozy. I'll get you some juice and you can lie down. We'll keep you under observation till we get your blood sugar back up and can proceed with the exams."

Gina's nurse said, "Your first trimester may be a dizzy one as your progesterone surges. They call it 'pregnancy dementia' or 'baby brain.'"

"I'm not dizzy and I don't have..."

The nurses exchanged understanding looks as Raphielli struggled to get her tight pants zipped up and Gina's nurse finished helpfully, "Baby brain."

Raphielli was staring at Gina, willing her to be silent. When Gina caught sight of her, she blinked, gave her a questioning look, and stopped making a fuss. Raphielli jerked her head to the door, scooped up their purses from the hooks on the wall, and held her hand out. Gina got up and came over to her.

The oblivious nurse asked, "What juice do you like? Apple? Or we have orange-cranberry?"

Raphielli grabbed Gina's hand and said in as casual a voice as she could muster, "Can we sit with Juliette? We're just really excited. Can Juliette have juice too? I think we'll all take apple. Three apples, *per favore.*"

When her nurse turned to dispose of her supplies in the receptacles on the wall, Raphielli practically jerked Gina off her feet as she hauled her out of the room and speed-walked her past a room where the contessa was talking to someone they couldn't see. *The doctor? Don't say anything! Run!*

They burst out of the doctor's suite and Raphielli looked at the elevator's indicator. The carriage was down on the first floor. "We're not waiting here." She pulled Gina toward a *la scala* sign. "We've got to get out of here," she hissed through her teeth.

"We need to get Juliette."

"No, we need to grab a water taxi."

"But it's freezing outside and raining," Gina objected.

"Our adrenaline should keep us warm, or maybe he shot you with antifreeze."

"*You saw?*"

"*Sì.*"

"That bastard! I'm calling a lawyer!"

"I've got a handful of people I trust, and right now I'm calling one of them."

"The police?"

"Er, no."

If they hadn't been dizzy before, running top speed in circles down flights of stairs did it. They staggered out onto a slim *calle* and moved with unsteady strides to the nearest taxi pier, clutching at the posts to keep from falling into the choppy water.

Raphielli flagged the driver of the first *taxi acqueo* in line. The boat was small and, sadly, didn't have an interior cabin, but right behind the driver was a hard canopy with a zippered canvas enclosure around the vinyl passenger seat. She clambered aboard and helped Gina in while directing the driver over her shoulder, "Scortini Palazzo, *per favore*." He nodded and lazily turned the wheel. "The photos will not be good today."

She stuffed Gina under the canopy behind the canvas drape and then tapped him on the shoulder. "We don't want a sightseeing cruise, we've got an emergency. Get through this traffic and I'll give you a terrific tip."

"Terrific?" He looked at them like they were schoolgirls pulling a prank.

"I'm Raphielli Scortini and I'll make it worth your while," she said.

He shrilled his horn and yelled at other drivers to move as he pulled away from the pier.

Raphielli nudged Gina. "Call Juliette, tell her to get to my place, top speed. Then get Vincenzo over to my place, now!"

Gina reached into her sleek little bag and then with the phone pressed to her ear she called to the driver, "Do you have a blanket?"

He pointed to a small lap blanket folded on a shelf in the enclosure. Gina snatched it up, draped it over the shoulders of her thin blouse, and hugged it close. "Anything else?"

He shook his head and throttled forward to shoot between boats, and the girls had to grab for railings to keep from being pitched onto the soaking floor. Raphielli wiped the rain off her phone and stabbed a speed-dial icon.

Gina yelled into her phone, "Juliette! Get over to Scortini palazzo right away! Don't tell anyone but your driver. We'll meet you there. I'm calling Vincenzo."

"*Ciao Bella,*" said the smooth voice in Raphielli's ear.

"Gio, I'm in trouble!"

"Where are you?"

"I'm in a taxi heading home, and I need to know what you know about my father confessor."

He groaned loudly enough to be heard over the boat engine. "Cardinal Negrali and his outfit make la Cosa Nostra look like school children pushing each other around for marbles."

"You know this for a fact?"

"You're a Catholic, how can you not know how powerful they are?"

"Well, faith...damn it."

"You drank the Kool-Aid."

"For all I know, they just gave me a hypodermic full of Kool-Aid in my hip."

"What? Who? What have they done to you? All that shit about bloodlines, why would they mess with you? You're only related to Salvio by marriage."

She gripped her phone and hung onto the railing as they took a bone-jarring couple of bounces across the wakes of another boat. The spray felt like ice on her soaked skin. "Hang on a sec, Gio." She pulled her phone away and yelled to the driver, "I'll give you two hundred euros for your coat!" He hauled it off and tossed it into her waiting hands. When she pulled it on, it felt like an electric blanket. She put the phone back to her ear and heard Gio cheer, "That's my girl!"

"Gio, I'm pregnant."

"You? You're...*you* are. I'm a father again?"

She ignored his question and blurted, "Can you come to my home right away?"

"*Sì*, I'm over on the Lido." She heard him say, "Primo, call Drea. We're leaving *subito adesso*." Into the phone, he said, "I'll be right there."

"*Grazie!*" She clicked off the call and tried to zip the coat, but instead had to grab the back of the passenger seat with both hands as the driver throttled back and then reversed, trying to turn into a narrow canal. Both girls were thrown to the wet floor where water sloshed over them as they tried to help each other up. The driver cursed as they drifted toward a flotilla of rain-slickered gondolas and a commercial vessel stacked with cargo. Their drift halted in a crescendo of prayers by their rain-soaked driver, and both girls were back on their feet. Gina had taken a hard fall and her knees were bleeding, but she didn't seem to notice. She'd lost her blanket, which swirled in the water on the floor at her feet.

Raphielli now felt certain she hadn't been suffering PTSD. She *was* being hunted, and so were the Veronas.

She thought about the bloodlines and the fact that both of these old Italian families had been choked down to one son—highly unusual. She put a foot up to brace herself as the boat roared forward again and juggled her phone to call Alphonso. When he picked up, she said, "Grab five hundred euros out of the safe and come to the front door to pay my driver!"

The driver's head swiveled in her direction, and he was grinning from ear to ear.

"What's going on?" Alphonso asked.

"We have a situation," she answered.

11

Mateo had been waiting for Doctor G to call. Juliette Verona's mysterious appointment could mean one of two things. One was almost too good to hope for: that she was bringing Giselle in for a prenatal exam. Or two—and there was nothing Mateo wanted to hear less—that Gabrieli had gotten Juliette pregnant before he died. Of course, the good doctor was ready to exterminate either child over a period of time so it would appear to be a natural miscarriage. He'd employed the technique successfully over the years with Juliette, who suspected nothing. It had been some sort of fluke that Vincenzo had survived. Doctor G had been planning to smother him immediately after birth but had never gotten alone time with the baby. The nurses and every nun in Catholicdom had swarmed Vincenzo in the delivery room as if he were the second coming of Christ.

The phone shrilled, and Mateo juggled it as he grabbed it. "*Pronto.*"

"Okay, the playing field has changed. La contessa kept her appointment, but she wasn't sneaking Giselle in as I'd hoped." Doctor G sounded uncharacteristically excited.

"Then what?"

"She brought Raphielli Scortini. Raphielli's pregnant! Salvio wasn't as estranged from her as we believed, or he took her one last time before he was killed! We have another Child of Sinope! Two Madonnas!"

"Wonderful news!" Mateo recalled that Salvio had gone to the Scortini Palazzo on that final night but hadn't killed her. Had he decided to try again for a child? Mateo cursed the fact that he knew next to nothing about that little convent girl. "We have two children to carry on the holy lineage. If, God forbid, we should fail to get a hold of Benadetta, we'd still be back in business. I could snatch Raphielli and hold her until the baby is born then send it off to be raised where no one would look...Nautilus Island."

"Over in Maine with Nejla? Excellent idea. I'll set up regular appointments and get control of her," the doctor was saying.

Mateo felt wary. "I had no idea Raphielli was so close to the Veronas."

"We have another issue."

"Oh?"

"Juliette had another girl with her—also pregnant."

"Uh-huh."

"Juliette says it's a Verona."

Mateo saw red as he realized what Doctor G was saying. "God damned it! Vincenzo got another girl pregnant?"

"Apparently. Juliette was very clear this girl is carrying a Verona baby."

"He doesn't get his wife pregnant for years, and now he gets her and *another* woman pregnant?"

"Or Gabrieli could have had a mistress, but Juliette didn't act like that was the case. I didn't get the chance to gauge how far along either pregnancy is, but I'm trying to get the girls back in the morning. I'll examine them and determine how far along they are. Either way, I'll get Raphielli to trust me, and I can take care of the Verona children. It's the first pregnancy for Giselle and this Gina girl, very common to lose the first baby. I already gave Gina the first micro-dose of the 'release' drug, and a few more scant doses will cause the embryo to detach. But I'm more focused on the good news. Suddenly we have two children of Sinope on the way." He sounded giddy.

Mateo knew this wasn't insurmountable. It was just a shock. He hoped the doctor could just terminate the Verona pregnancies. He didn't want to have to kill anyone, just rid the world of the Catholic parasite. He'd feel a whole lot better if he could discuss these developments with Benjamin.

"*Grazie,* Doc. Keep me informed."

Mateo called Benjamin's phone but there was still no answer. The one good development was that the Veronas had hired Noah, one of their most devout Alithiníans, as a boat driver. Currently, Noah was only willing to spy on them and report their movements—he would take no part in harming them. But Mateo was starting to indoctrinate him on the critical mission before them: the Verona line must end if there was to be any hope of world peace. He felt he could turn Noah, and they'd have a leg up on getting rid of Vincenzo, who was going out less and less these days.

<hr />

Gina used to think of the Scortini palazzo as eerily romantic and darkly mysterious. Now from the inside, it was just eerie and dark. It felt forbidding and permanent as a grave. An ancient butler and maid had assisted her and Raphielli with towels while Alphonso and Zelph, his look-alike cousin, hovered with blankets.

Gina was thinking a mile a minute as she wrapped the blanket around her shoulders. She wasn't going to let some chemical kill her baby. She had no idea what had been injected into her vein, and her mind flew over natural compounds that could be a broad antidote. While the little old maid tut-tutted about her bloody knees, Gina asked, "Raphielli, could I have several heads of garlic, a big pot of mint tea, and a jar of honey?"

"Of course." Raphielli turned to the old woman. "Rosa, bring them to the receiving room." The old woman trotted away down a cavernous hall. Raphielli turned back and asked, "What's that stuff for?"

"Garlic and honey can fight off almost anything if taken in sufficient quantities early enough. The mint will help keep my stomach settled."

Raphielli turned to her butler. "Dante, several guests should be here momentarily." He nodded and stood at attention at the door as she led the way down eerie marble halls with Alphonso and Zelph at her side. It was like walking into some dark overlord's version of Versailles. Their footfalls echoed down the silent corridors like kids in a museum past closing hours. Gina eyed the portraits of unattractive and forbidding people who stared down from frames on the walls.

When they arrived in the receiving room, it looked like someone had put furniture in a mausoleum, for all its cold austerity. Zelph went to start a fire in the enormous fireplace. There were probably eighty floral still-life paintings on the towering walls, all spectacular in their faded glory. The floral-patterned sofas were pretty in a neglected antique sort of way, but the cushions felt like sitting on uneven rocks.

Rosa, who had more stamina and speed than Gina had estimated, came hustling through a hidden door bearing a tray with a honeypot, a basket of garlic, and a teapot. She set everything before Gina and poured a cup before stepping back into the shadows. Gina pulled the basket onto her lap and began peeling and chewing. She was swallowing the first garlic cloves as everyone arrived in a rush. The man she'd seen in the flower shop, who Horace had called a Mafioso, came running into the room with someone at his heels who had to be his son based on the striking resemblance. They approached Raphielli looking wary. "Are you all right?"

She nodded and looked relieved, while Alphonso and Zelph went on edge as if the Mafiosos were pets of Raphielli's who may bite.

Next, Juliette swept in. "You were in the middle of an appointment! Explain yourselves." Then she noticed the impeccably dressed Mafioso and assumed the role of mother in the room. "I have not had the pleasure. Juliette Verona. And you are?"

"Giancarlo Petrosino, and my son Primo."

Juliette's eyes widened. "You gentlemen saved Raphielli from hanging."

"*Sì.*"

Giancarlo approached Gina. "I saw you at the flower shop." He had a heavy Sicilian accent and smelled wonderful—she could smell him over the garlic—like nutmeg, bergamot, cardamom, and something mouthwatering...perhaps papaya? She wanted to lean into him.

"Gina." She liked him instantly.

His almost-black eyes dropped to the bowl in Gina's lap, then Juliette said, "Giancarlo, I believe Salvio ordered you to kill my husband."

He turned his attention back to the contessa. "Salvio made a demand, but I don't take orders."

Next through the door came Vincenzo, Leonardo, and the pope.

Giancarlo didn't look surprised. "Gentlemen, we have to stop meeting like this."

Vincenzo grinned at the Sicilian, Leonardo looked captivated by him, and the pope came forward to clap the Mafioso on the back. Gina wondered why the pope looked grateful to see him. A Vatican security officer and Vincenzo's bodyguard finished their sweep of the room and stepped back out into the hall.

Raphielli broke in by clearing her throat. "Now that we're all together..." She proceeded to tell the group everything that had happened in the doctor's office. She finished her recitation by saying she'd witnessed Doctor G inject an unidentified substance into the port in Gina's arm.

"Then cool as a cucumber, he held up his empty hands like a magician's trick. It looked like the performance of a man who's never been caught and felt invincible, even as Gina yelled at him."

"You say he assumed you were carrying Salvio's child?" the pope asked Raphielli.

"Absolutely, and he said Salvio's name with...reverence, is the best way to describe it."

Giancarlo squinted at Raphielli. "And he gave you a shot?"

"*Sì.*"

Then the pope and Giancarlo turned their eyes to her. "Gina, he believed your child was Vincenzo's?"

"*Sì.*"

"But you both got the injection?"

Gina said, "*Sì,* but Raphielli's was administered by a nurse in her hip, while Doctor G snuck in and slipped something into my *vein,* then performed a sleight of hand while *lying* about it. Vitamins aren't pumped into veins, drugs are."

Alphonso turned to Juliette. "Tell us about Doctor G."

She stood up and began to pace. "He's the best OB-GYN in Venice. He's been my rock through miscarriages, a stillbirth, and he succeeded in saving Vincenzo."

"You couldn't have more children?" Raphielli asked.

"Doctor G said neither the child nor I would stand a chance, and I would be committing suicide...the ultimate sin..." her voice became small, uncertain. "He made me promise never to get pregnant again. So Gabrieli and I were very careful. You don't suppose that he..." she sat down abruptly, clamping her hand over her mouth.

The room fell silent until out of the quiet came the barely perceptible squeak of wheels and the butler and maid appeared with carts stacked high with stylish trays of sandwiches, hors d'oeuvres surrounded by boughs of holly, and edible decorations.

Raphielli got to her feet. "Goodness! The cook did this?"

Juliette cleared her throat and then said. "No, I texted Ippy, who called Marilynn Bergoni. She sent over some food from a party she was catering nearby."

Gina looked down at her lap full of garlic peels. "I'm going to have to keep eating these, but I could use a whole lot more mint tea and a washcloth for my hands, *per favore*." The fresh cloves were sticky, but that meant they had more of the allicin enzyme, which could eradicate practically anything from her system at this concentration.

"Gina needs to eat something besides garlic." Giancarlo placed his handkerchief into her hand, and Primo sprang into action. Within moments she had a plate piled with delicacies, and he'd thoughtfully spread a napkin across her lap.

Vincenzo flipped up the edge of her skirt. "Gina! Your poor knees!"

"They're just scraped," she shrugged.

He rocked back away from her. "I'm so used to your smell, and now you smell like a delicatessen."

"*Sì*, I smell like a salami, but my family has used whopping doses of this nightshade as an antidote to everything imaginable—even the plague."

Vincenzo looked impressed. "Seriously?"

"It's miraculous," she assured him.

Leonardo reached into her bowl and began peeling another clove for her. "Then *mangia, mangia!*" He pulled back, "Woo! You do smell like a salami."

"Eh, this salami is the mother of our child." Vincenzo squeezed her shoulder. "As long as garlic won't hurt the baby, I say eat as much as you think you need. But Doctor G isn't stupid. I don't think he'd terminate your pregnancy the moment he laid eyes on you. He must have bided his time with my mother or she'd have suspected something." He glanced at Juliette and her brows drew together in consternation, but she said nothing.

Gina popped the garlic in her mouth and chewed the fiery bud, but her tongue had gone numb. Giancarlo turned from handing a full plate to Raphielli and said, "He pulled a pretty desperate act squeezing into the nurse's lab and plunging a chemical into Gina's arm when four people could have seen him."

The pope said, "Raphielli *did* see him."

Leonardo went to investigate the sideboard where Dante and the maid were placing more trays of *anti-pasti* and desserts. "Isn't there a doctor we can trust to test them and find out what they've been given?"

Alphonso said, "You've been watching too many medical dramas. We don't know who to trust, and I don't want anyone doing any tests on Raphielli."

Gina watched Giancarlo and Primo exchange looks.

The pope said, "I agree. The girls have been targeted, but now we will keep them close and protect them."

Alphonso picked up the thread of conversation. "Assuming that Doctor G is in the habit of terminating babies without Juliette's knowledge, why would anyone—other than Salvio for jealous reasons—want to kill the Veronas? How does it benefit a respected doctor?"

The pope said, "Anyone wishing to undermine me and the Catholic Church."

Petrosino said, "Oh, so someone understands your..." He waved vaguely between the pope and Vincenzo. "Alliance."

Gina watched eyes communicating silently around the room at the depth of the Mafia don's familiarity with the family, then mouths dropped open when he looked at Vincenzo and said, "Does he know about your preference?"

Vincenzo stared at him, but the don waved the subject away and looked at the pope. "What about the Alithiní?"

The Holy Father came alive and said, "Apparently Salvio's forefathers founded the Alithinían Church. Are you thinking maybe the doctor is a member?"

"It makes sense," Zelph said.

"Then it would be a terrible way to learn the truth," the pope said. "But if nothing happens to Raphielli's baby and Gina's is adversely affected from whatever he injected, we'll know it's a conspiracy against the Veronas."

"The doctor didn't kill Juliette. Is it just male Veronas?" Zelph asked.

"No, female Veronas are particularly powerful," Vincenzo said. "But mother isn't a Verona, she's a Clairvaux. No reason to kill her."

"And what are the Verona's powers?" Giancarlo asked.

Vincenzo looked the Mafioso in the eye. "We love."

"They love," the pope and Leonardo echoed at the same time.

"Ah, well that's good," Giancarlo said with admiration and a look of relief.

"What should I say to Doctor G?" Juliette held up her phone and asked. "He has called Ippy twice asking why the girls left during their appointment. He wants to see them again tomorrow."

"Don't tip your hand," Alphonso said. "He'll cover his tracks and we won't be able to nail him."

The pope said, "Tell him the girls were just excited, that everything is fine."

Juliette nodded and texted Ippy to that effect.

Giancarlo said, "I suggest you keep the appointment, and we can send a young man with you. Say he's one of your distant relatives, contessa, and the father of Gina's child. Someone on *your* side of the family, and while you want to raise it as a Verona, it's not a Verona by blood."

Gina liked how practical the Mafia don was, and asked, "Who could we trust?"

Vincenzo was looking at Primo. "Would you do it?"

"Sure, he'll be good," Giancarlo said. "He can act as bodyguard while Alphonso checks the place out."

"I'm going?" Alphonso asked hopefully.

The Mafioso turned his back as he selected a plate of food from the table. "You'll present yourself as the father of Raphielli's child and find a way to search the place. You are a private detective, after all."

Juliette's phone pinged, and she said, "We've got an appointment tomorrow morning. He squeezed us in before his first patients."

The pope moaned, "I am relieved Giselle is in hiding."

"Hey, that's right," Zelph said. "If she's not carrying a Verona, can't it be leaked she's carrying Markus' baby? To keep her safe."

"I will not ask how you know that," the Pope snapped. "Not yet." He glanced meaningfully at Vincenzo.

Zelph waved a hand to encompass the room. "Hey, I'm part of the club, too. I know things." But when he looked at Giancarlo, he dropped his eyes. "Just a few things."

The pope said, "*Sì*, Giselle has her *Group Français* helping her. Now we have formed *il Comitato di Venezia* to end this war."

"Speaking of our committee, where's Ivar?" Raphielli asked.

Juliette wrinkled her nose at the coffee she'd just sipped. "Running Verdu Mer business while I took the day off to focus on you two. Raphielli, I must send you some Passero's beans. This coffee is no good." She tapped out a text, no doubt to Ippy.

Everyone got down to the business of eating, and Raphielli said, "On a different subject, Holy father, I need your help with Cardinal Negrali. He's holding up the permits for my new shelter..."

Alphonso broke in. "He's extorting her and strong-arming her to get control of her estate."

Gina saw Giancarlo's face darken, and then a quick glance at Zelph's face told her she wasn't the only one who saw it. *What a group we make* she thought. Vincenzo, Leonardo, Juliette, and the pope were focused on her, while Alphonso and the Petrosinos focused on Raphielli. Zelph was watching Giancarlo like his life depended on it.

The pope was saying, "Raphielli, I will free up your permits. And as for Negrali trying to get control of you, send a note saying he is no longer needed, you will have regular prayer sessions with me."

Hearing about cardinals extorting money, Gina felt it was important to add a bit of information. "Holy Father, at the Vatican I heard a cardinal say he was getting Raphielli's estate. He said it to a cardinal named Marconi."

"Marconi?" The pope's eyes went wide.

"Uh-huh. He also said that when he was pope, he'd deliver Germany to this Marconi."

Vincenzo choked on his food. "*Dio mio!*"

"Would you recognize him?" the pope asked.

Vincenzo grabbed his phone and scrolled to a photo. "Was it either of these men?"

Gina took a look. "The older one with the big cross said it."

"Negrali," the pope and Vincenzo said together.

Gina continued. "I'd like to know more about the intense man at the Vatican. I can't recall his name, but now *he* gave me the worst feeling."

"An intense man?" the pope asked.

"*Sì*, he wears grey suits and his tie tack has broken arrows."

"Could it have been the Swiss Guard's two keys crossed on a shield?"

"No. It's a bird clutching the arrows."

"Must be Hierotymis Karno, Ecclesia Dei," the pope said.

Gina confirmed, "That's him, Karno."

"The symbol is a crow clutching lightning bolts. He's a member of a secret intelligence order."

Gina continued, "He started taking a creepy interest in me when he heard I was with the Veronas. He might have seen the three of us go into a room together." She gestured to the boys.

"We-we were oh-oh-only *praying*," Leo stammered in such a guilty way Gina was certain everyone in the room figured out what they'd been doing. "But Karno couldn't know *that*," he finished lamely.

Everyone's eyes widened and Raphielli looked away embarrassed while Giancarlo and his son quirked their brows at Gina in interest.

Giancarlo said, "Sounds like having Primo step up as the father of Gina's baby needs to happen sooner rather than later if the criminal element in the Vatican could be conspiring to bring down the Veronas and the Pope."

"Apparently Vatican intrigue isn't just for the history books," Zelph said. "But I'm not gonna stand by while innocent women and children are poisoned."

Leonardo asked, "How can we find out if Doctor G is Alithinían?"

"I could ask a resident of mine," Raphielli said. "She's Alithinían."

"What?" The pope slammed his hands onto his arm-rests, heaving himself up until he was hovering over his seat awkwardly. "I must see her!" he thundered.

Everyone froze.

Gina sensed that the atmosphere had become danger-ous. "What's that?"

"It's a secretive religion," Raphielli said firmly. "They've been hunted by Catholics, she'd never speak to you."

"God will open her mouth. I must see her!" he ordered.

Juliette jumped to her feet. "Oh Raphielli! Call her, at least ask her about Doctor G!"

Everyone watched as Raphielli produced her phone and called the shelter. "*Ciao,* Kate. I need to speak to..." She looked around the room and then shrugged. "Benny."

Primo muttered, "Benedetta? The missing girl?" and shot his father a worried look.

Raphielli said, "Ah, *sì,* Benny. I was looking into doctors for your baby. What do you think of Doctor Gugliemoni?" The look on Raphielli's face conveyed the hysteria on the other end of the call.

"Okay, no, I won't. Don't worry. I promise. Forget I mentioned that name. Okay, *ciao.*" She hung up and said, "She's worshipped with him. He's Alithinían and would take her child to be raised by them."

"It's a cult," Primo said.

"It is not a cult," the pope corrected.

Just then a woman came into the room saying, "I finally gave up on you guys. If you wanted to have a party and not

invite me, you just had to say so...*holyshih-hih-hih! Pope!*"
The last word sounded like a cork coming out of a bottle.
The redhead stood frozen before the pope, hands covering
her mouth. She was wearing a sweat suit with the words
Porto delle Donne over her left breast and down one leg.

"Paloma, I'm so sorry!" Raphielli cried. "We forgot to
come get you."

"Oh-mih-gawd-oh-mih-gawd-oh-mih-gawd" the shivering woman repeated under her breath as she stared at the
pope. "Excuse the life outta me! Oh my God, sorry, sorry..." She swayed where she stood.

Raphielli said, "Paloma, please forgive us. This wasn't
planned. A last-minute situation arose."

"Hey, it's cool."

Gina could tell the woman was looking at the decorated
party platters and not sure whether to believe Raphielli's
story. Paloma shifted awkwardly from foot to foot, arms
going out to steady herself, and said something that
sounded like, "Whew, super embarrassing" under her
breath.

Gina suddenly felt sick and set her empty garlic basket
aside. "I'm not feeling well."

Eyes regarded her with alarm and she tried to reassure
them. "Nothing specific, just clammy. Maybe I'm not close
enough to the fire. And my knees are throbbing, and my
best skirt is ruined..." She suddenly felt on the verge of
tears. "Excuse me, *per favore*. I think I'll go home."

Vincenzo helped her up. "I'd feel better if you came to
stay at our place, Gina. I'll give you some of Giselle's
clothes."

Despite her fear that perhaps it wasn't just nausea from the whopping ton of garlic she'd forced down, but that she was suffering the ill effects of Doctor G's poison, she actually got excited at the prospect of wearing Giselle's fabulous designer clothes.

As Vincenzo, Leo, and Juliette followed Gina to the door, the pope began again, "Raphielli, you must take me to see this Benny."

"*Sua Santità*, let's do it another time. She isn't going anywhere. *Per favore.*"

He said, "Then I am going to Rome to start getting Cardinal Negrali under control," and hurried after them.

This time Gina didn't feel nervous traveling the dark halls, because the pope was so incandescent with righteous rage he practically lit the way.

———⊙———

Hiero was facedown and hovering in a state of bliss when his phone blipped. He retrieved it from the nearby table and waved off the masseuse as he propped himself on an elbow to answer.

"*Pronto.*"

"Where are you?"

"Getting a massage."

"Where? Are you close?"

"Baan Thai on Borgo Angelico. What's up?"

"Hard to tell. Americo Negrali is camped outside your office door and the helipad crew is expecting His Holiness at any moment."

"I'll be right there, say ten minutes." He rolled to a sitting position and the masseuse began wiping oil off him using hot towels.

Once in the Vatican offices, Hiero could feel an air of urgency, so he went straight to his favorite font of information, Clovis, at the concierge's desk. The horsefaced little man was so enamored of power, he lived to gossip with the head of Ecclesia Dei.

"*Buonasera*, Clovis," Hiero said warmly.

"Are you back to meet with His Holiness?"

"Why do you ask?"

"You know, because he's really mad."

"You astound me," Hiero said and leaned over for their usual conspiratorial chat.

Clovis leaned in, smelling of contraband cigarettes. "No one's talking about it, of course, but apparently His Holiness could be clearly heard yelling that he'd uncovered a plot to oust or kill him...over his pilot's microphone...you know...in the background when they were communicating their coordinates to land."

"Pah, nothing new," Hiero said. "If there wasn't some sort of drama over these recent brouhahas, then the cardinals would need to be checked for vital signs." Hiero chuckled and walked off with a wave.

As he approached his office he saw Negrali pacing, a bright red penguin with his head bowed. "The place is old, try not to wear a hole in my floor."

"We need to talk, and you need to get moving." Negrali stood by as Hiero unlocked his door, and then he hurried inside to resume his pacing in front of Hiero's desk.

"Move? I'm not going anywhere."

"Into gear! Mobilize!" Negrali shrieked.

"I don't have my paintings."

"I'll snatch the damned paintings off Raphielli's wall tomorrow!"

"What's with your hysterics?"

"Raphielli just called me to say she's leapfrogging over me and will be confessing directly to the pope! She's trying to keep me away from her."

The phone light on Hiero's desk started blinking, and he held up a finger to silence his frantic visitor as he picked up the line his operatives used.

"*Pronto.*"

The voice said, "A number of developments: The bug inside the papal apartment just picked up what sounded like the pope telling someone that Vincenzo's gotten a girl named Gina pregnant, Raphielli Scortini's carrying Salvio's child, Contessa Juliette is probably fertile, and he's overheard Negrali promising Marconi favors once he ascends the throne."

"You're certain?"

"The audio broke up several times like he was pacing out onto the balcony. But confusing as it was, *sì*, those were the topics."

"Keep on it." Hiero hung up. "Americo, I agree with you. We need to get moving."

"Finally! What's happened?"

"Vincenzo's made another heir with that little plaything he's been diddling since his wife took off."

"Woah! Maybe he's not gay after all."

"And Raphielli's carrying Salvio's child."

"What? She didn't say anything! But come to think of it, she's been feeling poorly."

"How pregnant can she be?"

"Hard to tell with her figure, she's all round curves."

"*Sì*, not my type at all," he said as a dismissal. "And things are also looking up for Juliette. Apparently, not only has life after Gabrieli proven her to be a capable and popular construction manager, but she may be fertile."

"I don't care about her fucking uterus, she's not got any of those weird brainwashing powers. I want Verdu Mer! Kill her!"

"You want to watch your volume. I don't like yelling."

"*Spiacente.*"

"Okay, I'll get my men down to Venice, where our best bet will be a boating accident with the whole Verona family onboard."

"Don't forget the wife in France. I don't want to have a single Verona left to derail my plans when I'm pope."

"We'll get her, too."

"And I want Raphielli dead within the week! I've got a will I've made for her, and it leaves me everything."

"Oh?"

"I've made sure everyone who matters has seen us together. I even went along with her to dine at the mayor's home. I put her signature on it. I've picked up a couple of papers with her signature on them, and this document is codified by a very expensive lawyer. Now she just needs to die so I can take the will to a probate court."

"Hold onto that skullcap there, Americo." He pointed

to the silk headpiece Negrali had placed on the corner of his desk. "We're not a smash-and-grab operation. We are exacting professionals. You can rest easy that they're all as good as dead."

"I don't plan to hold onto this skull cap, Hierotymis, not when the crown is within my reach. I want these people ended."

The angry cardinal slammed out of the office, muttering that he'd kill the heiress himself if he got the chance.

Hiero still felt loose and relaxed from his massage as he called his team for a planning meeting. He had a feeling Giselle Verona hadn't gone far from her home turf, so he would plant a team in Gernelle before the night was out. He had two men who were experts at flushing out prey. They'd go underground and wouldn't be heard from again until they sent word of her elimination.

In Venice, he had three of his best operatives infiltrating the top security firms in the hopes of getting assigned to the Verona and Scortini palazzos. It would be easiest if he had men on the inside who could arrange a tumble down the stairs or food poisoning. The boat tragedy would take a few more days to play just right. It didn't matter if it looked suspicious, it'd never be pinned back on the church. More likely the Mafia would get the heat, like it happened so often when his department pulled off an audacious operation. And if the pope should take a ride with the Veronas, so much the better.

12

Gina wished she still drank coffee as she sat in Doctor G's waiting room. She hadn't slept much the night before, but now felt bolstered by the solid presence of Primo. He held her hand reassuringly and, in turn, he was being attended to by Juliette pretending to be his doting relative. The young Mafioso had been hilariously funny when he'd greeted the Contessa outside. To get into character with her, he'd revealed an agile mind and wicked sense of humor, riffing in equal parts French and Italian about embarrassing things they'd done together at family reunions. Juliette took an obvious shine to him and seemed grateful that he'd lifted the mood.

As they sat staring at the tasteful prints on the walls in the empty waiting room, Gina tried to take her cue from Alphonso and Raphielli, who looked cool and collected. Everyone was set to play their parts, and Alphonso was ready to use his private-eye skills, but Gina couldn't help feeling a bit weak and sick. She'd had some blood spotting this morning and had told the boys, who were now beside themselves with worry. After this appointment, *il Comitato di Venezia,* as they now called their group of confederates, was reconvening at the Verona palazzo, which was light years more comfortable than the Scortini Palazzo, maybe because it was literally lighter.

"Doctor will see you now," the receptionist announced and pointed down a hall indicating the door to his large office. Gina saw the woman's longing look as Alphonso walked past her, and she could have sworn she saw him give her an interested look in return.

Doctor G looked at the men in surprise. "It seems we have guests."

Primo beamed a disarming smile. "I would have come to the last appointment, but Gina was keeping it as a surprise." Extending his hand across the desk he said, "Louis, Louis Dubois, soon to be Verona." His accent was an amalgam of privileged European pronunciation and French inflections.

The doctor looked confused. "Monsieur Dubois?"

"Call me Louis. You are bringing our baby into the world, no need to be formal. Am I right, Toni?" he said turning to Juliette. He'd pronounced it in a quick throw away, so casually French, *doh-NEE*.

The doctor looked alarmed at the contessa being treated so improperly, but Juliette grinned and patted Primo's knee. "*Certainment le médecin est notre bon ami.*" Then to Doctor G she said, "Louis is one of those modern fathers who wants to help with every facet of Gina's pregnancy and birth."

"I'm sorry, did he just call you 'Tony'?"

"Oh, my family, we have so many Juliettes, we use our middle names to avoid confusion. Mine is Antonia."

"You are related? I thought your last name was Clairvaux." He stared at her.

"Louis is not my brother, he is my cousin."

"Poor cousin, to be honest," Primo cut in. "Tony has always taken care of me. She is going to adopt me. I know I will not get a title or anything like that, but Gina and I plan to have lots of kids and that will cheer up Tony since she has become a widow. I want to be in the delivery room, you know, coaching. We are going to take classes." He kissed the back of Gina's hand with gusto, and she found herself giggling. He was bowling the doctor over with bullshit.

"Juliette will have Giselle and her child soon, too," the doctor said.

"Oh, for certain she will. But Gigi and Vincenzo prefer Paris, while Gina and I will be moving right in with Tony here in Venice. Hearing the patter of little feet every day will do her good."

"I see." The doctor looked at Juliette. "And when is Giselle coming back to start her pre-natal care? We need to get her onto a schedule of checkups."

"She says to tell you she is feeling fine and begs your indulgence while she takes a bit more time on her art before she gets too big to climb around with a welding torch. She promises to be here soon."

"M-mm, where is she at the moment?" he asked casually while scratching a few notes on a pad.

Gina felt them all tense at the probing, but Juliette lied like a pro. "Kópavogur. She's overseeing the installation of a large sculpture at a collector's home."

He made a note. "Kópavogur. Where is that?"

"Iceland. I spoke to her just yesterday, and she feels tip-top."

Gina was impressed at Juliette's improvisation, but Iceland sounded far-fetched.

"Travel poses undue stress on the fetus. Press Vincenzo into getting her settled back here in Venice until their baby is born."

"I will."

Doctor G turned his attention to Alphonso, who would have been hard to overlook in a room twice the size. With his sheer bulk and long hair, he looked like a big barbarian next to the tiny Raphielli. "And you are?"

"Alphonso Vitali. I'm Raphielli's baby daddy."

Raphielli looked so genuinely surprised at the moniker, she blushed and looked at her hands to compose herself.

"Mm-really?" Gina could see the skepticism on the doctor's face as he looked between the two. "All right then, let's get started with the examinations."

Primo grabbed Gina's hand. "I can be in the room for this, right?"

She felt unnerved at this darkly intense acquaintance being present while her feet were in medical stirrups and her breasts were examined. But it'd be a goldmine of opportunities for Primo to keep the doctor busy with questions or baffled with bullshit, so she got on board with the plan. Sure, he'd be seeing her body, but in for a penny in for a pound. Besides, he was quite attractive in a dangerous sort of way. She gulped and nodded, "Of course dear, absolutely."

The doctor looked ready to object when the contessa said, "I love Louis' devotion. Reminds me of my husband." She choked up, and Primo patted her back as she dabbed at her eyes and continued, "I am so grateful for your understanding and attention to our needs."

Doctor G nodded, got up, went around the desk, and leaned out the door. "Nurse, please see Miss Verona and Monsieur Dubois..."

Juliette cut in, "Refer to him as Verona. He will be soon enough."

He continued, "The Veronas into examination room B and Signora Scortini into C." He turned to Alphonso and Juliette. "Both of you can relax in the waiting room."

When Gina and Primo were alone, she started undressing to put on the gown she'd been given. He turned his back, but there was a mirror over the sink on the opposite wall, so he closed his eyes.

"Where did you learn that posh Euro accent?" she asked him.

"When I'm around posh Eurotrash, I study them. I study everyone."

"You've studied me?"

"Absolutely. It's how I stay one step ahead of people." He smiled, and with his eyes closed he looked sweet, very different with his intense black eyes hidden. "People have a misperception of my family. We're more chess players than thugs. We get to know people and anticipate their moves."

"You think Juliette is trash?"

"No. She's as posh as can be, not a trashy hair on her head. She's a real lady."

Gina folded the clothes she'd borrowed from Giselle's closet and placed them over the back of a chair. "So, we'll keep the doctor in here with us as long as we can and give Alphonso plenty of time to snoop around."

"Uh-huh. And Raphielli knows to keep the doctor with her until she can't keep him any longer. Let's settle in."

She closed the paper gown. "I'm decent. You can open your eyes."

He opened them, and when their eyes met in the mirror Gina felt a momentary respite from the nausea as desire lapped at her in warm waves.

His voice was husky when he said, "You look good in paper."

"You won't look at my...me...down there will you?"

"Not if you don't want me to."

"*Grazie.*"

She found herself wondering what would happen if she told him she wanted him to. She thought about how awkward and exciting that could be, and then remembered they weren't there to make a naughty experiment of things. This was deadly serious and Primo needed to keep his mind on waylaying the doctor, who was most likely a cold-blooded killer.

Raphielli was relieved when they left the doctor's office. No one had tipped their hand to Doctor G that they were on to him, which was difficult because Gina was furious at having been given a shot and Juliette was clamping a lid on her rage with only varying degrees of success. It was still early morning, and most of Venice was shuttered as they all piled onto the Verona's boat and got on their phones. She felt Primo's eyes on her as she sat next to Alphonso, who placed a call to Vincenzo asking him to go to his late father's bathroom cabinet, and then started tapping searches on his smartphone and reading chemical names to him. The opulent boat cut smoothly through the icy waters as Juliette conducted Verdu Mer business through her earpiece while simultaneously texting Ippy.

Raphielli was grateful for the opportunity to return calls before they all started hashing out what Alphonso had discovered at the doctor's office. She listened to a message from Ava about sending costumes along with the invitations to her ball and called her to discuss it.

"*Ciao*, Elli. What do you think of providing costumes for your guests?" The designer sounded unbelievably calm for someone who created hundreds of designs each season that were judged by the fickle fashion world.

Raphielli was reluctant. "I thought I'd just have Marilynn send out invitations. She offered to. Won't people be offended if I send them something to wear?"

"They'll love you for it! You've never been to these balls, but I can tell you, many people have moth-eaten costumes they've worn for years. They'll wear the damned things to like six balls this season alone. They'll be thrilled to wear something new!"

"Won't that be too much work for you?"

"Are you kidding? It's a designer's dream to put clothing onto these people's bodies! Marketing 101! My team can whip up the whole lot in forty-eight hours. Marilynn already sent me your guest list and they're all people who are in the society pages, so I've got a photo board with their pictures. Sizes are easy, and I'll make everything tie or Velcro closure. Colorful morning coats for the men with outrageous hats and masks, dazzling gowns, gloves, and fake jewels for the women with outlandish wigs and masks. I can have them to Marilynn in time for her to affix the invitations on top of each box and have them delivered."

"You can?"

"You're speaking to a woman who's standing inside a cargo container full of paste jewels, and the next container over is wigs. I'll have everything you need as soon as you approve it and I point my finger."

"If it's all that easy, let's do it."

"Done. And according to Marilynn, you're going to have the most outrageous ball in the history of Venice. I hear she's got a company from Las Vegas installing Poseidon in the canal in front of your palace, and he'll rise up out of the water at the finale. Now you'll have the most beautiful guests, too. *Ciao!*"

Raphielli felt the beginnings of excitement as she scanned important emails from Kate. One was a notice that Paloma had met with the shelter's attorney and was going to press charges against Milos, her ex-boyfriend. It was a courageous decision, since he'd stomped her almost to death last fall and had killed their unborn child in the process.

"You did an excellent job of keeping the doctor in with you," Juliette was saying to Primo and Gina.

"Oh, *sì*. Primo, aka Louis Dubois, invented all sorts of things that I was worried about," Gina said. She turned to Primo, who broke into chuckles with her as she continued. "Apparently, I've been terrified I'll need an epidural and needed to understand every aspect of that procedure. Also, episiotomies, piles, colostrum, and a host of breastfeeding fears because I have no boobs. He was quite an advocate for all the issues I'd shared only with him."

"Well, it worked. You had him in there for almost an hour." Juliette smiled at Primo.

"He got impatient, but Primo wouldn't shut up," Gina said, and then bit her lip to keep from laughing. "He finally walked out while Primo was asking about sex positions during pregnancy."

"Rude." Primo pretended to be miffed. "I told him she was afraid we'd injure the fetus. But he kept repeating that I needed to make Gina take shots, which I promised to talk to her about."

"I'm never setting foot in that place again if I can help it. I'd like to see him in court." Gina's mood turned somber again. "He noticed I was spotting, and actually looked happy as he told me there was nothing to worry about." Then she squeezed Primo's knee. "Louis, be a good fiancé and kill him for me, would you?" She looked half serious.

He shook his head good-naturedly. "Petrosinos don't take orders. Remember?"

Raphielli arched a brow and said, "Let's not talk about having people killed," then felt like a big fat hypocrite since she'd asked Gio to kill her husband. Primo was gentleman enough not to say a word.

When they arrived at the Verona palazzo, the pope, Gio, Zelph, Vincenzo, and Leonardo were waiting for them in the salon.

The pope asked Alphonso, "Did you find anything about the doctor's plan?"

"I got into Doctor Gugliemoni's filing system."

Gio's eyes narrowed. "Just like that, eh?"

"The moment Doctor G went in with Gina, I went to talk to the young file clerk. She's in the market for a boyfriend, so I was able to maneuver around her workstation with surprising ease. She also lacks imagination. The password for their filing program was on the corner of her desk blotter."

"Ah!"

"Then I excused myself to use the restroom, but instead went to the doctor's office. He'd left his computer on."

"What'd you find?"

"He believes Salvio Scortini is the father of Raphielli's baby. He listed Salvio as the father."

"His patients have a below-average rate of prenatal mortality—I just cross-referenced what I found with government records." Alphonso waved his phone. "We can't report him for bumping off babies in utero, but I looked up the Verona files which contained almost no notations other than Juliette's appointment dates."

"So maybe he did give Gina vitamins?" Juliette asked.

"Not a chance. You don't administer vitamins intravenously," Gina said dejectedly.

"Whatever compound he gave her, there was no notation in her file. But back to the Verona files, I found

Gabrieli's name in a spreadsheet with dates going back years."

Juliette said, "Doctor G discovered that Gabrieli had a condition called pellagra and needed to take medicine for life. He took it faithfully every morning."

"Gabrieli took medicine from a women's doctor?" the pope asked.

"Doctor G was like family. He'd noticed some inflammation around Gabrieli's neck and did a quick test. Then he prescribed the medicine."

Alphonso continued, "I just looked up the ingredients that the compounding pharmacy had on file for Gabrieli, and mostly it contains dosages of normal vitamins. But there are scant dosages of..." He consulted a photo of the doctor's computer screen on his phone. "Phthalates, bisphenol A, and NPEs. Those are endocrine disrupters and most likely the reason you've been childless, Juliette. The count was being chemically sterilized while you were being told it was your infertility that accounted for your lack of children."

Raphielli's heart broke for Juliette and Vincenzo as they took the news like a physical assault.

"No!" Vincenzo jumped to his feet, then doubled over and began crying.

Juliette's face went white as a sheet and her nostrils flared. "That bastard," she seethed from between her teeth.

Gio spoke up. "It feels like the Alithiníans to me. If they've been hunted by the Catholics, it would appear they've started to target the Veronas to hurt the Catholics. It's time to act. Do we know where they meet?"

"Go to where they meet? To what end?" the pope asked.

"I'd like to pay them a visit."

"I believe they are peaceful faith...except for Salvio who had become a terrorist."

Gio shrugged. "Wouldn't be the first peaceful religion to attract terrorist-minded disciples. Primo and I can find the rogue members and put an end to this."

Raphielli said, "Benedetta's not certain of the location. Her parents always kept her covered and hidden when they traveled to 'the safe house.' Apparently, they hide from the neighbors to keep from being discovered. She's only seen the inside of a water garage on her way down into a small temple for worship. When she was brought there to serve as Salvio's surrogate, she was locked in a back bedroom. When she escaped, she discovered she was near Parco Savorgnan."

"Parco Savorgnan is a densely populated area for something secret like this to be going on," Alphonso said.

Zelph nodded. "Like a needle in a haystack."

Raphielli continued, "Detective Lampani said that in a quieter area, comings and goings would be noticed, but it's so busy, they've gone undetected. He searched that whole neighborhood and came up empty. She doesn't know exactly where the safe house is."

"Right, then I'll start my friends scouring the Parco Savorgnan neighborhood. She can't be that far off," Gio said and stood up.

Juliette nodded her head in agreement, but her jaw was set. Raphielli could only imagine her fury at having children murdered in her womb and then her husband sterilized.

Alphonso stood up as well and the rest of the group followed suit. "We'll leave now and wait for word on Gina's condition."

Raphielli went straight to the shelter and, not for the first time, registered that she was at her best when she was there with the women. When she arrived, she found Paloma hard at work in the office.

"I've been busy reviewing candidates for the new shelter, and I've held some interviews this morning," she said.

"Not here..."

"No, I took a pop-up office space over in Dorsoduro, a renovated building, and it comes with a receptionist and security. Very reasonable and rents by the hour."

"I'm impressed." She looked over Paloma's spreadsheet with names and qualifications of the people she'd interviewed. She patted Paloma's shoulder. "This is great. Maybe add a column with notes about your reference checks? Another for comments you'll go over with Dante?"

"*Sì*, good idea."

"So, on to another subject. You're pressing charges against Milos?"

"Attempted murder for trying to kill me, and murder for him killing our unborn child. I'm doing what's right. I'm moving forward so I can start a new chapter in life. I can't have what he did just swept under the rug."

"I'm behind you, whatever you need."

"Well, since your shelter is already paying for my legal defense, I'll let you know if there's anything else." Her expression became serious. "Now that you're pregnant, what're you going to do about your love triangle?"

Raphielli panicked. "How is this common knowledge?"

"Come on, I live with you, and I see you sneak off during the day. Judging from the way that Mafioso looks at you, I can see he's completely spun by you."

"I'm wrecking my life," she lamented, overcome with humiliation. "But I can't help myself."

"You're creating drama and you need to stop."

"You make it sound easy."

"I can fix your life."

"Am I so transparent?"

"Like glass, kiddo. You came out of a convent…"

"Abbey."

"Whatever…where you were told what to do, you hadn't had any love since your father died, and you were forcibly married off to a monster who tried to kill you. You're an actual damsel in distress who's barely twenty with a body that won't quit. Why wouldn't you be tempted by hot men who're crazy about you?" Paloma rattled it off so matter-of-factly, it didn't even sound shameful.

"Wow, you're good."

"I pay attention to everything Mia and Doctor Risinger say in our sessions."

"But you didn't solve my problem. I don't know which one I love more, and Gio's married. I don't even think I want a husband."

"You gotta make up your mind. You're not the devious kind, and it'll fuck with your head—pardon my French. I never see you meditate, and for all of that confessing you did with that creepy Cardinal, I wonder if you actually pray. Contemplation is getting lost in the shuffle."

"Contemplation." Raphielli looked at Paloma in disbelief. "Who are you?"

"Hey, Mia's right. Spending some silent time every day helps me know who I am and what I want. You should try praying for guidance and then sitting and listening for the answers."

"The answers?"

"Apparently they come from within. Go up to the third floor and get quiet in the meditation room with the other women. They just went up after breakfast. You need to get your life in order."

"But I've got to review plans for the ball and find a gynecologist for Benedetta and me."

"Let Kate find the gynecologist—her mother's probably one—and let the professionals work their magic with your party."

She fiddled with the fine links around her wrist, a gift from her father when she was a girl. "Right. I'll go meditate."

Paloma's eyes were kind. "Read your own bracelet. *The truth shall set you free.* Your men can handle it."

Raphielli thought about that bit of parting advice as she headed for the meditation room on the third floor.

———— ✦ ————

Luigi was dressed and ready for work when he put his arms around his wife. "Gladys, would you like to do some undercover police work for me?"

Her eyes lit up. "I'm your girl! Do I get to wear a disguise?"

"You'll literally be under a cover."

"I'll make the coffee, you tell me the plan."

He pretended to enjoy her coffee—somehow, she managed to ruin espresso—as he explained that Kate would take her for a boat ride and bring her to him over by the stadium. All she had to do was keep herself covered—especially her head.

"Uh-huh, what are we hoping to accomplish?"

"There's a mole in my department. They're the one who kept Salvio one step ahead of me, and now they're trying to find Benny."

"Oh! Luigi, are you in danger?"

"No, but they may try to shove me into the canal or something."

"Uck! I'll bring the eye drops and the antibiotic ear solution."

"Spoken like a true wife." He had to get out to a café for some proper coffee. "Okay, Kate's gonna come get you."

"You can count on me."

He made a beeline for a café and tossed back a double espresso while he called Kate to give her the go-ahead. She agreed to cover Gladys with blankets and bring her to Stadio Penzo on the Rio Sant'Elena side at two o'clock.

Next, he went to the office and pretended to be on the phone. He spoke loud enough for anyone to hear.

"Listen, don't worry Benedetta, I've got a safe place for you. She'll bring you to me. I'll be waiting near the closed stadium vending booths on Fondamenta Sant'Elena at two o'clock. It's deserted this time of year. Everything's gonna be fine."

He hung up and saw that everyone seemed to be working diligently, oblivious to his performance. He crossed his fingers and went into Laszlo's office.

"We have a mole here in homicide. They assisted Salvio and now have been breaking into my desk. I'm gonna flush them out. I've set a trap at two o'clock next to Stadio Penzo's vending booths. Can I get back up?"

The inspector did a double take and then gave him a disdainful look. "No. What're you watching *The French Connection*? Set a trap for a dirty cop? I think your headaches and all-nighters have finally caught up with you. Take some time off. Turn around and go back home."

Fine. I'll go it alone.

At two o'clock he was pressed up against the stadium wall in the freezing shadows behind a boarded-up souvenir kiosk. He saw Kate approaching in a boat, and behind her his petite wife was shrouded in blankets.

When the boat docked, he stepped out, calling, "Benedetta, over here." Then everything happened at once.

Kate was helping Gladys up, steadying her and he reached out, helping her up onto the *fondimenta* when he felt a searing pain slam into his left buttock, taking his feet out from under him. Then a hot knife skittered down his left leg. *I'm being stabbed? What the fuck?*

Two figures appeared out of nowhere and grabbed Gladys, one trying to press a cloth to her face as she twisted and tripped on the blanket. There was the sound of breaking glass, then police everywhere. A woman was hollering, "Benedetta! She's my daughter!" and others were saying, "Smells like chloroform! Get them away from that!" and Gladys was yelling, "I'm not your daughter, you dumb bitch! Let go of my hair!"

Luigi rolled onto his side. Lydia was lying on the ground holding a Taser, and the tines of her Taser were rattling alongside Luigi's left leg. Inspector Laszlo was standing on her hand. Bruno was gasping for breath as he grappled with Benedetta's father. Another cop was simultaneously trying to hang onto Benedetta's mother, who was flailing a rag while trying to keep the fumes from knocking her out. Other police officers stepped over to cuff both Amendolas and place them under arrest. Another officer was saying something like "assault of police officers and attempted application of an unconscious-inducing substance in the commission of an attempted kidnap," which sounded made-up to Luigi, but he commended their quick thinking.

Gladys stood with her hands on her hips, hair wild, her blanket across her shoulders like a cape. Laszlo leaned down, tapped the Taser handle out of Lydia's hand, and then depressed a button that retracted the probe with a *crack*.

Luigi looked up at the big man. "You came."

Laszlo shook his head. "Why is it you're never wrong, Lampani?"

Gladys crunched over glass to help Luigi up. "I want you to retire! You could have been killed!"

He felt a searing pain in his buttock and flopped back down onto the other hip. "Christ!"

Bruno came to stand over him as the police boat arrived and took the Amendolas and Lydia into custody. "Let's get you to the hospital. You've still got one or both Taser barbs lodged in you."

"That mole bitch!" He gritted his teeth as Bruno helped him up. Standing on his right leg, he looked for Kate's boat. When he saw her face, her expression said it all. She would move Benny before anyone else tried to chloroform her.

He kissed one of Gladys' clutching hands and whispered, "Go with Kate, she needs your help to move something precious."

Gladys gave him a long look that said she understood, but that they'd be having a talk tonight, before she jumped back into Kate's boat and the two women zoomed up the canal.

Laszlo said, "I have a two-part question. Who is Benedetta, and why'd you think she'd make good bait for Lydia?" Laszlo lifted one of Luigi's arms and tried to drape it over his shoulder to support him, but the big man was so tall, he'd have needed to lift Luigi off the ground. Instead, he offered his forearm.

"She's the missing teen," Luigi said through gritted teeth.

"*That* Benedetta? How's she connected with your Scortini case?"

"While Salvio was evading me, he had her locked in a bedroom and was raping her."

"*Maria madre misericordiosa!* This goddamn case!" Laszlo raised his voice, causing pigeons and seagulls to take flight from their perches on the stadium wall. "What're you going to do now?"

"After I get this metal out of my hip, I'm going to ask Benedetta to tell me the truth about the anti-Catholic movement afoot in Venice."

"Back to the Catholics?"

"And this has to be kept absolutely secret."

"I couldn't agree more," the inspector muttered to himself as he helped ease Luigi down into the ambulance boat. Overhead, a seagull made a full-throated "Woah-ha-ha-ha-ha!" sound and Luigi felt he was being laughed at.

Benedetta was sitting in her favorite therapy session at Porto delle Donne—the Gratitude Circle—when Kate appeared at the door and knocked on the doorframe, signaling to Doctor Risinger.

"May I take Benedetta?"

"Of course, off you go."

Benny went into the hall where she was surprised to see Gladys Lampani standing near the door. Raphielli was pulling on her boots and seemed languid from meditation.

Kate beckoned her toward the door. "Benny, it isn't safe here for you now. We're taking you..."

"Where's Luigi?" she broke in.

"In an ambulance, honey," Gladys answered.

Raphielli said, "You'll stay with Paloma and me for a while."

Kate waved her forward. "Come, we've no time. Let's get you into the boat."

Benedetta felt a thrill cascade through her body and skipped over to the door. *I'll get to see the temple!* "Fantastic!"

Gladys snatched a coat off the foyer peg and handed it to her as Kate hustled them off.

On the short ride, Kate told them about how Luigi had exposed a mole within the department, and Benny's parents had been arrested with chloroform. Gladys showed her pessimistic side by pointing out that her parents were probably on the phone to their lawyer, who was already spinning the story that they were going to use the dangerous drug on Luigi and not on Benny.

"Could that be the case?" Raphielli asked.

Kate shook her head. "No, the mole tased Luigi, and the Amendolas were trying to chloroform Gladys."

"Your mother had me by the hair and was shoving a chemical-soaked rag in my face," Gladys agreed.

"Sounds like them," Benedetta said.

As they approached the Scortini Palazzo, Benedetta felt overwhelming reverence knowing she was finally going to get inside the home of the children of Sinope, and she was carrying one inside her. The Alithiníans had been barred from this palazzo for two long generations.

They slid into a fancy stone water garage which was colder inside than out in the elements. A deep ancient cold seeped through her coat and the blanket they'd wrapped her in. They hurried up the steps, then across the black stone pavers, then up a grand flight of steps and under the stone entry canopy that was more perfect than any Catholic Church door. The carvings of horses and boats told the stories of Paul and his ministries throughout the Mediterranean as he spread the teachings of Jesus the Christ and then Paul's grandson, Marcion of Sinope, gathering up Paul's letters.

Raphielli fumbled with her key, but Kate twisted the bell ring, and an old man opened the door, bowing in a courtly manner.

"Dante, this is Benedetta. She'll be staying in my suite with me."

Benedetta was dying to see the temple, but she couldn't say anything in front of Kate or Gladys, or for that matter, what did this guy Dante know? Everyone looked at each other, as if wondering what to do now.

Kate spoke first. "Well, I need to get back to the shelter. Gladys, can I drop you at the hospital to check on Luigi?"

Gladys had been staring around the enormous entryway with its brooding statues which seemed to look down their noses at you.

"Oh! *Sì!* If you don't mind. Or just drop me at the nearest *vaporetto* stop. I can take a water bus."

When they were gone, Benedetta threw her arms around Raphielli's shoulders and whispered, "Can I see the temple now?"

"I don't see why not. I'll call a friend who visits our temple regularly and ask him to join us."

"Great." She followed Raphielli through the biggest, darkest halls she'd ever experienced. Even where light came from an open door, the halls seemed to pool shadows so black it felt as if you could fall down a hole into...the underworld. No one else was around, but Raphielli moved with ease, as if the dark silence was part of her. They passed portraits of some of the ugliest people Benedetta had ever seen, but they certainly liked their jewels and silks by the look of it. Either they were fond of pets, or they had spectacularly ugly children in past generations who resembled monkeys or pale dogs.

Suddenly the décor changed, and they were in a fresh blue space with a towering fountain that had bowls of flowers bobbing in the splashing raindrops. Then they entered a glorious white apartment with big sofas and fireplace and a massive desk. Near the windows was another fireplace and an enormous bed. Beyond all the furnishings were windows that went from the floor all the way up, like two stories or however tall the ceilings were, and the best view of Venice's waters on display with the Lido in the distance.

"This is totally different from the rest of the place! I get to stay here with you?"

"I'll invite Paloma to stay in here, too."

"The bed's big enough for like ten people."

"We'll keep each other company," Raphielli said while texting—probably the person who was going to join them in the temple. "I don't know if you've heard, but I'm pregnant, too."

"Won't Paloma and I be in the way? I assume that guy who picks you up, Alphonso, is the father..."

"I don't want to talk about that now. No, there's nothing to get in the way of." She wasn't mean about it, but she sounded like she shouldn't be pushed. "Now, I've got a couple of bathing suits in my closet, all too big for you I'm sure, but we'll make do." And then she blushed. "You're not used to worshipping naked or anything are you?"

Benny was caught off guard for the umpteenth time today. "No, but then Nejla never mentioned anything about how the Scortini family worships in the temple or what we used to wear when we came here."

Once suited up, they walked through the silent halls bundled up in long dark bathrobes like two monks. After a long walk with so many turns and stairs, Benedetta gave up trying to memorize the way. She helped Raphielli push open a metal door and was exhilarated when they were hit with warm air and the scent of spring water. *I've come home!*

After hanging their robes on pegs next to a lone robe and men's swim trunks, she followed Raphielli down the green marble steps into the warm water, and they both took a deep breath before diving under the crystal water toward a tunnel that was emitting light.

The short swim through the tunnel took them past Alithinían symbols in gold, and they surfaced in the temple that was the same as the drawings she'd seen all her life— but in person, it looked like heaven. Tears came to her eyes and she choked up. She and her unborn child were in the holiest water.

A soaring golden dome glittering overhead, and symbols in mosaic tiles adorned the floor of the huge disk-shaped pool underfoot. Benedetta's eyes were everywhere at once as they swam to the shallow end toward the marble steps and the altar. There were captivating images of Marcion of Sinope in his boat with the eclipse overhead, Paul on the road to Damascus, and Jesus on the Mount of Beatitudes.

She was thrilled by the *scivolo*. Its water tentacle wavered as she passed, an almost undetectable column rising out of the ship design in the floor.

They had just walked up the steps to the altar when a splash sounded by the tunnel and an old man surfaced. The look on his face was rapturous as he called, "Praise Jesus!"

Raphielli smiled broadly as the man swam closer. He looked like...he resembled...*No! It couldn't be! The pope? It's a trap!* Benedetta bounded down the steps and dove into the water making for the *scivolo* as fast as her arms could stroke, but the pope beat her to it and hauled her away kicking and screaming. *Fuck he's strong!* Then Raphielli had hold of her, too.

"*Smettila!*" Raphielli yelled in her ear. "Quit it, Benny! He's converting to Alithiní!"

"*He what?*" she sputtered.

Even the pope stared at Raphielli, and then he nodded. "I believe that is what I am in the process of doing."

"He's the pinnacle of evil!"

The pope said, "I am trying to live long enough to re-form the Catholic Church. My religion has gotten too far away from the teachings of The Christ."

Benedetta's hands made circles in the water as she tried to get around them to the *scivolo*, but they blocked her. "Is that what you call it? Waging war against other religions, killing innocent populations all the way back to murdering Marcion of Sinope, even Peter getting Paul killed. I'd say you Catholics started about as far away from Jesus' teachings as you could get."

"That is fair," the pope conceded. "The more time I spend in this temple, the more I see that. May I worship with you? Would you lead me?"

Benedetta felt her jaw unhinge. "Elli, do you want to?"

"*Per favore*, lead us."

"Okay then." She stepped up to the altar, and Nejla's words poured out of her. When she was done, both of them were staring at her in appreciation. She almost felt like curtseying.

"You know that by heart?" the pope asked.

"We all do. It's an oral tradition. Nejla, our orator, is the best."

"And the water." He swept his hand through it. "It is a holy element."

"It's God's divine intelligence, giver of life. We are creatures of water," she said. "When we're born, we're composed of nearly eighty percent water. When we become dehydrated, we die—quickly."

"So, for my church to drown Marcion of Sinope..."

"An indescribable crime and a defiling of our sacred source."

The pope approached the altar, took her hand and kissed it. "I am so relieved that Paul's precious blood was not lost, and you now are carrying the next child of Sinope."

"Speaking of my child—maybe it's because I'm pregnant—I'm so hungry, I'm suddenly having trouble concentrating. Can we get something to eat?"

"Of course," Raphielli said. "We rushed you over here before you got lunch."

On their way back to the main wing, Benedetta saw a painting of Nautilus Island and almost tripped.

"What is it?" Raphielli asked.

"I know that island."

"There are so many paintings of islands in the palazzo. I own quite a few."

"How do you know this one?" the pope asked.

"It's Nautilus, where the first temple of North America was built."

"A temple like this?"

"As far as I know. It's in Maine, just offshore from Castine where a lot of our faithful live."

Raphielli gasped. "Gosh! I put that island in a trust and was planning on leasing it, along with the others, to charities. I'll need to check them all out before I do. I don't want some animal conservationists to stumble on an Alithinían temple and start using it as a veterinary clinic."

"Whoa! No! Don't loan out Nautilus!"

"Oh, well, certainly, I won't loan out any special properties. I'll need your help identifying them."

"I'll help any way I can," she said and then her stomach grumbled loud enough for even the pope to hear.

———※———

Giselle could feel how tense Markus, Yvania, and Daniel were as they headed out onto the property for some animal husbandry and some creative art time. They'd all gotten a scare this morning when Fauve called and, over speakerphone, delivered some news that had the locals buzzing.

"A couple of strangers, Italians by their accents, were in Bazeilles this morning asking a grocery store clerk how he came by the "X" sliced in his hand. People standing behind them overheard the clerk say that some crazy grandma had done it with a giant cooking knife."

"Oh no!" They all looked at Yvania, who became the picture of regret.

Fauve continued. "Did Yvania mark this delivery guy?"

"Er...well..." Giselle didn't want to say.

"Because the clerk said that he used to occasionally deliver items to Abbaye d'Orval's kitchen..."

"Shit!" Markus dropped his head into his hands.

"...but since that old Ukrainian bitch showed up, he's not going near that place. He said he bet she's an escaped mental patient they've got up there. And the Italian strangers said, 'Pardon me, did you say Ukrainian grandma?' And he told them, '*Oui!* Short, round, with red hair in a bun? Sparkly glasses! *Elle est fou!* She's crazy!'"

Giselle crossed her fingers and asked, "Did the Italians seem to care?"

"Oh, they surely did and asked for directions right to you."

Daniel spoke up at that point. "You did right to alert us Fauve, but we've withstood armies here. We can protect Giselle. Today we'll close the grounds to visitors, and at the first sign of anyone, we'll put Giselle in the keep. No one can get to her there."

With that, Daniel arranged to have the grounds closed to the public. The guards posted a sign on the locked gate apologizing for the inconvenience. The access road and fences to the property were firmly locked up.

Frankly, Giselle couldn't tell the difference with the place closed because she hadn't been anywhere near where the public roamed. And despite Daniel and Markus' tension, she was in a good mood crunching through the snow and breathing in the fresh air. This timeless place was quiet, and must have felt this way since the 1100s when it was founded. The same great forest trees stood along the property. While Markus and Daniel went to patrol behind the main buildings, Giselle and Yvania went to the animal barns to spend time with the young livestock and gather eggs.

About forty-five minutes later, Giselle was gathering eggs when she heard cautious footfalls outside the coop. She went on the alert and parked her crate in some straw before dropping into a crouch and peering through the slats. *Am I being paranoid? Will these flights of fear ever stop?* But the boots that stepped stealthily into view didn't belong to anyone on the property, they were expensive all-weather boots. She wondered if she could get back to Yvania in the piglets' barn, but she didn't dare move. She snatched her phone, flipped the switch to silent, and texted Yvania:

I'M IN COOP
MAN OUTSIDE

Yvania replied:

FREEZE

Giselle stayed crouched and soundlessly closed her hand around a little iron hand rake. The man's cautious footfalls on the snow-covered wooden walkway were loud in her ears. He was just the other side of the wall, and if it weren't for those flimsy slats, she could reach out and touch him. He'd stepped toward the coop's door when she saw Yvania's clogs sneaking soundlessly up behind him. Giselle held her breath as the man whirled around and then screamed, "*ARRGGHH!*"

There was a pneumatic sound as a bullet whizzed through a wooden slat in the coop. *He has a gun!* Giselle leaped up and slammed out of the coop door, poised to swing the rake like a claw, and saw a man with a thick layer of bubbling white glue covering his eyes and nose like a mask. He and Yvania were juggling a pistol with a silencer when he ripped it out of her grasp and yanked it back. Yvania cracked him under the chin with a vicious upward blow of her liquid skin canister, and he fell backward. She leaped on top of him searching for his weapon, her skirt riding well up to reveal the seat of her thick grey tights. He grabbed fistfuls of her hair, slammed her sideways, and heaved himself on top of her. *Mon Dieu! He'll kill her!*

Giselle scrambled forward with the claw when the man went flying feet-over-head, and she had to duck to avoid being kicked. The gun sailed past the corner of the coop and disappeared into a drift of snow. Giselle staggered to keep from falling and noticed the man's lower lip was no longer attached where it should be. Yvania sprang to her feet as Daniel and Markus came running between the buildings. The man was still.

"They never are expecting Hemi's move!" Yvania crowed as she straightened her glasses. She looked wild with her hair yanked out of its bun.

"Who's Hemi?" Giselle asked as she used the claw to dig through the drift for the gun.

Yvania was panting slightly but looked energized, even ecstatic. "A friend. He was Slovak-born. Nobody could fight like him. Taught me how to fight when I was a girl."

"Oh." Giselle was back at her side with the gun, thinking this little woman had never had a childhood.

"Do not give me the pity look. I wanted to learn from him. He taught class in his underpants. Very nice lookink, also."

"Well, I saw your underpants, too." Giselle gave her a conspiratorial look.

Markus said, "While patrolling we found two sets of footprints."

"We tracked this guy's partner and put him down the oubliette. I tried to get him to follow me toward a forest pit," Daniel gestured toward the tree line. "But he caught sight of Markus, who lured him around the stone cider house wall, and down the intruder went."

The man behind Yvania suddenly hopped blindly to his feet, but Giselle didn't want to shoot him as he swung in the direction of their voices. His fist whistled through the air—it would be game over for someone if his fist had connected—but Markus took a step forward and tapped him on the Adams' apple, which sent him down onto the hard ground again. Now he was having trouble breathing, and his gasps made whistling sounds.

"Uh-oh," Yvania said, shaking her head. "You have hurt his voicebox. Whistling with his mouth open is no goot. We will put him with his friend and let them get a bit weak from hunger before we question them."

"I'm going to get something to tie him up with." Daniel eyed the man who was now being held on the ground by Markus' foot on his forehead. "Can't gag him or he'll suffocate now that you've sealed his nose shut."

Markus said, "We will keep them here in secret. Their contacts must not know they have failed. Giselle should stay out of sight now. No more going outside until Daniel hears from Juliette that the danger is over."

Giselle eyed the love of her life and his charming surrogate mother. "Okay, but one of you has to teach me the throat chop. I've seen Markus use it now twice. It looks like something I can manage."

Markus shrugged. "It is mostly the element of surprise."

"Nobody expects the Spanish Inquisition, eh?" Giselle said as Daniel disappeared into the nearest barn. Giselle looked to the Ukrainians, but they didn't get the Python quote.

"This could all be over. Meh-be we have got the last hit men." Yvania brushed her hands together.

Giselle looked at the man on the ground who'd turned onto his side in the fetal position, Markus' foot now firmly on his temple. "He's not dressed all in black like the last ones. He's wearing grey and green, no bag with a rope to drown me."

Markus bent over and plucked a small pin from under the man's coat collar. "Any of you know this symbol, a raven holding lightning bolts?" Then he reached back into the man's coat pocket and produced a small disposable phone.

Giselle said, "Anyone want to guess how long it'll take to make him give us his code?"

13

Gina felt serene as she worked away in her laboratory-cum-greenhouse-cum-herb- garden just off Juliette's kitchen at Palazzo Verona. She finally felt like family. It had been over a month now since Juliette had asked her to take time away from school while the Alithiníans were still at large.

"I will speak to the Head Master and request a sabbatical," she'd said with her finger poised over her phone, no doubt to make it happen.

"But I've only just started my college career." Gina had done a poor job of disguising her disappointment. She didn't want to have her career derailed because of a pregnancy. What a cliché. "Do you really think something'll happen out in public or in front of schoolmates? I think I'll go a bit stir crazy if I have to stay here all day every day."

"Think of how Giselle feels."

That made Gina feel like an ingrate for even objecting.

"You're right, of course. But it feels so oppressive to have to lock up all the fragile pregnant women."

"I could not agree more, but it will only be until we stop the terrorists trying to exterminate my family. I feel so guilty for putting you in danger along with us."

"Don't worry. I feel certain nothing bad will happen to me."

Everything had gotten more complicated with Giselle's discovery that the assassins who'd come for her at the abbey either worked for, or wanted her to think they worked for, Ecclesia Dei because they were wearing their insignia. After the attack, *il Comitato di Venezia* had come together and agreed with Giselle's *Group Français* that they wouldn't tell a soul about Karno's men in the oubliette in Belgium. The pope and the Veronas were under attack from not just the Alithiníans, but a coup was underway within the heart of the Vatican the likes of which the church had never seen. Typically, that meant the pope was the sole target. This was much more.

As a result, as the weeks passed, when the pope wasn't tirelessly working with the children of the world, he was at the Scortini Palazzo with Benedetta. With each passing day, he sounded more drawn to the Alithinían philosophy. He'd sit at the dinner table extolling the virtues to eschewing church dogma and simply following Jesus' teachings with one's whole heart. He even veered into pure Marxist philosophy that capitalism was a hungry alien entity that was consuming human workers at a terrifying rate. The key to freedom was for humans to stop buying into capitalism and consumerism. Gina agreed with the pope and could see he'd finally given up on adults understanding the necessity for radical change and why he was so focused on the world's youth.

Unexpectedly, far from going stir-crazy, Gina had found plenty to do in the fairy tale palazzo with the family, not the least of which was exercising with Juliette. Gina was learning some old martial art that women did with fans instead of weapons. It was elegant, so Gina wanted to do it well. She tried to emulate Juliette's long graceful lunges and fluid low kicks, which were slow and precise but made Gina's legs and arms ache after only a short session. A few times when Juliette sped up a sequence of moves to show Gina a transition, Gina was so impressed she could hardly contain herself and redoubled her effort to learn. Each day she'd be drenched in sweat only from moving at a stately pace. Maybe part of the exhaustion was from intense mental focus, but clearly Juliette was a badass.

"How long have you been doing these *travail d'épée* exercises?"

"Since I was five. But before then, I ran around hitting everything with my toy sword."

"I'd imagine no one messes with your family."

"No, we are descendants of Mark, or his Greek name, Martkos, meaning consecrated by the god of war. My family founded the Knights Templar. We protected people on their pilgrimages to the Holy Land."

"Wow. All I can say is...wow. Mark, like as in Saint Mark?"

"*Sì*. And while lineages are important, I am particularly partial to my own which you are carrying. Now, raise your fan and begin again or you will never be ready for the rigors of childbirth, or a sword for that matter," was how that topic was closed.

Now Gina looked around her laboratory at Juliette's carefully potted herbs in the greenhouse and got back to work. The headmaster of Ca' Foscari University had agreed to let her do a special lab project for full credit, and she knew what she was working on would wow her instructor. She took the beaker of spearmint essence off the warming rack and inserted a clean thermometer: 40 degrees Celsius. She withdrew the thermometer, inserted a pipe, drew out six drops of liquid, and transferred it to a transdermal patch where other compounds were cooling. She peeled off the backing and then applied the patch to her arm.

This was the best of all worlds, getting credit toward her degree while working on her own line of natural products. As an added benefit, this patch contained spearmint's powerful limonene, dihydrocarvone, and cineol to cure her nausea and suppress any excess hair growth that pregnancy may bring.

The OB-GYN that she, Raphielli, and Benny were now seeing was a trusted cousin of Porto delle Donne's manager, and the first visit had put all three of them at ease. Benny's child was conceived first and had a strong heartbeat. Raphielli's embryo was a bit further along than Gina's, but both looked good and their hormone levels were perfect. The doctor had gone over everything they could expect, and all three groaned when they'd learned about hair changes during pregnancy. Raphielli had squawked, "I'm going to get it on my belly? I'm hairy naturally! I'll be a gorilla!"

With the fresh-scented patch firmly in place, Gina made

more for Elli and Gina before sealing her beakers and making notes in her school book. Then she checked her other project, an herbal ingestible tincture called 'shrubs.' She poured a shot of shrubs into a tall glass and headed to the kitchen to add cold water and ice.

She was just taking a sip of the puckery-yet-refreshing drink when Juliette appeared in the kitchen looking outraged. "*Presto, vieni adesso!* My dear, you must stop your work and come."

"*Certamente.*" Gina was getting used to big things happening in the household and handed her the drink to try.

Juliette took a sip and said, "*Il Comitato di Venezia* is coming over to hear the news. I am livid!" Then her expression changed, and she stared at the glass. "*Assolutamente delizioso!* More of your shrubs?"

"Uh-huh. It's apple, cardamom pods, dried peach, vinegar, and honey."

"You must send some to Yvania. Use that warehouse address Daniel gave us. I will ask her to use it in a sauce." Then she refused to give up the glass. "Bring this batch with you. We can make a pitcher for *il Comitato* to enjoy. Just because we have bad news to share does not mean we cannot be gracious hosts."

Then she turned to her cooks, who had flown into action behind them. "Ah, *grazie*, plenty of little sandwiches. And Ivar has requested you make salads we can eat without a fork, something on an endive leaf."

When the now-familiar group of the Vitalis, the Petrosinos, the pope, and Raphielli had joined her, Ivar, Leonardo, Vincenzo, and Juliette in the family parlor, everyone began sipping their drink and smacking their lips in pleasure as Juliette stood and began to pace.

"Ivar has just received a formal notification that our Verdu Mer accounts have been frozen. We are being audited for criminal transactions!"

"Negrali!" the pope said angrily.

"The notice demands a halt to all work and our books be turned over to the IOR!"

Raphielli made a face. "Ee-yore?"

"Instituto per le Opere di Religione—the Vatican bank. We're being accused of embezzlement!"

Ivar said, "Cardinal Negrali has planted seeds within the European Housing Authority that Verdu Mer is a money-making scheme with no plan to honor its promise to the original residents!"

"He's getting bolder," Gio said. "And when you confront him now, *Sua Santita*, I'd keep your head of security..."

"Alberto."

"...Alberto between the two of you. Negrali's after everything he can grab: Verdu Mer, your crown, Raphielli's estate."

The pope nodded and looked at Ivar. "This audit is ultimately a challenge to *me*, Ivar. I am the one who directed Vatican funds to Verdu Mer."

"Negrali paints Juliette and me as your henchman who are stealing at your behest! I am not handing those books over to anyone," Ivar said with real venom in his tone. "That little cardinal will learn what happens when you slander a Ukrainian." He eyed his drink. "I love this, but right now it could use a shot of vodka."

As Vincenzo headed behind the bar to oblige, Raphielli said, "Well, now this sounds petty, but Cardinal Negrali stole two paintings from my home."

Everyone but Zelph and Alphonso turned to stare at her.

Don Petrosino and Primo asked, "How?" in unison.

"The whole place is a bit of a...well...circus what with preparations for the ball being such a big production."

"She's not kidding," Zelph said. "Marilynn Bergoni and Domina are installing huge party fixtures, furniture, twenty-meter pillow pits, and they're stringing a matrix of invisible fiber optic webs for lights and visual effects all across the four-tiered theatre with a fifth story balcony that has become the party space."

Alphonso nodded. "They've had temporary generators installed for the party and a temporary motor house for a motorized submergible head out in the canal. Not to mention the pyrotechnic barges on either side of the palazzo and the stunt barge."

Raphielli joined in. "The new shelter dorms are temporarily being slept in by a troupe of circus performers, riggers, and stunt safety team."

This news upset the don, and no one wanted to see that. "Fuck the ball! Those crazy broads are gonna get Raphielli kidnapped or killed! Not to mention Benedetta *who they're tasing police trying to get to!* How many unexplained boat fires have you Veronas had in the past four weeks?"

Gina shuddered, recalling two close calls when Vincenzo and his bodyguard came home blackened from smoke and they'd lost a driver who was still in the hospital.

Raphielli countered, "I *am* safe. The theft happened when I was at the shelter. Ghost and Mister Fox had to disrupt my security system when the new generators were installed. It was for an afternoon. Cardinal Negrali had been seen near the property. He's been quite a pest stopping by with ridiculous excuses."

"What?" The don glared at Alphonso and Zelph, then softened as he looked at Raphielli. "That guy wants your money and he'd prefer you disappeared or dead."

"Then it's good I haven't seen him. Dante takes messages and puts him off. Our best guess is that he saw the commotion as an opportunity to make off with some art. My security system is back up now."

Gina asked, "How do you know it wasn't some of the masquerade people?"

"The masquerade crew are over in the theatre wing. They can't even get to the wing I live in from their side—it's locked. And the two paintings are by Caravaggio that I'd caught Cardinal Negrali's staring at while he was on his phone describing them. The police art expert is trying to determine their value."

Ivar raised his now fortified glass. "To the return of your art and may we all celebrate the cardinal's downfall soon." Then he downed it in one long gulp.

"*Così sia.*" They all raised their glasses.

Then don Petrosino said, "Doctor G won't be playing God anymore. He died recently."

Gina literally shivered at the news so casually offered in that heavy Sicilian accent.

The pope said, "We will not ask how you know that."

"Best not. But I can tell you he believed the Catholic Church was the ultimate evil and the Veronas were some supernatural papal enforcers who needed to be stopped. He'd been planning to poison Giselle and Gina's babies the same way he'd done with Juliette. Said Gina's baby would be fine because she needed about four more shots to be effective."

"*Grazie a Dio!*" Vincenzo and Leonardo cried. Gina felt a free-floating relief.

"He also believed to his dying breath that Salvio's children will save the world," he finished.

"Children, plural?"

"Yeh, he believed Benny and Raphielli were both carrying Salvio's children. Unfortunately, the doctor died without giving up a single name of another Alithinían. He had some deep reserves of mental strength. Didn't crack."

"Like the saints who disappeared into their faith as they were killed?"

"Yeh," he said and seemed impressed in spite of himself. "Just like that. The police will find an Ecclesia Dei pin in his closed fist."

Now it was Gina's turn to smile in spite of herself and she saw a look of triumph settle onto Juliette's face.

"Would Benedetta know of any more rogue Alithiníans?" Primo asked.

"She said all the ones she knew are caught or dead. Short of taking her out into the *calles* in disguise to stare at passersby in the hopes of spotting someone she's worshipped with—which is no plan at all—there's little hope of identifying any others."

"How do we stay safe if powerful Catholics and some rogue Alithiníans or some hit men Salvio hired want to kill us?" Gina asked the committee in general.

Raphielli said, "And don't tell us to stay alert and close to our bodyguards. Salvio struck twice while guards were present."

Don Petrosino soothed, "We're not saying not to live your life, Raphielli, but keep alert. You and Benedetta have Alphonso and Zelph, plus for extra coverage you have me and Primo. Gina, you have professional security, and when any of you are near the pope, you've got his security contingent headed by Alberto, so...let's stay vigilant. Now you all know what it feels like to be me," he said and took a sip of his drink. "If you stay on your toes, you'll be ready to strike the instant you see them coming, and seconds before they expect it."

As Raphielli left the Verona's, she felt Gio's hand on her arm. "In light of recent incidents with the Verona's boats, how do you make sure no one plants an explosive on your boat?"

"Well, when I'm here, the Verona's attendant watches it, and when we're out, Zelph hires someone."

Alphonso and Zelph stood listening and then eyed the boat Gio and Primo had been using since they came to the islands. Drea, the cool blonde driver, stood at the wheel looking capable, and yet somehow managed to blend in with all the other Venetian pilots.

"I'm suggesting you hire a trusted driver who stays in

the boat," Gio said. Then in a nod to civility, said, "Not that you're not trusted, Zelph. You've got a lot on your plate overseeing the security of her home."

"No offense taken," Zelph said.

With that, she let Zelph and Alphonso guide her to her boat while Gio and Primo hopped down into theirs. Drea gave her a little salute.

Raphielli had been pulling away from both of the men in her life for the past several weeks, pouring herself into shelter work and preferring to spend time with Benedetta and Paloma in the evenings. Her emotions and hormones whipsawed her head and heart in two directions. She would no sooner make a decision about her future, when the next moment she wouldn't feel that way at all. Just this week, Gio had called her on it when she'd refused his invitation for the umpteenth time.

"What is it? Have you had your fill of me?" His voice was soft and unguarded.

"Wuh-no! I..."

"What then?"

She looked at her bracelet. "Gio, I don't know if the baby is yours or Alphonso's."

"Oh." He didn't say anything for a beat. "I knew he was nuts about you, but I'd taken you for the kind of girl who wouldn't do that."

"You took wrong."

She was surprised when he'd laughed and said, "I didn't take wrong. You're a good girl and that baby's mine. I know it, and I know how I feel about you. I'm here until you and our baby are safe."

"You're not thinking of killing Cardinal Negrali are you?"

"It's not just Negrali. Those Alithiníans want our baby, so while they don't want to kill you, they'd kidnap you in a heartbeat."

"I feel like one of those Hollywood actresses with stalkers."

"I'll be keeping an eye on you. Let me know when you miss me."

"*Grazie*, and I do miss you. I...it's complicated."

"Not for me it isn't. Are you still sleeping with him?"

"No. I've been putting you both off."

"I don't like to be played with, so don't mess around."

"I won't," she'd said. As she disconnected the call, she felt like she'd made him a promise not to sleep with Alphonso, which she hadn't meant to make.

Now, as Zelph pulled into the palazzo's water garage, Alphonso asked her, "You're off to find Benny, right?"

"No. Can you come to my suite?"

A flicker of anticipation flashed across his face before he read her expression, and then it was gone. "*Certamente.*"

When they got to her private living area, she ignited the fire and joined him on the couch. "Alphonso, I'm not sure the baby is yours."

He looked crushed. "What?" His face fell and he shook his head in disappointment. "The don. I knew he wanted you, I just didn't think you'd succumb."

"I don't know what to say. I'm crazy about you, and you're sort of my best friend..."

"But you don't know if you love me?"

"I've been all messed up in the head. I even tried to get

my marriage annulled. I'd have lost my estate. I must have been in shock."

"Evasion...answer my question."

She looked at him, uncertain of what she should say, and feeling a bit resentful at having to defend her actions. She was, after all, a modern woman who didn't need to be married to have sex.

He said, "I don't doubt that you've been out of your mind. But I assumed none of this was you." He waved his hand around to indicate the palazzo. "I figured you'd come live with me, you'd keep running your shelter, and you'd fundraise like a normal person. Not be this power player you've become."

"I feel like I'm doing what I was born to do."

"Speaking of being born, I was born to parents who had no business getting pregnant. I was raised by my *nonna* and aunt. I don't want our child to be..." He seemed to be in terrible pain, and for such a big man, it was hard for her to witness.

"This baby would be raised by the Dour Doublet over my dead body."

"No, I know that. Well, I want to thank you for being honest with me. And I don't know what's going to happen between us, but these short months I've spent with you have been no ordinary time."

Just then her phone pinged with a text message from Marilynn:

URGENT! POSEIDON TESTS UNDERWAY
IN FRONT CANAL.

BOAT CAPTAINS FURIOUS IN TRAFFIC JAM.
WE SHOULD OFFER THEM GIFTS!
HOW MUCH CAN I SPEND?

Alphonso stood. "I know you're busy."

"What're you going to do now?"

"You're the mother of my child. Until you're safe, I'm going to stick by your side and try to keep the Catholics or Alithiníans from getting you."

She walked him to the door where Paloma, who looked transformed in a tailored suit, intercepted them. She had her hand-held device and the slick folio of paperwork that went everywhere with her now. "Elli, there you are. Can I get you to go over the staff picks? We're less than a month from opening and I'd like to notify our hires in the next day or so."

"Shoot," she said as Alphonso stood his ground at her side, clearly not wanting to leave their conversation as it was.

"Kate and I thought you'd want the same staff-to-woman ratio at the new shelter."

"*Sì*, that sounds right."

"And Signor Tosca just confirmed we can accommodate one hundred live-in residents."

"Correct."

"So, the only question is what kind of coverage you want to achieve with your personal household staff?"

"It'll just be you, me, perhaps Benny, and the baby living here. We don't need much staff," Raphielli replied. She felt Alphonso's interest pique with that statement.

"Dante has some suggestions," Paloma said.

"I defer to him. Come in, we can sit down at my desk." She waved Paloma past Alphonso and then stepped closer and hugged him.

He hugged her fiercely and whispered into her ear, "I'm hurting so bad right now, I can't tell you. But I love you and our child so much...let's not make any rash decisions." With a final squeeze, he let go of her and walked away.

She watched him disappear around the big fountain with the sick feeling that she'd experienced the last of his affection. For all his earthiness, he was a very pious man. Had it only been this fall when she laid in bed so desperate to have him visit her and reassure her while she communicated via notepad? Now he'd probably take a detective job and start going out a lot more. She focused on the tasks at hand.

Raphielli held up a finger to Paloma. "I need to send Marilynn a quick text about the traffic jam out front, then I'm all yours." She tapped away.

"Have you seen it? Poseidon's head is the size of a house. It rises out of the water, and the eyes move! They look real! And the tines of his trident come up, too!"

"*Sì*, I wish we could keep it, but it blocks traffic when it surfaces. Have you seen Benny anywhere?"

"Uh-huh. I passed her, the pope, and his security heading off for their usual worshipful splash-about in the temple I hear you guys whispering about."

Raphielli tensed. "What do you know about that?"

"Nothing, actually. Don't worry. I don't need to know everything. How're you feeling?"

"Great." She patted her spearmint patch. "Thanks to

professor Gina, no more nausea. And with a little luck, I won't start sprouting hair on my belly."

Paloma opened her folio and made a face. "Uh-well, that's good. Now let's get started. Miriam is our top candidate for head nanny at the new shelter, but Dante likes her for your baby's nanny here in the residence...your private nanny. She worked at an orphanage in Switzerland and the top administrator I spoke to couldn't say enough good things about her."

When they'd finished reviewing candidates, they went to find Dante, who was in the next wing. They retrieved their jackets from the cloakroom and went outside past the entertainment wing's entrance. Out of nowhere, a man latched onto Paloma's arm, causing her to juggle her device and folio.

"Milos!" She yelped. "Get away from me!"

"You fucking bitch, you'd better drop this lawsuit." He enunciated every word. "If you tell anybody that I hit you, I'll break every bone in your body, starting with your face."

"I'm telling my lawyer about this!" Paloma wrenched her arm away, and Raphielli threw her arms protectively around her as they pressed themselves against an outer wall of the palazzo.

"Paloma, are you hurt?" It was Gio's voice. Primo was suddenly leaning into Milos with a gun pressed to his neck. The Petrosinos had the brute sandwiched.

"I'm not hurt, he was just threatening me," she said.

"I heard." Gio's tone was ominous. "Milos, do you know me?"

Milos' eyes strained sideways to look at him. "*Sì*, Petrosino. You were on trial this summer."

"Paloma has become very dear to me, like a sister."

"Why the..."

"Stop talking. You make me angry when you talk. You need to listen. You're going to go to jail like a man. At your trial, you're going to own up to every single thing you did to Paloma. You're not going to try to defend yourself or intimidate her in any way. You listening?"

"But..."

"If you don't do what I say, I'll end you in a very ugly and painful fashion. A fitting end for a man who *stomped* his own woman and unborn child. If you want to find out what I have in mind, just shoot her a dirty look. You'll find out."

"Do my whole sentence?" Milos wheedled.

"You stay in jail as long as the judge wants you to. And when you come out, you move as far away from Paloma as you can manage. Relocate to the other side of the planet and stay there. *Capisce?*"

"*Sì, inteso.*"

Primo put his gun in his pocket and took one of Raphielli's arms while Gio took the other, scooped an arm around Paloma, and said, "Milos, go find your lawyer and plead guilty right now."

Milos walked away unsteadily.

Raphielli turned to Gio. God, he smelled good. "*Grazie.*"

"*Prego.* Now, where were you ladies off to?" he asked brightly.

"Heading over to the next wing to see Dante." Just then Raphielli's phone pinged and she looked down at the text from Kate:

DETECTIVE LAMPANI SUFFERED BRAIN ANEURYSM! HE'S IN HOSPITAL!

"Oh! *Dio mio!*" She showed them her phone screen. "I have to go to him! I have to get Benny! She's in the temple!"

"Primo, get Drea over here," Gio said. "Now, don't worry unnecessarily. Brains are tricky to diagnose, maybe he just dropped from exhaustion. Get Benny, throw a disguise on her, and we'll take you to the hospital."

Raphielli felt tears hot on her cheeks as she hurried back to her door. *My secrets have killed this good man. For months he's begged me to be honest, but I lied and lied. Come to think of it, I haven't even been truthful in confession for months now. Who have I become? A murderer!*

———————◈———————

Mateo had spent the last hour making the case to Noah that the Veronas needed to die so that the Catholic church could implode. It was God's will that Noah's sterling reputation had gotten him hired by them. The conversation had been going well until Noah stood up and said, "I've got to leave now if I'm going to be on time for my shift. I'm absolutely clear that the Veronas are devout Catholics and that Salvio, God rest his soul, saw them as a threat, but I won't do anything to harm them. If you need to know their location or something, I'll tell you. But that's as far as I'll go."

Now Mateo sat in his kitchen thinking about his next step. Doctor G had been found murdered, and something terrible must have happened to Benjamin. He didn't want to be on his own, but after striking out with Noah, it was time to reprioritize. He couldn't do it all. He'd have to postpone the plan to kill the Veronas and focus solely on getting Salvio's children.

He felt in his bones that Benedetta must be pregnant, and while he didn't know where she was, he felt certain that Raphielli did. It only made sense. The girl wasn't at the shelter, but of course, two women who were bearing special children would band together. He had to get his hands on Raphielli and make her tell him where Benedetta was.

All of Venice was abuzz with conjecture about the season's final Carnevale ball, which was Raphielli's debut as a party-throwing hostess on what was rumored to be an epic scale. He'd heard that the mayor's wife, Elene Buonocore, was responsible for the invitations. He'd served with Elene on the Water Preservation Society's board for more than five years, and while they only socialized when that society came together, she was always very friendly with him, pleasantly flirtatious. He grabbed his phone and called her.

"Mateo! How are you, dear?" She sounded pleased to hear from him. "Congratulations on getting the MOSE project hearings televised."

"Oh, you know, the more the public knows about saving the lagoon, the greater the pressure to prevail."

"I agree. What can I do for you, dear?"

"I heard a rumor that you're helping Raphielli Scortini with her ball."

"Just helping with the guest list. I do what I can. She doesn't know many people, but I'm about to change that. I'm filling her party with fun new friends."

"I'm fun."

"That you are! I was short on eligible bachelors. Consider your invitation in the mail. It'll be coming with a costume, so be sure to wear it. Ooh! I'm so glad you're coming. You must save a dance for me. Remember our Society's party at that Moroccan place?"

"Are you going to belly dance again?"

"*Attempt* to belly dance," she said, and then giggled delightedly.

"Raphielli is a big deal now. Will the other big family be attending?"

"The Veronas? Juliette RSVP'd, and if Vincenzo and Giselle are in town they'll come, I'm sure. They can always be counted on to make a splash."

His heart hammered at the thought of getting a crack at Giselle, but he forced himself to stay focused on Raphielli. "What can you tell me about the ball?"

"It's a masked affair. The party planner is Marilynn Bergoni, and it's going to be a spectacle inside a big theatre in a wing with its own entrance, so guests won't get to set foot inside Raphielli's private home. The venue has lots of levels all stacked, so like a good nightclub you'll be able to move around to find the action. Um, what else? It's a Poseidon theme with fireworks and a DJ from Sri Lanka. Um, let's see…great food, and a big ship just docked in the lagoon to unload plenty of liquor for the party. Oh! That's my other line, must jump. See you at the ball, dear."

"Can I bring a boat?"

"No mooring anywhere near Scortini Palazzo during the ball, they have too much going on. And she's got something against *carri di carnevale*, so no show boats. Absolutely refused to consider them. *Ciao.*"

Mateo decided to keep it simple. He didn't dare try to smuggle a bottle of chloroform into the ball, so he'd have to improvise, maybe a presoaked cloth in a zip bag. As for the Veronas, he hated to miss an opportunity, and he had some poison he could slip into one of the Veronas' drinks, but only if an opportunity arose that was so foolproof he couldn't pass it up. He'd be on the lookout for Giselle.

But perfect opportunity aside, he wasn't leaving that ball without Raphielli. He'd get her out to the Verona's boat—they were always the exception to any rule—there was no way the first family would be forced to walk. Everywhere mooring was forbidden, the Veronas were welcome to dock. Noah would be waiting in their boat, and while he drew the line at harming a Verona, Mateo felt sure he could get him to borrow their boat for something as important as getting one of the Madonnas of Sinope back to the safe house. Mateo would make Raphielli tell him where Benedetta was, and if it came to it, trade Raphielli for Benedetta. Then he'd take the girl to Nautilus Island.

———⊙———

Hiero was sitting at his desk when a light on the secure relay switchboard next to his desk started blinking. He hoped it was one of the operatives he'd sent to France calling to report that their job was complete. Picking up the phone he said, "Cellular service, what is your account number?"

"Sixty-eight eleven seventy-one, N as in *nada.*"

It was Negrali calling on a secure line. Karno's voice changed to his usual flat delivery. "*Pronto.*"

"I want you to tell me that you'll be here to kill the Veronas and Raphielli tonight!"

"Where are my paintings?"

"I stashed them in my apartment in Rome. They're safe. You need to move now! Everything is going sideways! And to make matters worse, the entire Veneto is anonymous! They're all wearing masks!"

"We don't do anything in a rush, and masks don't affect our operations. I've succeeded in getting men inside both the Veronas' and Raphielli's palazzos. They'll strike when they can get away with it, and not before. They've got another device to blow up a Verona or two in their boat. If they can do it during Raphielli's ball tomorrow night they will, but otherwise they can strike when the Veronas and Raphielli are asleep. Now bring me my paintings," he said and hung up on the pompous ass. The nerve of him, holding those paintings just out of Hiero's grasp and yelling, "Kill! Kill!" like he was a trained attack dog. Negrali was going to be a nightmare as pope.

Luigi opened his eyes and looked around a strange hospital room. The digital clock on the wall of his private room said four o'clock PM. He recalled an explosion had gone off in his head. It felt like being hit with a shotgun blast, and then everything went black. Right now, he didn't feel any pain and felt miraculously well-rested.

Someone was holding his hand and he looked sideways. Benny and Raphielli were kneeling at the side of his bed. Benny was praying, barely recognizable in a disguise, and Raphielli was whispering fervently with her hands clasped and her eyes closed.

"I didn't mean to kill you. Please forgive me. I never meant to cause you so much stress. *Dio*, please don't let him die. I'll tell him everything if you save this good man."

"*Grazie*," he croaked, his mouth parched. "Start talking."

Raphielli jumped up, her face smeared with tears, and threw herself across him in a hug. "*Grazie a Dio!* Where do I start? Um, I believe Salvio killed Reynaldo, and uh..." she stammered as Benny pushed Raphielli off him, placed a glass of water in his hand, and pressed a button on the hospital bed to raise his upper body into a sitting position.

"Forget the stuff I know. Who killed Salvio?" he said and took a sip.

"Gio...Giancarlo Petrosino...who also may be the father of my baby...I'm pregnant."

He didn't like the sound of that. "Woo-ho-kay."

"Gio was trying to keep Salvio from killing me. He kidnapped him and held him in Palermo."

"Salvio didn't go on a religious quest?"

"No."

"Uh-huh," he said. "Then Salvio came back, hung you, went on his first rampage, and Lydia was helping him?"

"I don't know anything about that." She looked desperate.

"No, it wasn't like that," Benny spoke up.

They both looked at Benny. "We were waiting for a

Scortini to lead us against the Vatican, but peaceful, like always. It wasn't until you brought Salvio to the hospital a few weeks after that rampage that some people in our church—my parents, Ben, Carlos, Matt, Rajim, and Lydia—went off the deep end. They started helping him, and Lydia got herself moved to your department to keep an eye on you. Monitor the case you had against Salvio."

Luigi looked back at Raphielli. "What was going on at your home the night Salvio was shot? You were lying to me."

"Salvio had found us in the Scortini temple and escaped through this suction valve..."

"The *scivolo*," Benny said helpfully.

"But the temple is a secret."

"Why?" he asked.

Benny was holding his shoulder. "I'm an Alithinían, and the Vatican has been hunting us. We worship in secret. Please don't tell anyone."

"You worship Salvio?"

"No, we follow the teachings of Jesus. We worship God. But the pope is no longer against us, he's been worshipping with me every day in the Scortini Temple."

"You're Christians, eh? What's the deal with your shiny black shoes?"

"It reminds us of standing in water."

"Like baptism?"

"Very much like that."

He turned to Raphielli. "Is your Cardinal Negrali happy about the pope's change of heart?"

"He doesn't know. He hates the Alithiníans. Cardinal Negrali has attached himself to me—trying to get my estate. I think he'd like to get me out of the way."

"*Salvio* sure wanted you out of the way. And his hit men, Rajim and the rest, they certainly had orders to either kill anyone necessary while kidnapping you, or kill you themselves."

"They killed enough of my staff trying," Raphielli said.

He set his water aside. "Salvio smashed Vincenzo's head in, killed Gabrieli, and they were looking to kill Giselle, too. Where do the Veronas come in? And what about Nejla? Why'd she go to Maine?"

Benny leaned forward almost frantic. "Veronas can influence people, their family is born to support the pope and, uh, fix things for the Catholics within the Vatican and...everywhere. Ben and his brother Bernardo want Vincenzo's child dead, so they're hunting Giselle. But now a girl named Gina is carrying Vincenzo's child. They'll hunt her if they find out. And please don't go after Nejla, she's the repository for our holy tradition. If she went to Maine, she went there to hide from the Catholic death squad."

"Repository?"

"The Alithinían religion has never written anything down," Raphielli enthused. "So, no documents could be found and used against them by Catholics. The orators pass down and memorize the words spoken by Paul, and even Jesus' words as told by the disciples who were there!"

"Nejla is very special," Benny said desperately.

"What's special about the Scortinis?"

"Their bloodline came from Paul."

"Paul who?"

"The Apostle Paul."

His mouth dropped open and he stared at Benny in shock. "You're carrying a child descended from the Apostle Paul?"

She beamed. "That I am." Then her face darkened. "It was a horrible process, but I am."

"So simple. A holy war. Catholics attempting to wipe out Salvio's people..."

"The Alitinínían Church. For centuries," Raphielli clarified.

"And Salvio's people...the Alitinínían are trying to..."

"Topple the Vatican, and it's the Veronas who have helped the Vatican survive," Benny chimed in.

"What's the motive? Greed? Power?" he asked.

Benny looked offended. "Not for us. My people have been hunted and murdered almost to extinction by people who are trying to overpopulate the planet. We just want to survive."

Raphielli looked disgusted. "I was raised Catholic, but the Church has a terrible history."

"Power. Oldest motive in the book," he said.

Gladys came through the door with *panini* and sodas and ran to him. "Luigi! Oh, honey! The doctors didn't know...if you'd wake up!" She stashed everything on a table and kissed him all over his face. "Let me get the doctors!"

"Wait, *per favore*," Raphielli said as she dragged Benedetta forward. "I have to tell him some very important things."

He tried to hug his wife and discovered his other hand had tubes in it. "Gladys, give us a minute, okay?"

She nodded and stepped out, pulling the door closed. But she stood staring through the glass window at him.

"There are no new motives," Raphielli continued. "Man just repeats mistakes the old teachers warned us against. While the world has changed dramatically where technology is concerned, mankind hasn't changed since the beginning. Even Socrates, four hundred years before Christ, tried to get people to stop power-grabbing in the name of the gods and pursuing wealth for wealth's sake."

Luigi groaned. "Religions trying to prevent children from being born, it's so biblical. Am I still unconscious?"

"You're not dreaming, and people do away with children who have special birthrights all the time. Especially in royal families."

He had a terrible thought. "Benny, no one in your church knows about your baby, do they?"

"No, I don't think so, but they made sure Salvio was on me at least once a day while he had the chance. I'm certain my church *thinks* I'm pregnant."

"Ah, I recall hearing them say maybe you'd been stolen. By who? Catholics?"

"If I hadn't run off, that'd be the other option they'd consider."

Raphielli interrupted. "I had an Alitininían doctor for a minute, and he absolutely thought I was carrying Salvio's baby."

Luigi was grateful they'd added their missing pieces to his puzzle, but what a fucking picture! "I was so close to getting this, but there's no way I'd have believed it. And I figured you for Alphonso's girl. Does he know about Petrosino?"

She looked embarrassed. "*Sì*."

Gladys opened the door. "The doctor's coming."

"So, I'm coming to your ball tomorrow night. I highly doubt anyone is audacious enough to try something with a palazzo full of witnesses, but if so, I need to see who's trying to kill who."

"We'll all be masked. They won't be able to see who's who."

"I'll be there just in case."

"I'll put you on my private guest list if you're up to it."

"I feel great, and I've got a good mask I haven't used all season."

"We'll have dressing areas where you can pick up a hat or morning coat, anything you need."

"Benny, are you going?" he asked.

"Nope, sounds creepy. Uh...well...sexy, and Salvio put me off sex. Not my thing."

Raphielli asked, "You're not going to arrest Gio are you?"

"For locking up Salvio and then killing him while he was on a rampage? No. I'll pretend I'm still in the dark on that one."

Just then the doctor and a nurse came in and asked the girls to leave so as not to tire Luigi out.

"Doc, they just helped me more than you could ever know. I feel good."

"Glad to hear it. But after your cerebral event, I'd still like them to leave."

"What was it?"

"We have no idea. We're just calling it an event."

On her way out, Benny pointed to a big basket in the corner. "Luigi, that's your Christmas present from me. It's filled with every coffee candy imaginable."

He was touched.

"It's late because I had to special order most of it, and some of the packages didn't arrive until yesterday. They don't make Pocket Coffee anymore, but I found one called Espresso-Filled Dark Chocolate."

So, while they checked his vitals, he had time to chew on the confessions and he got Gladys to give him an espresso-filled dark chocolate. It hit the spot. He felt reborn. The Scortini mystery had been a festering splinter in his brain. No wonder he'd had a cerebral event!

Tomorrow night was Raphielli's ball and the biggest party as Carnevale ended. He wondered what would happen there. Did the Catholics know Benny was carrying Salvio's child? If so, she was in danger. Was Raphielli in danger from them? He had a feeling that storm fronts were about to collide that could change the landscape of world religion.

14

Raphielli was becoming frustrated with the logistics of safety. Getting around was becoming more of a hassle the longer this siege went on. Zelph and Alphonso were either at her side as transportation and protection, or she was stuck cowering somewhere "safe" while she called to summon them. *Dio mio!* She recalled Giselle once saying she'd met Markus in the Metro because she hadn't wanted to call for her driver. Now Raphielli could relate. She just wanted an independent life.

When the doctors shooed her and Benny out of Luigi's hospital room, Raphielli just wanted to go home, so she signaled for Benny to follow her. Obediently, Benny pulled the scarf up to her nose and pulled her long coat's hood down over the whole disguise. Then she followed Raphielli wordlessly out of the hospital and to the public *vaporetto* pier where they jumped onto the water bus and were noticed by exactly nobody.

When Raphielli had her safely back at the palazzo, Dante took her coat saying, "Your friends from France have arrived." Benny excused herself to take a nap saying she'd meet them later.

"Who made it?" Raphielli felt her mood lift.

"Carolette, Fauve, Henri, Laetitia, Robert, Auguste, Fabrice, Selma, and Solange."

"Great, pretty much the whole gang."

"I've settled them in rooms just here." He indicated the nearest staircase leading to old family bedrooms. "Ava arrived with her team. I gave them three rooms for dress fittings, accessories, and alterations. That is in addition to the costume rooms adjacent to the ball space where guests will have costumes altered during the party if necessary. They arrived with an entire department store of clothing. The freight boat just left."

"*Grazie.*"

"Marilynn Bergoni has been sending food for the Carnevale performers and crew, quite delicious, and she has provided overly generous portions for the household as well. I have never seen such bounty. Also, His Holiness is here meeting with Ghost and Mister Fox. He wants to borrow their services immediately after the ball."

"What for?"

"To take them to Rome for his Ash Wednesday sermon."

"Of course, anything he needs."

"They'll fly via helicopter with His Holiness and Vincenzo."

"If he needs audio and visual assistance, he's welcome to them."

Just then, Carolette came gliding down the staircase looking like something on a naughty 1920s Berlin cabaret poster. She seemed naked except for cascades of pearls that swayed and shimmied as she moved. "Elli! Hell of a place you have. So dark. Anyway, guess who I am?"

"You're not wearing a mask. I can see it's you, Carolette."

"I'm Poseidon's consort Amphitrite!"

"And the lovely Hestia..." She beckoned the beauty with the jeweled mask and headpiece who was carefully descending behind her. "Poseidon's sister is Paloma."

Paloma was grinning, but her mouth was all Raphielli could see beneath the mask. Her costume provided more coverage and fell in shimmery folds.

"The boys are all wearing capes and *baùtta* masks with big hats, so you can't tell one from another. The *baùttas* are a big hit because they can eat and kiss with them on."

The doorbell shrilled and Dante answered it. Cardinal Negrali bellowed, "I must speak to Raphielli! I cannot be put off!"

"Let him in," she said. The cardinal pounced around Dante like an angry cat, stopping next to her at the foot of the stairs.

"There you are! I've been looking for you everywhere! We need to talk." He lost his train of thought as he goggled Carolette's peek-a-boo pearls. Recovering himself he said, "In private."

"I don't have time for this," she said flatly. "I'm exhausted and have too much to do in preparation for my ball."

"You need confession." He stared at her hard.

"Nope, freshly confessed," she stifled a yawn.

"*I* am your father confessor, and in this time of upheaval in the Church, I'm warning you, you need to align yourself with me. The current pope has been found out for the brutal despot he is, and you'll regret distancing yourself from me."

"Do you regret stealing my paintings?"

"I did no such thing!" His voice went up an octave.

"The Carivaggios you had your eye on are gone."

"I'm not surprised. They were the most valuable items in that room and easily portable. Anyone could see that, even those long-haired fellows who are always hanging around you."

"I'm too tired for this little charade, I have a big charade to get ready for. Now if you'll excuse me, I'm late for my fitting."

"You're not going to just sprinkle on some pearls, are you?" he spat.

"If that's my costume, I hope they're bigger pearls." She found herself chuckling but gave Carolette a worried look.

"No, you're going as the golden sunrise," Carolette said as she turned to help Paloma back up the stairs. "Other than a plunging neck and back, you're fully covered."

With that, Dante showed Negrali out. Looking on, Raphielli saw the almost imperceptible air of satisfaction with which her old butler gave the mighty cleric the heave-ho. She then turned and followed her friends up the stairs to where she could hear Fauve and the others laughing and singing to music. What a different place this was with lively people in it.

"Paloma, you are stunning," she said, and her friend turned slowly so as not to dislodge the elaborate headpiece.

"*Grazie.*" Her smile got bigger, and up close Raphielli noticed a chipped tooth. Must be from one of Milos' beatings. They'd make her a dental appointment to get that fixed.

Half an hour later, all her friends were dressed as Poseidon's court, and Raphielli was the sun. Her mask was magnificent with flame-colored feathers floating upward from her cheekbones around her eyes like rays of the sun. Her golden costume was glorious, but the amount of dress tape that held the plunging front and back to her body made her uncomfortable. She pictured sneezing and both of her boobs tumbling out, or her back fat causing the whole back to open up and show her bottom.

"Ava, I look like a fat goldfish. Why can't I wear that one?" Raphielli pointed to a stunning costume that was all shimmering neon shades of greens and black with wings. "The dark flying fish. It looks so flowy and easy to move in."

"The neon tetra was my second choice for you, but the sunrise is so perfect, I have to insist, Elli. You're the glory of the heavens."

I don't want to look like a slutty goldfish. I'd rather be a fighting fish who can breathe without a boob popping out. But she didn't want to be ungrateful for all Ava had done, so she nodded. "I'm just tired, I could use a nap," she said while stepping behind a curtain to let Ava's team help her out of her dress.

"Will your new roomie, Benny, be attending?"

"I invited her, but she said she didn't want to see old people in drag getting their freak on and would prefer staying on this side of the palace." She pulled on her clothes.

"But she'll miss the fireworks and the big show out front."

"I told her that, too, but apparently she's already seen Poseidon's head going up and down, and fireworks aren't her thing. Now if you'll excuse me, you all party on. I'm going to go nap beside her."

"We'll send some of this food to your suite," Ava said.

Raphielli waved at her crazy friends through the open door of the sewing room and wished she had the energy to keep up with them.

They called, "Rest up! We're going out to dinner tonight! We've taken over al Covo. Very cozy, we'll have a blast!"

———※———

Casimir Vaskovsky aka Pope Leopold XIV was ready to make the speech of his life. Tomorrow at sunrise, he would step out onto his balcony high above Saint Peter's Square and give his message for Lent. He had come to see the Vatican as a dysfunctional nest of vipers. He had prayed about the decision he had to make and had been led to spend his energy empowering the world's youth. Now he had everything in place, but he needed to make sure tomorrow's speech was heard even when they tried to silence him.

He left the underwater temple, and after getting dressed, he asked Raphielli's maid to take him to her. When he entered the modern pristine feminine space of her suite, she and Benny were just waking from a nap.

"How is the detective?" he asked.

"We don't know. He looked good."

"*Bene, bene.* I have come to ask you to loan me some staff."

"Dante told me. Anyone you need, you're welcome to. But what could you possibly need with Ghost and Mister Fox?"

"Powerful people at the Vatican will want to silence my message, and I need a backup plan with people I trust."

"You're not in danger, are you? They won't try to silence *you*, will they?"

"Being the pope is to have a target on one's back. They have tried—and many would say, successfully—to ruin my reputation. Tomorrow, they may try to kill me. I have taken steps to prevent it, but I will not let fear stand in my way. After your ball, at sunrise, watch my speech on your phone, *per favore.*"

"Why on my phone?"

"Because I expect some interference with the television feed. My new team will stream me live."

"I'll watch on my phone. May God be with you, *Sua Santità.*"

"And also with you."

He kissed both her and Benny on the forehead before leaving.

Gina sat with Ivar and Leonardo as Juliette and Vincenzo showed off their costumes.

"Those are not real jewels, are they?" Ivar asked.

"Goodness no! There is one thing for certain at a Carnevale ball, I will be kissed and petted. If a sapphire should come away in a stranger's hand, better it be glass."

Gina thought Vincenzo looked dashing in his dark blue morning coat and top hat. His full-faced mask of white material had intricately painted designs around the eyes and a glitter blue stripe down the center of the mask's full lips as if someone with paint on a finger had tried to silence him.

"Guess you won't be kissing anyone with your full mask," Gina said.

"No," he said from under the material. "The only person I care to kiss will be here keeping you and Ivar company."

Leonardo smiled and waved a hand in embarrassment.

"Are you both wearing kohl makeup around your eyes?" Ivar asked.

"Of course. One cannot wear a mask with a naked eye," Juliette said.

Juliette's elaborate painted mask covered three-quarters of her face, and over her mouth was a fetching swath of blue lace, somewhere between a demure shield and a kinky gag that she was able to speak through. "I find a full mask too hot, and I intend to dance. Marilynn tells me the music will be captivating. What will you three be doing?"

Gina said, "We'll have a relaxing evening. But His Holiness made me promise I'd watch his sunrise speech, so if I fall asleep, wake me up as you two return home."

"Oh, we'll be home before sunrise, "Vincenzo said firmly. "Balls tend to have their finales around two o'clock."

"But this is Raphielli's first ball," Ivar said. "And rumor has it she is breaking all the rules."

———— ⸙ ————

Giselle sat in the abbey's reading room, trying to make herself cozy in one of the gothic stalls that must have been state of the art back when they were built. The bench seats were worn smooth by hundreds of years of bottoms sheathed in rough wool, and vents within each foot compartment piped warm air from the basement furnace. But her book couldn't hold her attention. She wanted to be in Venice with all her friends at Raphielli's masquerade ball.

Now that they had Spratman and two Catholic hit men safely in custody, Giselle was convinced the danger had passed and she'd lobbied hard to be able to leave Abbaye d'Orval. But everyone she'd tried to convince had given her the same firm reply. "Absolutely not! You've gotten a few hit men out of the way, but we're more convinced than ever that the conspiracy which drove one or more people to hire them is still in motion. Stay put!"

She'd tried Vincenzo, Juliette, even Leonardo and Ivar but she felt they were all a bit jumpy since the unfortunate mishaps on their boats. Maybe they didn't notice the frequency of boat mishaps in the Venetian islands, but in her opinion as an outsider, boats had frightening calamities all the time. *Give me a horse any day,* she thought as she flicked back a page and began the chapter for the third time. She hadn't retained a single word she'd read in the last half hour.

Her phone buzzed and she felt a wave of gratitude for the superior cell access as she looked at the photos coming through from Fauve.

There was Ava looking happier than Giselle had ever seen her, surrounded with glittery costumes and boxes of enormous feathers, and sipping from a glass of champagne. Next to her stood Carolette holding the bottle and wearing only what appeared to be silvery bubbles. *Ooh! That daring darling is wearing nothing but pearls!* The next photo was Fauve in shimmery blue swirls of chiffon and sprays of green and gold coming off her shoulders. Either she had lost all her inhibitions, or the swirls were adhered to some delicious body stocking because she was almost as naked as Carolette as she perched happily on Auguste and Robert's shoulders. They looked like male models in their suits. They were grinning at something off camera and their three-quarter *baùtta* masks dangled from strings around their necks.

The next photo was of women in full face masks but two of them were immediately recognizable by their figures. Laetitia's outrageously long limbs and torso were encased in reddish nylon with a cutaway dress in the shape of a shell, and her red squid mask swept upward in delicate tentacles. Next to her had to be Raphielli looking like a golden goddess that belonged on the top of a casino in

Monte Carlo. Her gown left nothing to the imagination and her figure was sheer gilded decadence with a neckline that plunged far enough to make it clear that those youthful boobs of hers should be on the cover of every men's magazine for the next hundred years. *Move over Marilyn Monroe!* Elli's face was hidden beneath feathers in a gradient of flame colors, and the result was so brilliant that Giselle could see why Ava looked so happy. This was another level for her career.

Soon this'll all be over. And the moment I get the all clear, Marcus, Yvania, and I will hop into The Tank, drive straight back to Gernelle, and throw the biggest party our château has ever seen. Then they can all whoop it up at our place!

She set her phone aside, licked her thumb, flicked the same page back, and started her chapter over in the perfect quiet of the deserted reading room.

———— ••• ————

Karno was sitting in his office when the secure line rang and Negrali rattled off his verification code.

"What's up?" he asked the next pope.

"You don't sound desperate! Why not?" Negrali demanded.

"Everything's in place."

"The Verona's keep surviving their boat accidents."

"Not a problem. No one suspects anything, boats have issues all the time. It's not like the Veronas are going to stop using the waterways and start walking everywhere in Venice. I have a man who'll plant another type of device on their craft while it's docked at Raphielli's ball. It'll be foolproof. The propeller turns and *boom*. Not just a fire, total oblivion."

"It won't be easy. You should see the Scortini palazzo. The party director has security everywhere and more coming by the minute."

"I'm not worried. My men tell me she's got an army of people coming and going with food deliveries and flowers."

"Your men?"

"*Sì*. The party director hired a security company, and that company needed more men for this job. They subbed one of my men over in the wing where Raphielli lives. He'll be taking over when the butler retires at midnight."

"Do you have anyone who can get me into the party?"

"What am I, a doorman? Figure your own way in. I thought you'd ingratiated yourself into Venice society. Hang on some influential arm or charm the mayor's wife. My men say Elene Buonocore invited the movers and shakers because Signora Scortini doesn't know anyone but battered women."

"Fine, I'll get myself in. A plan just came to mind."

"You're filled with plans for an old man."

"You don't know the half of it. Tomorrow after you take care of Leopold, I'm coming back here and claiming Peter's throne as my first plan of business."

"Here, meaning?"

"Venice, where I am now. I'm going to have it removed from Basilica di San Pietro di Castello, ship it up to Rome, and when Leopold is out of the way, I'll rule from it!"

"What's Peter's throne been doing in the Castello of Venice all this time?"

"What indeed!" Negrali snorted.

"Anyway, I have more good news," Hiero said. "The Verona residence will be momentarily vulnerable when the Pope and Vincenzo leave for Rome early tomorrow morning. Two of my men have a plan to get inside in those wee hours of Ash Wednesday before sunrise. They'll get Juliette in her sleep."

"At sunrise the boy scout leader, I mean, pope, will be delivering another scintillating speech about conservation and pollution. We have a plan to take care of him when he comes off the balcony into his residence," Negrali bragged.

"Uh-huh, that should be interesting," Hiero said and hung up on the maniac.

15

Her ball was in full swing when Raphielli and her friends made their entrance into the party wing. The theatre space was a perfect square of four balconied floors with two stairways on each floor climbing to the next level all the way up to a fifth-floor perch with a knee-high balustrade. The main stage was on the second level where tumblers in alluring neon leotards were performing. A light show kept colors chasing through the air on fiber-optic wires while the lighting in the whole party space kept changing from bright to dim. One moment the place was sparkling and vivid with flashing colored lights bouncing off fractal screens, and the next the whole space was moody, shadowy, and darkly romantic. Music was booming on the ground floor but became quieter the higher one climbed.

Marilynn took Raphielli by the hand and led her on a tour of the space, climbing the levels, making brief intro- ductions, giving people the opportunity to thank her for inviting them, gush over their gifted costumes, and exclaim over the golden sheath and headpiece she was wearing. As the golden sunrise, she stood out because Ava had made sure no one else wore gold.

To Raphielli's horror, she recognized Donatella, Alphonso's friend, the mistress, her face easily recognizable with a skimpy lace mask not really covering her orange features and the same fake lashes she'd been wearing that morning after the murders. Elene was at her side, and Donatella extended her hand.

"So nice of you to invite me." She eyed Raphielli's glued-on dress and leaned forward to snark, "I see how you got Alphonso, with goods like that on display."

Raphielli suddenly felt cheap and ridiculous. She wanted to turn and run back down the stairs, but Marilynn continued to usher her upward.

On the darker fourth floor, they passed an enormous pit of pillows that some people were busy rolling around in...with purpose. Ugh, having sex right here...sort of in front of other people? They continued climbing to the fifth-floor perch at the top of the space, where Marilynn handed her a microphone and spotlights found her. She remembered Juliette's advice. "Establish yourself as the great woman you are. Think of yourself as the Unsinkable Molly Brown throwing her first party for Denver society."

The music stopped as Raphielli stepped to the edge of the perch and spoke into the microphone. "Welcome to Casa Scortini. Tonight, we celebrate Poseidon and the glory of our Venetian waterways. It's the last night of Carnevale, and tomorrow is Lent, so enjoy yourselves to the fullest. *Facciamo festa!*" Everyone whistled and clapped and stomped their feet enthusiastically.

Raphielli handed off the microphone as the music kicked into high gear, and out of nowhere performers tumbled through the air in front of her in the middle of the space on rings and clinging to silks. Instead of pressing the flesh with guests on the way downstairs, she evasively ducked in and out of people. It was easy to get lost in the crowd with everyone looking at the performers. She stormed into the dressing room and started stripping the dress off her body. An assistant hurried forward to help her with the feathered headpiece. "I want to wear the fighting fish," Raphielli declared.

The team flew into action and had her in the flowy tetra costume in a flash. The swirling Pisces three-quarter mask was in place, and as she turned to go, she bumped into several women entering the dressing room. Donatella was one of them but this time the hussy didn't recognize her. "I need help to cinch my dress tighter," she whined to an assistant. Then she and the other women started pawing the racks of extra clothing like they were at a sale.

Raphielli slipped out to the dance floor where she found Carolette, resplendent in her ropes of pearls, dancing with Zelph, who wore an heirloom Scortini mask he'd coveted from the *baùtta* room in her home. Paloma was swaying gracefully amidst a group of people who had abandoned themselves to the music. As the lights dimmed, Raphielli had nothing more to do than to enjoy the fruits of so much production. She felt her shoulders loosen and she began to move. Song after song kept them dancing and everyone lost their inhibitions. Raphielli felt young and bold. She was anonymous even from her friends in this new costume. Bodies glided past her, some closer than others.

At one point, as the lights went to almost total black, she smelled Gio and felt fingers on the back of her neck. He pulled her in for a kiss that melted her completely, and she threw her arms around him, offering her body through the filmy material. They swayed, mashing and grinding together and she offered her tongue for erotic kisses. As he cupped her breasts and grazed his teeth along her neck, she threw her head back and clung to him. Everyone around them was an anonymous throng of beautiful masks and peek-a-boo flesh. As the silver pins of light strung across the space started to pulse and grow brighter, he was gone.

Raphielli ate, drank, watched show after show, and danced all night. Around one in the morning a trapeze act began way up toward the ceiling, and everyone's eyes were glued to the death-defying leaps of the three acrobats flying high above the black stone floor. As Raphielli's eyes followed the action, a flash of gold on the fifth-floor perch caught her eye. *Someone's wearing my discarded sunrise costume!*

She was miffed as she watched the woman step over to the low railing. In the next instant, a man in a plague doctor's mask appeared behind her and shoved her over the balustrade into the void! Instead of plunging to her death, she was caught by the lighting web and bounced just a few feet down onto the fourth-floor passion pit of pillows as neatly as if the webbing were a safety net. None of the busy people in the pit noticed.

A woman standing next to Raphielli caught the flash of falling gold out of the corner of her eye and clapped absent-mindedly without looking, then went on watching the trapeze over the other side of the party. Raphielli watched in horror as the man in the plague doctor's mask got into a tussle with a man whose hat was knocked off revealing a shiny bald head. The bald man deliberately shoved the plague doctor off the perch. He didn't catch on anything, but fell five floors straight down, landing in the shadows near the performer's backstage area. The party's safety team rushed over and slid him back-stage. No one noticed the man fall because an erotic peep show of dancers had begun undulating inside fish tanks on the main second-floor stage.

Looking back up, Raphielli saw the bald man had made it to the stairs where he was now fighting with a man in a painted red and silver mask. She darted past people and raced up the stairs toward them.

When she got close to the fight she heard someone say, "Take it outside, you two macho assholes."

The man in the red and silver mask took a punch to the face that split his mask. He tumbled down a couple of stairs, losing his mask along the way. It was Luigi Lampani, and there was blood on his face. She ran to him. "Don't move! Have you broken anything?"

His eyes widened as he recognized her voice. "I'm fine, just bloodied my nose. I thought he'd killed you!"

"Who?" she asked.

"Stay here, Elli!" Primo said in her ear, and he ran after the bald man who was making his way down the far staircase.

"I don't know, some guy in a plague doctor's mask," Luigi said as she helped him to his feet. "But the bald guy threw him over."

She felt Alphonso's arms close around her.

Luigi's hands went to his face and he said, "It's kinda refreshing to have a completely different pain in my head."

Alphonso ushered them to the next staircase, and they made their way past people having sex in the darkened recesses of the stairs. No wonder Benny wasn't up for this.

The lights began to flicker and then the house lights came on. The party was over. A deep horn sounded, and all the fractal screens flashed a message.

CLAIM A CAPE AND PROCEED TO THE CANAL
FOR POSEIDON'S ARRIVAL

Doors opened to the outside *calles*, and Marilynn's staff stood at each exit handing out a final gift from Raphielli: dark green capes to keep the guests warm while they watched the fireworks and the big god's head rise from the deep. Alphonso kept a tight grip on Raphielli as they moved along with the crowd.

"How did you know it was me under this new mask?" she asked him.

"I'd know your body and the way you move anywhere. It seems Primo figured it out, too." Alphonso's voice was unemotional.

"I have to see who tried to kill me," she said and pointed to where her attempted murderer had landed.

They followed Luigi to the backstage area where the

performers' safety team had covered the body with a white sheet. "He's dead," the safety captain said. "We called the police. They'll be here soon."

Blood was seeping through the sheet from the man's head and trunk area, and the plague doctor's mask lay on the floor. She lunged forward and pulled back the sheet. Cardinal Negrali's dead eyes stared up at her, and the back of his head was gone.

Who was the bald man who'd shoved Negrali off the perch?

———⟨●⟩———

Paloma had never had so much fun. Rich people were crazy! This party was total decadence. In the past, she'd only ever attended lame Carnevale parties where people in bad costumes tried to solve half-assed murder mysteries and everyone ended up drunk. This ball was magical! She'd danced, or mostly swayed and shimmied because her hip was still messed up, and at one point, someone came up behind her and trailed the softest kisses along her shoulder and neck. They didn't grope her or anything, and she'd never been kissed like that before. It was a great night of gorgeous mostly-naked bodies performing super-human feats. Even the fight on the stairs looked like something out of Phantom of the Opera. Maybe it was a performance, who could tell?

When the lights came up the Frenchies found her and started dragging her along. "Come, get a cape! We don't want to miss the big finale! We'll see the fireworks before Poseidon's head comes out of the water!"

"I'm coming," Paloma said.

Carolette had love bites on her shoulders and Zelph was attached to her at the hip. "We've been invited to an enormous yacht for sunrise breakfast. You're coming, right?"

"How're you getting to a yacht?"

"It's some member of some royal family. They have a *carri di carnevale* somewhere. We'll party our way out to the lagoon where their yacht is moored," Fauve said.

"No, my hip's killing me, I'm wiped out. I'll go back to the home wing and keep Benny company. Where's Raphielli?"

"Mixing with all her new society friends. She's got to mingle, she's the hostess."

Once outside in the dark, Paloma snuggled down in her cape and the crowd clustered together as showers of golden fireworks started appearing over the palazzo, dazzling embers raining down weightlessly like stars falling. Then ominous music swelled from speakers that sounded like a giant was blowing a ram's horn, and spotlights started searching the water. Bigger and brighter fireworks launched from barges on either side of the palazzo, the explosions became more dramatic, and the music got louder as Poseidon's crown became visible under the green water. The crowd gasped and shrieked in surprise and pleasure as the god rose from the deep. Performers dressed as neon sea creatures started sailing down from the palazzo's roof on wires and landing on a pontoon boat decorated as a coral reef.

After shoving the plague doctor over the balustrade and getting into a scuffle, Mateo had scrambled through the crowd staying low. He had to get out. He snatched someone's cloak off their shoulders, dragged it over his head, and ducked away in the crowd before they could stop him. He skirted the throng through an exit door. Coming to this party had been a catastrophe. It was like a Roman orgy inside a...well...a Carnevale! Raphielli had been killed, and he'd killed her murderer, but no one seemed to notice except two men, one who'd started punching him and the other guy who'd chased him.

A police boat cruised past. *I have to get out of here!* He'd get over to the Verona's boat and Noah would get him to safety.

He ran down the little *fondimenta* and saw the Verona's sleek boat around the corner from where the crowd was gathered staring in the opposite direction. Noah stood looking up at the fireworks. Mateo jumped aboard and over the music he shouted, "Change of plans! Get me out of here!"

The last thing he saw were acrobats in neon fish costumes flying down from the roof. He didn't hear, see, or feel the explosion that touched off when Noah started the motor. Parts of them flew through the air. But around the corner, everyone was watching Poseidon break the surface, and no one witnessed Mateo's spectacular finale. The intensity of the fireworks decreased and, as a beautiful rendition of "*Venezia, la Luna e Tu*" swelled over the sound speakers, the palazzo's security came running to see two sections of the Verona's boat sinking beneath the canal's surface. One of them stopped to look at the leg lying across the *fondimenta*. It was bare except for the glossy black shoe still neatly laced.

<hr />

Raphielli stood watching her party's finale. Fireworks boomed all around and neon fish came sailing down on zip lines landing on the opposite sides of la Ponte di Smeraldi. Finally, Poseidon's trident appeared, causing everyone to cheer and scream as his eyes moved back and forth slowly sweeping the rowdy crowd. The biggest fireworks launched into the sky, and one final explosion ended the spectacle. The boom caught her off guard, and she shrank inside her cape within Alphonso's arms.

Quite a bit of smoke was carried on the wind, and the emergency fireboat that had been standing by revved its engine and burbled its way around the corner of the palace to check on things.

"I'm done for the night," she told Alphonso. "I want to leave the crowd behind."

"Okay. I'll take you around to your wing and let your security take over." His voice was tight.

They met up with Paloma at the front door and a security guard stood back to let them in. Raphielli gave Alphonso a searching look.

He said, "I figured out who you were because I knew what Petrosino was wearing. I watched you two together on the dance floor." He turned away and raised a hand in farewell as he walked back down the steps and into the crowd.

She knew how she'd responded to Gio and was mortified that Alphonso had witnessed them together.

"Just you and your friends in residence tonight," the security guard said, more of a statement than a question.

Paloma answered for her. "*Sì*, our visiting friends have gone to breakfast. They'll be back in a few hours."

He tapped his clipboard. "I've got the approved list of people allowed in. Rosa and Dante are gone for the night."

Raphielli knew Marilynn had taken care of everything. At the moment, she was probably personally taking care of Negrali's body removal, which Raphielli preferred never to see again.

"Well, if that was your first ball, you've set the bar pretty high for yourself," Paloma said. She took hold of Raphielli's arm as they walked alone down the dark corridor. "Wanna tell me what's going on with you and Alphonso?"

"No, I'd die of shame."

"Wanna go get Benny and raid your kitchen for some of that tiramisu?"

"Absolutely. Right after I take off these shoes."

After they stripped off their costumes and put on their flannel pajamas, they took a very interested Benny off to the kitchen where they liberated a big silver tureen from one of the refrigerators and ladled big mounds of tiramisu into bowls.

Around mouthfuls, they told Benny about the party.

She rolled her eyes. "Yep, sex on display, that's what I wanted to avoid."

"Mercifully, they were all wearing masks, or I'd never be able to look at these people around town."

"Cardinal Negrali tried to kill me, and a man shoved him off a balcony. He's dead."

Paloma's spoon hung in the air. "How'd I miss that?"

"Were you watching the last aerial act?"

"I sure was!"

"And the skin show in the fishtanks?"

"That was so cool. I wonder if they were really under water."

"That's how. The Carnevale people got the body out of sight and called the police."

Paloma thoughtfully spooned tiramisu into her mouth.

"That last big firework was scary," Benny said. "I heard that one from inside. We lost lights temporarily."

Just then, all the lights went out.

"Like this," Benny said.

They heard a man's voice echo from far off. "Raphielli? Sorry to disturb. Could you come here for a moment?"

All three of them put their bowls down and crouched behind the big kitchen island like caught children. Then Paloma scrambled to the light panel and tried the switches. Nothing.

"Raphielli?" The man's voice was louder.

"Let's get out of here," she whispered. She thought of the spider-filled crustacean-scuttling secret passage off of the back pantry and shuddered.

"We're buried in the center of the palazzo," Benny said. "Which way?"

"Follow me!" Paloma hissed.

"Can you run?" Raphielli asked.

"Watch me!" she yelped, and they ran after her.

"Raphielli?" the man's voice echoed through a hall by the butler's pantry.

They ran silently in their slippers, and then a set of footsteps started to pound behind them. Paloma banked around a doorway into the Baùtta Room so quickly, yanking Benny behind her, that Raphielli had to grab the doorjamb and slide around with her slippered feet to keep from overshooting the door.

Paloma raced across the room and straight for the dark maw of the fireplace. "Stay right behind me!" she said. Reaching up, she started to climb an iron-rungged ladder inside the chimney. She disappeared upward, and then Benny was gone, too.

Raphielli grabbed the rungs and started climbing as the man laughed from across the great room. "What are you doing? You'll get stuck. Come on down, I won't hurt you."

Raphielli climbed as fast as she could, reaching for rungs in the dark, and the man below started to climb, too. She had just reached some sort of a deck in the darkness as a bullet clanged off the metal flue next to her. Paloma pulled her to safety on a deck, which turned out to be a floor. They were inside the corridor Paloma and Zelph had described. *Why's he shooting at me? Who wants me dead? Is this "Kill Raphielli" night?*

"Stay low and hug the left wall," Paloma hissed in a whisper. "If you go too far to the right side of the passage, you could fall down a chimney. There are lots and lots of them."

With that, they ran and ran and ran the length of the palace, dodging around warm spots where lazy smoke billowed upward in columns like ghosts. They heard the man with the gun behind them and at one point it sounded like he fell. Paloma led them off into a recessed chamber and skidded to a stop.

"Careful, I have to feel my way. Got it!" she whispered triumphantly as she reached up into the darkness. "Don't bang your head, we're going to crawl up this master flue. It'll take us to the roof. Benny, you first. Push the door at the top, it'll swing up and over. Don't pinch your fingers. Elli, go up after her. Don't look down. It's quite a fall down to your palazzo's sub-floor."

"Why are you bringing up the rear?" Raphielli asked.

"I'm going to lock the damper behind us. Now go!"

They climbed through more spider webs than Raphielli thought possible. Benny didn't complain, but she was making a high keening sound like, *"Ieeeessh-eeee-iiii-ieesh!"* as she went. This air tunnel had stayed cold for so long, it was now a thriving habitat for the critters they brushed past. Almost to the top, winter-stunned bats started flapping confusedly around and Benny slipped back a rung, kicked Raphielli who caught her, and they both would have plummeted downward if she hadn't been clinging to each rung with a death grip.

Benny continued climbing and then bumped her head. "Found the door at the top." She said to herself, "Swing it up and out, don't pinch my fingers..." And then the cloudy night sky was above them and the clang of the door roused more bats. A whole colony of the flapping furry creatures took to the sky, and the three of them staggered out onto the cold rooftop near the greenhouse. Paloma threw the door shut and fiddled with a latch before standing up.

"He can't get up?" Benny asked.

"No, I bolted it. But we can't get down."

Raphielli started across the roof. "We have two elevators. The freight one is over here." They tried the button, but nothing happened. They ran to the formal elevator, but it didn't respond, either.

"I don't suppose either of you has your cell phone in your pajama pocket?" Raphielli asked.

They shook their heads, and clouds of soot and crawly things fell out.

"No one knows we're up here, and it'll be hours before the French contingent comes home. We have to warn them."

"How long till the sun comes up?"

"A couple hours."

"Think anyone can hear us?"

They hurried across the rooftop to the edge nearest the canal and formal entrance. Way off to the side they saw a lone staff person from the party crew talking to someone inside the palazzo's theatre door.

"Hey! Call the police!" they screamed, but the man went inside the theatre.

"Where's the goddamn security?" Paloma howled.

"Inside the venue? Cuz apparently the one Marilynn hired to guard your wing is trying to kill you," Benny said.

"Hey! Help!" Raphielli yelled. "We need something to wave to get someone's attention."

They looked around and then, in a fit of desperation, despite the February cold, Raphielli unbuttoned her flannel pajama jacket, whipped it off, and began waving it as high as she could over the edge of the roof. "Help! Help us!"

Benny looked at the rigging on the corner of the roof. "Hey, we can zipline down."

"Not with my hip," Paloma protested.

"If you fell you'd die or lose the baby for sure," Raphielli said and continued waving.

"I've ziplined before," Benny said eagerly.

"Take my word for it," Raphielli said, "the performers came down like lightning. Those cables are deceptively steep. HELP, ANYBODY!" She waved her arms frantically above her head.

A dark figure appeared from the shadows below. It was Gio. He waved.

"There's a hit man inside!" Raphielli screamed down, too intent on communicating to think about covering her breasts with her jacket.

He raised his hand telling her to stay put and jogged toward the theatre. Raphielli put her top back on, and in less than a minute Gio came running back out with police, who all looked up.

"Oh! The police were here investigating Negrali's death at the party," she said.

"There's Luigi!" Benny yelled.

Paloma said, "Now, they'll get in and get the fucker with the gun."

Raphielli flubbered her lips and stomped off toward the elevator to wait. "My ex-father confessor just tried to throw me to my death! What's going on here? I'm not a Verona and just a damned Scortini by marriage!"

Gina had spent a quiet evening watching Ivar and Leonardo play chess, and then playing several hands of gin rummy with them. The pope had worked on his speech. When Ghost and Mister Fox had arrived around midnight, Alberto and the Swiss Guards showed them all to the pope's study where they were deep in the planning of whatever was going to happen in Rome. Ivar had excused himself to bed about a half hour before Vincenzo and Juliette came home with the bodyguard.

"Our boat was blown up. Our new driver was killed," Vincenzo declared.

"How did that happen?" Leonardo gasped.

"According to the fire department, it was a fireworks misfire."

"I'm just glad you two are home safe," Gina said.

Vincenzo beckoned Leonardo. "I'm running behind schedule and need to get changed before I fly to Rome." They headed up the stairs to Vincenzo's room.

Leonardo blew a kiss goodnight to Gina. "Once he's packed, I'm going to bed. See you in the morning."

Juliette turned to Gina. "Come while I get changed and I will tell you all about the ball."

"Did anyone kiss you?"

"I was kissed more than once, and I saw the largest penis you could imagine."

"Really?" Gina almost tripped as she followed the contessa up the stairs. "Up close?"

"Too close, if you must know."

"Whose was it?"

"I have no idea."

"Did you see any balls at the ball?"

"No."

After the pope, Vincenzo, Ghost, Mister Fox, and their security contingent departed for Rome, the palazzo was completely quiet. Everyone was asleep, and staff was in the staff housing on the far side of the palazzo. Gina sat with Juliette in a windowed room designed to view the city. Gina was bundled in a thick cotton nightgown, plush robe, and slippers, while Juliette wore dove grey silk pajamas with a matching grey robe and fancy grey slippers with a low heel. She looked divine.

The night had become cloudy and snow was starting to fall when Juliette stopped mid-sentence and put a finger to her lips. A question died on Gina's lips as Juliette slipped her feet out of her slippers. She jerked Gina out of her chair just as Gina saw the silhouettes of two male figures in the hall motioning to each other.

She and Juliette ran out the door on the other end of the room, down a long flight of stairs, and down a long hall. As they got to the hall with the suits of armor, Juliette grabbed a long sword off a stand with her left hand, palmed a smaller blade in her right, then froze behind a big suit of armor. She hissed, "Get up those stairs to Vincenzo's room! Bolt the door!"

Gina ran on alone as two men brandishing guns burst into the hall of armor. She started up the stairs as fast as she could run. Vincenzo's room was one of the only rooms with a solid bolt and it was at the top of these stairs. From below she heard a man's scream as he went tumbling and his gun went flying. She turned and saw there was a dagger in his leg. Juliette stepped out of hiding and with one stroke of her sword she took the right arm off the man who was whirling to shoot her with a gun held in his right hand. Blood flew in an arc across the white marble space as he fell.

The man with the dagger in his leg wrenched it out, got back on his feet, and raced after Gina. She ran top speed and could hear him and Juliette giving chase. Even with his injury, the man was demonically fast. Gina got to the top of the stairs and was reaching for the doorknob of Vincenzo's room where Leonardo lay sleeping when she felt her head yanked back. *He has me! No!* She tucked in her chin and used the only move that came naturally. She ducked backward, grabbed hold of his shirt and jacket as he raised the dagger, then spun and used her momentum to throw him off balance. He crashed into the big stained glass window next to them, which promptly swung open. The man hovered in the air for a moment before he fell to the *calle* stones below. The sound of his impact was grotesque even if not very loud.

Leonardo came out of Vincenzo's door and looked at the window. "Ugh, it's freezing out. Must V open every window in the house?" He saw Gina and Juliette, gave them a sleepy look, mumbled, "Wake me for the pope's speech, okay?" and sleepwalked back to bed.

"Come Gina, we will keep Leonardo company as we call the police."

"What about the man in the hall of armor?"

"He is bleeding to death from his brachial artery."

"Juliette, are you a warrior?"

"No. Tonight was poor form on my part. I am tired."

Juliette took her into Vincenzo's room and shot the oversized bolt. Gina crawled into bed beside Leonardo as Juliette called the police, then alerted the staff that there were intruders in the house, and instructing them to lock themselves in their rooms. Leo roused, held Gina close and said, "You're safe. I got you. I don't want you to go home ever again, I want you to live with us."

"I'm not going anywhere." She slid her arms around him and snuggled close. "Say, did you know our child is a descendant of Saint Mark through Juliette?"

He shrugged. "Every person on this planet comes from an ancient lineage. I'm not going to love our baby any differently because of a blood line."

In the Vatican, Casimir stayed close to Vincenzo and Alberto and well behind the phalanx of Swiss Guards on the walk from the papal apartments to the balcony over-looking Saint Peter's Square. The sun was blushing over the buildings, and as he stepped out by himself, he reached up and fingered the secret microphone Mister Fox had fastened under his chin. He looked at the little dot on the balcony's railing and had faith that Ghost's tiny camera would transmit his image to the farthest regions of the world when the official feeds were cut as they certainly would be.

He had placed Vincenzo just inside the doorway, who was working harder than he'd ever done to send out love in service of God and pope. There was a chance that someone would try to kill him during his speech, but most likely they'd just kill his microphone or disconnect the official cameras mounted on the building. Behind a curtain by the doorway were Ghost and Mister Fox standing by to reset or reboot their equipment when News.va tried to silence his message.

Casimir stepped out, and the crowd below roared as the first rays of sun blinked atop the colonnade and shone on his face.

"May the blessings of our creator be upon us all." He raised his hands to the crowds below, who reached back to him in a sea of hands and cell phones.

"I welcome the youth of the world and those who are young at heart. It is Ash Wednesday, and humanity *must* rise from the ashes of our home—our mother earth—that we are currently burning down around us. I have asked that you all watch this message via cell phones or internet connection because there will be an attempt to silence what I am about to say. My last act as pope..."

A collective gasp sounded from below.

"...has been to fulfill my promise to the displaced people of Verdu Mer. We will restore your homes. They are yours. I have signed a decree with the Italian president and Venice's mayor that the deeds to each of your homes are still in effect."

"I am under unprecedented attack and therefore must step down as head of the Catholic Church. I beg that the faithful among you undertake the courageous work of reform rather than revolution. I charge that a new College of Cardinals be immediately elected through a blind ballot of ordinary church members from every diocese, and a new college of untouchables begin to dig out the rot, greed, and corruption from within our walls. Our current college has again proven that absolute power corrupts absolutely. Moments ago, I approved a search warrant sought by the Venetian Police Department allowing them complete access to the apartment held for Cardinal Americo Negrali and the Vatican Secret Securities office of Ecclesia Dei."

A roar of outrage rose from the interior of the Vatican behind him, and Casimir heard cardinals yelling at Alberto. "The Holy Father has lost his mind! Get him off that balcony! He's undermining the Holy Church! Let us through! Cut off his microphone!" There was a shriek of feedback as the News.va's microphones were cut.

Casimir prayed his little microphone and camera were still functioning and continued. "I leave you with these words: Love is the highest power, the highest good. Only love can save humanity and our world. People must marry whom they love, no matter their sex. When I think of the people who have been murdered for, or committed suicide over the shame of loving someone of their own sex, it breaks my heart, and the deepest part of my soul howls for the loss of them. Look around you. We are overpopulating. Procreate purposefully, but before you do, I beg you to adopt every single child currently without parents. *Every single child!* Take in your elders. Build community! This life is not just an exile from Heaven to be endured, it is a short sublime adventure of purpose and growth surrounded with wonders and majestic natural beauty. Love one another and put down the fighting over borders and our vanishing resources. Talk to one another, find understanding through discourse. Improve yourself by helping others. Be generous and end the mindless production of material things which man does not need. Cast aside the constant use of money. Barter, trade, and donate your crafts.

Blessed are the humble, for theirs is the kingdom of Heaven.

Blessed are the compassionate, for they will be comforted.

Blessed are the generous, for they will inherit the earth.

Blessed are those who hunger and thirst for righteousness, for they will be filled.

Blessed are the merciful, for they will be shown mercy.

Blessed are the pure in heart, for they will see God.

Blessed are the peacemakers, for they will save God's creations.

Then Casimir blew a kiss and said loudly, "*Ti amo!*" He gave Mister Fox the signal, and Queen's gospel anthem "All God's People" rang out across the square below from everyone's phones and portable speakers. Casimir turned with Alberto and his Swiss Guard, hurrying into the building, which was now a swaying mass of red vestments like dancing painted cobras, and Vatican employees dashing around with phones clamped to their ears looking for where the music was coming from.

He felt Vincenzo take his hand and he slung his other arm around Ghost's slim shoulders, who in turn had her arm around Mister Fox's waist. Alberto was matching them stride for stride as the song built in intensity. When Casimir caught sight of his secretary hovering at the assigned spot, he did a quick do-si-do maneuver, and his secretary moved on with the group while Casimir ducked into a recessed corridor behind Monsignor Nuur. In just under two minutes, they were locked together on a motor-cycle plunging through the dark sewer tunnels, then out of the Vatican via an alley and racing through the sleepy streets of Rome.

"Now can you tell me where you're headed?" Nuur asked.

"I'm going to Castine, Maine."

Hiero sat at his desk, rigid with shock and rage. The pope had ripped the veil of secrecy from the Catholic Church, and then pulled the ripcord on his reign. Where was Negrali to galvanize the College of Cardinals? They needed to refute the pope's sanity and restore the status quo by applying pressure on the politicians in each of their pockets.

He'd been in his office all night but had yet to hear from a single one of his operatives. Still no word from France, and now the team he'd sent to Venice had gone silent. Since four o'clock this morning, he'd been dodging calls from a Detective Lampani in Venice.

Without a word to his staff, he walked out of the Ecclesia Dei's offices. While he was trying to get into his car, he heard a voice behind him. "Hierotymis Karno, you are under arrest for the murder of Doctor Gugliemoni ..."

———≈•◦•≈———

Giselle was on top of the world as she drove her grandfather's big truck across the border into France. Yvania and Markus were in the mood to celebrate, and Yvania was clutching her satchel containing the manuscript of her and Juliette's cookbook and a couple of bottles of Gina's shrubs. Veronique was waiting for them at the château, and her friends would be back from Venice tonight.

She knew Yvania would love Gernelle, and even when Ivar was working in Venice, she'd have Veronique as a new friend. They had promises from Juliette that she, Ivar, Vincenzo, Leo, and probably Gina would come for a vacation early this summer when the Verdu Mer project didn't need her and Ivar there constantly. When Verdu Mer was complete, Ivar would come to live on the estate. Daniel had spoken to Juliette and made plans to come, too. From the look in his eyes when he got off the phone, Giselle could guess at the next chapter for those old friends.

Her next sculpture was dancing in her head and she was itching to donate it to the monks. Instead of the way she'd seen the men locked together in her original vision, she would sculpt Vincenzo and Leonardo in each other's arms and she would call it, "Mankind".

Traffic was light as people all over the country were sitting in churches wondering what to do, and Giselle took full advantage of the open roads.

"Do you have a nice kitchen there at your castle?" Yvania asked them.

"It's a château," she and Markus answered at the same time.

———◦◉◦———

Sleep-deprived, Luigi returned to headquarters while the entire police force—except for Lydia, who was sitting in jail with the Amendolas—was out at multiple crime scenes, not for the first time where the Veronas and Scortinis were involved. He had just plugged his phone into an outlet and pulled the bag of espresso chocolates out of his jacket pocket when he heard Chief Inspector Laszlo's voice bellow, "Lampani! Are you here?"

Luigi went into the sweatbox and straight to the window.

"Looks like you took quite a punch," Laszlo said. "Where'd that happen?"

"At Raphielli's Poseidon Ball. It was a Carnevale ball to end all balls."

"Brawling agrees with you. I haven't seen you so alive since...ever."

"Nah, a couple of angels gave me the kiss of life."

"Oh? Good for you, cuz from where I'm sitting, we've got an angel of death making the rounds again. La Serenissma's greatest palazzos are littered with crime scenes *again*."

"It's all over. The Scortini case is solved. I finally know the who's and why's. And my soon-to-be-foster-maybe-one-day-adopted-daughter Benedetta found these!" He pulled the bag of espresso-filled dark chocolates out of his pocket, unwrapped one, and popped it in his mouth.

"Pocket Coffee?"

"No, but they'll do."

"So, you're gonna bring Benedetta out of hiding?"

"She's got a new spokesperson who is going to put out a statement that she ran away from an abusive situation and is asking the court to transfer guardianship to Gladys and me."

"I wish her luck," he said. "So, we're done with this crime spree?"

"*Sì*. It was a war between the Catholic Church and a Christian sect called the Alithinían Church."

"Never heard of them."

"That's because the Catholics have been exterminating them since the first century."

"Why?"

"The Alithinían Church, or in Greek, the True Church, was founded by the Apostle Paul's grandson, guy by the name of Marcion of Sinope, a wealthy boating merchant who sailed the Mediterranean gathering up all of Paul's letters. Paul was the one who spread Christianity— supposedly directed by God—because the disciples weren't getting the job done."

"So?"

"Peter was the first pope of the Catholic Church and he found Paul threatening."

"This fight goes back that far?"

"Yep. Apparently, Jesus tapped a Verona to help Peter, like a sidekick to Peter's superhero, and that relationship continued to present day with Leopold and Vincenzo."

"No shit? Gimme one of those." The big man pointed at

the espresso chocolates. "How does Doctor Gugliemoni fit in? He was my wife's OB-GYN! He delivered my kids!"

"He was Alithinían, and according to Juliette Verona was systematically murdering her children in her womb to try to stamp out the Verona bloodline. We can only guess that the Alithiníans have been doing this surreptitiously for some time."

"And you like the head of Vatican Security for Doctor Gugliemoni's murder?"

"*Sì*, Doctor G was killed by the head of the Vatican's secret service Ecclesia Dei, a guy named Hierotymis Karno."

"How did that amber-colored rope fit in?"

"The Alithiníans revere water as holy, and apparently Peter's men killed Marcion of Sinope by drowning him underwater exactly as Salvio killed Count Gabrieli Verona, with an amber-colored rope around his left ankle."

"The French police have more of that same rope in the kill-bags found with the dead hit men at Giselle Verona's château in Gernelle," Laszlo said as he savored his candy.

"Yep, Salvio was trying to make a point. If he'd succeeded in killing Vincenzo last fall, then when he'd killed Gabrieli, he'd have killed off the Verona line."

"Did Giselle lose her baby?"

"No, but Juliette told me in confidence this morning that it isn't Vincenzo's."

"So now it's over."

"*Sì*. It's over, and after I type up my report, I'm typing up my resignation letter. Gladys, Benny, and I are moving to Sorrento."

"What're you gonna do down there?"

"For a while, relax with my family and go snorkeling with Benny in Praiano."

"Retiring to become a father...and soon a grandfather...you'll extend your life by about fifty years. But I hate to lose you."

"Hey, I need to enjoy life before I have an actual aneurysm. And after a case like this one, it's time to drop the mic and walk off stage."

"Go put an ice pack on your face and then gimme my report."

Luigi swiped his precious bag of candy off Laszlo's desk and walked back to his desk feeling on top of the world.

———⊰◦⊱———

Raphielli was exhausted, and her third wind of energy had dissipated. She'd had enough of crime scenes around her home. Benny had solved the puzzle of who killed Negrali. Luigi had let her see the head of the bald man in the boat, a man she called Matt. He'd been the leader of the Venetian branch of the Alithinían Church.

The pope had quit, and the news was saying that Ecclesia Dei had killed Doctor G, but she knew that wasn't true. Her tipsy French friends had just dragged themselves back to the palazzo and gone to bed.

When Raphielli got to her room, she found the massive shades had been drawn and it looked like night. Benny was fast asleep in one corner of the vast bed, while Paloma was working at the desk in the office part of the suite. She looked up with bleary eyes as she set her phone down.

"You're not working, are you?" Raphielli asked as she staggered toward the bed.

"I just had to take that call," Paloma said. "Your new nanny just accepted the job."

"Great. What's her name again?" Raphielli asked around a yawn.

Paloma flopped into bed next to her and drew the covers up to her chin. "Miriam."

Yes, it's true, St. Peter, while buried inside The Vatican, his throne is in The Cathedral of Castello in a quiet neighborhood in Venice.

Yes, it's true, Santa Maria dei Miracoli, Venice had all of its marble cladding removed and desalinated at the cost of approximately 4 million Euros.

Yes, it's true, there is a special statue at the Abbaye d'Orval just across the border from France in Belgium inside the Ardennes Forest—make your own decision whether it's Leonardo and Vincenzo.

Yes, it's true, Passero's espresso in Philadelphia is the finest in the world.

Anna Erikssön Bendewald is the author of *Meet Me At Père Lachaise, Stealing Venice,* and *Storming Venice.*

She is married to Mason, and they live in Los Angeles and New York with their daughters Jem and Julia.

Anna is a bookworm, a foodie, and a passionate champion for animal issues.

Made in the USA
Monee, IL
08 April 2025